"I don't want a bodyguard or some cop following me around, if that's what you're getting at."

Quinn dropped her hand and gave it a friendly pat as he returned to the file. "Actually, you don't have much choice. My commander has already made it clear that you're our priority right now."

"There's no way you are going to follow me around for a month, Quinn! Absolutely not!"

He shrugged.

She stood up from the chair and glared down at him, seeing that he now grinned from ear to ear.

"There will be no kissing, are we clear on this?" She put her hands on her hips. "You're delusional if you think I'm interested in you, Detective."

She abruptly turned to go, and caught the buckle of her sandal on the chair leg. She toppled over and went belly-down on the shiny linoleum.

He came behind her and grabbed her by the waist, pulling her to her feet. She slapped his hands away and walked out in a huff, not looking back. . .

KNOCK ME OFF MY FEET

Susan Donovan

St. Martin's Paperbacks

ISBN: 0-312-98374-3
EAN: 80312-98374-1

Printed in the United States of America

St. Martin's Paperbacks edition / December 2002

St. Martin's Paperbacks are published by St. Martin's Press, 175 Fifth Avenue, New York, NY 10010.

10 9 8 7 6 5

This book is dedicated—with love—to Bub and the Squids.
Thanks for putting up with me.

ACKNOWLEDGMENTS

The author would like to acknowledge the kind assistance of Patrick McNulty, Joseph Brady, and Jack Ridges of the City of Chicago Police Department, and John Palmieri, curator of the Herreshoff Marine Museum. Also, thanks to Marilyn K. Swisher, Irene Williams, and Vicki Boone for reading early drafts and to my agent, Pamela Hopkins, and editor, Monique Patterson, for their enthusiasm. I thank John Reed, Beverly and Sean Lewis, Lizard and Matt-D, and many others for their friendship, encouragement, and help with the kids. Thanks to Arleen Shuster for bowls of pureed squash soup and sight-seeing trips to the Empire State Building.

KNOCK ME
OFF MY FEET

CHAPTER 1

Detective Stacey Quinn stood in the shadows of the television studio and watched her. She glowed in a proper pink suit jacket that reminded him of frosting on a party cupcake. Her hands were folded primly on the desk in front of her.

That voice, however, came from a full, luscious mouth that was anything but prim and proper, and he listened to the flow of it—honey-smooth, rich, and god-awful sexy.

With those lovely lips, she spoke of the best way to remove water spots from glassware, and the detective felt his pulse quicken.

Could it be that here she was at last—the woman of his fantasies, the woman his brothers claimed could not possibly exist? Could it be that this woman under the studio lights was one part Martha Stewart to one part Carmen Electra?

"Unfortunately, the spots may be tiny pits in the glass itself." She smiled sadly, sharing the heartbreak of scratched stemware with her fans. "So if this trick doesn't work, then I assure you, nothing will."

Detective Quinn swallowed hard.

With a little tilt of her head and a friendly grin, she held the camera's gaze. "And as always, thank you, viewers, for

another wonderful week of handy comments and suggestions."

"And thank you, Helen! We'll have more Homey Helen
next Monday. Stay with us, Chicago. We'll be right back
after the break."

The anchorwoman flashed a smile until they were off
the air, then turned to her guest. "Nice segment, Audie.
Good luck tonight. Who're you playing?"

"The *Sun-Times,* and we're gonna kick some serious
butt, let me tell you." She unclipped the tiny microphone
from her lapel. "What time is it?"

"Five fifty-four."

"Crap!" She popped up from behind the long curved
desk, jumped off the platform, and ran across the studio,
shouting good-bye to the news anchor and crew.

The detective watched as she did a header over a cable
and landed flat on her face, giving him ample opportunity
to notice that Autumn Adams—"Homey Helen" to the rest
of the world—wasn't wearing a skirt with that jacket.

She wore a pair of baggy black soccer shorts, shin
guards, thick socks, and cleats.

The detective looked down. OK, so maybe she wasn't
exactly the fantasy, but she'd just skidded to a stop spread-
eagled, her nose at the tip of his polished tassel loafer, the
soccer shorts riding up her rather extraordinary bottom.

"Watch out for that loose wire," he whispered.

Autumn let her forehead fall to the floor and closed her
eyes, pausing to gather her wits and what remained of her
pride. She had a feeling she'd need both when she met the
owner of that gravelly, smug voice.

"Need a hand?" He reached for her, and Autumn looked
up, scanning him from the tips of his fingers, up the long
arm, all the way to the green eyes sparkling with suppressed
amusement.

The face was just as smug as the voice.

"No thanks." Autumn hoisted herself up and gave an indelicate yank on her shorts. With a huff she began to walk past the man, but he placed a hand on her arm.

"Miss Adams, I'm Chicago Police Violent Crimes Detective Stacey Quinn. I believe you were expecting me."

Autumn's mouth fell open and she snorted. "But that's a woman's name! They said Stacey—I was expecting a woman!"

Detective Quinn was unfazed. "Yeah? And I expected you'd be wearing a skirt. We'll call it even."

She blinked at him, stunned, watching as a corner of the policeman's mouth curled up in delight. It was completely involuntary, but she smiled back.

"OK, Mister Detective Stacey," she said, laughing. "You get twenty minutes, but you have to take a ride with me because I'm late. Can you drive a stick?"

Detective Quinn followed the pink suit jacket through the lobby of the WBBS-TV station, but his eyes were riveted to the woman beneath it. Two parts of her, to be exact: the nape of Autumn Adams's slender neck, where delicate question-mark curls clung to the damp skin under a neat twist of hair, and the identical globes of her butt, swooshing full and firm beneath the soccer shorts.

They walked through the double glass doors, out onto the sidewalk, and into the sweltering parking lot. She suddenly turned to him, and Stacey Quinn got his first real close look at her face.

"Whoa."

"What?"

She looked like she would be nice to touch. Silky. Her hair and her eyes were the exact same shade of rich brown—smooth like milk chocolate or coffee with cream. Her skin was a dark peach, and those lips—Holy God, those lips!—they looked plump and juicy and he bet they tasted like some kind of rich, sweet fruit.

The little pink jacket didn't suit her at all, he decided. She should be in leopard print underwear. In his bed. To hell with spotted stemware.

"Here. Drive." Autumn tossed him the keys while she grabbed a gym bag from the trunk of the Porsche convertible. "Lakeview High School, Irving Park, and—"

"I know where it is." He got behind the wheel. "But why am I driving?"

Autumn plopped down in the passenger side and smiled at him. "Don't you want to drive my Porsche? I was under the impression that all men like Porsches."

He turned the ignition and felt the sports car rip and rumble to life beneath him. As he pulled onto Walton Street, he retrieved his shades from inside his sport coat and slipped them on one-handed.

"I didn't say I minded driving, Miss Adams. I just asked why."

Autumn shrugged indifferently. "I need to change my shirt in the car."

She began pulling pins from her chic French twist and tossed them one-by-one into the ashtray. She used her fingers to ruffle up her shoulder-length waves.

Next, Autumn Adams yanked off her pink suit jacket, wadded it into a ball, and shoved it under the car seat.

Quinn laughed as he turned north onto Lake Shore Drive. "I hope you got a secret way to get wrinkles out of linen."

"As a matter of fact, I do. It's called the dry cleaner." Autumn leaned her head back and turned her face to the evening sun. "God, I love Chicago in the summer. Don't you?" She was in the middle of a long sigh when she suddenly shot him a suspicious glance. "Hey, how did you know it was linen?"

"I notice things."

She'd noticed a few things herself—like how Detective

Quinn didn't talk much or fidget at all. She got the feeling he was saving up for later—for what, she had no idea.

Autumn ran her fingers through her hair and let her arms rise above her in the wind, her sleeveless white blouse rippling around her ribs. She always seemed to be rushing somewhere. There was never enough time just to be—like this—the sun on her face and the air on her skin.

She sighed deeply and pulled the blouse up over her head.

It was safe to say that when he woke up that morning, Stacey Quinn never imagined he'd be behind the wheel of a Porsche convertible while a gorgeous, rich, and famous woman stripped to a sports bra in the seat next to him. That's what he liked about this job, Quinn thought—something different every day.

He risked a quick glance at her. "I could arrest you for indecent exposure."

Her face opened up in laughter just as she pulled a soccer jersey down over her head, and her chuckle was muffled by the red mesh fabric.

"Please, Detective. More of me is on display every time I go to Oak Street Beach." She abruptly thrust out her hips to tuck in the shirt, then reached down to adjust her shin guards. "Go ahead and ask your questions, Mister Stacey. I've only got a couple minutes."

Quinn was wondering how he'd manage to get out to Oak Street Beach more often when he saw her bend and twist in her seat again. Now what? Didn't the woman sit still for a second?

She surfaced with an elastic band and haphazardly bunched and twirled her thick hair into a heap at the back of her head. Those little damp curls appeared on her neck again, and he had to turn away.

"I read all of the letters you dropped off, Miss Adams. Sixteen notes in all, beginning last summer, right?"

"Unless I got another one today. I haven't been to the office to check my mail." Autumn crossed her arms over her chest and looked out at the calm summer-blue water of Lake Michigan.

"All were sent to your office on Chestnut Street, is that correct?"

"Right—which I don't make public. I tell readers to write in care of the *Banner*." Autumn jolted up again and rooted around in the gym bag at her feet. She produced a little pot of lip balm and dipped her finger inside. With eyes heavy-lidded in concentration, she ran a slick pinkie over lips that formed a perfect O of wet, soft flesh.

Quinn couldn't watch. His chest hurt. "And you reported that before the letters there were other incidents? Slashed tires, the delivery of dead flowers?"

"Yep. Dead roses. Creepy. It started right after my mom died last spring."

"And you have no idea who is doing this to you?"

She tossed the lip balm into the gym bag and gave him a sassy shake of her head. "That's your job, isn't it? I tell people about one hundred and one uses for dryer lint. You solve crimes."

The dark cop sunglasses hid his expression, but Autumn could see his face strain to suppress an outright smile.

"You know, Miss Adams, you're not exactly what I expected."

She groaned. She'd heard that one before.

Wrigley Field now loomed over them and Autumn turned in her seat as they drove by, feeling a huge silly grin spread over her face.

The crowds were already milling around Clark and Addison for the night game. She could smell the roasting peanuts. The doors to the neighborhood taverns were flung wide, and raucous music and the sharp tang of draft beer floated out into the streets.

Autumn closed her eyes and breathed it all in, letting herself remember.

The spring afternoons she had spent at Wrigley Field with her father were by far the happiest times of her childhood. Her dad would skip work at the Chicago Mercantile Exchange and take her out of school to catch a Cubs game, a forbidden thrill made all the more thrilling because Helen never once found out. They used to giggle together the whole way home to Winnetka.

Autumn giggled with pleasure now—because the smells and sounds of Wrigley Field still made her happy.

"You can call me Audie," she said, turning back around in her seat as they drove past the ballpark. "And puh-leeze don't tell me you don't know I inherited the column from my mother, the *real* Homey Helen. It's not exactly a secret."

"I knew. I just didn't expect . . . well . . . you."

"Sorry to disappoint," she snapped.

Detective Quinn didn't respond. How could he? Everything he wanted to say would sound ridiculous, because, Holy God in heaven, she didn't disappoint him at all. She just amazed him.

He wanted to tell her he couldn't remember the last time that fifteen minutes with a woman had left him unhinged. He wanted to tell her he could barely prevent himself from reaching over and letting his fingertips brush the back of her neck. And most of all, he wanted to tell her that he was her biggest fan, that he kept many of her columns in a recipe organizer in his kitchen, sorted by date and topic.

"We'll need to discuss who you might have offended, Miss Adams, who it is that might hold a grudge against you. I'll need a list of husbands and boyfriends, current and ex-."

Autumn burst out laughing. They were driving north on

Ashland Avenue now, almost at the school. It took several moments for her guffaw to die down.

"Sure, Detective. No problem." She pursed her lips and frowned. "Let's get right to it. Never was a husband, and at this rate there never will be. There's no current anything. And how do you want the others—would alphabetical work for you? Or how about according to the way I got the bad news—E-mail, beeper, voice mail, answering machine, or telepathy!"

She perked up a bit and waved her hand in the air. "Wait! I know! How about I organize the names by the man's neurosis—fear of commitment, fear of boredom, inability to stop lying, unclear sexual orientation, like that?"

Detective Quinn pulled up alongside Lakeview High School and cut the engine. He methodically removed his sunglasses and tucked them inside his jacket pocket. He waited for her to turn to him, and when she did, he saw tears in her eyes.

Despite the attitude, she was scared.

"Someone is threatening to hurt you, Miss Adams. I need to ask questions if I'm going to find him. Do you think we can work together on this?"

Autumn nodded slightly and brushed the tears away with a quick sweep of her hand. "I'm sorry for the snide comments. I'm just so incredibly pissed about this whole thing."

"About the letters or the boyfriends?"

Autumn exhaled sharply and noticed that his uneven grin had returned. "Both, since you asked."

It startled her when he reached inside his jacket and offered her a crisp white handkerchief.

"Thanks." She blew her nose with enthusiasm. "Look, Detective, I don't have a very good track record with men, OK? Nothing ever lasts very long. It's like after seven or eight weeks some green slimy and hairy thing with eleven eyeballs suddenly jumps out of the top of my head and the men start running for the nearest exit."

She sniffled and sighed and rubbed her forehead. "But I don't think I ever did anything to make any of them mad at me. They all seemed pretty glad to see me go."

"Uh-huh. Green and slimy, you say?"

She cast him a sideways glance—he was scribbling in a small notebook. Was he laughing at her? "Hairy, too."

He nodded soberly.

Autumn looked down at her hands. She'd been biting her nails again. "I think I scare men," she sighed. "I'm kind of a spaz."

"Really?"

"Look, I've got to go warm up. You can stay for the game and I'll take you back to your car after, if you've got time. Maybe we can talk more then?"

"I've got time."

She cocked her head and looked at him closely. "You're not much of a conversationalist, are you?"

What color were those eyes? she wondered. Hazel? That word hardly did justice to the complexity of color there— an olive green iris with a sunburst of gold around the pupil. They were dazzling.

The rest of him was *way* above average as well.

Detective Quinn had a head of straight, neatly trimmed light brown hair that the sun had kissed near his forehead and temples. His face was handsome as much for its self-assurance as its strong, even features and wily grin. He was probably a good four inches taller than she was, and she could see the outline of his solid body beneath the light-weight sport coat.

"Everything's relative," he said.

"Meaning I talk too much?"

"I didn't say that."

"Right."

"Audie?"

She stopped before she opened the door. "Yeah?"

"You did say I can call you Audie?"

"Yes, I did."

"Then please call me Quinn. My friends call me Quinn."

"Not Stacey?"

"Nope." The grin was back. "Stacey's a girl's name. I'm not a girl."

Autumn laughed. "You know, I think I noticed that at the TV station. See you after the game."

She didn't fall once, Quinn noticed. In fact, she ran with speed and grace, soared over toppled bodies, bent and twisted to get a good angle on her kicks, and pivoted with quick and sharp agility.

And the whole time, Autumn Adams was smiling.

She scored again and, with two other women, jumped high into the air to slap hands—a sight he found amusing. These women were all professionals from the thirty-and-over Chicago Parks and Recreation Women's Soccer League, yet they were running around like a bunch of boys.

"Go, go, go!" Audie screamed a few moments later as her teammate slashed the ball through a tangle of legs and into the net.

"Yes!" Audie punched her fist into the air and jumped into the middle of a cluster of women hanging on one another like monkeys. Quinn watched Audie's hair fall out of its tether as she bounced around on a teammate's back.

He stepped farther from the sidelines and tried to put some distance between himself and Autumn Adams.

Who the hell was this woman? How could he reconcile what he'd seen and heard today with the public persona of Homey Helen, the world-famous household hints columnist?

Quinn had to laugh. He knew too well how whacked-out celebrities could be. For the last few years, he'd been working mostly celebrity cases out of District 18, which encompassed Chicago's Gold Coast, Michigan Avenue, and the ultrachic towers of black glass and steel along Lake Michigan. Talk show queens lived there, as did professional athletes, politicians, and film stars, and he'd handled stalking or harassment cases on a bunch of them.

But compared to Autumn Adams, most other famous types seemed pretty easy to peg.

True, she wasn't the original Homey Helen, but she had taken over everything the job entailed, hadn't she? She still toured all over the world. She still did the television segment. She still wrote the column. So how was it that she was nothing like her image?

Quinn sighed. It had to be a real bitch to pretend you were someone you weren't, day after day.

And then he smiled to himself. God, he loved the way his brain worked! No wonder he'd made detective at the age of twenty-nine.

Obviously, Autumn Adams was sending those notes to herself. If she didn't enjoy doing the column, if the job cramped her style, which it clearly did, then these letters would be a way to bow out without anyone accusing her of failure.

He had to give the woman credit—it was certainly worth a try. Too bad he was so good at his job.

Autumn was walking toward him, and he watched her lift the front of her jersey to wipe her sweaty face, exposing a stretch of flat, smooth, and golden skin.

She smiled up at him. "I could really use a beer. How about you?"

Quinn pushed aside the starched cuff of his oxford shirt and checked his watch. So she wanted to play with him a little, did she? He was up for that. He grinned at her. "Sure. Why not?"

"Can we go to my regular watering hole?"

"Sure."

"Great. That would be Field Box Seats Two-oh-five and Two-oh-six, Gate D, Section One-thirty-four, along the first base line. The game starts in ten minutes."

Stacey Quinn stopped dead and stared at the pretty, flushed face and the toffee-brown eyes wide with a question. Homey Helen had just asked him for a date—to a Cubs game!

"I'm not sure I can do that, Audie."

Her face froze in a smile. "Why not? Are you still on duty? Or aren't you allowed to go to sporting events with taxpaying citizens?" Her smile suddenly collapsed and she shook her head. "Whoops. You've got a wife or girlfriend to go home to."

He kept grinning. "No wife. No girlfriend. I'm off duty. And yes, I'm allowed to accept your offer."

Her brows knit together. "Then what's the—"

"I'm a White Sox fan, Miss Adams, born and bred."

"Oh, is *that* all?" She slipped her arm through his and pulled him to a walk beside her. "It'll be our little secret then."

Stacey Quinn tried to keep his head down as much as he could. There were television cameras tucked away all over the friendly confines of Wrigley Field, and there was no way he could allow his mug to end up on television. If his father and brothers ever found out he had gone to a Cubs game, his life would be barely worth living.

"Do you want a hot dog?" Audie tapped his knee. "I'm starving."

"Sure, I'll go to the—"

Audie suddenly stood up, brought a thumb and middle finger against her tongue, and let a piercing whistle rip through the ballpark. "Yo! Hot dog here!"

The kid with the metal box of steaming Eckridge red

hots caught her eye and nodded. He was on his way, taking two steps at a time to get to her.

This was too much. Quinn let his head fall into his hand and starting laughing for real now. Martha Stewart, Carmen Electra, and what else? Athlete. Beer drinker. Whistler. A sense of humor and a sharp, albeit criminally inclined, mind.

He should probably just get down on his knees now, in the middle of the second inning, and ask her to be the mother of his children.

She took out a wad of bills from some hidden interior pocket of her shorts and began to pay for the hot dogs.

"I've got this," Quinn said, standing and pushing her hand away. He gave the kid a ten-dollar bill and handed her one of the warm bundles.

Audie stood very still, feeling the blood thump in her veins. "You got the beers. I should get the hot dogs."

Quinn sat down with a shrug and began squeezing out a neat crosshatched layer of mustard along the inside of the bun. "I got it."

Audie collapsed in her seat and left the foil-wrapped package untouched in her lap. She'd suddenly lost her appetite.

"We're not dating, Detective. I just wanted to split the costs."

"You don't have to."

She laughed a little. "I know I don't have to—but I want to!" She stared at him, incredulous. "I'm the one who invited you to come, and I can pay for anything I choose."

Quinn raised the hot dog and bun to his mouth and took a large, but tidy, bite. He looked out on the emerald green grass and watched the Padres take the field. He could hardly believe he was sitting in a National League park, watching a National League game. He'd probably go to hell for this.

"Are you listening to me?" Audie whacked him in the shoulder.

Quinn turned slowly toward her, one eyebrow arched high in surprise as he looked at his arm and then at her. "That's assaulting an officer," he said calmly. "I might be forced to use my handcuffs on you."

Audie rolled her eyes. Maybe this wasn't such a good idea. She just wanted company for the game, and he was extremely cute. And they did need to talk. But it was clear he was the kind of man she'd clash with on a regular basis. This was a mistake.

"Detective. I can see that you're a wildly progressive man, so it must have occurred to you that I might enjoy paying for half of our purchases this evening, that I might even prefer it."

Quinn took another bite, then dabbed at the corner of his mouth with a napkin. He reached for the large plastic cup of Old Style beer below his seat and took a gulp. "Not really."

He watched absently as Sammy Sosa hit a little hopper over the head of the second baseman for a single. It seemed everyone was on their feet cheering but them.

Audie glared at him—what a jerk this Stacey Quinn was! She unwrapped her hot dog and ate in silence as the Cubs ended the inning with Sosa on base. A wasted hit. A wasted evening.

"I'm sorry."

Audie's eyes popped and she stared in disbelief at the detective, a mouthful of hot dog now lodged in her throat. Nothing—absolutely nothing—would have surprised her more.

"They're your season tickets, so I thought I should pay for everything else," he said. "I didn't mean anything by it."

She blinked. My God, he was a fine-looking man, but

then, she'd always found men at their most attractive during an apology.

Audie was about to say something nice to him when he smiled wickedly and added, "So how long did you plan to let me squirm?"

"Huh?"

"When were you going to admit you wrote those letters yourself?"

A hot and electric shiver ran up Audie's spine and she wrestled for command of her voice. "What are you talking about?"

"The letters. You wrote them and mailed them to yourself to give you an out."

The blood was pounding in her skull, hot and blinding. "An out?"

"So that you could stop writing the column. It obviously doesn't come naturally to you."

The pounding had mellowed into a quaking rage, and Audie stood up over him. "Go to hell, Detective." She turned, knocking over her beer in the process, and barged down the row of seats to get to the aisle.

Quinn was right behind her, climbing up the ballpark steps toward street level. "Audie, wait!"

He had no choice but to look at her lovely round butt, right in front of him. This was not working out the way he'd hoped. Not at all.

"C'mon, Audie! Wait up!"

She was running now, and Quinn had to push himself to keep up with her. She was fast, ducking and weaving through the crowd, searching for an open exit gate. Quinn knew she was probably scared, but a decent lawyer could get the charges dropped. Filing a false report wasn't exactly homicide, after all.

They were out on Addison Street now, and she was slicing through the tangle of pedestrians and souvenir vendors to get to Clark Street and their parking spot four blocks away. He really didn't feel like chasing her, but he'd do it if he had to.

There she went. She didn't even wait for the light, and now she was directly across the street from him. "Audie! Please!" he yelled over the traffic.

She flipped him off and ran faster.

Quinn made a break across the traffic and nearly got a hold of her arm as she made a hard left and headed into the tree-lined streets of Wrigleyville.

He was right behind her, shouting, "I can run all night, Audie! But I'd rather talk!"

She slammed to a halt and turned toward him, and he bashed into her. A *wumph* escaped her lips as she fell flat on the sidewalk beneath him. Quinn heard the unmistakable sound of a skull hitting concrete.

Her very female body went limp under him, and for an instant Quinn feared she'd been knocked out. But then she screamed something shrill and unintelligible in his ear, pushed him away, and brought a right fist to the side of his jaw.

Quinn went sprawling, half of him in someone's tiny front lawn and half on the sidewalk.

"You jerk! You idiot!" She was on top of him now, pummeling him in the chest and arms.

Quinn put his hands over his head and absorbed the blows until he could sort out the situation. He couldn't remember the last time he had let a female beat him up.

Without warning, the punching stopped and she went still, sitting on top of his legs. She began to cry.

Quinn was paralyzed by the feel of her body on top of his, softly rocking back and forth with her sobs. He opened one eye to peek at her.

"I didn't write the letters, you dumb ass! I want a different detective on the case—someone with half a brain!"

She took a gulp of air and rubbed the back of her head. "You hurt me!"

Quinn felt her begin to rise and suddenly knew exactly how to handle this situation. He sat up, grabbed Audie by the hips, and pulled her down into his lap.

"What are you—?"

His mouth was on hers so fast and hard that she didn't have time to catch her breath. It was beyond a kiss—it was a verdict, a claim, an assault—and he tasted like beer and hot dogs and something else, something powerfully male.

Audie was dizzy. Her head hurt. She was crying. And she felt her body catch fire. She took a quick gulp of air and then gave as good as she got, even as it began to go black around her.

She couldn't help it—if it was the last thing she ever did in her life, she had to open her mouth to this man and take everything he could give her. She pressed hard against him now, clutched at his back, felt his moan fill her mouth and his hands tug on her disheveled hair.

Not a word was exchanged between them, and all Audie wanted was the pushing and seeking and taking. She wrapped her legs around his waist and grabbed the back of his neck. She was suffocating. She had to have more of him. She was blacking out . . .

"Yo, Romeo and Juliet. This is a family neighborhood." A uniformed officer stood on the sidewalk next to them, trying to hide his amusement with a serious frown.

When Quinn pulled his lips from hers in surprise, Audie lost consciousness. She fell backward in his arms, her head hanging limp.

The patrol officer tensed.

"Area Three Violent Crimes Detective Stacey Quinn," he said, out of breath. "My badge is in my jacket pocket. I can't reach it."

The officer still frowned. "Then you might want to ascertain if you just killed your girlfriend, sir."

Quinn nodded. He rolled with Audie until she lay back in the grass. He pulled out his badge and flipped it open, then put it back in his pocket, all the while running his fingers along her scalp.

"She hit her head on the sidewalk," Quinn said, leaning over her.

The officer squatted on the other side of Audie's lifeless form. "Do you want me to call an—"

Audie suddenly sat up, smacking her forehead against that of Detective Quinn.

"Aaaah!" she screamed, bringing a hand to her head. "God! Get the hell away from me!"

The patrol officer stood up and adjusted his leather holster. "Take this inside somewhere, OK, folks?" He turned and strolled down the sidewalk.

Quinn and Audie sat on the grass cradling their foreheads, stunned, breathing unevenly.

Audie started crying again. "How could you do that?" The words were muffled but full of fury.

"I didn't mean to knock you over, Audie."

"Not that!" she yelled. "God!"

Quinn glanced over at her. His jaw was throbbing. "I'm sorry I accused you of writing the letters."

She groaned in frustration. "Not that, either!"

"Then I'm not sure—"

"Why did you kiss me?" she yelled. "Why did you have to kiss me *like that*?"

Quinn wondered if he looked as wild-eyed and confused as she did—he certainly felt that way. He raised his knees and let his wrists dangle over them.

"God, I'm sorry. That was inexcusable. You can file a complaint, but I . . . damn, I just had to do it." He rubbed a hand over his jaw and looked up at her with a frown. "Why did you kiss me *back* like that?"

Audie sat cross-legged in the grass, her head hanging. "Same reason, I guess." She sniffled. "I just had to." She caught his eye. "I didn't write those letters, you know."

"OK." Quinn stared absently at the tidy houses along the north side of Grace Street, his pulse and breathing slowly returning to normal. He could hear the cheers inside the park, not a block away.

"It never even occurred to me to do that," Audie continued. "But it's a good idea."

"What, kissing me?" Quinn was confused.

"No! Writing the letters!"

Quinn nodded, giving her the nicest smile he could manage, given that his face felt like it was broken. "You hate being Homey Helen, don't you?"

A single tear streaked down her face as she nodded slightly. "You could say that."

"Then why do you do it, Audie?" Quinn scooted closer to her on the grass, and she leaned against him, as if it were the most natural thing in the world to do.

"I can't talk about this right now," she said, turning her face into his shoulder. She breathed in the clean smell of him—a mixture of soap and fading aftershave and male summer skin.

"Is it too complicated?"

She laughed a little and looked up at him. "Not hardly, Detective. But my head hurts so bad I can't think straight, thanks to you. I think I should go home."

"Come on. I'll drive you." He was about to get up but paused, kissed her very gently on the forehead, then stood and reached down for her hand.

This time, she took it.

CHAPTER 2

Thank God for Marjorie Stoddard.

By the time Audie stumbled up the stairs and through the reception area to her private office, she felt as if her head would fall off. But on her desk was a steaming cup of coffee and a little packet of Tylenol. That woman was amazing—a little too controlling sometimes, but positively clairvoyant.

After taking her medicine like a good girl, Audie reappeared in the reception room to greet her staff—all two of them.

"Rough game last night?" Griffin Nash was leaning against the doorjamb to his tiny office, and Audie nearly spit out her coffee.

"Good Lord, Griffin! What are you wearing?"

"Isn't it happenin'?" Griffin tugged at the snug vest and did a little spin, sending the long strips of suede fringe twirling out around his waist. "Found it at that funky little boutique in Wicker Park."

Audie gawked at him. "Just don't tell me what you paid for it, because I'll just yell at you again."

"Fifty."

"We're talking cents, right?"

"Stop it, you two." Marjorie whipped around in her desk chair and tried to produce a frown of reprimand beneath her laughing eyes. "I swear, I think you two actually get satisfaction out of making each other miserable."

Griffin smirked at Audie.

"And really, Audie. The pants are far more hideous than the vest." Marjorie slowly raised her head to catch Audie's eye, and the two women began to howl with laughter.

Marjorie was right, as usual. Griffin's purple velvet bell-bottoms were uglier by far than the black suede vest. Audie simply hadn't had a chance to comment on them yet.

Griffin crossed his arms over his mostly bare chest and ignored them both. "You got sixty-seven E-mails to your site yesterday, Audie. You had more than four thousand hits, which was a record. I think it's 'Pet Corner'; I really do."

Audie took another soothing sip of coffee and nodded at him. "Great."

"Pet Corner" was a weekly compilation of pet-related hints and something Audie never wanted in the first place. It had been Marjorie's idea, and like most of her ideas, it had proven an instant hit with the readers.

"You gonna tell her, Marjorie?" Griffin stood up straight and walked toward the large walnut reception desk. His hand reached for the stack of fan mail.

Audie felt her shoulders sag. "Not another one?"

Griffin and Marjorie nodded.

"Oh, crap. Hell."

"Did that detective show up at the television studio yesterday?"

For some reason, Griffin's simple question startled Audie, and she just stared blankly at her friend. "Who?"

"The police detective."

"Oh! Yes. He did." Audie reached for the letter and cradled it, nearly weightless, in her palm. It was the same white business-sized envelope, the name "Homey Helen" neatly typed front and center, a single generic stamp placed in the corner, covered by a Chicago postmark. It was just like all the others. Her hand trembled slightly.

"Did you guys read it?"

Marjorie avoided Audie's eyes and turned to Griffin.

"What's going on?" Audie demanded.

"We read it. It's bad, Audie," Griffin said. "This one's twisted. I think the guy's a head case."

Audie blinked at him. "Well, of course he is! No normal person gets his ya-yas out of threatening a household hints columnist!"

"Honey," Marjorie said softly. "This one is very weird, and frankly, I'm starting to get worried about your safety."

Audie sighed and walked around behind Marjorie's chair. She brought her lips down to the chic and short gray hair, fragrant with expensive hair spray, and kissed her on top of her head. "But that's your job, Marjie," she said sweetly. "Without you, I wouldn't have anybody to worry about me, right?"

Marjorie brought a hand up to stroke Audie's forearm and offered her a brave smile. "I've always done more than just worry about you, and you know it, Autumn."

Audie hugged her tight. "I know, Aunt Marj." She sighed again, gathered up the rest of the mail, and headed for her office. "What else did I miss yesterday? Anything?"

"Well . . ." Marjorie adjusted her bifocals. "Russell called. He wanted to remind you that the *Banner* contract is up for renewal and you can't keep putting him off."

"Great." Audie's lawyer and former boyfriend was the last person in the world she wanted to see, and her contract with Banner News Syndicate was the last thing she wanted to think about.

"Anybody else?"

"Well, honey, I'm sorry, but Tim Burke called again and he sent more flowers yesterday—with a note. The boy is besotted." Marjorie handed Audie the card.

"Ugh." She didn't think it was possible, but her headache had just gotten worse. This man would not leave her alone! How blunt did she have to be with him? She tossed the card in the trash can without bothering to read it. "You told him I was dead, right?"

"Autumn!" Marjorie shook her head with exasperation.

"Where'd you take the flowers?"

"The nursing home, as usual."

"Excellent. That it?"

"No. You also had a message on the main voice mail this morning from a Stacey Quinn—a woman's name but a man's voice. Do you know him?"

Did Audie know Stacey Quinn? She stopped in the doorway to her office and closed her eyes.

She knew that his lips were soft but demanding. She knew how good it felt to wrap her legs around his waist and have him pull her hair. She knew approximately how long and thick he became when sexually aroused, because it was difficult to miss something that big jammed up against the inside of your thigh!

But she didn't know him at all.

"He's the detective working on my case," Audie said hoarsely, taking another sip of coffee so she'd have something to do for three seconds. She felt dizzy again.

"I see." Marjorie offered her the slip of paper. "He said for you to call first thing. He inquired about your headache."

Audie chuckled to herself and caught the flash of humor in Marjorie's eye. So much for clairvoyance. She grabbed the message. "I'll call him right now."

"And you'll tell him about the latest note?" Griffin's voice was edgy as he called after her. He seemed more shaken up by this than she did—how bad was it this time? she wondered.

Audie turned to him and smiled. "I will, Griff." She let

her eyes take in the full effect of his wardrobe, and she giggled—the bald truth of it was, Griffin Nash looked gorgeous.

With his thick shoulder-length dreadlocks and that innocently sexy face, he drew women to him without effort. The man could wear a lawn and garden bag through the streets of Chicago and women of all shapes, sizes, colors, and professions would still be sucked into the gravitational pull of his charms.

"It's actually very Jimi Hendrix," Audie admitted.

"I realize that, mon," he said with a grin.

"Care for a mint?"

Detective Stanley Oleskiewicz shoved the box of Frango Mints under his partner's nose, but Quinn batted it away with the back of his hand and snarled low and deep until he backed off.

Not once in their four years together had Stanny-O altered his routine. He came in the doors to the District 18 police station, got buzzed through, and immediately reached into his top right desk drawer and pulled out a bright green box of Marshall Field's Frango Mints.

And every morning he shoved the box under Quinn's nose and offered him one, apparently oblivious to the fact that Quinn had never once taken him up on his offer.

Stanny-O shrugged and put the box away, but not after grabbing a few to savor with his coffee. "What's happenin', buddy?" He leaned back in his chair comfortably.

"Not much."

"How'd it go with the Homey Helen babe?"

Quinn shook his head and started to laugh.

"That good or that bad?"

Quinn looked up at his perpetually cheerful partner and wondered how much he dared tell him. Stan was not exactly famous for his tact. Plus, they had a long history of giving each other massive amounts of grief just for the sport of it.

"She's a real piece of work," Quinn said. "I thought at first she was writing the notes to herself. You know, to get out of having to do the column."

"Why would she want to do that?" Stanny-O narrowed his already beady eyes. "She's got quite the scam goin', don't she?"

"Yeah, but she's . . ." Quinn shrugged. "She's not what you'd think."

Stanny-O popped the last of the chocolate-covered mints into his mouth and swirled it around, thinking. "I've seen her on TV. She's a total biscuit. She never really struck me as the happy homemaker type, either. Is that what you're getting at?"

Quinn looked at him blankly for a moment. "Her heart's not in it. She hates it, really."

Stanny-O watched his partner carefully and straightened up in his chair. Something wasn't quite right about this exchange. "She told you all this, or this is just your take on the situation?"

"A little of both."

Stanny-O leaned his elbows on the desktop and rubbed a hand over his neatly trimmed goatee. A smile oozed across his face.

"So how hot is she in person, Stacey? On the standard one-to-ten scale."

Quinn shrugged. "I don't know. Five."

"You, my man, are lying." Stanny-O got up from his chair and came over to sit on the edge of his partner's desktop, his polyester dress slacks straining at the seams.

"Get your kielbasa off my work space." Quinn shoved him in the hip, but he didn't budge.

"Did you make it with her or something, Stacey? What's going on?" His face was wide with wonder now.

"God. Of course not." Quinn got up from his chair to

get coffee just as his phone began to ring. Stanny-O waved him on magnanimously and picked it up, still smiling.

"District Eighteen, Detective Stacey Quinn's desk, may I help you?"

"My head still hurts."

Stanny-O pursed his lips and tried not to snicker. "I'm sorry to hear that, ma'am. Is there something the Chicago Police Department can do for you? We're here to serve and protect."

"I . . . uh . . ." The woman seemed confused. "This isn't Stacey Quinn, is it?"

"No. It's his partner, Stanley Oleskiewicz, but here he comes right now." He handed Quinn the phone. "I think it's her."

"Her who?"

"Horny Helen." Stanny-O doubled over in a laughing attack as Quinn ripped the phone from his hand. Quinn succeeded in shoving his partner off the desk and quickly turned his back to him.

"This is Quinn."

"Hi. It's Audie. Was that really your partner?"

"Unfortunately. How's the goose egg this morning?"

"Sore. Uh, I got another letter."

So this was a business call. Quinn had assumed it was going to be social.

The whole thing had ended rather awkwardly last night—she had refused to get checked out at the emergency room and left him standing in the middle of her building's underground parking garage. Not that he expected her to invite him up, but still . . .

"Did you read it?"

"I just finished reading it. It's awful."

"We'll be right over."

"No!" Audie nearly shouted. "Look, I'm sorry, Quinn, but can I just fax it to you? I feel very strange about what happened yesterday and I think you're a very . . . uh . . . unusual man, but I'm really not sure we should take this any further because I'm really not interested in—"

"Fingerprints, Miss Adams."

"Huh?"

"I need the original letter so we can look for fingerprints. That's why I wanted to come over."

The line was silent for a moment.

"Oh."

"But we can hash out that other part later." Quinn looked over his shoulder to see Stanny-O finally recovering from his laughing jag. "Are you at your office, Audie?"

"Yeah."

"Are your coworkers there?"

"Yeah, but—"

"Great. Keep everybody around. We'll be there in about fifteen minutes."

Audie's outfit fell somewhere between the proper pink suit jacket and the soccer uniform, Quinn decided. She was wearing a short black skirt and a gray silk blouse. Simple, and simply stunning on her.

Audie's hair was loose and wavy around her face, and she wore just a hint of a rich shade of lipstick. At the end of her long and shapely legs were pretty clear-polished toes in a pair of black leather sandals.

She nervously greeted Quinn and his partner at the door.

"Five my pimply Polish ass," Stanny-O whispered to Quinn as they entered the reception area.

Quinn and Audie orchestrated the introductions and Marjorie politely offered the detectives coffee.

Quinn caught Audie's eye and she looked away.

He casually examined the place. Like all the other brownstones on Chestnut Street near Michigan Avenue, this onetime Victorian mansion had been converted into posh

offices. It was decorated in subtle mauves and greens, and
the furniture was a cheery floral print. A crystal bowl of
fresh pink roses sat on a low table. The sunshine poured
through a cozy set of bay windows.

Obviously, it had been the original Homey Helen's office—all over the walls of the reception area were photographs of Audie's mother posing with celebrities. There
was Helen Adams with Mother Teresa. Helen Adams with
Margaret Thatcher, Nancy Reagan, and Princess Diana.

In each of the photos, Helen Adams wore pink and
looked poised, polished, and perfect.

Quinn checked out the rest of the place and spied
through a set of wide paneled doors what seemed to be
Audie's personal office. It was a freakin' mess.

"Thank you, ma'am," Stanny-O said to Marjorie as she
handed him a delicate bone china cup and saucer. "This is
a beautiful setup."

Quinn snickered at the sight of fine china in the grip of
Stanley Oleskiewicz's sausagelike fingers.

"Oh, thank you, Detective," Marjorie said graciously,
motioning to the sitting area. "Shall we all get comfortable?"

The group chatted casually for several minutes and then
Marjorie explained how the Homey Helen office worked.
Regular mail was delivered about ten every morning and
went directly to her desk, where she sorted it. As managing
director of Homey Helen Enterprises, Marjorie ran the office, handled all the fan mail forwarded from the *Banner,*
and conducted research, scheduled public appearances, and
generally kept the column going.

"She's been the backbone of the business since the beginning," Audie said, smiling at Marjorie. "She and my
mom were college roommates. They came up with the idea
for the column when I was about six."

Marjorie nodded demurely. "I was the business major

and Helen was the English major—I was the brawn and she was the beauty."

Quinn grinned at Marjorie appreciatively. "I don't know about that," he said, noticing how the fine-boned older woman with pale blue eyes blushed under his compliment.

"At any rate," Marjorie continued, "we've managed to stumble along quite well this last year, everything considered." She smiled sadly at Audie, and Quinn watched as Audie grabbed the older woman's hand. Marjorie took a breath before she went on.

"I was quite pleased that Audie decided to keep it going, and I'm sure the sentiment is shared by her millions of readers."

Audie grinned politely but avoided Quinn's eyes.

"So you've been the first person to see all the letters, Miss Stoddard?" Stanny-O asked.

"Yes, although Griffin helps me go through the mail if it's particularly busy. I think he might have found one or two of them, didn't you?"

Griffin crossed a purple velvet leg over the opposite knee and jiggled his foot nervously.

"I did," he said, frowning. "How long is it going to take you to find out who's sending these threats? Could it be the same guy that sent the dead flowers last year?"

"Not long and it could be," Quinn answered. He gave Griffin Nash a careful once-over. The guy's outfit clashed so badly with the decor that Quinn's eyes were watering. The accent was from some Caribbean nation, he thought. The guy seemed agitated.

"And how long have you been with Audie, Mr. Nash?"

Griffin suddenly smiled. "I've known her for almost ten years. I've worked for her here since she took over the column, about fourteen months or so."

"And you are . . . ?"

"Her *friend*," Griffin said with irritation. "And Web site

manager. I update the page every day and put up the weekly features. I run her interactive chat site and her live on-line appearances. I answer all her E-mail inquiries and send out reminders and greetings to everyone who visits her site. I handle any technical problems."

"Does that keep you busy?" Quinn was jotting down some notes in a palm-sized notebook.

"Yes. The Homey Helen site gets thousands of visitors every day, from Milwaukee to Moscow."

"Really?" Quinn kept scribbling.

Unless she was imagining it, Audie detected some kind of subtle tension between Quinn and Griffin, and she sought out Griffin's eyes. He gave her a nervous smile.

Audie stood up. "I'll go get the letter."

"Here, allow me, if you don't mind." Stanny-O stood and walked with Audie to her private office, catching her elbow when she nearly tripped on the thick carpeting. He used a pair of long tweezers to pick up the envelope and carried it to Quinn on the sofa.

Touching only the edges, Quinn unfolded the note. It was computer-generated, like all the others. He saw immediately that it was printed in a standard font on the kind of generic white paper stocked at any office supply store.

Quinn scowled. The letter may have looked benign, but the words sure weren't. He read it as Stanny-O leaned over his shoulder:

August 20
Dear Homey Helen:
   I've found that human remains keep longer in the deep freeze if each section is first wrapped in waxed paper, then sealed inside a zip-closure freezer bag.
   Before sealing, be sure to press out any air pockets. With indelible marker, indicate the exact body part and date the

columnist was hacked to pieces—that way, you can always be sure of the freshness!

Quinn looked up from the note at this point to share a wince with his partner. Then he continued.

Let's plan on getting together on September 22. No need to RSVP.

Fondly,

Your most loyal reader

PS: I simply loved your column on how to remove stubborn underarm perspiration stains!

"Man, that's nasty," Stanny-O said, looking at Audie. "Human remains?"

"And they're giving you a date," Quinn mumbled.

Stanny-O rubbed his goatee. "He don't sound too happy with you, Miss Adams. Any idea why?"

"No."

Quinn looked at Griffin and Marjorie, noting the worry in their faces. Marjorie was now gripping Audie's hand. Quinn moved his attention to Audie.

She sat primly at the edge of the chair, her knees tight together and her eyes cast down. Quinn watched her thick dark lashes flutter against her cheek.

Her face was a fascinating combination of curves and angles, he thought. The cheeks and chin were round, almost plump, and that fullness was echoed in her very kissable mouth.

But the shape of her jawline was more precisely cut, and the very tip of her nose ended in the most adorable little tilt.

Audie's lashes suddenly flickered and she looked right at him. Quinn inhaled audibly at the sight of the liquid, catlike eyes.

Stanny-O cleared his throat.

"Miss Adams, we'll need that list from you as soon as possible, the one Detective Quinn mentioned yesterday."

She nodded.

"And then either Detective Quinn or myself will sit down and have a long chat with you."

She nodded again.

"Then we're going to need to get everyone's finger-prints, so we can isolate any unknowns," Stanny-O continued, "and we'll need to take a hard look at your past columns for any connection between the threats and what you were writing at the time."

Griffin chuckled lightly. "Yeah, mon. All that talk of how to clean bathtub grout can really send a guy over the edge."

Stanny-O chortled in appreciation, but Marjorie shot Griffin a look of reprimand.

The detectives stood and thanked them for their time. It was then that Audie realized she'd intentionally avoided looking at any part of Quinn except his face, and she looked there only briefly and only out of necessity.

But she'd blown it now.

She'd just noticed how his button-down shirt opened at the throat, exposing ruddy, smooth flesh. She'd seen how his jacket hung straight from his broad shoulders and how his crisply pressed chinos clung to the long muscles of his thighs. She'd noticed he wore a delicate gold ring on his left pinkie finger, which struck her as odd—he didn't seem like the pinkie ring type.

Autumn released a soft whimper of appreciation and tried to hide it with a yawn.

"Audie?" Quinn stood close to her now. Everyone else had moved toward the door. "Are you free for lunch?"

"No." Her eyes flew around the room and she shifted her weight nervously. She could smell his aftershave! She remembered how hot his lips had felt on hers!

"I need that list from you and we need to go over it. We can do it at lunch."

She nodded and tried not to look at him.

"Here's my card. Call me later this morning and tell me where we can meet."

She took it from him brusquely and saw him to the door. Without another word to her, Quinn walked out.

Audie eventually looked down at the business card she held in her hand. Under his name, he'd drawn a big arrow and written: "See back."

She flipped it over and read the words written in a tidy, modest hand: "Are you falling for me, Miss Adams?"

Audie's mouth gaped open as she stared at the closed door in disbelief. Wow—and she had thought Tim Burke was the biggest egomaniac she'd ever known.

"Dream on, you cocky bastard," she whispered.

"This is an impressive list." Quinn leaned back comfortably in his chair. "And the time line is handy, too."

"Wonderful."

This was pure humiliation. Audie was glad she'd at least had the presence of mind to suggest they meet at the police station instead of a restaurant. With all the noise and motion and phones and talking in this big open room, there was little chance for personal remarks, let alone personal contact. She felt safer this way, if not less embarrassed.

As Quinn busied himself with her list of ex-lovers, she let her eyes wander over his orderly desk. A computer and keyboard sat on a small side table directly behind him. A five-tiered metal in-box held stacks of files, neatly labeled by category. A black plastic desk organizer held pens in one tube, precisely sharpened pencils—points up—in another, and little compartments of paper clips, pushpins, and rubber bands. A pair of scissors labeled at the handle with the words "Quinn—Paws Off" was tucked in with the pencils.

An ornate silver picture frame sat to the back center of his desk, but Audie couldn't make out the image in the glare of the office lights. She turned a little in her seat and leaned forward, as if to stretch. She almost had it . . .

"My family," Quinn said, grabbing the frame and handing it to her. He scooted his chair closer and reached over the top, pointing, so near her now.

"This is my da, Jamie Quinn, retired from the force in 1996, a beat officer for thirty-two years in District Twenty-two, on the South Side. This is my mother, Trish—she died not long after this picture was taken."

"I'm sorry."

"Me, too."

Quinn pointed to the faces, all handsome and flushed, pressed together in a casual tangle of arms and shoulders and hugs. It was an outdoor setting—maybe a summer barbecue. They had the openmouthed smiles of laughter, and she could almost hear it. It must have been a raucous, rolling sound. They all looked like accomplished laughers, these Quinns.

About as different from her family as you could get, she thought.

"This is my baby brother Michael, an assistant state's attorney, and his wife, Sheila, and their two kids, Kiley—she's two here—and Little Pat. He was about four at the time."

Audie nodded, noticing the pinkie ring again. It was one of those Irish rings in the shape of a pair of hands holding a heart—it had some strange name she couldn't remember.

"The kids are six and four now." A huge smile lingered on Quinn's face before he resumed the tour. "And this is my brother Patrick. He's a parish priest at St. Aloisius on the Southwest Side, but he's a vicious liar, so don't ever believe a thing he says. And that's me. You know me."

It was the longest string of words she'd heard Stacey Quinn put together, and she noticed his voice had a charming cadence to it, somewhat scratchy but musical nonetheless. She looked up and caught his eye, their heads still quite close together.

"So your family's Irish?"

Audie didn't think it was the world's stupidest question, but the look Quinn gave her clearly indicated it had been.

"I see you picked up on that right away."

Should she just get up and walk out, or should she laugh at herself? She was still deciding when his green-and-gold eyes crinkled in amusement, and she heard her laugh escape without her permission. "Maybe I should be a detective, too."

He raised an eyebrow. "Hey, if Stanny-O can do it, I see no reason why you couldn't."

She giggled. "It was your ring, Quinn."

Quinn looked puzzled for a second before he glanced down at his left hand. "My mom's wedding band. It's a *claddagh*—you know those?"

"I've seen them before." She smiled at him, noting the sweet, shy expression in his eyes. Then she abruptly stopped smiling, because the sweetness left and it was replaced by something hungry.

Then she recalled the ridiculous words he'd written on his card, sat up straight, and pulled away.

Quinn put the frame back in its place and returned to her list. "This is a regular who's-who of Chicago's most eligible bachelors, Audie. Can I ask for their autographs when I talk with them?"

"Talk with . . . ?" Audie's mouth fell open. "You have to talk with them? In person?"

"Either myself or Detective Oleskiewicz."

"Why?" she cried.

He cocked his head a bit. "To try to find the bad guy."

"But I told you none of these guys would do something like that! I told you they were happy to get rid of me!"

Quinn narrowed his eyes. He didn't believe that for a second. "We still have to check," he said with a shrug. "We wouldn't be doing our job if we didn't."

Quinn began to read out loud. " 'Russell Ketchum, attorney,' your steady up until six months ago. Nobody since then?" He looked up, his face a mask of professional politeness.

"No one."

A tiny satisfied smile crooked up the corner of his mouth. He went back to the list. "WBBS anchor Kyle Singer—I just assumed he preferred men."

Audie had no comment.

"Then we've got University of Illinois–Chicago professor Will Dalton, the guy who wrote that famous book on TV sitcoms and childhood depression, right? Wasn't he on *Oprah*?"

She nodded.

"And then there's Chicago Bears placekicker Darren Billings—is he coming back this season? How'd the knee surgery go?"

Audie rolled her eyes—she knew Darren could use a brain transplant, but she didn't know squat about his knee. "I have no idea."

Quinn suddenly stilled. She watched his whole body go rigid. He looked at her, his face stiff and completely unreadable.

"Chicago's illustrious vice mayor, Mr. Timothy Burke," he said, his voice flat. "And how's Timmy these days?"

"I really don't know. Look, is there a point to this?"

Quinn placed her list inside a manila file and closed it. He sat back in his chair, tucked his hands behind his head, and studied her.

She studied him, too. He'd taken off his jacket, and Audie could see how the long muscles of his upper arms tugged at the sleeves. She noticed how his gun holster cut snugly across his big shoulders.

"How the hell did you end up with Timmy Burke?" he blurted out.

Audie watched Quinn's chest rise and fall in rapid breaths. He was positively vibrating with some kind of unfriendly energy, and it alarmed her.

"We met at a ribbon cutting a couple months before my mom died. Why?"

Quinn shrugged, and Audie saw him close his eyes for a moment to switch gears. Then he smiled pleasantly. "So, how did you come to do the column? What kind of work did you do before?"

She shook her head, trying to figure out how he'd gotten from Tim Burke to her job résumé.

"Before?" Audie gave her wavy hair a nervous fluff. "I was a teacher at Uptown Alternative School, a place for high school kids who aren't making it in the traditional setting. They sign a contract to graduate and stay out of trouble."

"I'm familiar with it. It's a good place."

"Really?" Audie was pleasantly surprised. "I was one of the founding teachers. I taught physical education, sociology, and anger management; plus I coached girls' soccer, basketball, and softball."

"Anger management?" Quinn's lopsided grin spread. "As in how to manage a wicked right cross to the jaw?"

She pursed her lips. "I said I taught it. I didn't say I actually *did* it."

Quinn laughed loudly at that. "OK, Miss Adams. So how long were you there?"

"Since right after college—seven years. That's where I met Griffin."

Quinn's eyes lit up. "OK. So tell me the story with him."

"Why?" Audie scowled, shifting in the chair and crossing her legs defensively. "Do you have to know everything about me? Aren't there some things I get to keep private?"

He shrugged a little, reaching for his tiny notebook. "Sure. Lots of things. Just not this."

Audie looked down at her hands and took a breath. "He's my best friend, Quinn, the best friend I've ever had. There is no way in hell he's sending me those letters."

"That's good to hear. Then I'll be able to cross him off right away."

She grunted. "I don't like this."

"How serious was it?"

She closed her eyes. "We were together for over two years. We broke up when he turned pro—soccer—and was traveling all the time. But we're still close. We'll always be close."

"Two years is longer than seven weeks, Audie."

She smiled a bit. "I think we stayed together a lot longer than we should have because it felt safe, comfortable. It was the first serious relationship for both of us. Besides, I think that was before I had the green slimy problem we discussed."

Quinn nodded, letting his eyes trace the line of her cheek and jaw. "Do the letters scare you, Audie?"

She looked around the room again, a blur of activity. Quinn seemed so calm compared to the rest of the cops in here, she thought. He seemed to move slower—not a lazy kind of slow but an intentional hesitation.

"There's definitely something about the letters that bothers me," she said, biting her bottom lip and gazing at her sandals—anything to keep from looking in his eyes. "It's not so much what he's saying. It's the way he's saying it. There's so much hate there, but it's like he's laughing at me, too. Like he knows me, like the joke's on me." She looked off into the room again. "Do you know what I mean?"

Quinn dropped forward in his chair and leaned his elbows on his knees. He scrutinized the softness of her face in profile. "I do, Audie. And I think you're right—whoever it is knows you. That's why we're starting where we are."

She turned to face him, feeling a bit shaky. The fear must have been broadcast in her eyes, because Quinn suddenly reached out for her hand. She slipped her fingers inside the safety of his warm, steady grip.

"Your apartment is safe, Audie. That place is a fortress."

She nodded. She knew Lakeside Pointe was a forty-six-story citadel. Her neighbors were the kind of people who demanded their privacy and security and were happy to pay dearly for it. Her mother had been one of those people, and along with the column, Audie had inherited the $6 million condominium that overlooked Lake Michigan and the Gold Coast.

"It's the rest of your life that concerns me," Quinn said suddenly. He squeezed her hand a bit. "You're by yourself a lot."

"I like it that way. I refuse to let these letters take away my privacy. And I don't want a bodyguard or some cop following me around, if that's what you're getting at."

Quinn dropped her hand and gave it a friendly pat as he returned to the file. "Actually, you don't have much choice. My commander has already made it clear to Stan and me that you're our priority right now."

She shook her head slowly and emphatically. "No way in hell."

"Just until September twenty-second. To be on the safe side."

"No! That's . . ." She waved her hand, thinking. "That's a month away! There's no way you are going to follow me around for a month, Quinn! Absolutely not!"

He shrugged. "Detective Oleskiewicz then."

"Well—"

"But you should know that Stanny-O's got a wee bit o' the gas now and then."

How extremely vulgar he was. So why was she laughing? It had to be the brogue he'd slipped in for effect, and she couldn't stop giggling to save her soul. Several moments went by before she reclaimed her composure. "You're disgusting, Quinn."

"Thank you, lass."

She stood up from the chair and glared down at him, seeing that he now grinned ear-to-ear.

"There will be no kissing, are we clear on this?" She put her hands on her hips. "I regret that kiss. You're delusional if you think I'm interested in you, Detective, so don't grin at me like that. I think it's best to be honest about this from the beginning so nobody gets hurt. Understand?"

"Honesty is good."

She made an impatient clucking sound, abruptly turned to go, and caught the buckle of her sandal on the chair leg. She toppled over and went belly-down on the shiny linoleum, giving Quinn another look at what he believed was one of her best assets.

He came behind her and grabbed her by the waist, pulling her to her feet. She slapped his hands away and walked out in a huff, not looking back.

Quinn watched every swaying, ripe, and round step she took.

"Jee-ay-sus," he whispered to himself.

Audie decided to walk from the station to her office, taking a detour along Michigan Avenue. She needed the exercise. She needed to take in big gulps of heavy, humid Chicago summer air. She needed to get a grip on herself.

There was something about Quinn that completely unnerved her. He was a very basic man—not as smooth as Griffin or as charismatic as Tim Burke or as devastatingly handsome as Kyle Singer. What he was, she decided, was incredibly male. He oozed it. He knew it. He swaggered. Probably an illness found in all Chicago cops. And the way she'd caught him looking at her—like a lion looks at breakfast. She really should file a citizen's complaint against him for that kiss. She should be revolted by the whole situation.

The problem was, she wasn't revolted and she wasn't complaining. In fact, the man sent chills through her. Quinn could be categorized as one of those dangerous quiet types, she decided, and she'd just have to keep him at arm's length.

Audie sighed—this was going to be a long month.

She stopped at the corner of Michigan and Chicago Avenues to wait for the light. There were nearly 3 million people in this city, and one of them wished her harm. Quinn was right—it was someone who knew her. She could feel it. But who?

She glanced quickly at the sweaty faces so near her, yet so far away, absorbed in their own inner worlds of troubles and desires. They all just stood there, as if in a trance, waiting for the light to change.

She'd be damned if she'd stand around waiting for something awful to happen on September 22. Of course nothing would happen. She refused to even think that way.

Audie crossed the street and picked up the pace. She probably should call Drew to tell him about all this nonsense. She should probably call her brother anyway—it had been at least a couple months since they'd spoken. His latest divorce should be final now, if she remembered correctly.

Audie stopped at the Tiffany's window just to look and

to catch her breath. She'd been power walking, it seemed, and her reflection in the dark glass showed sweat pouring down her neck and sticking to the silk blouse.

She crossed the street and walked down Chestnut, smelling the Indian food from the Bombay House and suddenly realizing she was ravenous. She would just run up to her office and get her wallet and—a man was waiting for her on the stoop.

"Hello, Autumn."

"God, Russ! You scared me to death!"

"What a coincidence, then, because you are scaring the living hell out of me lately—do you realize we've got just over a month to renew your contract? Do you realize how many millions of dollars are involved? Do you have a good reason for not returning any of my calls? And why is a police detective harassing me?"

"Wow. Already?" Audie looked up into his gunmetal gray eyes filled with impatience. She pushed past him and bounded up the marble steps to the massive oak-and-leaded-glass doors.

"Just now on my portable," he said, staring at the phone in his palm. "He said he wants to question me about some letters or something. What's this all about, Audie?"

She shrugged, holding the door open for him. He stepped up into the dark, cool foyer and looked down at her. "God, what have you been doing, playing soccer in your skirt? You're dripping wet."

"It's hot, Russ. I sweat when it's hot. I'm a warm-blooded creature, unlike you."

He started up the steps in front of her, ignoring her insult. When they entered the reception area, a blast of icy air conditioning pummeled them and Audie sighed with relief.

"I see he's found you." Marjorie smiled at the two of them and handed Audie a few phone messages. "I made some fresh-brewed raspberry iced tea; would anyone care for some? Next month's columns are all done, Audie, and I need to know if they're good to go. I also need you to OK the travel schedule—it's on your desk. And I just ordered sandwiches for all of us. Will that be all right?"

"Yes," Audie muttered, staring back at Marjorie. "To everything you just said."

"So the syndication numbers are way up over last year— sixty-seven new U.S. newspapers and twelve international. I think it's the modern, sexy twist you bring to the whole concept. I really do. Book sales are steady. Oh, and the feedback is very positive on the new publicity shot— they're going to start sending it out on the wire next month. I think you look fabulous with your hair down."

"Great." Audie fumbled around under the haphazard stacks of paper on her desktop, looking for any stray Tylenol packets. She found one beneath an empty Fritos bag, which she crumpled up and tossed in the wastepaper basket across the room.

"Nothing but net, baby," she said with a smile.

Russell stared at her. He had that pinched look of disapproval on his aristocratic face, the look that had made her cringe when they'd been a couple—the one that made her cringe still.

"Mind if I smoke?" Audie opened her desk drawer and pulled out a pack of Merit Lights. "I'm down to about three cigarettes a week. Isn't that great? For some reason I'm desperate for one at the moment."

Audie eyed him through the smoke, noting with satisfaction the subtle change in his face. She'd succeeded in making him just plain angry now.

Russell Ketchum, partner in Ketchum & Clinton Entertainment Law, Inc., was an attractive man by anyone's standards, with those cool eyes and dark hair and fine bones.

Audie once had found him terribly attractive—right up until she found him in bed with a paralegal named Megan Peterson. Then it had disintegrated into weeks of begging for forgiveness and another chance. He even said he loved her! What a mess! What a joke!

She knew she owed him a debt, however. Thanks to the Russell Ketchum debacle, she'd sworn off men entirely, and it had been the most peaceful six months in memory.

After just a few puffs, she ground down the cigarette in the ashtray and picked little flakes of tobacco off her tongue. "Yuck. I really don't even like these things anymore."

"How marvelous for you." Russell pulled a legal-sized folder from his briefcase, a pained expression on his face. "It's just a standard extension, another three years with the same thirty percent signing bonus your mother received and a ten percent increase in syndication fees. I've already got it drawn up, and all you need to do is sign."

Audie flashed her eyes at him. "You mean you haven't learned to forge my signature yet?" She laughed loudly. "Why not? You do everything else!"

A polite tap was heard at the door, and Marjorie carried in a tray of chicken club sandwiches, coleslaw, and more iced tea. She delivered the goods and left after a few friendly words for Russell and an understanding smile for Audie.

Audie's hunger took precedence over her anger and she reached for a sandwich. "Look. I'll have to think about it, Russell. Just leave it here."

"There's nothing to think about and you can't sit on it, Audie. You don't have time."

"I won't sit on it." She took a huge bite and closed her eyes in pleasure. "I was starving. You want a sandwich?"

"No. I don't want a sandwich. I want you to sign the damn contract." Russell rose and took the file to the credenza below the bay window. He pushed aside a stack of newspapers to find a place for it. "Don't forget, Audie."

"I won't," she said, her mouth full. "Thanks for stopping by."

Russell had his hand on the doorknob but turned to her. "The detective said somebody's been sending you threatening notes for a year. How come you never told me, Audie?"

She reached for the coleslaw. "I didn't think it was a big deal. Griffin finally convinced me to call the police."

Russell chuckled. "Ah, yes, Griffin Nash—your adviser and moral compass."

"At least I have one," she snapped.

He smiled sadly. "Bye, Audie. I'll call you next week to remind you about the contract."

"Later," she said, not looking up.

CHAPTER 3

August 27
Dear Homey Helen:

Have you ever noticed how some stains just never come out, no matter how hard you scrub? I think you owe your readers the truth. I think you should tell them that not everything can be made nice and tidy, that some things never come out right—in the wash or in life.

Perhaps I'm just bitter.

Fondly,
Your most loyal fan.

PS: I so enjoyed your tip on how to remove furniture indentations from deep pile carpet.

"At home? This came to your home address?" Quinn's frown lines deepened as he went from Audie's face to Stanny-O's.

"It was in my mailbox last night."

"Why didn't you call me?"

"I . . . uh, you were off duty."

"You've got my card. You call me anytime, all right?" Quinn made sure she saw that he meant it.

She nodded.

"I don't get it." Stanny-O rose from his desk and held an open box of candy under Audie's nose. "The guy threatens to drop you in the Bass-O-Matic with the last letter, then gets all philosophical about it in this one. Care for a mint?"

"Wow! Yes!" She grabbed a Frango Mint and tossed it in her mouth, feeling the chocolate melt on the back of her tongue.

"Another?"

"Sure! Thanks, Stanny-O." She smiled at him until she saw the surprise in his small blue eyes. "I'm sorry, Detective. I heard Quinn call you that."

"Ah, no problem, Audie." He grinned at her. "One more?"

She nodded happily and snapped another mint from the box. Stanny-O seemed quite pleased with himself.

"Hey, Willy Wonka, any report from the state police lab yet?" Quinn asked.

"Yeah. All of them are off a midline ink-jet printer, nothing fancy, nothing high-powered. Like from a home office kind of setup, one of the major brands. Nothing unusual that would make it traceable."

Quinn nodded. "And where are we on fingerprints?"

Stanny-O looked down at a page of handwritten notes. "Griffin Nash, Marjorie Stoddard, Audie here, we got Tim Burke's on file, along with Will Dalton, Kyle Singer, and Darren Billings, who apparently ran with a bad crowd as a juvenile. And we had Mr. Russell Ketchum come in. He didn't like getting his hands dirty, by the way."

"Little late for that," Audie mumbled to herself.

Quinn heard her and raised his eyebrows in amusement. "We had a nice long visit with Mr. Ketchum last evening," he said.

"You going to arrest him?" Audie looked hopeful.

"Nah," Stanny-O said. "Being an asshole lawyer isn't a chargeable offense last time I looked. Besides, we can't seem to come up with a reason he'd do this. I mean, what would Russell Ketchum have to gain if you got scared and quit the family business?"

Audie looked at both the detectives. "Nothing. He'd actually lose quite a bit, personally and for the law firm. Homey Helen has always been one of their biggest cash cows."

"Exactly," Stanny-O said. "So, we'll put him on the back burner."

"Thanks for bringing this in," Quinn said, placing the latest note inside a manila envelope. He rose off his desktop and cupped her elbow. "I'll walk you to your car, OK?"

"Sure—" Quinn was already hustling her across the room, his palm now flat against the small of her back. "Bye, Stanny-O."

"See ya," he replied.

Quinn spotted her Carrera 911 in the parking lot without much trouble, and they walked together toward the car. He put his hand on her upper arm as she opened the driver's side door.

"What are your plans today?" Quinn asked.

Audie shrugged a little. "Stuff at the office. I thought I'd go for a run this afternoon after lunch. Then I've got a book signing and talk at the Newberry Library tonight."

"Where do you run?"

She pursed her lips. "Lincoln Park. Why?"

"Today you've got a partner."

"Quinn, I don't think—"

He very softly brushed his knuckles across her cheek, and the jolt of his touch made her eyes fly wide.

"He knows where you live, Audie, and my commander doesn't want another Homey Helen getting hurt on our watch—bad for the city's image and all. End of discussion."

He dropped his hand, but the whole side of Audie's face

tingled. She looked into green eyes filled with determination—and concern—and she sighed.

"Am I right in assuming that if I tell you to go to hell you'll just follow me anyway?"

Quinn smiled and nodded.

"Meet me at three o'clock at the main entrance to Lakeside Pointe, then. I usually do a loop up to Montrose Harbor and back, sometimes wander through Lincoln Park Zoo, about ten miles or so. Can you handle that?"

"I can handle it." He let his fingers barely graze the top of her hand and whispered, "See you then."

He was precisely on time, appearing from behind a massive black marble pillar, already grinning.

"Do you need to stretch?" she asked him.

Quinn tried not to look at her below the neck, and God, it wasn't easy.

"Already did. You?"

"I'm ready. Let me know if you can't keep up." She shot him a smile.

They took off side by side down the paved pathway, through the green ribbon of public parkland along Lake Michigan. This afternoon, the water shimmered in the sunlight and absorbed the blue of a cloudless sky. It was hot but less oppressive than the last few days had been.

Once they'd hit a comfortable pace together, Quinn decided he'd risk looking at her. She wore a pair of high-cut running shorts and a torso-length black sports bra. Her hair was pulled back in a ponytail. She had nice wide shoulders. And her legs were muscular and trim—the legs of an athlete.

"I like running *with* you better than running *after* you," he said.

"Yeah, but I bet it's harder to look at my butt this way." She kept her eyes in front.

"Maybe you should be a detective," Quinn mumbled.

The lakefront was crowded that day, and a steady parade of cyclists, joggers, skaters, and walkers streamed by.

"Do you play any sports, Quinn?"

"Hoops now and then. Pickup hockey. A little soccer with the guys in the neighborhood."

"Where do you live?"

"Well." Quinn fell behind her for a moment to let a group run by, then returned to her side. "I live on the North Side now, but I meant the neighborhood where I grew up."

"And where's that?" She glanced over at him. He wasn't even breaking a sweat.

"Beverly. You've probably never even heard of it."

"Sure I have. The stronghold of the Irish South Side. Nineteenth Ward. Alderman Paul Ryan."

Quinn looked at her in shock before it dawned on him. "Oh, yeah, Timmy Burke. How could I have forgotten?"

She grinned at him. "He talked about it sometimes. So how long have you two known each other?"

"Too long. We grew up about a block apart and went to school together, from kindergarten all the way through Brother Rice."

Quinn dropped back again to avoid a bicyclist.

"Having trouble keeping up, Detective?" She increased her pace a bit.

"I'll let you know, Homey."

Audie's head whipped around and she laughed outright. "Homey? That's funny, Stacey."

"Point taken," he said. Suddenly Quinn darted around a dog walker and took off a bit faster. Audie pulled up alongside.

"Are we racing, Quinn?"

"Nope. Just out for a nice jog."

Quinn tugged at the neck of his Police Athletic League T-shirt and jerked it forward over his head with one hand.

The gesture struck Audie as an overtly macho thing to do, and as he tucked the shirt inside the back of his running shorts she tried not to look at him below the neck. God, it was hard.

"Don't you worry about skin cancer?" Audie asked. "You're very fair."

"All the time. I wear SPF thirty."

She cast him a sideways glance. He was a soft peach color and covered with pale freckles and light brown body hair. He was lean and hard and she could see the ripple of muscle through his back and shoulders. His upper arms looked powerful. "So how Irish are you, Quinn? Your grandparents or something?"

He laughed and caught her eye. "Them, too. But Da and my mother were both born there. They came over in the sixties. I'm first-generation."

"Oh, I see."

"Do you now?"

Audie chuckled. "No, not really. I don't know much about Ireland. I suppose you're Catholic?"

"I suppose I am. You got something against Papists?"

She blew out air. "No. Are you trying me make me hit you again or something?"

He laughed. "Just making conversation. How about you? My guess would be Presbyterian."

Her mouth fell open and she glared at him. "Why do you say that?" Was it her imagination, or had he just kicked up the pace?

"Well, there's growing up rich in Winnetka. The name Adams. The general upscale North Shore WASP thing you have going on."

"Upscale North Shore WASP thing?" She huffed. "That's pretty insulting, Stacey. If you must know, I'm nothing, really, but my parents were married in the Presbyterian Church. Don't tell me you're prejudiced against Presbyterians?"

This time it wasn't her imagination—he'd just sped up again.

"I've got nothing against Presbyterians in particular, just Protestants in general."

She narrowed her eyes at him and shook her head. "You're mocking me."

It was a marvel to her how slowly his grin spread and how much smug sexuality was conveyed in the gradual curl of his lips. "I'm just playing with you, Homey. It seems you've got a fine sense of humor for a Protestant girl."

She rolled her eyes and made a break for it, turning on the heat now. She began to weave and pivot through the crowd of people, skateboards, scooters, bikes, and dogs, leaving Quinn in the dust. It served the cocky bastard right.

Then he ran right by her.

As she chased him, Audie knew she was being childish. She knew he was teasing her, testing her. She realized she should just turn around and have a nice, peaceful, quiet run home. She didn't need this aggravation.

But instead, she focused on the white T-shirt bobbing along his compact, muscular butt and the really nice set of his shoulders and poured it on.

Just as she reached him, he slowed considerably, and Audie had to twist sideways to avoid slamming into him.

"You're very graceful, Homey. And fast. You play a mean forward, too."

Again he surprised her. A compliment—several of them in a row, in fact.

"Thanks. You're pretty fast yourself." Audie was sweating up a storm now and she wiped her forehead with the back of her hand.

"Here." Quinn tossed the shirt to her and she mopped her face with it. The clean, bracing scent of him nearly made her topple over. She slowed almost to a walk and raised the shirt to her face once more before she tossed it back to him.

"I'd like to talk to your brother sometime soon," Quinn said.

Audie stopped dead. "Drew? Why? You think he's writing the notes?" She placed her hands on her knees and leaned forward, catching her breath. "That's ridiculous."

Quinn grabbed her arm suddenly, pulling her off the pathway before she was flattened by a kid on Rollerblades.

They stood in the grass staring at each other, breathing fast. They'd been sprinting for quite a distance.

"Not necessarily, but I need to check it out."

She nodded, swallowing hard, staring at the muscles in Quinn's chest and his little pale pink nipples. "Drew wouldn't do something like that," she breathed, letting her eyes travel down Quinn's rippled abdomen and then out over the lake, anywhere but at that body! "Anyway, there have been, what, eighteen letters now?" She let out a laugh. "Andrew Adams is incapable of that kind of scheme, Quinn. It would mean coming up with a plan and sticking to it—you know, commitment. Not his strong point."

Quinn took her hand and they walked together across the grass, toward the water, and Audie stared at his striking profile. This man left her bewildered. In a span of thirty minutes, Stacey Quinn had insulted her, aggravated her, mocked her, complimented her, made her laugh, and saved her from harm.

And now he cradled her hand with such tenderness that she couldn't bring herself to pull away. In fact, she found herself moving closer to his side.

What was he doing to her?

Quinn faced her then, the sun behind him turning him into gold, and he smiled. "You really are extraordinarily beautiful, Audie—for a Cubs fan."

"Ha!" She stood in front of him, smiling back. "And you're the most aggravating man I've ever met in my life."

He thought about that for a moment, exploring her face with his eyes. "Would you believe me if I said I don't mean to aggravate you?"

"Hell, no."

Quinn leaned his head back and roared, and the gesture reminded her of the family photo she had seen on his desk.

She wondered what it was like to grow up in a family like his, where people laughed and smiled and threw their arms carelessly around one another, sure that they were loved.

As if he read her mind, Quinn draped an arm loosely over her shoulder. "My brothers would love you. What do you say we go see the lions, Homey?"

She was running late. They shouldn't have stopped for ice-cream cones near Lincoln Park Zoo. They shouldn't have sat under the tree and talked as long as they did. Now it was after six o'clock, and she still had to get showered and change into the Homey Helen uniform and get to the library in less than an hour.

"Can you wait while I get my clothes out of the car?"

Audie cocked her head at him, confused. "What? Your car—?"

"It's in a visitor space in the garage. I'll get a shower at your place and go with you to the book signing."

She closed her eyes to gather her patience.

"Three minutes," he said, already running off to the garage elevator, leaving Audie standing at the building's lakefront entrance, a bit confused.

She turned and stared at the water, dotted with after-work sailboats, and suddenly longed to be out on the family's forty-three-foot cutter. Alone in the wind. Alone where there were no threatening letters, no contracts, no book signings, no South Side Irish detectives who made her crazy.

He was so easy to talk to. She'd told him more in the last few hours than she'd shared with Griffin in the last ten years—and it scared her. She was a private person. She knew she could talk a lightning streak, but it was usually surface things. She didn't open up very easily. Yet she had with him.

"So what's the story on the column, Audie? How did you get where you are?"

He'd asked her that as they lolled in the shade just outside the zoo, licking their ice-cream cones. Seeing him apply his tongue and lips to the creamy white concoction had caused her insides to flip, and all she could think about was that wild kiss on the sidewalk. She'd probably think about that kiss for the rest of her life.

"You know how my mom died?" Audie had asked him.

He nodded, holding her gaze. "I certainly do. I know the guys that handled her homicide."

"Oh, of course," she said sadly. "Well, we'd never talked about the column, because I guess everyone just assumed Helen Adams would live forever. She was only sixty-two, still very energetic and busy—and fabulous, of course." Audie smiled a little.

"And then Marjorie called me that night to tell me she'd been mugged and beaten. So I get to see her on her way to surgery and she looks like she's dead already—she didn't even look like my mother. Her hair was all sticking up and her skin was gray and . . ." Audie closed her eyes for a moment.

"She made me promise I'd do it. She made me swear to her that I'd take over the column. We'd never even discussed it before, but, well, I agreed because I thought she'd get better and it wouldn't be an issue."

Audie looked up at Quinn and blinked. "Then she died. And poof—I'm Homey Helen."

Quinn was crunching on the sugar cone now, still watching her carefully. A thin trickle of ice cream slipped from the point of the cone and ran down his wrist. Audie watched him scoop it up with the tip of his tongue, and little black spots began to dance in her vision.

"Why would she ask you to do that? Didn't she know—?"

"That I'm a spaz?"

He frowned at her. "That the column wasn't something you were particularly interested in."

Audie chuckled and finished up her own ice cream before it liquefied in the heat. "What I wanted wasn't part of the equation. Never really was," she said, munching her cone.

Before she realized what was happening, Quinn leaned forward and licked softly at her forearm, removing a wayward pearl of melting ice cream from the fine hairs there. Audie gasped.

"So what happened with the estate?" he asked nonchalantly, as if his warm tongue hadn't just raked over her skin.

Audie blinked, trying to recover her composure. "Uh, I got the apartment, the syndication contract, the office . . ." He was licking his lips and smiling at her, which was completely unfair. ". . . the Porsche, and half of everything my mother and father had accumulated. Drew got the house on Sheridan Road, the summer house in Door County, the sailboat . . ." Quinn gently sucked on each of his fingers, never taking his eyes off hers. ". . . and the rest of the cash." She let out a breath when she finished.

"So how much has your brother managed to lose in the last year?"

Audie snorted. "A lot of it. I don't know how bad it is,

really, but if you think he wants to do the column, you're way off base."

"OK. Why's that?"

It was her turn to grin. "I think that will become obvious when you go talk to him."

"Fair enough."

Audie lay back in the grass and Quinn propped himself up on his elbow to gaze down at her.

"How long do you plan on keeping this up? How much longer can you do this?"

His words were hushed now, and the rough, musical quality came back to his voice. She liked that sound very much, and her eyes automatically followed it, entranced.

"I'm not sure," she said. In the afternoon light, she could see the fine lines around his eyes and at the corners of his mouth. Those remarkable olive-and-gold eyes looked right through her. "I'm supposed to be signing a new contract within the month."

"And?"

"We really need to be heading back."

Quinn returned from the parking garage and came up behind her. She spun around to see that he had a garment bag slung over his shoulder and that he stood very close.

"I got two bathrooms," she said, a hint of challenge in her voice. "And forty-five minutes."

It was ten till seven, and Quinn waited patiently in Audie's living room, looking out the massive glass wall to the blue expanse of lake, the long stretch of city, and the Ferris wheel at Navy Pier. It was so clear this evening that he could see the Indiana Dunes and the pale silhouette of the Michigan shoreline.

Quinn had been ready for a while now, but he could still hear Audie cussing and bumping into things at the other end of the huge apartment.

"Oh, crap! Hell!"

He smiled to himself again. So this was Homey Helen's abode. He wondered if the original Helen was flopping around in her grave like a mackerel.

It wasn't filthy. In fact, the guest bathroom was spotless, probably because it was never used. But the rest of the apartment was in a state of utter disarray.

Newspapers, magazines, books, and sweat socks were scattered on tables. A half-filled microwave popcorn bag had toppled over on the expensive Italian couch, leaving oily streaks on the leather. He'd seen how three soccer balls had rolled to a stop in odd places, like in front of the stove. He couldn't imagine the ball was in the way since the kitchen obviously wasn't used for much—there was nothing in the refrigerator but bottled water, a jar of jalapeño peppers, and what appeared to be some kind of shriveled moss-covered ball that may have once been a citrus fruit.

A thick layer of dust had accumulated on the screen of her high-definition television set. He knew this because he'd run his finger across it.

"Quinn!"

"Yep."

"Are you ready?"

"Yep. Have been."

"Do me a favor—do you see a pair of bone pumps out there somewhere?"

Bone pumps were either medical devices or women's shoes, Quinn thought. "You mean shoes?"

"Yes, shoes! Look in the dining room and toss them back here when you find them, would you please?"

Quinn headed into the formal dining area, another room strewn with newspapers and odd bits of debris. He saw the shoes sticking out from beneath a sleek modern sideboard—blond maple, he thought. As he looped his fingers inside the shoes and stood up, he saw a few family photos on display. Like everything else, they were sprinkled with dust.

He took a second to examine them—and his eyes fell on one group shot in particular. There was Audie—fourteen maybe—gangly and wearing braces and suffering from a fatal case of Big Hair, standing as if someone were holding a gun to her head. Quinn laughed at the angry look in her eyes until he saw that her brother possessed the same expression. They must have been fighting.

Audie's father looked absolutely lost, standing off to the side a bit, his hands shoved deep into the pockets of his suit trousers.

In the center was Helen, beaming into the camera like she had with Margaret Thatcher and Nancy Reagan, her hand resting on Audie's shoulder. It didn't seem to be out of affection as much as control.

And who was that? A younger, quite beautiful version of Marjorie Stoddard, standing with a protective hand on Drew's arm, holding the leash to a regal-looking standard poodle with a pompadour and a pompom tail.

Dear God. Out of the lot of them, Quinn decided the poodle looked the happiest.

"Did you find them?"

He straightened up at the faint sound of her shout and headed toward the other end of the apartment. A man could get a blister on his heel walking from one end of this place to the other.

"Whoa!" Quinn pulled back as Audie ran into the hallway outside her bedroom.

"Sorry. Thanks."

Quinn watched her balance one hand on the door frame, bend at the waist, and slip her feet into the shoes one at a time.

She looked elegant, refined, and professional. She'd chosen a simple pale pink sheath dress and wore pearls at her throat and ears. Her hair was twisted back in some complicated shape that left those little tendrils loose at the nape of her neck again. She smelled faintly of flowers and spice.

"You're lovely, Audie."

She straightened up, and her breath caught. "God, you clean up good, Stacey. You look downright . . . I don't know . . . Protestant!"

As Quinn laughed, she checked out his lightweight gray suit, simply cut, nicely fitted, and the starched white collar and a tie of watery blues and grays. The man was dazzling.

"I'm late. Let's go," she said.

Quinn couldn't remember the last time he'd enjoyed being in a library this much. It was a decent crowd, mostly after-work types and a few older retirees. He scanned the faces, looking for anything that might catch his eye—a little too much adoration or anger or resentment, anything that didn't fit.

"Perhaps I'm just bitter."

He couldn't get that sentence out of his head. There was something intimate in those words. He looked around the room again—was there bitterness in anyone's face here tonight? He didn't see it. These people were polite, excited, starstruck, and, at worst, a bit impatient that they had to wait in line for Audie's autograph.

But whoever was sending her those notes wasn't here tonight. Quinn was sure of it.

He moved around the large hall, watching her from every possible angle. He'd listened earlier as she stood at the podium to chat about the column and answer questions. He laughed to himself when he realized that most of her answers involved the use of club soda, baking soda, or white vinegar.

She was good, Quinn had to admit. She smiled pleasantly as she rattled off facts and tricks. She looked perfectly in control. She looked as if she enjoyed herself.

It was only when Audie stepped down from the podium that the spell had been broken. She tripped on a microphone cord and nearly fell on her face before the library director grabbed her arm.

About an hour had passed since then, and Audie sat at a long wooden table, her legs crossed daintily at the ankles, writing and smiling and nodding. At one point she raised her head, blinked, and looked around the room until she found him.

Quinn watched something pass over her face—relief, maybe. Whatever it was, it was just for him, and it made him smile.

The smile abruptly faded. Quinn felt the hard, cold stare of unfriendly eyes on him and turned in time to see a man disappear around the double doors of the hall. After a quick look Audie's way, Quinn followed.

He found nothing. No one. But he wasn't about to leave Audie alone to go chase after the guy. Besides, he had an appointment with him in a few days.

An appointment with Vice Mayor Tim Burke.

"I've got to eat something." Audie leaned back in the car seat, closed her eyes, and sighed. She flipped off her shoes. "I thought I'd never get out of there!"

Quinn was driving the Porsche north on La Salle Street. "I'll take you somewhere."

"I'm too tired to go anywhere."

"Then I'll take you nowhere."

"Perfect."

They drove in silence for most of the way as Quinn headed west on Division and north on Clybourn. He pulled into an alley off of Southport. In the dark, Audie had no idea where they were—until they whipped into a small parking space adjacent to someone's neatly landscaped backyard.

She turned to him, too tired and hungry to put up much of a fight. "Is the food here any good?"

"Always."

The first thing she noticed was how clean his floors were—shiny, flawless oak strips that ran the narrow length of the house, not a scatter rug to be seen in the whole place.

The next thing she noticed was that Quinn's house immediately put her at ease. There were big, overstuffed chairs, a soft-looking couch, photographs on the walls, and a nice old fireplace. She saw lots of green thriving plants near the windows and the bookcases filled with rows of books arranged by height.

"Make yourself at home," Quinn said, hanging his suit jacket in the hall closet. "Wine?"

She nodded. "Bathroom?"

He pointed up the set of stairs. "Down the hall and to the left."

When she finished in the bathroom, she ripped off her panty hose and balled them up in her hand. Wearing panty hose in the summer in Chicago was masochistic, and she sighed with relief to feel the air on her legs.

Audie caught the smell of onions and hot butter and headed toward the stairs, as if pulled by the rich and pungent scent.

But suddenly she stopped, blinked, and stared at the wall of framed photographs beside her—portraits, candids, baby pictures, weddings, communions, landscapes, cityscapes, graduations—all along the upstairs hallway from the chair rail nearly to the ceiling. The faces! So many faces!

The pictures made her smile. Quinn and two other boys in hockey uniforms, one boy missing a front tooth. Scruffy-looking mutts. Fishing trips. First cars.

Her eye moved to one picture, a wedding portrait from

what looked like the early 1900s. The man stood stiffly in a suit that didn't quite fit, one large hand clutching a cap against his leg and a sweet, shy smile plastered across his broad face.

His other hand rested hesitantly on the tufted parlor chair that held his bride. Her thick, dark hair was piled loosely on top of her head. Her light eyes danced in the camera flash. The bodice of her gown fit snugly against her tidy figure.

Quinn's great-grandparents, maybe? Audie gazed in wonder at all the people that seemed to radiate from this single old wedding portrait, their placement telling the story of a family.

Audie realized with a start that she was weeping, that a steady flow of silent tears now ran down her face. She swiped at them with the balled-up panty hose and scolded herself for the ridiculous outburst. It had been a long day.

With a deep breath she turned to go, but her heart was having none of it. She looked back and stared. There was joy on that wall. There was life and death and a reason for everything in between. She felt the jealousy stick in her chest like a knife, sending the pain of longing through her.

Damn it, how did her heart become such an empty, awful place? It wasn't right that she felt so disconnected when other people had so much . . . what was all this she was looking at? Belonging? Family? Love?

She'd always known she was different somehow, but standing here in front of these faces made the truth so obvious it was laughable.

Audie was alone. She always had been.

The tears came in earnest, and she bent her face to the panty hose and let her shoulders shake.

She caught a slight movement out of the corner of her eye and saw Quinn at the bottom of the stairs, watching her, his face pulled tight with concern.

She shook her head and started down the steps, waving her hand dismissively. "I'm fine. I'm sorry for crying."

He pulled out a crisp white handkerchief from his pants pocket and waited for her to reach him. With great gentleness, he dabbed at her tears and then handed her the folded cloth. Quinn placed a hand at the small of her back and bent his lips to her ear.

"I know we're not the prettiest bunch on earth," he whispered musically, "but I believe you're the first that's been driven to tears at the sight of us."

She laughed a bit and leaned against him, feeling his arm come around her. Quinn had removed his tie and rolled up his shirtsleeves, and his bare forearm rested warm against her exposed skin.

"Let's eat, OK, Homey?"

She nodded, still wiping at the tears, as he led her into the kitchen.

It was perhaps the most delicious omelet she'd ever eaten—light but rich with cream cheese, onions, green peppers, and mushrooms. He'd made rye toast, too, and orange juice. The meal raised her blood sugar, and her mood, dramatically.

When they were done, Quinn sat back and watched Audie pad around his kitchen in her bare feet, happily scrubbing pans and wiping the countertops, chattering all the while. Apparently, she *did* know how to clean a kitchen when the need arose, and the fact lightened his heart.

He enjoyed seeing her turn and spin and pivot on those smooth, uncovered legs. He smiled appreciatively when she bent over to fill the dishwasher. When she stood up, he could see the slight swell of her belly against the snug dress, and he wanted to run his hands across her there. He noticed the bone and muscle move in her ankles and soft-looking feet, and he wanted to put his hands on her there, too.

She turned to him suddenly, holding a small box in her hand. Her dark eyes were huge. "Quinn?"

He winced, then shrugged in defeat. "I'm busted."

Audie let out a delighted laugh as she flipped through the categories. " 'Auto,' 'Home Maintenance,' 'Household Organization,' 'Laundry,' 'Stains,' 'Thrifty Tips' . . .?" Her mouth fell open.

Quinn rose from his seat at the kitchen table and sauntered toward her. He gently took the box from her hands, closed the lid, and placed it back on the countertop. In doing so, he'd managed to reach across her body and pin her to the cabinets.

"It was my mother's." He pulled back just a bit, his eyes moving from her gaze to her fabulously full lips. "She was your biggest fan."

"You mean my mother's biggest fan, don't you?" Audie struggled to raise her wineglass in the narrow space between them and took a sip.

"I've always liked the column, too."

Audie grinned, then politely pushed past him into the middle of the room. She looked around his house again—charming, organized, clean, and comfortable. Her eyes fell to the gleaming floors.

"Damp mopped with two tea bags per quart of water, Quinn?"

He nodded.

"Wow."

"Yeah, my brothers think I'm a freak."

"Well, you are!" She laughed at him, suddenly spinning around to examine the spice rack over the stove. "A ha! Alphabetized! I knew it!"

He shrugged.

"The CDs, too?"

"Yes."

"Could I please look in your freezer?"

"Be my guest."

So what if she was giggling at the sight of his labeled and dated Tupperware containers and freezer bags? He got to stare at her sweet, round butt as she did so.

"Oh, my God!" Audie slammed the freezer door and spun around with her arms flung wide, the laughter pouring out of her. "You're me! I mean, the me I'm supposed to be! Hey, you wanna take over the column?"

"Nope." Quinn grabbed the bottle of wine off the table and gestured to the back door. "How about we sit on the deck?"

He put his palm against the small of her back and guided her to the door. She twirled away from him.

"You're always doing that, pushing me somewhere, steering me. Why do you do that?"

He dropped his hand and his eyes flashed at her. "I was being polite and escorting you to the goddamn deck."

She snorted and reached for the door before he could. "After you, Detective," Audie said. As he walked past, she placed her hand on the curve of his back and it was warm and hard—and Audie decided right then that she probably shouldn't have any more wine.

They made themselves comfortable in cushioned patio chairs at an oval cedar table. Audie looked out over a narrow manicured yard glowing under tastefully placed outdoor lights. The weed-free grass was cut short and looked like green velvet, and the entire space was set off with boxwoods and mulch along the fence line.

She sighed in appreciation.

"This is a very cute house, Quinn. How long have you lived here?"

"About five years now."

"Have you ever been married?"

"Nope. Unless you count Stanny-O."

Audie giggled and poured herself some more wine. One

more glass wouldn't make her lose her head over Stacey Quinn, certainly. "Have you ever lived with anyone?"

"I'm living with someone now," he said casually. "Why do you ask?"

Audie put down the wine bottle rather forcefully and blinked at him. "Is she at Ace Hardware stocking up on mulch while you entertain me tonight?"

Quinn shook his head and sniggered. "Nope. Rocky Datillio is at his fiancée's tonight. He'll be moving out for good when he gets married in a few weeks."

"Oh."

"Can I ask you something, Audie?"

"Mmm . . ." She was taking a nice long draw from her wineglass.

"Why were you crying upstairs?"

She put down her drink and began to remove the bobby pins from her hair, then tossed them in a pile on the table. She raked her fingers through her waves and massaged her scalp, waiting for her emotions to subside.

"I get a little sentimental when I'm hungry and my feet hurt," she finally said.

"I give a mean foot massage." Quinn took a sip of his wine and looked out into the yard, listening to the neighborhood night noises of cars, barking dogs, garbage can lids, and voices. He waited a long while before he felt her feet plunk down in his lap.

Quinn touched her ankles with reverence before he pushed her feet aside. "Wait. Come here to me."

He pulled Audie by the hands and guided her to the edge of the table, where she hopped up, letting her feet dangle. Quinn positioned his chair in front of her and sat down.

"There. That's better." He placed her feet squarely in his lap.

Audie giggled until she grew accustomed to his touch, then let her eyelids drift down in heavy pleasure. In silence,

Quinn rolled his fingers into the ball of one foot and pressed his thumb along her arch. Then he stroked the top of the foot, paying lavish attention to each toe—pulling, bending up, and pushing down—until little electric shocks of pleasure raced up from the thin bones of her feet.

Then he started the cycle of touch all over again, and soon Audie's breathing fell in sync with his movements and she felt her muscles uncoil from her soles to her shoulders.

When he went to the other foot, she giggled again but was soon returned to bliss with his rhythmic touch.

"This is wonderful, Quinn."

"Yes, it is."

Audie realized her eyes had been closed all this time, and she opened them to admire his efforts.

"Oh!" The little exclamation came out involuntarily. It seemed Quinn's lion-at-breakfast look was back, but this time she'd served herself to him on a plate. He held her gaze as his touch suddenly changed.

Audie felt the hot, firm pressure move to her ankles now, then to her calves. He stopped there and raked his knuckles hard down her muscle.

"Ahhh!" She nearly jumped off the table.

"You're very tight," Quinn said, still holding her eyes with his. She could've sworn he smiled at his choice of words, and she was once again impressed by the fact that Stacey Quinn was one damn fine-looking man.

Audie found herself scooting closer to the edge of the table to give him more of her legs, which clearly indicated she was out of her mind or wasted or both. He responded by taking long strokes from the soles of her feet to above her knees, still staring at her intently.

"Oh, wow," she whispered. The sensation was pure heat, and it tingled and pleased and hurt all at the same time. She found she couldn't breathe between strokes of his hands. "Oh, yes," was her next comment.

"How are those feet doing?"

"What feet?" she answered, smiling behind her closed eyes.

His hands were now fully inside her dress, pushing higher on her legs, leaving streaks of fire on her skin, moving higher still, and heading outward toward her hips. She groaned softly when his fingers brushed against the silk of her underwear and raced back down her legs, only to move back up, turning this time toward the painfully tender skin of her inner thighs . . .

Quinn's hands stopped. "Audie?"

"Yes?"

"What are we doing?"

"You're giving me a foot massage." She clenched her eyelids tight and didn't dare breathe.

"Not anymore I'm not."

Audie sat up, clamped her legs together, and felt sick with embarrassment. His hands slid away abruptly. "You're right. This is not a good idea. I've got to go home. Do you still have my keys?"

She was about to remove her feet from his lap and run like hell when Quinn jumped up, spread her legs apart, and stepped inside.

"I didn't say it was a bad idea." Quinn was leaning forward, his hands on the edge of the table by her hips, his breath hot on her neck. "I was making sure you knew what was happening, that's all."

"Thank you, Quinn, I . . . Oh, God, I appreciate that. I really do." Audie swallowed hard. "It would have been a mistake."

He smelled so good, so sharp and masculine. Every nerve ending in her body was screaming to touch him. His lips were so close to her neck, to her face. Her legs were opened to him.

"Just one kiss, Homey."

"One good-night kiss. Then I've got to go."

When Quinn pulled back enough to look her in the eye, Audie gasped. She was in for it now.

Technically, it was just one kiss. It started quite gently, a soft, careful touch of his lips against hers, moist and sweet and warm. Then came her tender response and her lips yielded to his, her hands lightly stroked the back of his neck, and she breathed his name into his mouth.

And it continued, as Quinn dared to ask for a little more, and Audie dared him right back, and the kiss deepened as Quinn climbed up on the table with her and gently laid her down, feeling her stretch out all soft and warm and willing beneath him.

And it continued, as she offered him her tongue and felt him suck it and pull it into his mouth and the flame licked low inside her and she felt his hands go into her hair, then down her neck to her shoulders, then wrap around her body, and the kiss grew wet and rough and she felt how very hard he was against her belly and she couldn't help it and just threw her legs around his waist and rolled with him.

They smashed into one of the chairs first, then tumbled onto the deck together, their legs askew but their kiss unbroken.

She scrambled on top of him, straddling his hips and devouring his lips, yanking his shirt from his belt, reaching up inside to get her hands on his bare chest, and raking her fingertips across his pebble-hard nipples.

"I want you bad, Quinn." She spoke, but her lips never left his.

"I'm going to tear off your clothes now," he mumbled, tugging on the zipper at the back of her dress.

"I'm going to rip off your pants," she told him, her declaration muffled not only by the ongoing kiss but also by the giggles now coming from both of them.

They began to shake with laughter while they pulled at

each other's clothing, their lips never parting—at least not until the back door opened and a man's voice called out into the night.

"Quinn? You home?"

They didn't dare breathe.

"Quinn? You're freaking me out. Where are you?"

"Uh, down here."

While Quinn answered, Audie zipped the dress and hid her face, hoping the roommate's eyes hadn't yet adjusted to the darkness.

"Jesus, Quinn, what are you doing down there? You scared me."

"My sincere apologies."

"Oh. Sorry. Well, I'm going to bed."

"Why aren't you at Marie's house?"

"She's got PMS. I'll lock the front door. Good night." He turned to leave but remembered his manners. "Hello. I'm Quinn's roommate, Rocky Datillio. And you are . . . ?"

"Going home now," Audie said.

CHAPTER 4

Quinn moved through the crowded, cavernous old city hall building at a no-nonsense pace, took the elevator to the fifth floor, and strode through the double glass doors to the reception desk.

He knew there was no need to show his badge, but he couldn't stop himself. "Area Three Violent Crimes Detective Stacey Quinn here to see the vice mayor," he said with a smile.

"Oh, certainly. Have a seat, Detective. He'll be right with you."

That son of a bitch.

Fifteen minutes, twenty minutes went by, and Quinn still sat there in the waiting room outside his office, seething, wanting nothing more than to get up, grab the little pecker by the collar, and beat him to a pulp.

Quinn took a breath and relaxed. He knew Timmy. He knew Timmy was making him sit out here simply because he could, and he'd prefer it if Quinn was good and pissed off so he could have the advantage right from the start.

Quinn wouldn't give him the satisfaction.

He could already see it—Timmy would come bursting out of his office soon enough, making up some sorry-assed excuse, apologizing like a gentleman, acting like it was pure joy to see him, and Quinn wouldn't believe any of it.

In fact, he pictured Tim right that second—probably peeking around the door at him, picking his nose, and snickering the way he did back in Sister Cecilia Edward's third-grade class.

Some people never change.

Quinn shook his head softly. Not today, he told himself. He was here to investigate Audie's case, nothing more. This was not the place to remember the day John died—how his baby brother stopped breathing and all Quinn could hear was Timmy's laugh.

It wasn't the time to start thinking about how Laura had made her point loud and clear from Tim's bed.

Quinn was here to do his job—and he planned to do it professionally, dispassionately, and be on his way.

Then when he got back to the station house, he'd take a hot shower and change his clothes, the usual precaution after any haz-mat spill—or a visit with Timmy Burke.

He heard the office door fly open and Tim appeared in front of him, flustered and apologetic, rambling on about how crazy his life had been this summer and about how he had a luncheon scheduled with a Lithuanian trade group and some other complete shit that Quinn didn't bother to listen to.

"Stacey! Come on in! It's great to see you! Have a seat. Can I get you coffee or anything?"

Quinn declined politely and sat down, crossing his legs comfortably in one of the leather club chairs.

"Nice digs you got here, Timmy." Quinn scanned the plush office with its dark paneled walls, flag stands, rich burgundy carpet, and massive, gleaming desk. "Looks like you've risen to the top."

Like scum in the Cal-Sag drainage canal, he thought.

"If I didn't know better, I would think you just paid me a compliment, Stacey."

Quinn smiled and said nothing for a moment. "Well

then, we've already pulled your prints, so I'm just here to chat about Miss Adams for a bit."

Tim blinked at Quinn and sat down in one of the chairs clustered in a casual sitting area.

"Let's chat then." Tim leaned back and produced one of his all-purpose smiles. "How's life in District Eighteen? You like the remodeled station house?"

"Absolutely. State-of-the-art and all that. Commander Connelly can't stop singing the mayor's praises."

"Good to hear," Tim said contentedly. "And the Quinn family?"

"Excellent. The Burkes?"

"Fine. Fine. Pop's doing great after his prostate surgery."

"Good."

"Did you hear Mrs. Geleski died?"

"Yeah, I went to her funeral. Apparently she had sixteen cats in the house."

"Must've smelled to high heaven."

Quinn smiled slightly. "So, Timmy. Know anything about these nasty letters Miss Adams has been receiving?"

"Yeah, you said something about threats. Is she still getting them?"

"Yep, she is. Anything you wanna get off your chest?"

Tim tossed his head back and howled with laughter. "Christ, Stacey, please. I just love you." He sighed contentedly. "You are the most humorless bastard I've ever known in my life. Honestly. So you think I'm sending these notes to Autumn? What on earth makes you think that?"

"Are you?"

"No, Detective. I am not. And she certainly knows that."

Quinn nodded. Timmy Burke seemed human enough on the outside—blond and blue-eyed and well dressed and well spoken. Quinn could see how Audie might have been momentarily hoodwinked. He couldn't hold it against her.

After all, much of the city had been conned by Timmy's act, apparently.

"So tell me how long you dated Miss Adams. How you met, what your relationship was like. Why you broke up."

Tim chuckled. "Don't you want to know if she'd go down on me in the car? As I recall, that was our standard of excellence at one time. You want to start there?"

Quinn reached in his jacket pocket for his notebook. It gave him something to do with his hands for a moment, enough time to remember it would be a felony to put a bullet in the vice mayor's brain and to remind himself yet again that this wasn't about Laura.

This was about Autumn Adams—who needed him to keep her safe and make an arrest. The fact that Quinn really liked Audie could not—and would not—interfere with the way he handled her case.

"Because she did, Stacey," Tim said with a sigh. "And Jesus, let me tell you, it was pure heaven! That girl knows exactly what those gorgeous lips of hers are for."

Quinn said nothing, but his insides were tensing, his blood was roaring, and his jaw went hard. He blocked the image from his mind—it was too horrible. Not Audie. Not with Tim Burke. Oh, God, why did it make him this crazy?

Maybe he could just shoot now and plead insanity later.

"I hope you weren't driving at the time, Timmy. That's a bit of a safety hazard," he managed.

Tim nodded, grinning. "So you want to know about Audie, do you? Am I really a suspect? Because the idea of being a suspect in one of your cases leaves me kind of skittish, as you might understand."

Quinn grunted. "Of course you're a suspect, Timmy, along with every man Audie has dated in the last few years. The letters are real nasty and personal. So what happened with the two of you?"

"Didn't Audie tell you?"

Quinn shrugged. "She told me you walked away after a couple months. Not much more than that."

"Oh, really?" Tim's eyes went wide in surprise. "How interesting."

He got up from his chair and made a lap around the perimeter of his office, his feet silent on the thick carpeting, his hands in his pockets. He was smiling.

"She really said that?" Tim came to a stop near Quinn and cocked his head. "That's what she told you?"

"Yep."

"Well, I'll be damned." Tim sat back down across from Quinn and leaned forward on his knees. "She dumped me, boy-o. That's how it ended. But she's slowly coming around. I'm trying to be patient, and we still talk."

Tim ran a hand through his pale curls. "The truth is I adore the woman, shortcomings and all. She stole my heart, Stacey, and she's driving me crazy. There. You can't say I never bared my soul to you."

Quinn glared at him and their eyes locked. There was a long moment of silence between them, and they both felt it—the electric crackle of old hate, resentment, and jealousy.

"Oh, holy shit." Tim was up out of the chair and began to pace along the broad bank of windows behind his desk. He turned his back on Quinn and looked out over the concrete-and-steel canyons of the Loop. When he turned around again, he was laughing bitterly.

"This is fucking hilarious. What are we, stuck in some kind of Greek tragedy or something? Are we cursed or something, Stacey? Answer me that."

Quinn said nothing.

"Please don't tell me you've got a thing for Autumn Adams, OK? I just don't think I'm in a good-enough mood to deal with that today—with the Lithuanians and all."

Quinn was scribbling in his notebook, trying to breathe

normally. "So she dumped you. You're pissed off. So you slashed her tires and sent her dead roses and a whole slew of letters and in your mind this all accomplishes what?"

"I'm not slashing tires or sending goddamned letters!" Tim's face was red. "I cannot possibly be considered a suspect. Give me a fuckin' break!"

"A jilted lover is always a suspect in a stalking case, Mister Vice Mayor."

"I told you we were working it out, that she's coming around!"

"And what makes you say that?"

Tim propped himself against his desk and crossed his arms over his chest, glowering. "Look. There was nothing ugly about the way we broke up, all right? She just has a little problem with commitment. She's the jumpy type. But we're working on it. I'm taking it slow. And I would never threaten to hurt that woman. Goddamn, Stacey—I think I'm in love with her."

Quinn stared at him in silence.

"Believe me, Quinn. I would die before I'd see her hurt."

Quinn let out an abrupt laugh. "And I'm to believe you because . . . wait. Because you're a man of integrity? Is that it?"

"Fuck you, Stacey."

"No. Fuck you, Timmy." Quinn was up out of his seat and his face was instantly in Tim Burke's. "God, this is sweet," Quinn said, turning to go.

Tim's words came out in an icy whisper. "Do you really think I'll let you stay on this case, you pathetic loser?"

Quinn spun around, his hand on the doorknob. "What?"

"Do you really think I can't have your ass pulled off this case and out of your fluff job at District Eighteen? Because it would take just a few phone calls to accomplish that, Stace."

Quinn didn't move a muscle.

"Which public housing assignment would you prefer? Cabrini Green? The Robert Taylor Homes?" Tim walked over toward the door to finish his point, his voice now sharp and angry. "I'll get your ass canned if you continue to harass me. Now get out of here, go find the real mental case who's bothering Audie, and leave my reputation alone."

"Your reputation," Quinn repeated, almost to himself, smiling. He looked Tim Burke in the eye. "As always, it's been a pleasure seeing you, Timmy." He opened the door to see a group of pasty-looking businessmen in the waiting room, all wearing visitor badges and nervous expressions.

"Your Lithuanians are here, big man. Oh, I forgot—" Quinn turned around and grinned at him. "Did you get your book autographed the other night? It was a shame you had to rush out like that. Urgent city business?"

A muscle twitched at the corner of Tim's lips. "Get the fuck out of my face," he said.

Audie didn't mind waiting for Griffin, because she was used to it. She knew that if she wanted Griffin to be somewhere at noon, she told him eleven, then she could count on him by twelve-fifteen. He always blamed his Jamaican upbringing for this affliction, explaining that when you live in a country that's stifling hot and you're hungry and have no job to go to, there's no point in rushing.

Besides, he'd always saved his speed for the soccer field.

At least she had a nice booth by the window and she could sip her iced tea and watch the Rush Street lunch crowd from her air-conditioned perch. She could let her mind wander.

That night last year when she found her tires slashed after a soccer game, she figured it was just random vandalism. When the dead flowers came, she shrugged it off. And at first, she thought the letters were a joke as well—weird, annoying, and sometimes a little creepy, but just a prank. For more than a year she'd ignored Griffin's pleas that she get the police involved.

Well, now the letters truly scared her. And she was angry that they'd invaded her life, made her worry, made her wrack her brain trying to figure out who in the world would want to hurt her.

Her stomach churned. Her head hurt. She felt very alone.

She knew the list of suspects she gave to Quinn was a waste of time. Will Dalton? He was an absentminded professor type—intelligent and wickedly funny but completely benign. The only thing that ever riled him was his belief that the American family had been destroyed by commercial television. Outside that topic, Audie never encountered a bit of passion in the man.

Darren Billings? He wasn't literate enough to write those notes. The letters just dripped with sarcasm, something he couldn't spell, let alone convey.

Kyle Singer was smart enough. Certainly snide enough. But he had no reason to send those letters—he couldn't have cared less for Audie and immediately had found someone else to escort to public functions. She'd been nothing to him but a distraction for the rumormongers.

Russell Ketchum was already ruled out. And Griffin was not even a possibility.

And Tim Burke. God, she wished he'd stop bugging her, but she doubted it was him. The letters didn't sound like Tim. His talent lay in putting a super-duper spin on just anything and everything! Audie could see Tim writing the press release for the grand reopening of the Union Carbide plant in Bhopal, but not those letters.

How pitiful that list looked when she put it in writing— six men in ten years, and yes, she'd left out a few nearly anonymous encounters she'd rather forget. But that list was the truth. It was fact. And if her love life was baseball, she'd have mighty lame stats: Six at bats. Six errors. Maybe a couple blooper singles but definitely no homers, no stolen bases, and no runs batted in.

Audie took a sip of her iced tea and sighed. She supposed she'd seen something she wanted in each of those men—wit in Will Dalton, an amazing body in Darren Billings, determination in Russell Ketchum, savvy intelligence in Kyle Singer, charm in Tim Burke, and a good heart and a killer smile in Griffin.

And she supposed some of them found something worthwhile in her, but it never seemed right enough. It never amounted to anything special.

Audie felt her stomach clench with dread. Realistically, if it wasn't one of those men, then who else could it be?

It could be her brother.

Oh, God, Drew. Why?

Audie stared out the window wistfully. No, she and Drew weren't exactly close, and she didn't especially admire her brother for his moral fortitude. But she never thought of him as a cruel person or an evil person.

Besides, why in the world would Drew do something like this? What would it accomplish? If he had something to say, why didn't he just come right out and say it?

Helen's will had stipulated that if Audie quit the column after the current contract expired, she had two choices—she could either give it to Drew or sell the rights and split the profits with him fifty-fifty.

Audie knew that Drew would never want the responsibility of the column. All his life, he'd avoided work like it was a flesh-eating disease. So was he trying to force her to sell so he could get his hands on half the assets? Was he that desperate for money these days? And if so, why didn't he just tell her what he needed?

Her brain hurt just trying to sort this out. Her heart hurt at the idea that her brother would do this to her.

Audie was startled out of her thoughts by the sudden

appearance of Griffin's face, his nose and lips squished up against the window glass.

"You're so strange," she mouthed to him, laughing, watching as he jogged into the door of the restaurant.

He was there in a flash, depositing a kiss on her cheek before he slid into the opposite side of the booth, his laptop slung over his shoulder and his smile brightening the whole room. He held something in his hand.

"The UPS guy brought this." He reached over the table and handed Audie a package the size of a hardback novel.

She stared at the return address—Detective Stacey Quinn.

"Since it came from him and it wasn't ticking, I figured it was safe enough." Griffin was grinning. "You going to open it?"

Audie just stared at the plain brown paper package. What in the world would he be sending her? She hadn't seen him in a week. Stanny-O had been with her instead, explaining that Quinn was busy wrapping up other work while interviewing suspects in her case. *Right.*

She knew very well what had happened—she'd thrown herself at Quinn, made a fool of herself, practically begged the man to put his hands up her dress. She'd scared him off.

Maybe he was sending her some kind of self-help book—*Nympho to Nun in Ten Easy Steps* or *Promiscuous No More.*

"Audie? You going to open it?"

She looked up at Griffin and blinked. "Yeah. Sure."

Her fingers tore at the outside wrapping to reveal a simple white gift box. She set it down on the table and pulled off the top, exposing a layer of white tissue paper. She looked up at Griffin, frowning.

"Don't look at me. Go on, girl."

Audie peeled back the tissue, to see what looked like

handkerchiefs—pressed white linen hankies trimmed with delicate lace.

"Good Lord," Audie muttered, and Griffin leaned across the table to get a better look.

"Wow. Those are pretty. Aren't you going to read the note?"

Audie picked up the piece of folded stationery and read: "So you don't ruin all your panty hose. Quinn."

She chuckled, surprised, to say the least. She picked up one of the hankies and held it in her hand—it was soft, feather-light, and feminine. It was lightly starched and ironed into a neat square with razor-sharp edges. She raised it to her nose and breathed in a soft scent, lavender maybe? Just then she saw Griffin's hand inside the box.

"I counted eleven in here, so there's an even dozen. I think they're really old, Audie, antique even. Look at the lace—it's handmade."

"How would you know, Griffin?" Audie laughed and tossed the hankie back in the box, replacing the lid.

"Because I spend half my life haunting consignment stores and antique shops, that's how. This is a really nice gift."

"Yeah." She pushed the box to the side and took a gulp of her iced tea. Her heart was pounding. Her eyes were stinging.

Why would Quinn send her such a personal gift? They hardly knew each other! And why was she on the verge of tears?

They ordered lunch and talked companionably, but Audie felt Griffin studying her, and it made her a little uncomfortable. She gazed out over the brass curtain rod toward the street, letting the sunshine hit her face. When she turned back he was still staring at her, frowning.

"What?"

He shook his head. "Nothing. I'm just . . . nothing."

"Griff, what? What is it? Are you worried about tomorrow?"

"Nah, not at all." He shook his head with a sad smile and Audie watched his dreadlocks tap against the sides of his face. "I just plan to tell the detectives the truth—that I only stalk you on Tuesday and Thursday afternoons and I'm more of an obscene phone-callin' man myself, not some anonymous-note-writin' wimp."

Audie leaned forward and admired his sweet face. "I've told Quinn all about you—about us—and he knows you're not really a suspect, so don't worry."

Griffin's eyebrows shot high on his forehead. "God, mon, I hope I'm not."

"So what's the problem, then? You look upset."

Griffin reached out and cupped his hand over Audie's and tried to smile. "I was just watching you sitting there, and I was thinking that I've never seen you more beautiful than you are right now—that you seem wiser, more sure of yourself, such a lovely woman."

Audie was shocked by this unusual burst of sentiment. "Uh, thanks."

"And I've never seen you sadder." He removed his hand and leaned back in the booth. "I really hate these letters, you know? I hate what they're doing to you, girl. Whoever is sending them is one sick mother, and I'm worried about you."

Audie exhaled deeply and produced a weak smile. "They're talking to Drew, too. Did I tell you?"

Griffin laughed. "I'd pay good money to eavesdrop on that party."

"Mmm . . ." Audie looked down into her iced tea.

"So what's the story with the Mighty Quinn? How much do you like him?"

Her head popped up and her mouth hung open. "How . . . ? What do you mean?"

Griffin smiled affectionately. "Damn, girl! How long have I known you? You've got a crush on your policeman, at the very least. So tell me all about it."

She shook her head, looking outside again.

"Audie. Come on."

She scowled at him. "I'm thirty years old, Griffin. Thirty-year-old women don't get crushes."

"Fine." He stared at her, unblinking.

She stared right back.

"All right. Since you asked, Stacey Quinn aggravates the hell out of me, OK? We've had these two extremely awkward groping sessions, including falling off a table. But that's it—not that I don't think about the possibilities every second of every day."

Griffin blinked rapidly and leaned back in his booth. "Really now?"

"And he doesn't talk a whole lot, which bugs me to no end, but when he does say something it either pisses me off or makes me laugh." She sighed. "We've got nothing in common, all right? And, Griffin, the guy's house is immaculate and his spices are alphabetized, and I can't stop thinking about him."

"I see."

"And out of nowhere he can be so sweet—like sending me these!" She waved her hand over the box, her eyes wide. "And the way he kisses me—my God . . . two kisses, that's all I've had, but . . . oh, God, they made me forget my own name. . . .

"And now I haven't seen him for days and days. I keep trying to come up with some excuse to call him, but I haven't gotten any more letters and Detective Oleskiewicz has been taking me home every night and it's like Quinn doesn't want to see me ever again and I don't know what to do."

Griffin gawked at her.

"But don't push me to talk about it, Griffin. I just can't right now."

He buried a smile in his coffee cup. "Of course."

"He makes me crazy. Completely insane. And I miss him. I'm lonely for him. What is *that* all about? Is that the stupidest thing you've ever heard me say, or what?"

Griffin leaned forward on his elbows and studied her carefully. "You're right, Audie. This is not a crush. It sounds like you're in love with the man."

Her mouth hung open and she blinked. "Oh, for God's sake," she said, standing up. "You know me better than that. I'm going to the ladies' room."

Griffin watched her start off in a huff, catch her heel in his computer shoulder strap, and crash into the unoccupied table for two across the aisle. He winced, then rubbed his mouth nervously until she was safely on her way.

"Be careful, girl," he whispered.

Audie drove the car along the semicircular brick drive and parked in front of the grand front door. The imposing brick-and-stucco Tudor looked exactly as it always had, as formal and as haughty as North Shore houses come, the thin steel blue line of Lake Michigan visible behind the heavily treed grounds.

She knocked on the door.

"Well, what an unexpected pleasure this is!" Andrew Adams swept his arm through the airy foyer as his sister scowled at him.

"I thought you knew I was coming."

"Oh, sure. I'm just teasing you. Come on in. Drink?"

"No thanks."

Apparently, the divorce was final, because it seemed a few more items had gone missing from the family estate: the antique Portuguese vase that had always sat beneath the hall table was gone, and so were the Impressionist landscape from the top of the landing, a mirror, and a few lamps.

Either these items were part of the latest ex-wife's settlement or Drew had been reduced to selling things for cash. Audie didn't care much either way. They were just things—Drew's things. He could do whatever he liked with them.

Drew handed her what looked like a gin and tonic. "Relax, Audie. How's the column going? How's soccer this season? How's Russell?"

Audie stared at the drink in her hand, carried it patiently to the bar, and set it down. Her brother had already deposited himself in a slipcovered chair, looking quite self-satisfied.

"I'm not seeing Russell Ketchum anymore, not for six months. We're seven-and-two. And some kook is threatening to kill me."

"So I hear." Drew gestured for his sister to have a seat near him in the library. Audie saw that he'd had the Oriental carpets and heavy draperies removed for the summer, just like Helen used to do. The property seemed well tended. Drew seemed to be staying on top of things, wife or no.

"The Chicago Police have already paid me a call—fine public servants they were, too. One of them seemed to be quite interested in your welfare." Drew brought the crystal tumbler to his lips and inclined his head a bit. "The macho Irish one. Finn."

Audie frowned at him. "Quinn. And I didn't know they'd already come to see you."

"Right after lunch today, actually. We spent quite a bit of quality time together, discussing sibling rivalry, my private financial affairs, my ex-wives, that sort of unpleasantness. Mrs. Splawinski was here, so it was like Warsaw old home week for the big Polish guy—they were jabbering in the kitchen while she made him brownies. You sure you won't have a drink?"

Audie felt her eyes glaze over for a moment, then tried to refocus. There he was—her brother, her flesh and blood—in his urban-chic eyeglasses, his Ralph Lauren khakis and Polo shirt and his Sperry topsiders, and she felt so little of anything for him.

Audie didn't hate Drew, but she didn't love him, either. He was just some man she never would have tolerated had he not been her brother, had he not shared a childhood with her and was now the only living relative she had in the world.

She saw that Drew's dark hair was starting to thin, leaving a shiny spot on top of his head. His skin was as tanned as it was every summer, but she saw a touch of gray beneath the brown this year. He was drinking too much, obviously, and he looked much older than thirty-three. He also seemed more arrogant and bored than the last time she'd seen him, if that could be possible.

It occurred to Audie that Drew was starting to resemble Helen around the eyes.

Audie studied him carefully. Did he look dangerous? She nearly laughed at herself for even considering the possibility.

"So how is Mrs. Splawinski?" Audie asked, smiling politely. "Any brownies left?"

Drew chuckled. "Yeah, sure. On the counter. Help yourself."

As Audie made the trip to the kitchen, she thought of the family's energetic cook. She'd stayed on with Drew after Helen moved to Lakeside Pointe, and Audie didn't see her often.

"Is her hip doing better?" Audie was back on the couch, two soft, chewy brownies in her hand.

"Oh, she's the Bionic Woman now, zipping around on all her plastic parts. Fit as a fiddle."

Audie smiled. "So what happened with the detectives, Drew?"

He sighed. "Well, I don't think they're quite ready to cart me off to Stateville, but they wanted to see my computer and printer and get my fingerprints. It was quite the *Starsky and Hutch* kind of experience, let me tell you."

Audie leaned back into the soft cotton slipcover on the sofa, crossed her legs, and munched. She watched his expression closely. "I'm sorry about the police coming here."

"Oh, for God's sake." Drew waved his hand around before he took another sip. "I was happy to oblige. It's truly awful. I can't believe you never said one word about it to me. Are the letters still coming?"

Audie stretched an arm along the back of the couch and wiped a few crumbs off her shirt. She'd inhaled those brownies and tried to remember how many were still left in the kitchen. Maybe she could take some home. "Nothing in the last week."

"Are you taking this seriously? I mean, why in God's name would somebody want to hurt you?"

Audie groaned in frustration. "I have no idea. But it's not going away on its own, so I have to deal with it."

"What exactly do the letters say?" Drew's eyebrows arched over the rim of the tumbler while he waited for her response.

She shrugged. "At first it was just snide insults. Now he says he's going to kill me, and apparently he's got a schedule to keep, because he selected September twenty-second to do me in." She ran a nervous hand through her hair. "You might want to keep that day open in case you have to identify my body—next of kin and all."

"Don't be morbid, Audie. Jesus." Drew abruptly got up

from the chair and made himself another drink at the long, polished cherry bar. He suddenly turned.

"That's rather clever, actually," he said, grabbing a handful of ice and tossing it in the tumbler.

"What is?"

"The twenty-second of September is the first day of autumn this year—get it? Autumn? Autumn Adams?"

She stared at him blankly.

"How refreshing—a psychopath with a dry wit." Drew relaxed back into the chair, chuckling, and raised his glass to that.

"That *is* pretty weird." Audie shivered slightly and hugged herself across the chest. "I wonder if I should tell the detectives."

"Why not? It could even be a clue—like in *Murder She Wrote!*" Drew cocked his head and blinked at his sister. "So what brings you up here? Not that I don't enjoy our visits."

Audie braced herself. The family's 1905 Herreshoff Yacht was the only reason she ever came to the house and they both knew it.

Helen was aware that Audie loved the *Take a Hint* with all her heart and had worked with her father day and night to refurbish the vintage boat just before he died. Helen also knew that Audie would have traded the apartment, the car, the column—everything—for the forty-three-foot cutter. Yet Helen had left it to Drew.

Audie often wondered why. She still couldn't decide if it was simply her mother's final cruelty or Helen's roundabout way of ensuring her children would have a reason to speak after she was gone.

Audie looked up, preparing herself for Drew's list of questions. "I'd like to take the boat out sometime next week. Would that be OK with you?"

He looked at her with casual interest. "Overnight? For

a few days? Mackinac Island or something?"

"Oh, no. Just a day sail. I was thinking of inviting a friend along. Will Saturday be all right?"

"Sure." Drew moved his wrist in a lazy circle, watching the ice cubes swirl around inside the glass. "I'll leave the boathouse unlocked. Be sure to wipe down the deck when you're done. Who's the lucky fellow?"

Audie forced herself to remain relaxed. Drew would see them anyway, since he was nearly always at home. It was either now or later.

"The macho Irish cop. If he'll accept my invitation."

Drew's hand flopped down onto the armrest and thin threads of mixed drink splashed onto the slipcover.

"Dear God, Audie! You've run quite the gamut with men lately. What the hell was wrong with Russell Ketchum? I've always thought he was a decent man and a damn good lawyer."

Audie sighed. "Actually, Russell is a—"

"But Jesus, a cop? This would be your first cop, right? I know it's not your first Irishman. What was that slimy Mick politician's name again?" Drew chuckled softly. "At least it's not another Jamaican."

Audie was already off the sofa and headed for the foyer.

"Oh, come on, Audie. Don't be such a cold bitch. Get a sense of humor."

She spun around and stared at him. He looked like a king on his slipcovered throne, his thinning hair a crown, his gin and tonic his scepter.

Maybe he *was* nasty enough to be sending those letters, after all.

"Do you need money, Drew?" Her voice was soft and polite.

"What?" His entire body stiffened.

"I asked you if you need money. Did what's-her-name

wipe you out? Are you having cash-flow problems? Is there something you need to ask me?"

Audie watched the superiority drain from her brother's expression. She observed how his entire body tensed. "You cannot possibly be suggesting that I wrote those letters," he hissed.

She tried to feel nothing, but the anger, sadness, and, yes, fear were boiling to the surface, and she felt herself tremble.

"I think you'd better leave," he said.

She turned into the foyer and headed for the door. Her shaking hand reached for the brass latch.

She heard Drew's voice echo through the huge rooms. "Make it Sunday instead, would you? I'm sailing down to the yacht club for a party Friday and may not get back until late the next day!"

Audie slammed the door behind her, got into her car, and turned south onto Sheridan Road. She watched her childhood home disappear behind her in the rearview mirror, right above the words "objects are larger than they appear."

And brothers weirder.

"Oh, hell."

She'd forgotten the brownies.

CHAPTER 5

Stanny-O was obviously thrilled that Audie let him behind the wheel of the Porsche that night. Though his knees were nearly in his nostrils, it didn't seem to detract from the driving experience.

"What year is this beauty?" he asked, pulling into the southbound lanes of Lake Shore Drive.

"A '96." Audie unwrapped her shin guards and fluffed out her hair. "Helen had the dealer custom-paint it this lovely champagne pink. It's your color, Stan."

"Baby, don't I know it," he said, shifting up and taking the curve a bit too fast.

"Hey, careful. There's always a cop waiting for speeders up here to the right."

He shot her a toothy grin framed in goatee and kicked up the speed.

"You're bad, Detective," she said, laughing.

They drove for a few moments in friendly silence. During the past week, Audie had come to enjoy Stanny-O's shy, earthy personality. They frequently argued about Cubs statistics and Chicago politics and listened to loud rock and roll on the car radio. They went out to Baccino's for deep-dish pizza one night. And another night they went to a movie, and tonight he escorted her to her game. She felt safe with him.

"Hey, listen, Audie. I'm supposed to tell you that I'll be hanging out with you for the next couple of days at least. Quinn's still got a bunch of other stuff he needs to do."

She narrowed her eyes at him. "What do you mean you're *supposed* to tell me? Did Quinn ask you to say that? He's hiding from me, isn't he?"

"No! No! That's not what I meant. Ah, shit." Stanny-O looked over at her a bit nervously. "Look. He's busy with work, that's all. Our commander told us to make your case a priority, but we had to clear up a whole bunch of other cases, that's all. Quinn told me to explain that to you and tell you he'd see you soon."

"That's it?"

"That's it."

Audie stuck her hand out into the summer night wind and inhaled the lake air. "Does Quinn hit on women a lot?"

Stanny-O's head spun around. "What? God, no. Not at all." He grinned again. "He don't have to."

Audie laughed. "No, I imagine he doesn't," she said softly. "Has he had a lot of girlfriends?"

Stanny-O adjusted himself in the leather seat. "That's the kind of thing you'll need to ask him about, OK? It's not my place."

"Fair enough."

"But not many. He's picky. The last one lasted about three years. I always assumed they'd get married, but she broke it off with him."

"Really?" Audie tried to hide her smile.

"She ran off to Miami with another guy."

"Oh."

They were quiet for a moment, and Audie leaned back against the headrest to watch the endless geometric blocks of light pass by, buildings clustered along the lakefront shoulder to shoulder in the night sky. "He's a good man, isn't he?"

"Quinn? Yes, he's a good man." Stanny-O looked a bit surprised by her question. "And a good cop. Why did you ask that?"

Audie shrugged. "I'm just trying to figure him out, I guess. Is he always so quiet? He just doesn't seem to talk very much when we're together."

Stanny-O chuckled under his breath. "He's mostly quiet, but that's because his brain is working overtime and he's listening real careful and keeping his eyes sharp.

"But I've seen him hammered and he can let it rip then, let me tell you. He gets all sappy and tells stories that don't have no endings as far as I can tell, and he sings those gut-wrenching Irish songs that make my skin crawl.

"And you definitely don't want to let him near his pipes when he's like that. God! The sound of those things makes me want to shoot myself in the head even when he's sober. But when he's hammered he can't play worth shit and it sounds like somebody's being tortured."

Audie stared at Stanny-O in confusion and disbelief, laughing. She'd just been handed a huge amount of information that didn't jibe with what she knew of Quinn. *And what the hell are pipes?*

"What the hell are pipes?" she asked.

"Bagpipes." He turned toward her. "You don't know about his pipes?"

She laughed again. "Guess not. You going to fill me in?"

Stanny-O smoothed down his mustache and looked up at the streetlights along Lake Shore Drive. "He plays with the Chicago Garda Pipe and Drum Band," he said. "His dad does, too—it's the official Chicago Police Department pipe band. They do police and fire funerals, parades, weddings, festivals, stuff like that. I think their shows sound like a whole herd of cows being slaughtered myself, but some people seem to like them."

"Bagpipes?" Audie shook her head. "Like with a kilt and everything?"

"Oh, yeah. Whenever I give him hell about that, he tells me only real men have the balls to wear a skirt." He winced at his choice of words. "Sorry."

Audie laughed loudly. "Well, what do you know?" She took a few moments to try to imagine the masculine Stacey Quinn in a kilt. She just couldn't do it.

"So what's *Garda* mean?"

"Quinn told me it's the name for the police in Ireland or something."

"Oh."

They drove for several minutes in quiet. "Hey, Stanny-O?"

"Mmm?"

"What about the women that Quinn meets in his work? I mean like me—one of his cases. Does he . . . hook up with, you know, get involved . . . with women he meets by being a cop?"

Stanny-O was slowing down to take the exit to Audie's apartment building, looming huge and bright against the dark lake.

"No. Not that I've ever seen, except maybe you," he said, giving her a shy glance. "You're pretty much the first one I've seen him interested in."

"He gave me a really nice present the other day. Did you know about that?"

Stanny-O smiled broadly. "Yeah. They were his mother's."

"What?" Audie nearly jumped out of her seat. She stared at him. "Are you sure?"

"Yeah, I'm sure."

"Oh, crap," Audie whispered, letting her head fall back against the seat. This was too bizarre, and she didn't know whether to be appalled or flattered—and wasn't that just perfect? Wasn't that the perfect gift from Stacey Quinn, the most exasperating man she'd ever met?

"Has he said anything to, you about me?"

"He don't have to." Stanny-O pulled into her parking garage. "It's obvious what he thinks of you."

Audie turned to him in the bright fluorescent light of the underground ramp and huffed with impatience. "And what is that, if I may ask?"

The detective sliced into Audie's assigned parking spot and cut the Porsche's engine. He grinned at her, his small blue eyes glittering. "That's another thing you'll need to ask him yourself."

Quinn opened the door to Keenan's Pub and immediately sensed the soul of the place: the incense of cigarette smoke and spilled ale, the celestial choir of laughter and jukebox reels, the reverence for something transcendent, larger than life.

"Over here, Stace!"

Quinn's eyes adjusted to the dim light and dark paneling to find the smiling face of his youngest brother, Michael, and then, as the other head turned, the grin of his middle brother, Patrick.

"Good evening, Stacey." The bartender had already drawn his pint of Guinness and placed it on the bar to sit. Quinn knew he'd repeat the process three times before he'd achieved the perfect balance of foam and liquid.

"Matt! Good to see you. How have you been?"

"Grand. Just grand."

And Matt did look grand, Quinn thought to himself— the same little spark plug of a bartender he'd known nearly all his life. He gazed around him—the whole place looked wonderful. Most of the usual Friday night flock was already assembled, and as he moved toward the booth he waved at a few of the patrons, slapped the backs of a few more, and shook hands with the rest.

Quinn reached into the booth and briefly tugged at Pat's shoulders before he joined Michael.

"Is Da coming?" Pat asked.

"What? The two of us aren't good enough for you?" Michael edged over in the booth as Quinn pushed harshly against him as a greeting.

"Move your wide ass," Quinn said.

Then he winked across the table at Pat and settled in with a sigh of pleasure. "Da stayed a little late at practice tonight," Quinn said. "He'll be here eventually."

"So is the band ready for CityFest?" Pat asked. "I hope to God you've got some new sets, because we're getting tired of the same old crap every year. Have pity on your fans, Stacey."

Quinn smiled at Pat, realizing it had been six years since his ordination, but it was still sometimes jarring to see his smart-aleck brother in a priest's collar.

"Sure, Pat. We thought we'd do some gangsta rap this year. Maybe a few calypso tunes."

Pat and Michael snickered for a moment before they launched into their favorite pastime—arguing with each other. Quinn sat back and expected to be entertained.

As he observed, he remembered how there'd been more than a few broken hearts in the neighborhood the day Patrick went into the seminary. It was as if God decided only one child would get the very best from the union of Patricia Stacey and James Quinn—and it had been Patrick.

He had Da's eyes—like Quinn himself—but Pat's were softer, kinder, and shaded in lashes that in a fair world would have gone to a girl. Pat's shock of light brown hair was thick and heavy, but it balanced out the elegant bone structure of his face. He had Da's ability to draw you into a tall tale like a lamb to slaughter. He had his mother's soft heart and curious mind but none of her idiosyncrasies.

Those had all gone to Quinn along with her family name, as he'd heard often enough.

Quinn looked over at his baby brother Michael, now vehemently pressing his case about something or other, and smiled. Michael had gotten Patricia Stacey's quick tongue and quicker temper, as well as her pale blue eyes. Yet all those traits dwelled in a carbon copy of Da's big, open face and husky body and were served up with a depraved sense of humor.

Lucky for all of Chicago, Michael had found his niche as a Cook County assistant state's attorney, where his fine brain and wicked lip helped keep the streets clean.

As Quinn half-listened to his brothers, he thought about where he fit in. He was the oldest, the quiet one, as he'd heard all his life. He was the one with his father's stubbornness, fierce sense of loyalty, and love of music—all wrapped up in his mother's need for order.

How many times had Quinn heard it? "If one of those boys were to be a priest, my money would have been on Stacey!" He never quite knew if that was intended as a compliment.

The Quinn boys were now men, ranging in age from thirty-three to twenty-nine, and as Da always told his pals: "My lads can bust 'em, prosecute 'em, and forgive 'em all in a day's work."

Michael and Pat's argument had deteriorated into a dispute over the name of a short-lived family dog from the late seventies. These two could argue about the color of the sky, Quinn knew.

"The damn dog's name was Caesar," Michael said, looking shocked. "I can't believe you don't remember that."

"Caesar?" Pat laughed. "Do you really think our father would have allowed an animal with that fruity name into our house? The dog's name was Jake."

"What are you, nuts?" Michael said, laughing. "If we ever owned a dog named Jake, then my dick is the size of the Space Shuttle . . ."

Quinn shook his head and wondered again what it would be like if John had lived, if he could sit here in the booth in the empty space across from him, where he belonged. As he did every day, Quinn wondered what it would be like if he hadn't let his baby brother die, and said a small prayer for everyone concerned.

Quinn was jolted out of his melancholy by Matt Lawler's delivery of his beer. "Perfect, Matt. Thanks."

He felt the dark, rich stout slide down mellow and smoky at the back of his throat and sighed. A pint was always best at Keenan's, in the company of his brothers and in the memory of John.

"So, how's lifestyles of the rich and fatuous, Stacey?" Pat smiled at him.

"Oh, it's rough," Quinn answered.

"Tell Pat about the household hints chick. He's gonna love it." Michael's eyes flashed above his full cheeks. "He's working on a stalking case with Homey Helen. Can you believe it? Is that perfect or what?"

"Really?" Patrick took a reverent sip of his own pint and eyed his older brother. "The new one or the dead one?"

"The dead one would be easier to handle." Quinn raised an eyebrow as his brothers laughed.

"The dead always are," Pat said broodingly. "It's the living that piss me off to no end."

"Bad day in the confessional, Father Pat?" Quinn asked.

"The usual." He waved his hand and sighed. "So somebody's stalking Homey Helen? What the hell for, to get their hands on her secret recipe for window cleaner?"

"Haven't quite figured that out yet," Quinn said. "Could take a while."

"I've seen her on TV," Michael offered. "She's a complete babe. Now tell Pat who she used to date."

Quinn leaned across the booth and whispered, "Timmy Burke."

Pat nearly spit out his beer. "Jaysus! No way!"

Quinn nodded. "A little over a year ago. Just after he oozed his way into City Hall."

"My God, is the poor woman daft or just a rotten judge of character?" Pat asked.

Quinn shrugged. "I think Timmy pulled his usual on her. She didn't hang around long. She's too good for him."

"My shit-stained drawers are too good for Timmy Burke," Michael quipped.

"Yeah, well I had to go talk to the man this morning."

Both Pat and Michael went silent.

"He's a possible suspect, like all her old boyfriends," Quinn continued. "Would you believe that bastard made me wait outside his office for twenty minutes?"

Pat cleared his throat. "How long had it been since you talked to him, Stace?"

"I don't know. Mom's funeral, I guess, so a couple years."

Pat nodded silently, feeling Michael kick him under the table. "What?" he whispered, scowling at Michael. "Stop it, you eejit."

Quinn shook his head at his brothers. "We were quite civil to each other, as far as Timmy and I go. No bloody noses or anything. He just threatened to fire me." He smiled. "Of course, I'd like nothing more than to arrest the dickhead, but Audie seems to think he's got nothing to do with the threats."

"Who's Audie?" Michael asked, confused.

"Oh. Homey Helen. Her real name is Autumn Adams—people call her Audie."

Pat set down his beer and smiled at Quinn, relieved to

direct the conversation anywhere other than Timmy Burke. He wanted to enjoy himself tonight.

"So did you tell this Audie person how important she was to Mom? How she made our lives an anal-retentive hell?"

Quinn laughed at Pat. "That was *her* mother, really, but I may have mentioned it. I kind of had to. She saw Mom's box."

Michael jerked back as if Quinn had slapped him. "The box at your place?"

"Shit . . ." he hissed to himself, rubbing a hand over his face. Quinn was toast now and he knew it.

"Need I remind you you're under oath, Stacey?" Michael draped a big arm around his brother's shoulders and grinned. "You had the squeaky-clean babe in your house and I bet you weren't reorganizing the linen closet."

"So he likes her, so what?" Pat said, frowning at Michael. "It's not a big deal. Leave him be."

"The hell it's not a big deal!" Michael's eyes went wide. "I think it's the first time he's brought a woman to his house since Laura took off. Am I right?"

Pat's eyebrows shot up. "Really? Is that true, Stace?"

He wasn't responding to his brother's taunts in his usual brusque fashion, and Pat wondered if Stacey still hurt over Laura—it had been more than a year since she'd had a fling with Timmy Burke and then left with the radio disc jockey. And good riddance to her, Pat thought. She wasn't right for Stacey, not that anyone in the family ever dared say so to his face.

Pat studied his older brother carefully, almost hearing the gears inside his brain as they clicked into place.

"Uh-oh," Pat whispered, turning to Michael, suddenly making the connection.

"Hel-lo," Michael said in singsong.

"Shut up, both of you," Quinn said, looking down into his pint glass. "I like her."

Michael's lips flapped together in a sudden burst of laughter and Pat joined in. "Well, of course you'd like her, Stacey!" Michael said. "She's your fantasy woman!"

"Martha Stewart . . ." Pat began.

"And Carmen Electra," Michael finished for him.

"So we were wrong—she does exist," Pat whispered respectfully, before he and Michael began laughing again. "No, really, I think that's great, Stace," Pat said. "So how *much* do you like her?"

Good question, Quinn thought to himself. What did it mean when a woman you'd just met monopolized your thoughts? What did it mean when you stayed away from her because you didn't trust yourself in her presence? What did it mean when you wanted her to have your grandmother's handkerchiefs and saw her face every time you closed your eyes?

"A lot, I guess." Quinn took another gulp of Guinness as his brothers exchanged glances.

"Have you winterized her yet?" Michael asked, and Quinn saw the glint in his eye.

"Jaysus, Mike. I've only known her a couple weeks. I think it's a little early for that."

"You can never do it soon enough," Michael said, quite serious. "I'll never forget what happened with Bridget Feeney—gorgeous woman, but she went totally psycho on me that winter. It was like a five-month-long case of PMS. I should've tested her in the fall, but I forgot. I was distracted by her ass."

Pat frowned. "What the hell does *winterized* mean? I have a feeling you're not talking about antifreeze."

Michael and Quinn nearly busted a gut.

"Actually, it *is* kind of like that," Quinn said.

"Look, Pat," Michael explained patiently. "You can

never really know a woman until you go through a Chicago winter with her, OK? The cold, the wind, the flu, scraping ice off the car, shoveling out your parking space—from November to March, that's when the real woman comes out.

"Incredibly bad things can happen during that time, let me tell you," Michael continued. "Ugly things. But if you can stand her during winter, you've got a good one. Sheila passed with flying colors. It's one of the reasons I married her."

Pat's mouth hung open. "Lovely. But that doesn't explain why in God's name the woman married *you*, Michael." Then he turned to Quinn, frowning. "Are these lucky gals aware they're being tested?"

"No," Quinn said. "That would skew the results."

Pat scowled at him.

Quinn held up his hands in defense. "It's nothing awful, Pat. All you do is ask a couple basic questions, like what she'd enjoy doing on a Sunday afternoon in February."

"And this accomplishes what?" Pat asked.

"Well," Michael said thoughtfully, "the best answers involve food, televised sports, beer, and sex in any combination."

"There's a range of good answers," Quinn added. "But if she mentions sex and beer, things are looking up."

Pat shook his head. "Good God, I'm glad I'm a priest."

They all felt him before they saw him—the room pulsed with energy when the door opened and Jamie Quinn strolled in, exchanging warm greetings all around.

"Hello, boy-os," he said, eventually sliding his big, sturdy body in next to Pat. "Did I miss anything?"

Pat nodded and gestured with his pint glass. "We were just talking about Stacey's new girlfriend, Da."

Jamie leaned toward his oldest and tapped a beefy fist on the table, grinning. "It's about damn time, lad," he said, settling back in the booth. "Well now. Let's just hope she's not the pain in the arse that Laura was, shall we?" He winked at Pat and Michael. "That woman gave me pontab of the gullet every time I saw her."

Audie lay sprawled out on the Italian couch, realizing yet again that she hated the feel of leather against her skin, especially in the summer, realizing yet again that for all its glitz, she hated this apartment.

It was sleek and huge and she felt insignificant and uncomfortable in it. The city lights and the dark lake were beautiful at night, beautiful and big and powerful—but all it did was make her feel small.

She thought of her old apartment in Wrigleyville, with the big oak tree in the backyard, its crooked little back porch, the neighborhood sounds and the cooking smells, the old clawfoot bathtub, the cozy bedroom. It fit her like a favorite sweatshirt—warm and comfortable and not trying to be anything it wasn't.

Why she let Marjorie convince her to move to Helen's place was anyone's guess. She was making a lot of stupid decisions around that time, if her memory served her correctly—one right after the next. She took on a job she didn't want and couldn't do. She agreed to pretend she was somebody she wasn't. She started living a life that belonged to someone else.

All for her mother. All for a woman who never loved her.

Audie closed her eyes at the awful memory of her mother's last hour. Her face was swollen and bruised from the attack and her hair was matted with blood. And the terror in her voice, the pleading . . .

It was the desperation that was Audie's undoing. The woman who was always perfect, polished, and poised was gone, and in her place was an old lady who was bleeding and trembling and could barely speak.

"I'm counting on you," her mother had whispered as they rolled her down the hallway. "Swear to me. Don't disappoint me, Autumn."

She was twenty-eight years old the night her mother died, but Helen could still slice her to the quick with those familiar words: *Don't disappoint me*. She said it, then reached for Audie's hand and died.

In her more self-pitying moments, Audie realized she had become Homey Helen to prove to her mother that she was worth loving, that she could be something other than a disappointment.

Stupid decisions, certainly.

And now what? Was a year long enough, Audie wondered? Did Helen ever look down from the Elizabeth Arden salon in the sky and feel rotten for putting her daughter in this position?

"Can I bag the *Banner* renewal and go back to my old life?" Audie asked out loud. "Will you forgive me if I at least *try* to be happy, Mom?"

Audie sighed. The woman was dead. She couldn't hear her and she couldn't love her. If Helen had ever wanted to do either of those things, she would have done them while she was alive.

With a sudden burst of energy, Audie hopped up from the couch and kicked a soccer ball down the long, dark hallway, hearing it smack dead center against the far wall.

"She scores," she mumbled to herself, "and the crowd goes wild." She heard her feet shuffle over what seemed like acres of carpets and wood floors before she reached the kitchen.

She walked around the long curved counter of teak and stainless steel and reached for the refrigerator handle.

"Gross." There were things in there that scared her.

"Crap." There was nothing to drink except water.

"Oh, hell." She opened the pantry to discover she was even out of tea bags.

Audie turned around and put hands to hips over her nightshirt—one of Griffin's soccer jerseys from his pro days. What was she doing? Was she nuts? It was a balmy Friday night in the big city and there she was—a reasonably attractive, pseudo-successful, still somewhat young woman, alone in her dark castle tower, talking to dead people, with nothing to eat or drink.

She was pathetic. She should be out enjoying her life.

Oh, wait. She had no life.

Her life lately consisted of following Marjorie's business plan, hanging out with Stanny-O and eating way too many Frango Mints, and waiting each day by the mailbox for the next death threat.

Oh, and let's not forget the best part about her life— Stacey Quinn! The intensely sexy cop who kissed her until her spine fused, then disappeared with some lame excuse, then sent her a gift so inexplicably sweet and personal that it made her cry.

Enough of that, she told herself—no more thinking of Stacey Quinn tonight. She'd see him Sunday. That would have to be enough. She was sexually frustrated. That was her problem. And Stacey Quinn was simply the hottest thing she'd ever seen in her life!

She covered her face in her hands and groaned. "You're such a jerk, Quinn," she whispered. Then she smiled in the dark.

It was beyond her control, so she gave in and wondered what he was up to right then, who he was with, what he was wearing, and whether he thought of her. She wondered who got to hear the sound of that gravelly voice and who was lucky enough to hear him laugh.

She hoped to God it wasn't a woman.

The buzz of her doorbell nearly sent Audie through the ceiling. She ran across the wide living room to the foyer and flipped on the light, slamming her eyes shut in the brightness. She peered through the peephole to see the smiling face of—Tim Burke?

"Tim Burke?" she whispered to herself, dropping her eyes from the door. It was beyond her how he thought it was OK just to show up here. It was beyond her how he got beyond lobby security. Why couldn't he just leave her alone?

"What do you want, Tim?" she shouted through the heavy double doors.

"Hey, babe! I was just at a dinner party in the building. I wanted to drop by to say 'Hi.' "

"Not a good time, Tim." As if there ever *was* a good time for Tim Burke.

"Oh. Well, sure. Not even a cup of coffee?"

"I don't have any coffee."

"Oh. Right. How come you haven't returned my calls, Audie? I miss you. You know I care for you."

She huffed. She leaned her forehead against the cool, smooth wood and began a light banging at a slow, even tempo.

"What are you doing, Audie?"

"Bashing my head in," she muttered to herself. "Nothing! Look, I've got company, Tim, all right?" She didn't like to lie, but this was an emergency. "Good-bye."

Audie was turning away from the door when she heard him say, "Is Stacey Quinn in there with you?"

"What?"

"He came to see me today. I'll give you a little advice, Audie. The guy's a hothead and a womanizer and nothing but trouble. Watch yourself."

Audie stuck her eye back on the peephole, but Tim Burke was gone.

She shook her head. Obviously, there was no love lost between Quinn and Tim Burke, and she wondered what had happened so long ago. She could just picture them in a playground scuffle, hurling insults and punches at each other, shoving and tearing at each other's little white Catholic school dress shirts.

She was rooting for Quinn.

"Men," she mumbled, heading for her bedroom. She might as well go to bed for the night. That way, when Marjorie asked her on Monday if she was getting enough sleep, she wouldn't have to lie.

CHAPTER 6

"What's your favorite thing to do in the summer, Homey?"

Quinn settled back on the varnished oak bench of the sailboat and stretched his arms wide along the edge of the cockpit.

"Take in a Cubs game." Audie threw him a teasing smile from her perch behind the helm. "And this—there just isn't much better than this, Detective."

She turned her face into the wind and closed her eyes, enjoying the peaceful sound of water lapping at the side of the boat, the whisper of air over the sails.

Quinn watched her. He didn't think he'd ever seen her truly relaxed, and his heart opened at the sight of it. He was perfectly content to sit there the entire day, just appreciating her face and the way the breeze tossed around her hair.

He'd never been sailing before, but if it meant hanging out with a beer and looking at Audie, he believed this was a pastime a man could grow to like.

It wasn't a stretch to say that Autumn Adams was the prettiest woman he'd ever known. He liked the way the light hit her out here on the lake, making her skin glow like copper and gold. He stared at the long, smooth, casually outstretched leg and remembered all too well what it felt like to touch each place on that leg—the solid calf muscle, the sharp shinbone, the hard knee, the soft thigh.

Holy God. That he wasn't jumping on her this very second, pulling her down onto him and devouring her, was proof of his superhuman will. Sixteen years of Catholic school probably didn't hurt, either.

And Holy God. The idea that Tim Burke may have ever put his hands on her was enough to make him lose his mind. He knew that he'd have to ask more about their relationship, but not right now. Not today. Today, he just wanted to enjoy being in her company again.

Quinn moved his eyes from Audie to the flat blue horizon line of Lake Michigan. He really had been busy last week. But the truth was, he had asked Stan to take care of Audie so he could cool his jets—pure and simple.

After that out-of-control kiss on his deck, Quinn found himself thinking with his dick instead of the perfectly fine brain God gave him, and that wasn't his style. And he was still responsible for Autumn Adams's case, which had to be his priority—at least for the time being.

But when she'd asked him to go for a sail, he'd accepted gladly. And now he wondered how the hell he'd managed to stay away for a total of ten days—ten very long days.

He took a swig of beer, put the can in the convenient beverage holder on this fancy North Shore sailboat—all gleaming wood and polished brass and bronze—and laughed at himself. He was sure this boat was worth more than Da's house in Beverly. He was sure he was a bit out of his element here.

He wondered how long it would be before he ended up at the fucking opera.

"Did you say something?" Audie opened her eyes and smiled at him politely.

"Nope." Those plump lips, wet from a recent slide of her tongue, and that rounded chin, perfect for biting. She looked delicious and juicy and he felt an ache in his groin.

Watching this woman did painful things to his chest, too, like his heart was being throttled, like his blood was backing up, like the oxygen couldn't quite make it up to his head.

"I used to sail a lot with my dad when I was a kid," Audie said, running her fingers through her hair and closing her eyes in the wind again. "It was nice to come out here on the water, away from everything, just the two of us."

He actually felt her voice touch his skin. It was warm and smooth and rich and he felt it fall over him, wrap around him in the breeze. It was the weirdest damn thing.

The satiny curve of her throat . . . had he gotten a chance to taste her there yet? It was all a blur. He couldn't remember if he'd yet run the tip of his tongue up her throat, and it bugged the hell out of him.

"Dear God," he muttered to himself.

"What?"

Quinn shook his head and tried to pick up the threads of the conversation—there had been words exchanged, hadn't there?

"Did your mother ever come out on the boat?"

"No. She didn't care for the lake all that much."

"Did she care for your father all that much?"

Audie's head snapped around and she stared at him in disbelief. "What kind of question is that?"

Quinn winced, annoyed with himself. He didn't want to piss her off already—they'd only been out here a few minutes and he wanted to stare at her for several more hours at least.

"I just saw some of your pictures, that's all. They didn't look too thrilled to be together."

Audie shrugged. "I guess they tolerated each other, like with any marriage. My dad was not a very demanding person, so he kind of let Helen rule the roost and did his own thing. He wasn't home all that much."

"What did he do at the Mercantile Exchange?"

"He traded in the pits for many years, then became a broker. Made a ton of money."

"Did he have affairs, Audie?"

She went very still and stared at him. He appeared perfectly innocent sitting there with one leg propped up on a knee, his arms draped across the back of the bench—but his eyes were insistent, intense.

She blinked at him in astonishment. "You know, it amazes me how rude you can be."

"I don't mean to be rude. I'm just trying to figure something out, is all."

Audie snorted. "What in the world would my father's indiscretions have to do with the letters I'm getting? You think one of his old lovers is sending them? That's a bit out there, don't you think?"

He cocked his head and examined her face for a quiet moment, aware that she was uncomfortable. There was no way around it. "So he did have affairs, then?"

Audie closed her eyes briefly and sighed. "I don't know for sure, Quinn. There was just something wrong. That I know."

"Wrong? What do you mean?" He leaned forward, elbows on knees.

Audie was rapidly becoming annoyed by this line of questioning and groaned. "Look, from what you've told me about your family, I don't think you'd understand even if I tried to explain it, so forget it."

Quinn gave her a small smile. "Try me, OK, Homey?"

The beer felt cool going down her throat, and Audie looked out over the water for a while. They were heading south, being nudged along by a nice steady breeze near the shoreline. To the right was one grand home after another, made of stone and brick or wood, surrounded by huge, heavy summer trees and tidy grounds. This back view of the North Shore castles of Winnetka, Wilmette, and Evanston was one she knew by heart.

"It was a big house, right?" Audie kept her eyes on the shore, watching the homes float by. "Everyone went to their own corners—you didn't have to see anyone else if you didn't want to. When Dad was home, he went to his den. I went to my room or down to the boathouse. Drew usually just left altogether. And Helen worked with Marjorie in the home office."

"Not Chestnut Street?"

"No. She didn't buy the building until I was in high school, so they wrote the column from the house for many years."

Quinn nodded slightly, trying to imagine what it would have been like to have so much room for so few people—the opposite of his experience as a kid. "Go ahead. I'm listening."

Audie sighed. "It wasn't so much that we didn't like each other—we just didn't know each other." She leveled her gaze and stared hard at him. "That's the part I don't think you'll get—how a family can be strangers the way we were. I think my dad and I were the closest, but that's not saying much, and he died when I was fifteen. My mother and I . . ."

Audie shrugged and looked up to the telltale fluttering against the jib. She adjusted the wheel a bit until the tiny streak of red cloth flew straight and smooth against the canvas. "Helen and I never really understood each other. I'm a lot like my dad, and that seemed to bother her to no end. She was always busy or traveling and didn't have much time for me. I think she was glad of that."

Quinn looked down at his hands and remained silent.

"Marjorie and Mrs. Splawinski were the ones who pulled me through." Audie flashed a grin. "For as long as I can remember, they were more my mother than Helen. I went to Mrs. Splawinski when I was bummed out, and she'd sit and speak Polish to me and feed me brownies. I didn't understood half of what she said, but God, she makes awesome brownies."

Quinn chuckled. "So Stanny-O tells me."

"And I went to Marjorie when I was in trouble and needed a plan. She covered for me when I came home drunk after my junior prom. She took my side in the whole Griffin fiasco."

Quinn's head jerked up. "Griffin fiasco?"

Audie sighed. "Helen nearly croaked when I brought Griffin home with me. You might have noticed that he's a black man."

Quinn grinned. "And a real snappy dresser. So what happened?"

"Oh, it was hell, basically. Helen would barely speak to me and threatened to cut off my inheritance if I didn't break up with him, all worried about maintaining her position in society. It was ugly. She was ugly. The funny thing is, I know now that Griffin and I hung on much longer than we should have—we make much better friends than lovers—but we did it to spite her." Audie scrunched up her face at the memory. "It wasn't a very mature thing for me to do."

The amusement showed in Quinn's eyes.

"I think that's why I started smoking, too. Just to piss off Helen."

"You smoked?" He looked shocked.

"Yeah. Just a few a day, but I'm pretty much over them now. I noticed smoking was affecting my lung capacity on the soccer field, that and getting older."

Quinn cocked his head and appraised her openly. "You do look downright elderly, Audie."

"Thanks."

"So you were talking about Marjorie and Griffin."

"Marjorie stuck with me. She told me to follow my

heart, fight for what I wanted, that sort of thing. She played go-between for Mother and me. She was wonderful. She did the same when I was dating Tim Burke."

Quinn sat quietly for a moment, and Audie watched his mouth pull into a grimace.

"You started dating Tim in late March last year, and your mother was killed in late April. You were dating Tim when your mother died. Is that correct?"

"Yes."

"And your mother didn't like Timmy, either?"

Audie saw where this was headed and smiled sadly. "No, she didn't particularly like him, and yes, the reason was because he was Catholic."

Quinn's expression remained quite grim. "And did Tim know how she felt?"

"Yes. I mentioned it."

"Did they ever argue or have words?"

"What? No. Of course not. They knew each other from city functions, but I don't know if they ever said more than two sentences to each other."

They sailed on for several moments in silence, Quinn lost in his own thoughts, staring at his hands, then staring out over the water. Audie watched him, wondering where he would go next in his questions, fascinated with Quinn the detective as much as she was with Quinn the man.

"Did Marjorie live with you?"

Audie laughed a little. "No, but she and Helen were so involved in the column that she was there a lot. I never understood why Marjorie never got married—she's such a great woman, smart and funny and adventurous. Did you know she went climbing in the Himalayas about ten years ago? But she only had the poodle."

"A fine animal indeed."

"Oh, there were more than one, Quinn! She went

through a bunch of them. As soon as one died, she got another, and they all had men's names."

Audie laughed to herself and checked the boat's trajectory and speed. "Let's see if I can remember them all—Bill, Ted, Frank. I think the one she's got right now is named Mark."

Quinn chuckled, too. "Her husbands?"

"Exactly!" He watched Audie's eyes sparkle in delight. "Marjorie and her gentleman poodles kept Drew in joke material his whole life, believe me. Still do."

"So what's your relationship like with Marjorie now?"

Audie smiled a little and shrugged. "She's my rock, both at work and personally. She does my research, writes the columns, deals with readers, runs the office. Plus, she knows me better than just about anyone, and is always willing to listen when I bitch and moan. She keeps me sane."

Quinn leaned closer and studied her face, wondering if she was going to cry or yell at him when he asked her this: "If she does all that, then what's left for you to do, Audie?"

She didn't cry *or* yell. Audie took a long sip of beer and chuckled.

"That's a very good question, Detective." She waved her hand dramatically up to the sky and projected her voice. "I pretend I'm Homey Helen, of course! I'm an actress—star of print, stage, and TV screen, all pink and cute and perky and . . . oh, hell . . . what a joke." Her hand fell down in her lap and she shook her head slowly.

"I'm a joke, Quinn."

"Your fans love you."

"They love Homey Helen. They don't love *me*."

"Then what are you going to do about it?"

Audie stared at Quinn as if he'd just fallen from the sky and landed in the cockpit next to her. "Do?"

"That's right. What would you rather be doing with your

life, Audie? I'm thinking more anger management classes, maybe."

Quinn realized that when she laughed the way she was doing right now, all throaty and loud, it sent ripples across his skin. Ripples of pleasure. Her laugh gave him an amazing amount of pleasure.

"Well, you're thinking right, Detective." She took another sip of her beer. "I'd love my old job back. I'd like to coach again."

"Then why don't you?"

"Because of the promise I gave my mother."

"The promise you gave a woman who didn't love you?"

Audie said nothing for a very long time, realizing that Quinn did indeed have half a brain and it worked just fine.

She took comfort in the soft rocking of the boat, the wind, and the silence around her. As aggravating as he was, she was glad Quinn was here. There was something about the man—his no-nonsense conversation, his rock-solid physical presence—that made her feel good.

She glanced at him slyly, at the defined muscles in his neck and shoulders under the thin T-shirt, the finely shaped arms and hands. It dawned on her suddenly that she'd not taken anyone on the boat with her in nearly eight years—not since Griffin. She had to look away.

"We haven't talked about what happened at my house that night." Quinn waited patiently until she turned back to him.

"That's because you've avoided me since then."

Quinn pursed his lips. "Not entirely true, and I meant we haven't talked about it yet today."

"I'm trying to pretend it didn't happen," she mumbled.

Quinn drummed his fingers along his beer can. "How's that working out for you?"

"Ha!" Audie glared at him. "It's not."

"Me, either."

She studied Quinn more directly, not caring if he caught her. She was allowed to look at how the wind tickled his sun-streaked hair. She could look at his wide, straight mouth and the keen eyes—it was her boat, after all, her brother's boat at any rate.

And the longer she looked, the more pronounced the pulling inside her became, an opening up that was unfamiliar but not completely unpleasant.

"I need some time," she said suddenly. Audie hadn't really planned on saying anything at all—let alone *that*—and her words surprised her.

"It's your call," was all Quinn said.

He continued to look at her, all crooked grin and dancing eyes, and Audie let go with a huge smile. She hadn't realized she was holding it in, and it was a relief to smile at him the way she needed to.

"I really do like you a lot, Quinn. It's the weirdest damn thing."

"I like you, too," he said, rubbing a hand over his mouth, as if hiding his smile. He shook his head. "We make an interesting couple, that's for sure."

They sailed for several hours, down to Hyde Park, where they anchored for lunch, and back to the North Shore. She taught Quinn the basics of sailing—how to read the wind, how to set the sails and determine right-of-way—and she let him take the wheel for most of the way back north. Then she sat back and watched him for a long period of comfortable silence.

Quinn was a quick study, and he was calm and steady behind the wheel. Despite the sunblock she'd seen him slather on at least three times during the day, he was slightly sunburned across his nose and cheeks, and his eyes sparkled in contrast to the rosy skin.

He cut a fine figure at the helm of the *Take a Hint,* broad shoulders held straight, the clean line of his nose, his trim legs covered in light brown man-fuzz.

She was thinking that Quinn had put his hands all over her legs, but she'd yet to do the same to him. Then she reminded herself of the truth—she wasn't quite ready for Quinn.

In silence, she once again thanked Rocky Datillio for his perfect timing.

"Hey, Audie. Can I ask you a question? It might sound strange."

She laughed. "You've been asking me strange questions since we left the dock, Detective."

"Yeah? Well, this one's personal."

"They've all been personal."

"I mean about you."

"Sure, Stacey. Go for it." Audie saw an expectant look in Quinn's eye and then watched as he hesitated—something she'd never seen him do. What in the world did he want to know? Whatever it was, it must be very important to him.

"My question is what do you like to do in the winter in Chicago—say, February, typical Sunday afternoon sort of thing?"

That was the big personal question? She was thinking underwear preference or prescription medications or maybe religion again.

But the man looked downright nervous about her answer, and Audie narrowed her eyes at him for a long moment. He was obviously up to no good.

"Winters can be rough, Quinn. You want to know what I'd consider my perfect afternoon?"

He reached down for his beer and took a long draw, nodding.

Audie locked her eyes on his. "I enjoy having wild,

sweaty sex on the floor and then popping out to a sports bar for a Guinness."

Quinn violently spewed his beer onto the boat deck and began coughing. Out of pity, she stood up and patted him—smacked him, really—between the shoulder blades.

"Did I pass, Quinn?"

"You could kill a man talking like that," he croaked, his eyes huge. "At least give me a warning next time, would you?"

"A warning? You mean when I'm about to mention sweaty sex? Or beer and sports bars?"

He thumped his chest. "How about 'em all, just to be safe?"

She laughed at the sight of him, standing there in shock. It was quite satisfying, really. She sat back down, crossed her legs, and smiled at him.

"And how about you, Detective? What do you like to do in the winter?"

The corner of Quinn's mouth twitched as he squinted into the sun, studying her with appreciation. "Well, if we could find time for some barbecue ribs in there somewhere, that would pretty much fill my dance card."

She laughed with him, trying her best not to imagine having wild, sweaty sex with Stacey Quinn on the floor—or anywhere, for that matter. Lord, the man bothered her, and she had to shut her eyes against the memory of him stretched out beneath her on the deck, his hands moving hot and demanding up her dress. She sighed and turned her face up to the setting sun.

"I bet I know what you were thinking right then, Audie."

Her eyes flew open at the soft sound of his voice, and she stared at him, caught red-handed.

"You know, we *are* grown-ups—we can talk about this. I'm actually pretty uninhibited for an Irish Catholic boy, so it wouldn't embarrass me."

Audie felt the blush spread like fire up her throat and across her cheeks. "Talk about wh—what?"

"About the attraction," Quinn said matter-of-factly. "What's happening between us. All the kissing. All the imagining."

She glared at him and crossed her arms over her breasts. Kidding around was one thing, but she didn't like the serious tone of his voice. "We'd better head back," she said, all business.

"Someday, Audie, when you're ready, I plan on making love to you. I'm real interested in finishing what we've started."

She swallowed, blinked at him, and clutched herself tighter.

"In the meantime, I'd like to know what you like best, what feels good to you, so that I can be prepared."

"What?" She stared at him, feeling a shudder move through her.

Quinn's hands were on the wheel, but his body was turned toward her, his green eyes locked on hers, and there wasn't a trace of smugness in his face.

"The moment I laid eyes on you, I started imagining what it would be like to have you in my bed. I'd like to know what it takes to make you crazy, Audie, get you wild, send you over the top. I just need a few details for the next time I find myself fantasizing about you—which would be right now, actually."

"God, Quinn. Please!" It seemed the man got downright talkative when it came to two subjects—his family and sex.

"It's just that right now I'm not quite sure about you, Homey. I get a feeling you want something you don't know how to ask for."

"What the hell are you talking about?" She twisted away from him, looking out over the water. She felt trapped on this boat, trapped in his stare.

"I get the feeling you're sexually frustrated."

"What!?" She stomped her foot down on the oak floor timbers and glared at him.

"Maybe you just haven't had the right lover, Audie."

She was dumbfounded, and for several long moments her mouth hung open. He stood there perfectly somber, looking down at her with those piercing olive eyes, not a hint of sarcasm on his fine lips. She felt her breath come much too fast for someone not doing wind sprints.

"I can wait, Audie. You asked for time, and I'll give you as much time as you need. Then . . ." Quinn shrugged and the grin reappeared. "Watch out, Presbyterian girl."

"You're unbelievable, Quinn."

"Not yet, but I will be."

"Arrogant. Cocky. Uncouth." She jutted out her bottom lip and glared at him. "I'm thinking of pushing you overboard."

One of his brows arched high, the grin widening. "And I'd take you with me. I think I'd like seeing you in a wet T-shirt."

And then something happened that shocked Audie as much as it did Quinn. Her eyes filled with tears and her chin trembled and she said very softly, "Please stop teasing me."

Quinn thought his heart would break. The heat rushed through him, his knees felt weak, and he groaned out loud at his stupidity. Apparently, he had a lot to learn about this woman.

She could kick the hell out of a soccer ball, put on a show for the world, make him laugh, kiss him hard—yet her heart was fragile, and apparently, he'd just stomped all over it.

"Jesus, Audie." Quinn held out his hand to her. "If I go over there, I might crash your boat, so please come here to me."

Audie brushed away her tears with the back of her hand

and stood close to him, melting as his arm wrapped around her waist.

"I was just having a little fun with you. I'm sorry."

She nodded and leaned against him. "I think it just got too close to the truth, is all."

"Which part?"

"Oh, I don't know . . . the part about me being sexually frustrated, not having the right lover—the part about me looking good in a wet T-shirt."

He tilted back a bit to gauge her expression. They started laughing together and he gave her a friendly squeeze.

"Let's go in," she said.

"You got it, Skipper."

"You actually did good today, Detective."

He looked down at her again. "Really? And here I was thinking I've got a hell of a lot to learn."

Audie smiled sweetly at him and dropped her gaze to his mouth and back up to his eyes. She rubbed his back. "You're doing OK, Quinn. The wind can be kind of fickle out here sometimes."

Quinn let go with a deep, satisfied chuckle, keeping his eyes locked on hers for a few moments, his arm snug around her waist. "Come over here, Audie," he said softly, guiding her in front of him. He pressed a hand to her stomach and pulled her against him while he headed for shore.

Audie closed her eyes, feeling the wind on her face, the heat of Quinn against her back, the pressure of his hand on her belly. The truth was she wanted to know exactly how unbelievable this man was. She *wanted* to be in his bed. She *wanted* to find out if there was a man who could love her for who she was, not who he wanted her to be—and she wanted to know if Quinn was that man.

But she wasn't sure she could handle one more disappointment. She didn't know if she had it in her.

Audie inhaled deeply and felt Quinn's hand rise and fall

with the movement of her breath. She felt him press closer to her. She wondered what he really wanted with her.

Tim Burke wanted arm candy for his political career. Will Dalton wanted to write a book about her and her mother. Kyle Singer wanted to convince the Greater Chicagoland viewing area that he was straight. Russell Ketchum wanted control over the business.

And Audie wasn't quite sure of everything Darren Billings had wanted, but she was sure it didn't require clothing or a college degree.

Something was different about the man she felt so solid against her back. He made her laugh. He could be sweet. He could be blunt. He was tidy. He was sentimental. And the force of his physical presence was overwhelming—a new experience for her entirely—because Quinn filled her senses, made her blood pound and her skin tingle.

He just felt good to her. He felt *right*.

Audie opened her eyes to the evening light on the water and felt Quinn's lips brush her hair. She snuggled back against him a little tighter.

There was no way to predict all the things he'd ask of her. But right at that moment, it seemed all he wanted was to be with her—just plain Audie—and that was a good place to start.

The sun had disappeared by the time the sails were neatly folded away and the *Take a Hint* could be tied down for the night. Quinn took a long time meticulously wiping down every bronze fitting on the boat with a shammy skin. Drew would be shocked.

They carried their gear and walked side by side up the wooden dock. The imposing house loomed in front of them, lit up from the inside and rising high and wide on the crest of the lawn.

The sensation was so soft at first that she thought a moth

had brushed against her skin—but it was Quinn's hand, reaching for her in the twilight.

"Audie . . ." He smiled sweetly at her. "I wanted to say thanks for today. And I wondered if I might kiss you."

Quinn laid down the things he was carrying and took the lunch basket and towels from Audie's frozen hands. She stood breathless, waiting.

His hand swept up along her cheek and came to rest in the soft hair at her temple. She didn't push him away. She didn't turn her face from him. She returned his gaze, and in her soft, dark eyes Quinn saw the permission he sought.

"You make me fairly crazy, Homey," he whispered, bringing his lips to hers in softness—such softness—as his fingers played along her cheek.

The gentleness of it stunned her. They weren't smashing heads on sidewalks or crashing into porch furniture this time. Quinn's kiss was tender and full of sweet questions, and it shattered her.

She closed her eyes and let him touch her, let him explore her mouth with his lips, her body with his hands. She felt his palm flat at the small of her back, but it didn't piss her off this time. And at that moment, somewhere in the recesses of her mind, she decided that she'd go wherever he was taking her. Maybe not today—but someday.

Audie tilted her head to yield to the tentative requests from his tongue, and the emotion welled up in her belly and spread hot through her, and a helpless little squeak came out of her mouth.

Quinn pulled away, watching her shut her eyes and smile, holding on to the shadow of his kiss. Then her dark lashes fluttered and she looked right at him.

"Nice kiss, Quinn."

"There's more where that came from."

The way he grinned down at her made him look like a little boy, Audie thought, cute and afraid and shy. But this was no little boy, she knew. Quinn was a man, with a man's desires.

Was she willing to get closer to all of him—the little boy's sweetness and the man's needs? Was she willing to try with Quinn?

"I need to be careful," she whispered.

"I know you do."

"I'm a total failure at this. You saw the list."

"Think positive."

"No. Quinn, listen. I suck at relationships. I'm trying to be honest here."

He laughed softly. "Honesty is good."

She grinned at him and sighed. "OK. You've been warned. Now what about you, Stacey Quinn? You're the cautious type, aren't you?"

He reached for her hands and held them in his. Quinn wanted to look at her, so soft and beautiful, so close. He wondered why this extraordinary woman stood here with him, scared but willing. He wondered if she had any idea how his heart was cracking wide open in his chest.

"Usually I'm cautious. But with you . . ." He pulled on her hands. "Oh, hell, Audie. Not with you. Come here to me."

He gathered her up in his arms and she felt him cradle her, protect her, give her a place in the world to stand for a moment, a place where she seemed to fit just fine.

Audie tucked her head into his shoulder and heard the lake stop rippling and the breeze stop blowing and her own heart stop beating. There was only Quinn, and he was a heady mixture of scents—water and wind, beer and sunscreen, and Quinn himself—and his body was warm and steady and sure against hers. She let the feel of Stacey Quinn sink into her bones.

"Thank you," she whispered. "It's been a long time since someone just . . . hugged me."

He chuckled softly and heard himself say, "I could hug you like this till we both dry up and blow away."

She pulled back and examined his face. There was no self-satisfied look in his eye—just surprise. Apparently this was something out of the ordinary for him as well.

The destruction was complete.

"What are you doing to me, Quinn?" she breathed.

The smile started small and spread slowly but eventually engulfed his whole handsome, sunburned face. "I'm not sure, but I hope to God it's something like what you're doing to me."

He kissed her again, and this time she threw her arms around his neck with enthusiasm. Quinn hugged her so tight that her feet lifted off the deck.

From his second-story bedroom window, Drew stared down the sloping lawn to the dock, where he watched his clueless sister throw herself at Mister Chicago's Finest. He took another sip of his Tanqueray and tonic.

"Jesus Christ, Audie," he muttered, spinning the ice cubes around with the rotation of his wrist. "We sure know how to pick 'em, don't we?"

He raised his glass to his sister and her latest beau, gleaming and giggling under the boathouse lights. "Two weeks, tops," he said, throwing back the rest of his drink.

"Do you have dinner plans for next Sunday?" Quinn could barely see Audie as they continued their walk up the dock in the darkness.

"No. Why?"

"I'd like to take you someplace real special."

She shook her head slowly. "You don't need to spend your money taking me to some fancy restaurant, Quinn. I thought you were getting to know me a little. I don't even like—"

"Audie."

"What?"

"I want to take you to Beverly for Little Pat's birthday party."

"You do?"

"I do. And you might want to wear something washable."

CHAPTER 7

September 10

Dear Homey Helen:

I've been thinking. September 22 is a dreadfully long way off. Could we possibly reschedule? I've tried to be patient— you have no idea how I've tried—but my patience is wearing thin.

I just don't think I can wait another moment for you to be dead. It's not like you'll leave behind a grieving family, now, is it? Why don't we just get to it?

—Your most loyal fan

PS: I thought your column on top fifty uses for transparent tape was to die for!

Her hands started to shake, and she felt a cold flash of panic race through her bloodstream. She handed the note back to Griffin very slowly, careful not to touch any part but the edges of the paper—careful not to meet his eye as she turned toward her office door.

"Audie?" Griffin placed the letter back on the reception desk, watching her walk away. "Shit."

Marjorie was shaking her head.

"Do you think I should talk with her?"

Marjorie wiped tears off her cheek with a trembling hand and sighed. "I honestly don't know what to do at this point.

Why don't you go in with her for a minute while I call those detectives, and then I'll try to talk with her, OK?"

Griffin nodded. "Are *you* all right, Marjorie?"

She pulled her mouth tight. "It makes me very emotional. I see these notes and Audie's sadness and everything that happened with Helen comes back to me like it was yesterday. I get so damn angry, Griffin! I feel so—God, I don't know—helpless, I suppose."

"I hear you," Griffin said softly. He patted the top of her hand and headed into Audie's office. He heard Marjorie sigh and pick up the phone.

Audie was sitting on top of the credenza near the window, surrounded by tall stacks of newspapers and file folders, hugging her legs tight and resting her chin on her knees. Griffin closed the door and leaned on the wall.

"Hey, girl. Is there anything I can do?"

She shook her head. "Just call Quinn and Stanny-O."

"Marjorie is doing that now. Anything else?"

"No."

"Do you want to be alone?"

"No."

"Would you like a hug?"

"No. But thanks."

Griffin sighed. This was an all-too-familiar state for him—not knowing exactly what Autumn Adams wanted or needed. It had always been this way with them, as a couple and as friends. When she pulled away like this he felt useless, the same as Marjorie. It was as if Audie wanted him but didn't want him; as if she needed something, but she wouldn't take anything.

She told him once that she believed she was missing some basic part of her heart—she just didn't know how to deal with people who wanted to comfort her, love her. She'd never had much experience with that sort of thing, she explained.

Griffin waited with her for many quiet minutes, watching her stare out the windows. "I'm sorry, Audie," he exhaled, letting his shoulders slump. "I wish there was something I could do to help you."

She nodded, and Griffin saw her jaw tremble and her shoulders shake.

"Oh, please don't cry."

The tears made his worthlessness complete. Griffin scanned the room for a box of tissues but didn't see one, though it could certainly be lurking beneath the layers of junk in there.

Just then, Marjorie tapped on the door and she stepped in, carrying a tray of hot tea, a box of Kleenex, and a slice of her German chocolate cake.

Griffin would just go out and wait for the detectives. Audie was obviously in competent hands.

"We should place a patrol officer here in the office and have one at her apartment when we're not around," Stanny-O said.

Quinn nodded silently, still balancing the latest letter between his fingertips, still reading, still thinking.

He glanced over at Griffin, draped across Marjorie's desk chair looking quite surly. His expression didn't go with the festive tie-dyed T-shirt and billowy cargo pants he was wearing.

The guy may have questionable taste in clothing, but Quinn and Stanny-O agreed—there was no question that Griffin cared for Audie, that he would do anything for her. Griffin Nash wasn't sending these notes.

"So, Griffin, what's your take on this?"

Griffin's head popped up, his eyes darting from Quinn to Stanny-O and back. "My take is I wish to hell you two would find out who's doing this. This one really ripped her up."

Quinn's stomach clenched, and a little painful surge moved through him at the thought that she was hurting. Then the inside of his skull began to throb at the thought that Timmy Burke may have done this to her.

He glanced at the closed door to Audie's office. He hadn't heard any crying from in there for a good long while, so maybe Marjorie had been able to calm her down.

"So? Any leads, mon?" Griffin stood up and moved in front of the desk.

Stanny-O and Quinn looked at each other briefly before Quinn answered him.

"Nothing new."

"Do you think it's Drew?"

Quinn and Stanny-O stared at him.

"You think it's her brother?" Stanny-O asked. "What's your insight into Andrew Adams?"

Griffin laughed, crossing his ankles casually as he leaned against the reception desk.

"We're not close. He didn't exactly welcome me to the family, if you know what I mean. So what I tell you, you got to realize doesn't come from an objective source, right?"

"Right." Stanny-O smiled.

"Andrew Adams is a spoiled, elitist, lazy, pussy-assed rich boy who hates anyone who doesn't belong to the Chicago Yacht Club. He drinks more than any man should be allowed. He doesn't give a shit about Audie or anyone but himself, for that matter. That about sums it up."

"Hey, don't hold back on our account." Stanny-O chuckled.

Griffin scowled at him.

"OK, so he's another asshole. We seem to have hit the motherlode in this case, don't you think, Quinn?"

"Absolutely."

"But that don't mean he's sending the letters. You really think he's our man, Griffin?"

"Probably."

Stanny-O frowned. "And his motive?"

"Money."

"As things stand right now, we've got no physical evidence on him," Quinn said. "He's lost a boatload of money in the last year, but he's managing to stay afloat. His printer doesn't match up and his prints aren't on any of the letters."

"And whose prints are?"

Quinn smiled a bit. "Well, Griffin, the letters that came before we arrived were covered in fingerprints—yours, Marjorie's, and Audie's. After we asked you to be careful handling the paper, there have been none at all."

Griffin frowned, and just then the door to Audie's office opened and Marjorie walked out, smiling, an empty plate and teacup in her hand. She gave Quinn a reassuring nod and gestured toward Griffin's office.

"Would you mind if I had a word with you, Detective? Can we use your office, Griffin?"

"Sure."

Quinn followed Marjorie, entered the office, and leaned up against the wall. He was surrounded by soccer action photographs—Griffin apparently played with the Baltimore Blast and the Chicago Fire. Above Griffin's desk was a photo of him and Audie, sitting on the stoop of an apartment building, their heads together, grinning.

Finally—Quinn had seen a picture where Audie was smiling.

"How do you think she's holding up, Detective?" Marjorie eased herself into the computer chair, smoothing down her stylish straight skirt. "It's obvious that you two have hit it off, and I thought maybe she was opening up to you a little bit. She's a difficult person to read sometimes."

Quinn nodded and studied Marjorie with appreciation.

She was a slim, attractive woman with nice pale eyes and fashionably short silver hair. She moved with surprising grace for someone her age.

Though she seemed devoted to Audie, he and Stan had checked out her background just to be sure, and found nothing that would indicate a motive for sending the notes. Marjorie's business partnership with Helen Adams had made her a very wealthy woman. She'd welcomed them graciously into her elegant La Salle Street townhouse and talked for hours about the Homey Helen column, answering all their questions and then some. Her computer equipment wasn't a match.

"I thought she was doing OK up until this morning," Quinn answered her.

"Are you with her all the time, Detective? Is somebody with her all the time?"

Quinn looked down into Marjorie's worried face and wished he had something more reassuring to tell her. He watched as Marjorie suddenly winced and brought her hand to her head.

"It'll be all right, Marjorie."

She shook her head and swallowed. "It's not . . . I'm sorry. I've got a horrible headache, and this has been a completely awful morning. You were saying?"

"We're going to post a uniformed officer here and one at her place when Detective Oleskiewicz or myself can't be with her. We'll keep her safe."

She nodded but continued to frown, apparently not satisfied with his answer. Then she sighed.

"I think she likes you quite a bit, Detective." She looked up at him quizzically. "Is the sentiment returned?"

"Are you always this nosy, Marjorie?"

She laughed. "Oh, well, yes, I suppose I am! Television is repulsive and I can only read so many hours before my eyes start to go haywire, so I have to find my jollies somewhere, don't I?"

They shared a brief laugh before her expression went serious again.

"I don't mean to pry, Detective, but has she told you about that Tim Burke, the vice mayor?"

Quinn's whole body stiffened and he felt the little hairs on the back of his neck prick up. "What about him?"

"That he's always bothering her. That he sends her flowers about once a week. That it's been more than a year since they broke up, but the man won't leave her alone."

Quinn stared at her, thinking through all the details—he'd get a search warrant. He'd confiscate Burke's home and work computer equipment. He'd—

"And Audie just told me he showed up the other night at her apartment. Uninvited, of course."

He'd kill him. The lying sack of shit—of course Audie wasn't "coming around." How could he have wondered for a moment that it was possible?

"Thank you, Marjorie. I'll talk to Audie about this."

"I was wondering what we should do about her road trip next week. Should we cancel, do you think? Russell will probably go postal on me if I suggest it, but I just don't know if going out of town is a good idea right now."

"Where's she supposed to be?"

"Los Angeles Tuesday through Thursday. Dallas Friday. Atlanta Saturday and Sunday."

"Would she be going alone?"

"Yes."

"Is it possible to cancel?"

"Oh, certainly."

"Then that sounds like a wise thing to do."

Marjorie sighed and stood, still rubbing her forehead. "Then I'll try to handle Russell." She smiled at Quinn bravely on the way out the door, but Quinn could see the discomfort in her eyes. "Maybe it's time I ask for that raise."

When Quinn stepped into the reception area, Audie was there, waiting for him. Her eyes were red and her face looked a bit puffy and all he wanted to do was cradle her in his arms, tell her everything would be all right, that he was right there and he'd keep her safe.

Instead he smiled at her and felt the relief wash through him when she tried to smile back.

"Got any plans for today, Miss Adams?"

She shook her head, her eyes so big and sad and beautiful.

"What do you say to lunch and maybe a nice long run? We haven't seen the lions in a while."

As he watched the edges of those lovely lips curl up in delight, Quinn thought again how much he wanted to hold her—but this time he also thought about crushing her with his mouth, covering her body with his, being inside her, protecting her from all the Timmy Burkes of the world, even if it were the last thing he ever did.

"That sounds absolutely perfect, Detective," she said.

And for a second, Quinn wondered what she'd just agreed to.

They had a long, exhausting run, and on the way back to the apartment they stopped at the grocery, and Audie was certain it was the first time she'd ever been positively giddy in the Dominick's produce section.

And now the man who made her that way was cooking for her, his hair still damp from the shower, his lean, muscled arms and hands chopping and slicing and mixing and stirring.

Audie remembered how she'd taken one home economics class in high school and the teacher had compared cooking to chemistry—the careful mixture of elements to achieve a predictable result, time after time.

Chemistry hadn't been her calling either, as she recalled, and so it made sense that her home ec projects boiled over, congealed, or exploded at random.

Helen had been very disappointed.

But right now, Quinn was showing her how to adjust the gas flame so that the onions would sauté clear, not brown, and she was actually interested—interested in standing close to him and hearing his voice, in breathing in his scent, in feeling him near her.

"Are you listening, Homey? I'll be testing you on this later."

"I'm just fascinated, Quinn. I didn't know what all those little knobs were for."

He shot her a sideways glance and pointed in front of him. "This is called a pan."

"Could you go over that one more time?"

"Just hand over the chicken, Miss Adams," he said. "Do you have a preference between breasts and thighs?"

As she reached for the plate of chicken Quinn had already seasoned, she felt her heart pound. "Which do you prefer, Detective?"

He turned to her, eyes searing like olive green lasers. "Don't make me choose, Homey. That would be cruel."

She nodded, feeling a rush of heat from her toes up through her solar plexus to the top of her head. She handed him the chicken, realizing she'd never been this nervous around raw poultry, or around a man.

All through dinner she kept wondering why Quinn hadn't kissed her that afternoon or that night. She wondered why he wasn't teasing her to the usual degree. She thought maybe it was because he was worried about her, and she wasn't sure if she liked the idea of that.

Later, they sat together on the leather couch, tucked into

opposite ends, their legs and bare feet stretched out along-side each other. It was just a leg, she reasoned with herself, and there was no reason that the warm touch of his skin and the soft brush of his body hair should be sending crack-les of electricity up her spine.

There was no reason such innocent contact should make her hands sweat. And there was certainly no call for her heart to slam under her ribs the way it was.

"Stop it," she whispered to her own heart.

"I'm not doing anything," Quinn said.

"Oh. Not you! I . . . forget it."

She watched helplessly as Quinn took a sip of his white wine, leaned his head back, and closed his eyes. Wow. Lightning bolt time. He was one damn fine-looking man. She saw the sharp line of his jaw, the lean muscles down his neck, his Adam's apple, and the peek of his collarbone beneath the T-shirt.

Audie knew all she had to say was, "OK. Now," and Quinn would be on her like a cheap suit. She took a sip of her own wine and cleared the thought from her brain, re-minding herself that this was uncharted waters for her. There was something waiting for her with Quinn—she could feel it. And it was big and scary and she didn't have a name for it.

The theme music from *Jaws* pounded in her brain.

OK, fine. She was attracted to him. But she could handle it. Besides, sex with him would probably be anticlimactic, run-of-the-mill stuff. She was building this up for no good reason. Quinn would be just like every other man she'd ever been with—somewhere between better than nothing and almost wonderful.

Wouldn't he?

She placed her wineglass on the coffee table. "Be right back," she said, standing up.

Quinn watched her do a header over the ottoman.

"You all right there, Homey?" He raised up lazily to see her scramble to her feet, yank down her tank top, and shake her hair.

"Couldn't be better," she huffed, walking toward the wine bottle on the kitchen counter. Quinn watched her straighten those wide, smooth shoulders and gracefully swing her arms. She looked extraordinary in a tank top, with all the good parts highlighted in case a man had poor vision.

Next he watched the sweet roundness of her body moving beneath thin cotton drawstring shorts. The shorts looked comfortable on her. His shorts were rapidly becoming uncomfortable on him.

Quinn slowly shook his head.

This woman was something else. She couldn't lie if her life depended on it. Obviously, every time she tried to be something she wasn't or walk away from the truth, she fell on her face.

She'd probably been sitting there telling herself she didn't want to go to bed with him. Then *bam!*—face-first on the floor.

Now that's the kind of woman a guy could feel secure with, unlike Laura. It still bothered him that here he was, a man who cut through lies and secrets for a living, and he hadn't noticed that his own girlfriend was unfaithful. She'd been a very smooth liar.

"Want some more wine?" Quinn looked up at Audie appreciatively. She was gorgeous—all soft and round shapes on a firm, solid frame—and right then he couldn't help but stare at the undersides of her breasts, and he was certain she wasn't wearing a bra.

Had he run his tongue over those breasts? Maybe the rise of her flesh just above her nipples? He couldn't remember. Did he get a chance on the sidewalk? No, not there. The deck? He might have. . . .

She was smiling down at him. They'd had another good run today, and he loved to have an excuse to watch her pushing herself physically, sweating, breathing hard, those little wet curls sticking to the skin on her neck.

Autumn Adams was definitely going to be worth waiting for.

"Yo, Quinn. Wine?"

He looked up at her warily. "Sure. Thanks."

Audie poured herself another glass and went back to her corner, returning her legs to their previous position—skin to skin. She sighed.

"Uh, can I ask you a question, Audie?"

Quinn watched her roll her eyes, just as he knew she would.

"What now, Stacey?"

He snickered a little, appreciating this little game they played. Audie pretended like she didn't want him inside her head, but she did. He could tell. She was only taking it slow, just like she said she had to.

"What part of the letter upset you the most this morning?"

She looked right at him but didn't answer.

"Was it the part about not having a family?"

She nodded almost imperceptibly. "Yeah," she whispered.

"I'm sorry, Audie. That was mean stuff."

She nodded again.

"I need to ask you how much you've talked to Timmy Burke about your family."

"What?" Audie jerked back. "Tim Burke?"

"Yeah. Did you tell him about your family? Would he know a lot of the details of what it was like for you growing up?"

"No, of course not." Audie was frowning. "Tim was

more interested in talking about himself. We never really got around to me."

Quinn smiled. "Sounds about right."

"He's not sending those letters, Quinn."

"Then how do you explain all the flowers, the phone calls, the late-night visits here to your place?"

Audie groaned and shut her eyes. "Marjorie has a really big mouth."

"She's worried about you, and I don't blame her. Why didn't you tell me about Timmy? It's a real important piece of information that I should have had from the beginning."

"Because he's not sending the letters, Quinn! God, you've got this thing about Tim Burke, don't you?" She tipped her head and stared at him. "What happened between the two of you? The day I gave you my stupid list I watched you practically boil over just at the sight of his name. What's the deal here?"

She watched Quinn hop up from the couch, taking his leg with him.

He paced for a moment before he came around and sat down on the teak coffee table right in front of her. Audie straightened up and looked at his face. She went cold.

Quinn leveled his gaze at her. "I'm going to tell you about me and Timmy."

"All right." She had a feeling this was about more than a schoolyard brawl.

"Part of it is old stuff. It happened seventeen years ago, but I live with it every day. It's about my brother John."

Audie frowned. "I didn't even know you had a brother named John. You've only told me about Patrick and Michael."

"That's because John died when he was eight years old. I let him die."

Quinn's expression horrified Audie. She'd seen arrogance, desire, anger, and humor in those green-and-gold eyes but nothing like this. She didn't know what to say, so she stayed quiet and just let him talk.

"John was the baby and he was a handful, let me tell you. He had a couple different learning disabilities and we couldn't turn our back on him for a second. He'd roam the neighborhood, go into other people's houses, eat food out of their refrigerators, disappear for hours. It drove my mother insane.

"I remember this one time he vanished at night, and from dinner to midnight we were scouring the neighborhood. My parents were a wreck and Da had half of District Twenty-two out cruising the streets, going door-to-door.

"Finally, our neighbor Mrs. Geleski comes over to the house. She'd been getting into bed for the night and heard somebody breathing next to her—the poor woman just about had a coronary. She looks over and sees John crammed down in the space between her bed and the wall. He was sawing logs, peaceful as could be."

"Good grief," Audie said.

"So that was John. And one day when I was seventeen, I was supposed to be on John duty when Timmy and I started fighting over a girl—Mary Beth Horan. We were busy beating the crap out of each other and John got hit by a car, right in front of me, killed instantly."

Audie stopped breathing. She watched him hang his head. "Oh, Quinn."

"Timmy and I had been at each other's throats since elementary school." Quinn kept his eyes down. "Hockey, soccer, academics, girls—we competed in everything—but by high school it was usually just girls.

"So that day he was telling me all this crap about what he did to Mary Beth—I was wild about her—and I completely forgot about John. He rode his bike right out into the middle of Artesian Avenue and got hit."

Quinn rubbed his face with both hands and groaned,

looking up at Audie again. "I ran to my brother and started screaming for help, and that's when I see Timmy walking down the sidewalk, real slow, with a smile on his face. Then I heard him laughing."

The devastation in Quinn's eyes blasted a hole right through Audie's heart.

"I wanted you to understand why I don't like Timothy Burke."

"I understand," she said softly.

"And that's not all." Quinn ran his hands through his hair and slumped forward, letting his elbows rest on his knees. His face was just inches from Audie's now, and she could feel the rage building in him again.

"Recently, I was with a woman named Laura. She and I were together for almost three years."

"I know," Audie said.

He looked surprised.

"Stanny-O told me."

He closed his eyes for a moment and sighed. "What else did he tell you?"

"That he thought you were eventually going to marry her, but she left you and moved to Miami. That's all he told me."

Quinn nodded slowly. "Mmm. Well, she did move to Miami, but as far as marrying her . . . no. I don't think so." Quinn's eyes stayed on Audie for several long seconds, and she saw him weighing something in his mind.

"In fact, Laura got very pissed when I said I wasn't ready to settle down with her. So she started seeing Timmy Burke on the side, for several months at least. I don't know all the details. I don't want to know them. But the juicy part is she knew all about my history with Timmy when she did it—kind of the ultimate kick in the nuts."

"Good God. When was this?"

Quinn's eyes looked so tired. He looked so defeated. "Last spring. I found out in April."

Audie stared at him and felt her face go hot. Then she hissed in disgust. "April? I was seeing Tim then."

He nodded a little and smiled grimly. "Small world, huh?"

"Wow." She felt sick to her stomach. "But we never . . . uh . . ." Audie shook her head. "Look. We weren't—you know—involved. He took me to dinner quite a few times and I went to a lot of functions with him, but I . . ." Why did she feel she needed to explain herself to Quinn? "I didn't like him much. I asked him not to call me anymore. And I was hoping that would be the end of it."

"He told me the other day that he was in love with you."

Audie's eyes went wide. "Oh, hell."

"He told me you went down on him in the car."

"What!?" She jolted to her feet in the narrow space between them, and Quinn was suddenly staring at her belly button and a narrow strip of exposed skin above her shorts.

"Audie. Sit down." He pulled her next to him on the table. She was shaking with anger.

"I'm sorry, but I thought you should know what he was saying."

"My God. The guy is absolute scum."

"I didn't believe him, though."

She stared at him openmouthed. "Well, thanks a million."

"He also said you were 'coming around' and that you two were getting back together."

"Like hell!" She tried to stand up again, but Quinn grabbed her wrists and pulled her down in his lap.

"So that's the story with Timmy Burke."

"God, Quinn." Her mind cleared and she remembered how this whole conversation had begun—with his little brother dying.

She placed her hand against Quinn's upturned face. "I'm so sorry about John." Her fingers brushed against his cheek. "I'm so sorry that happened. I don't know what to say."

Though his eyes were shadowed by old grief, it did nothing to dull the power there, the intensity, and Audie felt herself shiver in his gaze.

"Just say that from now on you'll tell me anything that might pertain to your case—about Timmy or anyone else—OK?"

She nodded, allowing herself to see things through Quinn's eyes. Maybe Tim Burke was more than just an annoyance. Maybe he was an honest-to-God stalker.

"I refuse to let anything happen to you, Audie."

She nodded again, helpless in his stare and burning up because she was touching him, because the backs of her thighs were pressed down into the hard muscle of his legs.

"Even if it's not Burke, it's somebody. But I'll keep you safe."

The hell he would. Audie was perfectly aware that she'd never be safe around Stacey Quinn—not when he made her heart pound and her blood throb and when he smelled so good and felt so hot against her skin.

Maybe safety was highly overrated.

She dipped her mouth to his because she just couldn't fight it anymore, and his response was serious and sure and Audie felt him moan deep in his chest as his hands cupped her bottom and he pulled her tighter.

Audie devoured him. She grabbed on to his shoulders and kissed the man like the world was coming to an end and this was the last kiss she'd ever be able to give him, her last chance to convince Quinn that it was good to be alive.

Her tongue slid into his warm, wet mouth, and she brought her teeth down on his lips and he tasted like hot wine and hot man. She could feel him begin to smile under

her kisses, and she felt his hand slide over the contours of
her hips.

Then his hands were up the back of her tank top and his
touch seared her skin, and suddenly she sensed that she was
moving up and coming to rest on the couch, Quinn now on
top of her, Quinn now covering her with his hard weight
and his clean smell. His hands were roaming up the front
of her shirt, and when his fingers touched the sensitive tips
of her breasts she groaned with relief.

"Oh, God, woman," he whispered. "Do you have any
idea how sexy you are?"

"Medium sexy?" she mumbled.

"Wrong. Very, very wrong."

Quinn put his mouth on her throat and she leaned her
head back so he'd have more room to do whatever it was
he was doing with his tongue and teeth and lips.

"I have a confession to make," Audie whispered between hard breaths, her head lolling to the side.

"Confessions cleanse the soul."

"This is not a clean confession."

"Those are the best kind."

"You are the sexiest man I've ever known in my entire
life, Stacey Quinn." She grabbed his butt and pulled him
against her, arching under him to feel how hard he was.

"You're a pushy little Protestant thing, aren't you?" He
reached behind him and pulled her hands from his ass and
pushed them over her head, pinning them to the armrest
with one hand.

"Do you like to play rough, Audie?" He laughed when
her eyes flashed wide beneath him, and he thought it was
time he let the tip of his tongue take that long, hot slide up
her throat.

When he did, all she could do was gasp.

Quinn raised up and used his other hand to shove the
soft cotton top up under her chin. No bra, just Audie, and

she was displayed beneath him and he could hardly believe he wasn't dreaming.

He brushed his palm over one fabulous, golden, round breast, then the other, enjoying how her toffee-pink nipples peaked with the barest friction.

"What are we doing this time, Audie?"

"You're giving me another foot massage."

"Wow." Quinn dipped his head and nibbled on a nipple "Then I should have been a podiatrist," he whispered.

The sound of her low, throaty chuckle made him close his eyes in pleasure. When he reopened them, he saw her sweet laughing face, those dark eyes and darker lashes, her plump mouth. She was beauty and softness and sex beneath him, and he'd never wanted a woman so much in his life.

"Would you kiss me again, Quinn?"

A wave of exquisite heat rolled through his groin.

"If you'd kiss me back."

The instant his lips touched hers, Audie lost whatever bit of control she thought she had. Her response was beyond control, beyond reason. She knew she wasn't ready for this, that this would likely end just as badly as every other relationship, but her body gave her no choice in the matter. At that moment, all she wanted was to give to him, take from him, die in the heat of him. It was exhilarating. It was scary and intense and it was building and building.

He dragged his lips down her throat, over the clump of tank top, and then down to her breasts. His tongue was hot and his teeth were gentle and skilled, and she began to writhe beneath him, her wrists still pinned above her head.

"You're very spicy, Audie." His voice was scratchy and low. "I've been wondering how you would taste and you taste spicy."

"But my spices aren't alphabetized."

"I don't give a fuck."

Her giggle turned to a moan when he bit down on a nipple, then caressed it with his tongue.

"Oh, God."

He released her hands and let his mouth travel down her smooth stomach. Her hands rippled along his shoulders and neck as he kissed her belly button and pressed his lips. against the front of her shorts. Then he raised his head to see her stretched out on the couch, reaching for him, half-naked and all his.

"Come here to me, Audie," Quinn said, and he cupped his hands under her bottom and pulled down on her shorts and underwear, until a mound of dark curls appeared before him.

He stopped to stare. He could hardly breathe. She was perfectly formed, opening with desire, dark and lush.

"Come here to me," he said again, as he yanked the clothing from her feet and reached for her hands to pull her to a sitting position.

"Quinn, what are you . . . ?"

"Relax, Homey. I'm going to take real good care of you."

Audie let her head fall back against the couch, telling herself this wasn't really happening. This had to be some kind of extremely wanton sexual fantasy. In all likelihood, Quinn had just excused himself to go to the bathroom and she was sitting on the couch, alone, making all this up in her head because she was so sexually frustrated. She should be ashamed of herself.

Because there was no way she was really sprawled on the couch with her shirt up around her neck like this. Stacey Quinn couldn't be bending her legs and spreading her apart like this. His fingers were not slipping into her and she was certainly not squirming against his hand like this or making these sounds in her throat.

He was not kneeling in front of her with his sun-streaked

head between her thighs like this, like he worshipped her, smiling up at her with his green eyes and doing things with his mouth that made her want to believe in God.

This could not be happening.

But then his tongue licked into her so long and slow and thorough that she heard herself cry out and she started to pant. When he licked her again, two things became very clear in Audie's befuddled brain—Quinn was, in fact, kneeling in front of her with his tongue and fingers hot inside her. And he would, in fact, take really, really good care of her. He already was.

Then a third thing occurred to her—the phone was ringing.

She stopped squirming under him.

"Don't get it, Audie," he breathed into her, not lifting his head. "Let the answering machine get it." He nibbled along the swollen rim of her.

"I don't have an answering machine anymore!" she cried out, panicked. "Oh, God, I don't have an answering machine!"

"I'll buy you one tomorrow. They're a lot more affordable than they used to be." His tongue landed hot and sharp on her erect little clitoris and she grabbed on to his shoulders to pull him closer, then push him away, right as she teetered on the brink of a sharp orgasm.

"Oh, God, yes! Yes! Wait! Stop! Crap! Oh, hell!"

Audie forced herself to breathe and forced herself to think. She wormed her way out from beneath him and lunged for the phone on the side table.

"Russell?"

Quinn watched in horror as Audie pulled the tank top down over those luscious breasts that he hadn't sucked on near enough and he thought he'd cry when she bent over to find her shorts and underwear and . . . suddenly she was gone. All of that soft, wet flesh was put away.

He could hear Russell screaming.

"Why haven't you called me? Why did you cancel your trip? It's going to totally fuck up your publicity schedule!"

Quinn collapsed face-first into the couch cushions.

"Why haven't you messengered the contract over to me? What the hell is wrong with you, Audie? Now we've got less than a week to agree to the terms!"

"Then get me an extension, because I'm not ready to sign anything yet!" she screamed. "And don't call me at home at . . . what the hell time is it anyway?"

"Ten-thirty," Quinn offered helpfully, lifting his head and turning as he plopped down on the floor.

Audie whipped around to look at him, startled by his appearance. He looked all scruffy and shell-shocked and his mouth was red and wet and he was leaning against the front of the couch like he'd been shot.

She'd just attacked the man again! And he'd just . . . "Oh, boy," she whispered.

"Audie?"

"What, Russell? Get me an extension and leave me alone—can I be any more direct than that? Jeesh! What is with people? It's like they don't take me seriously!"

Quinn stood up just then, and it was obvious that he took her quite seriously, because Audie's eyes were drawn to his nylon shorts, now straining around a rather impressive erection.

"My God, you're huge," she whispered involuntarily.

"What did you just say to me?" Russell screamed.

"Oh, crap. Hell." Audie closed her eyes and took a deep breath. "Work it out, Russell. And don't call me again."

She slammed down the phone and turned to Quinn, who was slowly advancing toward her, his eyes hot and green and serious. She brought up her arm, bracing it out straight, palm out, and she felt like Diana Ross doing "Stop in the Name of Love."

"Don't move."

"Why?"

"Because I don't want to do this."

"But I do." He moved a step closer.

"I'm not ready," she breathed. "Please."

"Not ready for what?"

"For you, Quinn." Once again she surveyed everything the man had to offer and she let out a little whimper. "All of you."

"You sure felt ready a minute ago."

"My body is. The rest of me isn't."

He stopped and brought a hand up to his forehead and rubbed furiously. "What are you doing to me, Audie?"

"Oh, God. I'm sorry. I don't mean to do this. I'm just scared, OK? I'm scared of you."

His eyes widened and he wiped his mouth with the back of his hand, aware that he might look a bit . . . damp. "Why in God's name are you scared of me?"

Audie stared at him, handsome and sexy and rumpled and hard as concrete. She closed her eyes.

"Because of who you are, everything you are, everything I feel—everything I'm not very experienced with." Audie's breath was coming in gulps and she dared to look at him again. "I need to be sure, OK? You're different, and I need to be sure. Can you give me one more chance to try to get ready for you?"

Quinn turned away and crumpled onto the couch. She watched him grind his palms against his closed eyes.

"Are you OK?"

"I'm fine."

"You're not hurt or anything?"

He laughed, letting his head fall back as his eyes swept over her from top to bottom. "Men aren't physically injured when we can't complete the act, you know. It's just something we tell women."

Audie put her hands on her hips. "I know. Like 'Size doesn't matter.' "

He chuckled. "Kind of like that."

"I'm sorry."

"Don't be."

"Why are you being so nice about this, Quinn? If I were you, I'd be calling me names right now."

Quinn sat up and put his elbows on his knees, staring at her. "Now why in the world would I do that, Homey?" A grin appeared on his stricken face and Audie's heart melted. "See, I want to get in your pants—and stay there—in the worst possible way, so how would name-calling accomplish that?"

She could see his logic.

"I'll put up with a bit more torture if I have to. I've already decided you're worth the wait." The grin spread wider. "I'll just think of tonight as an appetizer—a nice juicy appetizer at a restaurant with real slow service."

She laughed. "I'm pretty tortured myself," she said, smiling down at him, acutely aware of the truth of that statement. She was wet, trembling, and aching inside for him to fill her, but despite all that, he'd just made her laugh! How did he do that? Did he have any idea what a lethal combination that was for her?

"Everything you need should be in the guest room, Quinn."

"Not quite everything."

"I'll see you in the morning, Detective." She wanted desperately to kiss him good night but remembered the good-night kiss on his deck and knew they'd be right back where they started. With a sigh, she headed down the hallway.

"Hey, Homey?" He saw her spin around.

"Yeah?"

"Can I ask you a question?" He peered around the end of the couch.

Audie laughed outright. "Quinn, at this point I think you can ask me anything, so stop asking if you can ask me and just ask me."

"Great." He smiled broadly. "I was wondering if you'd come see our pipe band play at CityFest next week, since you're going to be staying in town now."

Audie had to giggle at how cute he looked, peeking at her, obviously wanting her to say yes.

"Sure. I'd be delighted. Kilts and all, Stacey?"

"Kilts and all, Homey."

An hour later, Audie was still wide awake, trying to sort out why she'd just run away from what had promised to be *outstanding* sex.

Did she want a guarantee of some sort?

No, she wasn't stupid. There was no such thing as a guarantee.

Did she need to know him better?

No, not really. She knew he had a kind heart and respected her wishes, no matter how crazy they made him. She knew the things he'd told her that night took a lot of courage. Stacey Quinn was a good man.

Did she trust him?

Yes, she trusted him.

Did she trust herself?

Bingo—that was the issue right there. It was a foregone conclusion that they wouldn't last long. Nothing ever did. It was just a matter of time before he'd want too much from her, before he'd expect something she couldn't give. It was only a matter of time before she hurt him, and she really didn't want to hurt Stacey Quinn.

She liked him too much.

On the dock the other night, she told him she sucked at

relationships, and it was the truth. She was giving him a chance to step away. But he didn't. He pulled her closer instead.

Why did he do that?

"I don't know the first thing about love," she whispered in the dark. "You should have listened to me, Quinn!"

She flipped over on her stomach and groaned with frustration, because that's exactly what she was dealing with here—love—whether she wanted it or not. For the first time in her life, she was thinking of possibly, maybe, trying to love a man, not just have a sexual relationship with him.

And *that* was what scared her about Quinn.

At the same time, Quinn was lying awake in Audie's chic gray-and-white guest room, staring out from the platform bed to the dark windows and the darker sky, wondering just how much longer she'd make him wait. His body hurt. He still tasted her. Everything from the waist down was throbbing and hard and ready.

Above his waist, in the region of his heart, there was another sensation entirely—a warm one, one that made him smile, one that made him feel like something was locking into place. It felt like that night by the boathouse, when he opened his arms to Audie and she stepped inside.

Quinn knew he had a tendency to set the bar pretty high for himself—personally and professionally. And he knew he'd always had a clear idea in his head about what love would feel like when it came into his life.

He wanted what his parents had and he decided early on that he'd settle for nothing less. He wanted the kind of love that was beautiful and resilient and funny. He wanted passionate love. He wanted love that would challenge him, complete him, make him a better man.

So why was he suddenly wondering if he'd found that in Autumn Adams, a rich, WASPy Cubs fan in the middle of a vocational crisis? A woman who decorated her apartment in the Neo-Landfill style?

It was so outrageous that he almost laughed out loud.

Just then he heard her outside the bedroom door. He closed his eyes and lay still, his heart hammering, wondering what was going to happen next. Would she dive into this bed with him, already naked? Would she drag him into her bed, ripping off his clothes on the way?

Nothing happened. And Quinn waited.

Audie leaned up against the doorjamb and stared at him in the dim light. His holstered gun rested on the nightstand by his head. His face looked lean and smooth and strong in the shadows, his mouth pulled into a straight line in sleep. He had such beautiful bones at his brow, around his eyes—and she wanted to touch him there, touch that sweetness she saw in him.

His mouth began to twitch into a smile—a dream, she thought—and she saw the little boy in him again. She shook her head in surprise. All the way back to her room she thought to herself, *Stacey Quinn has taken me by surprise.*

Later, when Quinn was satisfied she was asleep, he slipped into his holster and tiptoed across the football field of an apartment. He nearly broke his leg on the running shoes strewn in the middle of the hall, then stopped in front of her closed bedroom door.

He listened carefully, opened it without making a sound, and looked down at her.

She lay halfway on her stomach, the covers all twisted up and thrown off, which made complete sense to him. He remembered all the nervous energy he saw in her that first day. Of course she'd be the kind to toss and turn all night, but he'd find a way to live with that.

He smiled down at her. He'd pictured her in leopard skin, hadn't he? Well, here she was, wearing one of Griffin's old soccer jerseys, the name "Nash" in bold white letters across the back over a big number ten.

He saw a sliver of white panties where the shirt rose up over her bottom, the same little cotton things she'd worn earlier. No leopard skin there, either.

Quinn admired the long line of leg tucked up chastely in sleep, her thick wavy hair tousled out behind her head. She was so sexy and vulnerable that he had to hold his breath to suppress a sigh of contentment.

Damn, he wanted this woman. He wanted everything she could possibly give. And he startled himself with this next thought: Could Autumn Adams ever love him?

Eventually, he closed the door and leaned against the wall just outside, sinking down into a heap in the hallway. He let his head fall back, knowing there was a silly grin plastered on his face, and fell asleep.

In the morning, Audie woke up, opened her bedroom door, and tripped over something large. She banged her head on the opposite wall and started cussing.

Quinn had already pulled out his weapon and Audie went scrambling backward down the hall on her hands, like a frightened crab.

"God, Audie! You scared the shit out of me!"

"Me? You! You're pointing a gun at me! Put it away! What the hell are you doing in the hallway? Put away the gun!"

He holstered his weapon and groaned, rubbing a hand through his disheveled hair and over his scratchy beard, trying to calm his heart.

"I came to check on you last night."

She blinked at him and clambered to a stand, pulling down on her nightshirt, letting her pulse die down. "You were worried about me?"

"Yes."

OK, fine, Audie decided. He could be worried about her if he wanted. She'd find a way to live with that. She took a step forward and offered him her hand.

"Good morning, Quinn," she said, hoisting him to his feet. "Thanks for keeping me safe."

"My pleasure."

"And thanks for not shooting me."

"I aim to please."

CHAPTER 8

"Get the hell away from me with those things!"

Stanny-O backed off, returning the Frango Mints to his upper right desk drawer, eyeing his partner warily.

"All you had to do was say 'No thanks.' "

Quinn looked up at him, stupefied. *"No thanks?* I've been telling you 'No thanks' for four fuckin' years, and apparently you haven't heard it a single goddamned time because every day—*every day,* Stan—you ask me if I want a mint and the answer is *no,* I don't want a mint. I don't like 'em and I never fuckin' will."

"Jeez, Quinn." Stanny-O shoved his hands in his pockets and stared hard at his partner. "Are you hammered?"

"What?"

"Well, excuse me, but you don't usually ramble on like this unless you've been drinking."

Quinn closed his eyes and said softly, "Of course I'm not drinking." Then his eyes flew wide and in a much louder voice he added: "But I'm gonna start slamming heads if you ask me one more time if I want a Frango-fucking-Mint!"

Stanny-O began to nod slowly and smoothed his fingertips along his goatee, letting the understanding settle over him. He sauntered over to Quinn's desk, taking a wide, cautious berth before he plopped down on the edge.

"Not getting any, eh, buddy?"

Quinn turned to him and glared.

"I take it she don't want to go there."

Quinn ignored him.

"She's a beautiful woman. Hell, she's fun, too, just wonderful. I think I'm in love with her myself." Stanny-O began chuckling. "Want some coffee?" He walked across the room to the coffee island and came back with two Styrofoam cups.

"You know, Quinn, I thought I'd died and gone to heaven the night Audie and me went for pizza after one of her games. There she was, sitting across from yours truly, easily the prettiest woman in the place—even in her uniform with her hair up all messy the way she wears it—and she had me laughing so hard at one point, telling me stories about what a crazy mo-fo Darren Billings was, I thought I was going to choke to death. I haven't laughed that hard with a woman in I don't know how long."

Stanny-O sighed. "Did she ever tell you about dating Billings, Quinn? Did she ever tell you what he used to do at the Popeye's drive-through?"

Still no reaction.

"Oh, well." He shrugged. "I'm sorry she's making you nuts."

Quinn grunted.

"I think she's perfect for you. I really do. And I know it must be really hard to be close to gettin' some but not really gettin' any, if you get what I mean. It's gotta be tough, buddy."

"Are you done yet, Stan?"

"No, I'm not *done*, Stacey. You're going to tell me what's going on."

"No, I'm not."

"Sure you are. You're my partner and this is our case

and she's our responsibility. So you're going to tell me what's going on."

Quinn closed his eyes and wrestled with the fact that he was close to having a heart-to-heart with Stanley Oleskie-wicz. He trusted the guy with his life every day, true enough, and knew he was in good hands—but his ego?

"She's driving me completely crazy."

"What's she doin'?"

"Being Audie."

"I hear you."

"Being goofy and disorganized and sexy and tender-hearted. Being unable to tell a lie without falling over her own two feet. Being vulnerable." Quinn looked up to Stanny-O and frowned. "Did you request the Helen Adams files again?"

"Yeah. I got 'em. Kerr and McAffee should be here any minute." Stanny-O gave his partner a solid pat on the shoulder before he went back to his chair. "Rick Tinley's the uniform assigned to her until five," he said, tossing a stack of files to Quinn.

"Good. Tinley's a good guy."

"You going to keep doing the night shift?"

"As long as it's needed," Quinn said.

Stanny-O started snickering. "Can I just tell you what a privilege it is to know a man such as yourself—a man who can make that kind of personal sacrifice for the well-being of our fair city?"

"Blow me, Stan. Besides, you're on duty tonight until I get through with practice—probably ten-thirty or so."

"Yeah, I know. So, what's the deal—is she running around the apartment in one of those little Victoria's Secret French maid outfits or something? I mean, I think I need to be prepared."

"Sorry, no. She sleeps in old soccer jerseys."

Stanny-O let go with a long and low whistle. "And I bet

they don't got a number five on the back, no matter what you say."

Quinn looked up from the files, and for the first time that morning he felt himself smile. "You know what, Stan-My-Man? You're absolutely right—it's the number ten."

Stanny-O winked. "Told you."

Officer Rick Tinley was nice enough. He was about forty-five, soft-spoken, and had already shown her pictures of his three kids. But the idea of a policeman following her around made Audie terribly uneasy. Wasn't it supposed to have the opposite effect?

Audie was third in line at the coffee shop and kept glancing back at the officer as he leaned against the wall, nodding like one of those stupid wobbly-necked dogs in the back of a rusted-out car.

Good grief, she was bitchy this morning. Maybe once she got some caffeine in her system she'd mellow out. She rooted through her bag for some cash.

Tinley said he was on a diet and just wanted a medium house blend with skim milk, but Audie knew that only the big guns could handle her foul mood this morning. She scanned the menu on the wall until she saw the promise of deliverance—the double espresso mocha freeze grande.

She sighed. No, it wasn't hot sex with Quinn, but it *was* cold chocolate with whipped cream, and for now, it would have to do.

She was weighing the advantages of a carrot muffin over her usual cranberry biscotti when the man at the front of the line turned around with his order. It was Tim Burke.

"Well, good morning, Audie. What a pleasure this is!"

Revulsion slammed into her at the sight of him, and a chill traveled up her back. Rick Tinley instantly appeared at her elbow.

At that moment, Audie felt trapped. She imagined how

good it would feel just to scream at both of them to *back off*!

She saw the amusement flash through Tim's eyes as he smiled. "I'm glad to see that you're safe and sound. Bye now."

With a polite nod to the officer, Tim walked out onto Chicago Avenue, instantly disappearing into the morning crowds.

"This is nowhere near City Hall," Tinley said with disgust. "What's he doin' up here?"

Audie felt her heart pound and her stomach knot. With what she now knew about Tim, she couldn't bear to look at him! Was he following her? Was he dangerous?

The good part was that if Tim was threatening her, then Drew wasn't. That was a relief, right? So why didn't she feel relieved?

"He lives around here," Audie offered, still staring out the front windows.

"I'll let the detectives know about this little coincidence."

Just then, Audie realized she was glad Tinley was at her side.

She moved to the front of the line with a sigh and began to order. "Good morning. I need one medium house blend with skim only please, plus one banana nut muffin, one chocolate chip biscotti, and a double espresso mocha freeze grande. Oh—and if you could dump a big mound of those little chocolate shaving things on top of the whipped cream I'd really appreciate it."

To his credit, Rick Tinley said nothing. But his shoulders were shaking in silent laughter.

"Like I said on the phone, I don't got a crystal ball, Oleskiewicz." Detective Ted Kerr stood up from his seat at the conference table and stretched his hands toward the ceiling.

"Unless you got one laying around in your fancy new office here that we can borrow."

Stanny-O shot Quinn an amused glance and slapped the files closed. He stacked them in the center of the table.

"And if you recall, Helen Adams was one of eight hundred and seventy-six homicides in the City of Chicago last year," Kerr added, leaning his hands on the back of the chair. "We did what we could, then moved on to something that stood a chance in hell of getting solved. You know the drill."

They knew it well, Quinn thought. Just like they knew that Helen Adams's file had already spent several months languishing in the cold-cases unit, where it had plenty of company.

"Like we told you on the phone, we didn't have shit on Homicide Helen." McAffee smiled, enjoying his own turn of phrase. "None of our street weasels knew a thing about it—just your basic wrong-place-at-the-wrong-time mystery—and public figure or not, we had to eat that case for lunch, despite all those god-awful editorials in the *Banner*."

Quinn sighed. It was true that Helen Adams had made the quintessential easy target—an older lady, alone, at night.

He and Stanny-O had practically memorized these files by now, but they wanted this chance to meet face-to-face with the detectives who'd handled it, and so far, Quinn had no complaints with how they'd done their jobs.

The first cops on the scene had found Helen Adams sprawled out in an alley behind a warehouse on the Near West Side, barely alive. Robbery was the likely motive. Her purse had been ripped from her arm, and the bag and its contents were strewn on the asphalt around her. Any cash she'd carried was gone.

Her car keys were missing. A watch had been ripped from her wrist. Pierced earrings had been pulled from her earlobes and the little fourteen-karat gold clasps were found a few feet away on the concrete. Her Porsche was found the next day, parked along the Chicago River near the Merchandise Mart.

Autopsy results eventually showed blunt trauma to the back and side of the skull with what appeared to be pressure-treated wood. But the weapon was never recovered. There were no witnesses. No significant evidence was extracted from the car.

There were a few things that bothered Quinn about this case, however, besides the fact that the victim was Audie's mother.

First off, what the hell was a sixty-two-year-old woman doing in that neighborhood at night? The file said that earlier in the evening Helen Adams had had dinner with *Banner* CEO Malcolm Milton at Spago's on the Near North Side, and a number of witnesses saw them leave separately. But the security camera at Lakeside Pointe never recorded Helen arriving home that night.

So what had happened after the *tiramisu* and before the trauma unit? How did she get from point A to point B?

The four detectives had already discussed Quinn's main concern—a cell phone call Helen received a little after ten on her way home. It was the only loose end he could find in McAffee and Kerr's investigation.

They'd traced it to a pay phone near Lincoln and Fullerton, but it lasted just seconds and may have been a wrong number. They found no witnesses who recalled seeing anyone in the booth at that time. It was a dead end—and it bugged him.

Everything at the crime scene indicated she'd been attacked where she lay, and the Porsche was found without a scratch on it, not stolen or stripped, the keys in the ignition. Did the offender drive it there after attacking her?

Did Helen leave the car there and drive off with the offender to the scene of the crime?

There were no self-defense wounds on Helen Adams—no marks on her palms or forearms and no material under her fingernails that would suggest she fought against anyone. That meant she went to that parking lot willingly and was surprised by the attack.

So what was she up to? Did someone set a trap for her? Who would want her dead?

Quinn knew they might never get the answers to these questions, because Helen Adams hadn't regained consciousness long enough to talk about the events of that night. The files said she managed a few words to her daughter on the way to surgery, then died.

Whatever those words were, they'd been enough to convince Audie that she owed her mother, big-time. One last guilt trip for the road, apparently.

Quinn sighed, twisting his own mother's *claddagh* ring around his left pinkie finger, thinking, thinking. . . .

"Aside from the phone call, do you know what else really bothers me about this?" Quinn looked up at Kerr and McAffee, thinking out loud.

"I have a feeling you're going to tell us," Kerr said, returning to his chair.

"Yeah. I am." Quinn reached for the files again and gazed at the color postmortem photographs. "She was hit in the face. Not the first time, the second time." He ran his finger along the image of Helen Adams's brutalized cheek.

"First one to the back of the head—she's down. But that's not enough. Then one to the side of the face. Why? Wasn't her purse already on the ground? Why the extra hit?"

"And to the face," Stanny-O added. "Muggers don't usually go for the face."

"Exactly," Quinn said, turning to his partner with appreciation. "It's too personal. There's too much anger there for a random mugging, especially of an older female."

"What are you guys after?" Kerr rolled an unlit cigarette through his fingers like a miniature baton. "You saw the case files. We must have talked to half the city looking for someone with a grudge against that old bat."

Quinn grunted a little. What had Audie said the other day about her fame? "They love Homey Helen. They don't love *me*."

This homicide case may very well be about Helen Adams the person, not Helen Adams the public figure or Helen Adams the random mark.

As he'd wondered many times before, could the same person hate the mother and the daughter?

"But Andrew Adams was at the yacht club all night," Stanny-O said out loud, as if following Quinn's silent reasoning. "And there were about two hundred people to back him up on that, right?" He looked to the other detectives.

"Right," McAffee said. "And everybody else we talked to had an alibi as well, including Malcolm Milton, your girl Autumn, and the business partner, Marjorie Stoddard— about fifty people saw her at a dog obedience class that night."

"Which brings us exactly to shit, like we said." Kerr inserted the unlit cigarette between his lips and let it dangle there as he talked. "Which is exactly what you seem to have on your case, too. Which is why you're grabbing at straws trying to find a connection with her mother's case. But Helen Adams never received threats as far as we found."

"Nope. She didn't," Quinn said. "One of the first things we did was run an FBI database search for similar threats, and there wasn't anything, anywhere."

"DNA?" McAffee asked.

Stanny-O grunted. "Stamps were the peel-off kind. Wa-

ter was used to seal the envelopes, not saliva. We got nothing."

"Fingerprints?" Kerr asked.

"Nothing we can't explain."

They all turned their heads toward the tapping sound on
the glass wall of the conference room, to see Commander
Barry Connelly pointing at Quinn, then crooking his finger.
Quinn excused himself.

"Hey, Quinn?" Kerr called to him before he reached the
door. "Sorry we couldn't be of more help on this."

"Yeah. Me, too."

Quinn had barely opened the door before Connelly
started talking. "We got a little problem."

As they walked together through the squad room, Quinn
released a sigh of resignation. He'd been expecting this—
Timmy Burke had no doubt made those phone calls he'd
mentioned and slimed up the gears of Chicago politics. But
Quinn knew Commander Connelly and knew he didn't
bend over for anyone, not even vice mayors.

"Have a seat." The commander shut his office door and
walked around his desk, then locked his ice-blue eyes on
Quinn's. "Damn it, Stacey. What did you have to go piss
off Timmy Burke for?"

"I told you. He's a suspect in the Homey Helen threats."

"Says who?"

"Says me."

Connelly nodded slowly and eased down into his chair.
"And this is based on hard evidence, I'm assuming."

"Circumstantial at the moment. A gut feeling."

Connelly began shaking his head. "Your gut can't be
trusted when it comes to Burke, and you know it, boy-o.
I'm telling you to leave the good vice mayor alone or life's
going to get real unpleasant for you, real quick."

"Meaning?"

"Meaning I'll have to yank you off the case and run all over town kissing ass trying to keep you working out of my station house. And you know how downright disagreeable I get when I have to kiss ass."

Quinn smiled at Connelly. He knew that. Not only was Barry Connelly commander at District 18, he was also Quinn's commander in the Chicago Garda Pipe and Drum Band, one of Jamie's oldest and dearest friends, and Quinn's godfather.

"Don't worry about Timmy Burke," Quinn said, waving his hand dismissively and standing.

"I'm not worried about him, you stubborn Mick. I'm worried about you, so sit down while I'm talking to you."

Quinn stopped in his tracks to see Connelly scowling at him beneath bushy white eyebrows. He obeyed orders and sat.

"Now listen up, Stacey. You do a damn fine job, but you're walking a fine line here, and you need to watch your back."

Quinn listened quietly.

"Burke's been saying things. He says you're sleeping with Miss Adams, and—"

Quinn's protest didn't even make it out before Connelly stopped him with a big outstretched palm and a frown. "And if you are, you're off the case. Now you can talk."

"He's lying, as usual. I'm not sleeping with her."

Connelly's eyes narrowed above flushed cheeks.

"But it's not because of lack of trying on my part."

The commander snorted with laughter. "Yeah, well, keep me posted if the lovely lady succumbs to your charms and all, 'cause then I'll have to take you off the case. You know I wouldn't care except that with this being a high-profile victim and with Tim Burke involved—Christ Almighty, Stacey—there can't be a hint of conflict of interest anywhere. Burke's making a hell of a lot of noise. Are we understanding each other?"

"Sure."

"Now." Connelly squeezed the bridge of his nose between a thumb and index finger. "What the hell are you and the Chocolate Moose doing with this investigation? You two usually make quick work of these celebrity chasers. I've asked you to focus on the case almost exclusively, but it's been weeks. What's the holdup?"

"We've narrowed the field," Quinn said, leaning forward. "As far as motive and opportunity go, Burke looks like the best bet right now, along with Miss Adams's brother."

Connelly's eyes mellowed a bit and he leaned back in his chair. "OK. You get exactly one minute to tell me about Burke. Let's start with motive."

"Your standard jilted lover," Quinn said. "It's been over a year since they dated, but he calls her several times a week, sends flowers, follows her to her book signings, and comes to her apartment uninvited. He told me he's in love with her and she just needs some convincing, but Miss Adams thinks Timmy is scum."

Connelly closed his eyes. "And you're helping her reach that conclusion?"

"I just filled in some holes for her. She's smart. She figured that one out all on her own, Commander."

"And you're sure about the calls and the flowers and the visits?"

"Yep. I got the florist records this morning—forty-two deliveries since they broke up last spring. I've seen the phone records from her office, and the ones from her home are coming this afternoon. He's on the security video from her building, right there pounding on her door. So it's not like I'm up the guy's butt for no reason—he's a suspect. A real suspect. I'm just doing my job."

"But nothing else on him?"

"No. No prints. No match from his work printer. He claims he doesn't have a printer at home and I don't think we've got enough for a search warrant yet, unfortunately."

"You're right. Now tell me about the brother."

Quinn rubbed his chin. "Andrew Adams is a thirty-something slacker who's lost a shitload of the family fortune to three ex-wives and a string of bad day trades. He's got debts, but he's not desperate. Lives alone. Drinks too much. No drugs except for a juvy marijuana bust. And no gambling that we can see."

"You've lost me, Stace. I don't see a motive here."

Quinn laughed bitterly. "Yeah, well, we're still working on that. See, the way the original Homey Helen left it, if Audie—Miss Adams—decides to quit the column, Drew gets first dibs on it. If he doesn't want the job, they can sell the rights and split the profit. Right now, Homey Helen Enterprises looks like it's worth about twenty-four million dollars."

"That would pay for a hell of a lot of day trades."

"And maybe another wife or two." Quinn smiled. "But here's the problem with that motive: He and his sister aren't close, but he knows she doesn't even like the column and would jump for joy to give it to him or sell it. So why threaten her? Plus, his computer doesn't match and his prints aren't on anything. And when we interviewed him, I didn't get any feeling he was a particularly bad guy—just a rich jerk."

"So you've got close to nothing."

"The letters are coming more often, and our guy says he's ready to move. We've got Miss Adams covered twenty-four/seven. It won't be long."

Commander Connelly grunted. "Like I told you from the beginning, the last thing the City of Chicago wants is two Homey Helens dying under our watch. The big shots at the

Banner got wind of this and they're breathing down the mayor's neck. I've set you two loose and I expect you to take care of it."

"I understand."

"Any connections with her mother's case?"

Quinn shrugged. "Again, Burke is a possibility. Apparently Helen Adams didn't like the idea of a Catholic boy dating her daughter. But Tim was never interviewed in connection with her death."

Both Quinn and Connelly arched their eyebrows and stared at each other. "That's not much," Connelly said.

"But it's something, and it's more than what we've got on the brother, or anyone else for that matter."

Connelly frowned.

"Stan and I are going to keep looking for connections."

Connelly nodded. "Just don't go bothering Timmy Burke again without giving me a heads-up, understand?"

"Got it."

"And keep your drawers on."

"Yes, sir."

"And see you at practice tonight."

"I'll be there."

In the evenings after Mrs. Splawinski caught the El for home, Drew thought it got far too quiet in the Sheridan Road house.

Not that he missed his wife—any of them, for that matter. In fact, he recalled quite well that while they were with him, he simply couldn't wait for them to leave.

Drew knew he was funny that way—he didn't necessarily like being alone, but he didn't know how to deal with people who claimed they cared for him, even loved him.

Well, Lord, with his childhood it was no wonder. His sister was the same way, God love her.

Drew made himself another drink, this time with double

lime. He needed the vitamin C. He knew a man could not live on Tanqueray and tonic water alone, though he'd certainly been giving it his best college try.

He took the drink to the window and stared out.

He hoped to God that Audie had rebounded from the momentary loss of sanity that made her throw herself at that Chicago cop. Drew shuddered, remembering them down there on the dock under the lights, going at each other like hormonal eighth-graders.

How vile.

But that was several days ago, and he knew all too well that an Adams love affair could hit the wall and burst into flame in that amount of time.

His guess was that Audie had already been scared off by the street thug's ardor and had demanded another detective on the case. That would be like her.

Drew turned away from the windows and returned to the computer desk. He placed the drink near the mouse pad, within easy reach.

He had no idea why he'd started writing these diatribes. Perhaps it was just the right time. Perhaps he simply couldn't keep all the garbage inside anymore.

Sometimes he surprised himself with the quality of his writing. He knew he had a wicked sense of humor—he could bring the yacht clubbers to tears with his cutting commentary on modern life and human foibles. In fact, his sense of humor was perhaps his only redeeming personality trait. Thank God he was finally doing something constructive with his talents.

Drew took a nice long drink and created a new document file on the computer screen.

The most important thing to keep in mind was that *she* would eventually read this, and it had to be so good that it would shock her, devastate her, terrify her. God, he hated her.

Honestly, he wished she were dead.

CHAPTER 9

As they trolled for a parking spot along the Beverly side streets, Audie suddenly changed her mind. She was no longer annoyed that Quinn had spent the entire drive trying to explain who would be here today and how they were related and/or connected to his family.

She was glad. Because the street was packed. She could already hear the noise—the music, the loud voices, the sounds of kids screeching.

If only she'd taken notes. If only Marjorie could have come along to create one of her helpful computer-generated charts. Because without notes or a chart, there was no way Audie was going to remember any of this. Despite Quinn's efforts, she was doomed.

They finally found a spot on Campbell Avenue, and the moment Audie got out of Quinn's light blue Ford Crown Victoria, she noticed it was just one among many unmarked police cars.

She took a deep breath and joined Quinn in the middle of the street. He reached for her hand and they walked south for a couple of blocks.

"Welcome to the family manse," he said, nodding toward a simple two-story yellow brick house shaded by a large catalpa tree.

The Quinn home had dark green shutters, a small concrete stoop, and neatly trimmed hedges and grass—nothing frilly, just tidy and clean.

Audie wondered if it had looked different when Quinn's mother was alive, whether she put little pots of geraniums on the steps or hung a pretty wreath on the door. She wondered what she'd been like.

"Da's not much of a gardener," Quinn said. "When Ma was alive, she always put flowers in the window boxes."

Not for the first time, Audie wondered if the guy could hear her thoughts. Stanny-O had said Quinn was a careful listener, after all.

They turned down the shaded walkway along the side of the house and moved toward the back gate. Audie squeezed Quinn's hand tightly when she got a glimpse of the small backyard packed with people.

"They don't bite, Audie," he said gently. "Well, maybe Michael, but he says he's up-to-date on his shots."

She tried to smile.

"They're going to love you."

As he reached for the latch, Audie noticed a large hand-painted plaque wired to the gate. The words had to be Gaelic, because she had no idea what they meant.

She pointed and cocked her head and Quinn smiled broadly.

"Cead mile failte." The words fell off his tongue like a lover's whisper, and Audie was stunned by the beauty of his voice. "One hundred thousand welcomes."

Quinn leaned toward her and placed his hand on the small of her back while planting a friendly kiss on her cheek. "Ready to party, Homey?"

"Ready, Stacey."

The first person to see them at the gate was Quinn's brother the priest. Well, it was probably best to get the most awkward one over with first, Audie thought to herself.

On the drive down, she'd confided to Quinn that she had

no earthly idea what to say to a Catholic priest—she'd never met one in her life. Was she allowed to say the word *hell*? How about *damn*? What if she accidentally used God's name in vain and Pat heard her? Did he know she wasn't Catholic? Did he know she wasn't really anything?

Quinn had chuckled at her nervousness. "Don't sweat it, Homey. Pat's a regular guy, all right? He's been a priest for six years, but he's been my brother for thirty-one, and that's who he'll be today."

As Audie watched Patrick stride toward the gate—all smile and sparkling eyes—she knew, of course, that Quinn was right. That man was definitely his brother. He just happened to be dressed in a short-sleeved black dress shirt and a white priest's collar.

"Audie?" He opened the gate. "It's great to meet you. I'm Pat."

She felt herself exhale in relief as he shook her hand. His eyes were strikingly similar to Quinn's but softer, and his hand was warm and firm, and he just kept smiling at her.

The next person to see them was Michael—a stocky guy in a T-shirt that read: "Will Golf for Food." His smile was huge and his piercing light blue eyes danced with laughter.

"And you must be Audie!" He took her hand and leaned down to kiss it, grinning at Quinn the whole time.

Before Audie could respond, the horde descended on them. Within seconds, she and Quinn were pressed into the middle of a mob of faces and a little girl was hanging on Audie's left leg and there were hands to shake and names to repeat and laughing—so much loud laughing it made her head spin.

Before she could catch her breath, the sea parted and she was scooped up into the arms of a man—definitely not the one she came with. She felt his deep voice and rowdy laugh rumble from inside his chest as her face was squished against his polo shirt, her lungs nearly collapsing from the force of his embrace.

When he held her out in front of him, she saw Jamie Quinn.

"It's grand that you could make it, Audie. We've heard so much about you."

And apparently, that was all it took to fit in at a party at the Quinns'. And as Jamie brought his arm protectively around her shoulder and guided her into the yard, she felt welcomed—one hundred thousand times over.

She felt right at home.

"Get your own girl, Da," she heard Quinn say from the other side of his father's bulk. "This one's mine."

There were basically three categories of people at Little Pat's sixth birthday party, and as soon as Audie broke it down that way, the fog began to clear.

There were cops and their families, people of direct or roundabout family connections, and people from the neighborhood. Stanny-O showed up not long after she and Quinn arrived, bearing a box of Frango Mints and a case of Old Style.

Audie was sitting at a tablecloth-covered card table with Quinn's sister-in-law, Sheila, who had provided the detailed play-by-play for her.

"And that's Belinda Egan from two houses up—her claim to fame is coming back from a vacation in Mexico last winter with some kind of worm lodged in her brain, from the pork, they think." Sheila's deep blue eyes sparkled in her pretty pixie face. "Six hours of surgery—awake the whole time. Can you believe it?"

"Wow," Audie said.

"That's Ricky and Cindy Panutto—Ricky is Michael's best friend from Loyola Law School." Sheila craned her neck a bit to the right. "That's Esther O'Fallon, Jamie's

older sister—her husband Jim died a few years ago. That's
Bill and Tava Reingold—Bill was Jamie's partner for close
to thirty years. And that's—*oomph!*"

The little girl who'd clung to Audie's leg had just hurled
herself into her mother's lap.

"Mommy! Little Pat and Joey are peeing on the side of
the house!"

"What?" Sheila stood up and shot Audie a smile, then
started laughing. "I know I shouldn't laugh, but I can't help
it. Excuse me—be right back."

Audie watched Sheila run off across the yard in her
shorts and sneakers, weaving through the crowd, her nearly
black curls flying behind her.

"What are you looking at?" Kiley's fiercely intelligent
violet eyes scanned Audie up and down.

"I was looking at your mother. I think she's very nice
and very pretty, and you look just like her, do you know
that?"

Kiley's smile overwhelmed her face as she nodded. "My
mommy *is* nice and pretty. So are you. Do you love Uncle
Stacey?"

"Wha . . . ?" Audie wasn't used to young children. Were
they all this blunt, or was it just Kiley's Quinn-ness showing?

"Well, we're friends. I like him very much and I think
he likes me. Do you have friends like that?"

Kiley scrunched up her face. "Heather Morrelli was my
friend, but she called me a double butt face the other day."

"I see." Audie took a sip of iced tea, realizing that this
was one of those times when grown-ups shouldn't laugh.
"And what did you say to that?"

Kiley scrunched up her face and thought about it. "I told
her I deserved to be treated with respick."

"Respick?"

"Yes. Respick. Do you want to watch me get my treatment, Audie?"

Audie inclined her head and frowned. "Wha . . . ?"

"Sorry. Pissing contest." Sheila scooped up Kiley from her chair and set her back on the grass. "Why don't you go play with the McConnell girls for a little bit? Go blow the stink off you. Your next one is at four o'clock, OK?"

"Bye, Audie," the little girl said, and Audie watched her skip away.

Sheila sighed, settling her petite body into the lawn chair and crossing her legs. "Actually, it was not only a pissing contest, but they were comparing size. I fear for Little Pat's future. I really do. All the Quinns are too macho for their own good."

"Testosterone poisoning," Audie said.

Sheila's bright eyes landed right on Audie's and she nodded appreciatively. "You're familiar with the disorder?"

"I noticed Stacey has a fatal case of it."

"That he does," Sheila said with a giggle. "Well, I've got to say, Audie, you're doing quite well for your first Quinn hoedown." She poured them both more iced tea. "In fact, I think it was right about now that I started running for the car, not stopping to pick up any of my personal belongings. But of course, Patricia was alive back then." She wagged a dark eyebrow.

"What was she like? Thanks." Audie took a refreshing sip of tea and scanned the crowd. She spotted Quinn with a group of guys by the fence arguing about something and laughing. He was wearing a pair of khaki shorts, a baggy blue-and-white Hawaiian shirt, and a White Sox cap, and he looked adorable. Cute and approachable and fun and huggable—except for the gun she knew was tucked into his waistband.

Quinn's eyes moved from his friends and landed right on her, flashing under the brim of his cap. Then one corner of his lips twitched, and Audie was instantly transported to the moment they had met in the WBBS studio. It seemed like a lifetime ago.

She felt herself blush. She smiled at him quickly and looked away before she embarrassed him—or herself.

"Trish was a good person," Sheila was saying. "I'm sure Stacey told you all about her Homey Helen fixation."

"He did," Audie said with a nod. "And he seems to have inherited it."

Sheila let loose with a big laugh. "Yes, he did, and my God, there isn't a day that goes by that I don't wish Michael had some of that in him! I love him to death, but the man is a pig."

Audie giggled until she saw Sheila's expression sour.

"Trish was one tough cookie, let me tell you. She loved her sons very much, and she put me through the wringer before Michael and I got married." She shook her head at the memory. "We lived together in sin, you know, careening down the fast lane to purgatory."

Audie nodded, her eyes wide.

"I think I broke her in for any woman who might be lucky enough to end up with Stacey, but she died before that happened."

"Was she ill a long time?"

"About six months." Sheila let her eyes scan the crowd for a moment before she looked at Audie. "It was skin cancer and it had spread to her lungs. When she got sick, she got real sick and stayed that way."

"I'm sorry."

Sheila nodded quietly. "Jamie was lost at first. He seems to be doing better lately." She sighed and put on a smile. "So tell me. What do you think of Stacey?"

Audie shrugged and laughed a little. "I like him."

"I can see that." Sheila appraised Audie openly. "He's

talked to Michael about you. Michael thinks Stacey's in love with you."

"Oh, please," Audie said, waving her hand in the air. "We've known each other less than a month, and he's spent most of it either avoiding me, pissing me off, or interrogating me."

Sheila guffawed. "Sounds familiar. That's the method of seduction Michael used, and look where it got me."

Audie saw Jamie Quinn moving toward them, his broad pink face lit up with what could only be described as delight. He was headed right toward her, and she tried to prepare herself for another rib-crusher.

But he got waylaid by one of the clusters of cops and Audie heard herself exhale.

"Now Jamie is even more intense than Trish was." Sheila nodded toward the big man with a heavy cap of salt-and-pepper hair, and Audie followed her gaze.

Jamie Quinn had to be at least six-foot-three and he was solid and wide and loud. She could picture him in the dark blue Chicago Police Department uniform, a billy club hanging from his belt, scaring the bejesus out of anyone.

"Tell me about him," Audie said.

Sheila smiled. "Well, Michael has referred to Jamie's parenting style as 'knock heads first; ask questions later.' Things got pretty wild around here with a house full of boys."

Audie nodded. "A house full of Quinn boys."

"Exactly." Sheila reached over and patted Audie's forearm where it rested on the tablecloth. Sheila had a very soft hand. "But he's a great guy. Opinionated as hell. Very proud of his family and the life he and Trish made here. As long as you don't cross his family or Ireland, the Church, or the White Sox, Jamie is a big old softy. If you're stupid enough to go back on your word or hurt one of his boys, God help you."

"Yikes." Audie took a big gulp of her iced tea. "Quinn said his parents moved here in the sixties. Do you know what part of Ireland they came from?"

Sheila squeaked with laughter. "Dear God, of course. You don't spend much time with us Irish types, do you?"

"No." Audie shrugged.

"Well, we tend to talk a lot about Ireland and being Irish. It's like a hobby. It's what makes us the way we are, I guess. My parents are first-generation Americans. All four of my grandparents were born in County Mayo."

"Oh."

"On the west coast."

"OK."

Sheila smiled at her. "Trish was from a little town called Ballyporeen in County Tipperary in the midwest. Jamie's family was from Dublin. They met at a church dance at St. Cajetan down the street here, and apparently it was love at first sight."

Audie grinned at that, looking over at Jamie, trying to picture him as a nervous suitor at a church social, but not being very successful.

"My God, you should see pictures of the two of them when they were young. Jamie was one studly specimen, let me tell you—wickedly good-looking. And Trish was stunning—she had a very intense and lovely face."

"Kind of like Quinn."

Sheila tried not to giggle at her new friend. "Yes. Like that."

"I think I may have seen their wedding portrait actually. In Quinn's hallway."

"Did you now?" Sheila's eyes shot wide.

"Ladies? May I escort you to the servin' table?" Jamie stood in front of the women, blocking out the late-afternoon sun, his arms crooked out for easy access. "This bein' my house and my rules, I say I get all the pretty girls."

Sheila hopped up, spun Jamie around, and hooked her arm in his. "No argument here, Da." She went up on tiptoes to kiss his cheek.

Audie stood slowly and wound her arm around Jamie's elbow, a little embarrassed by how nice it felt to be on the arm of this man. "I'm honored," she said, smiling up at him, and it surprised her that she meant exactly that. Jamie's attentions made her feel special.

During and after the serve-yourself feast of ribs, hamburgers, chicken, corn, a variety of salads, and lots and lots of beer, Audie talked with nearly everyone at the party. She met the enchanting Commander Connelly, who admitted he was a big fan. With several of the neighbors she discussed the pros and cons of using crumpled newspaper to clean windows and the handiest ways to use old toothbrushes around the house. She'd butted heads with Michael several times, on topics ranging from baseball to "real" barbecue sauce. She somehow ended up talking politics and religion with Pat, yet came away thoughtful and smiling. And she'd been squeezed by Jamie more times than she could count.

Audie was having just about the best day of her life.

She was talking with Aunt Esther about her 1959 steamer ship passage from Ireland to New York as a new bride when she felt a little tug on her skirt. She looked down to see Kiley, smiling brightly up at her.

"Hey, kid!" Audie reached down for her hand.

"Wanna see my treatment?"

"What?" Audie looked up at Esther, but the older woman shook her head and whispered, "I'll tell you in a second."

Audie looked back down at Kiley. "Sure, honey. Where should I go?"

"The kitchen."

"You go ahead. I'll be right there, OK?"

"OK!"

Audie watched the little girl's legs churn and then carry her up the back steps. The kitchen storm door slammed shut behind her.

She turned back to Esther to see the woman's face lined with sadness. "What?" Audie's pulse quickened. "That's the second time she's mentioned that. What treatment is she talking about?"

"She's a sick child, though you wouldn't know it to look at her." Esther's voice was soft. "She has cystic fibrosis—can't breathe well and has all these problems with digestion and the like."

"What?" Audie nearly yelled.

"I think Jamie told me she's up to six breathing treatments a day now and she has to take three of the enzyme pills at each meal. It's a sad thing to watch. Sheila is a saint, and that's the God's truth."

"I didn't know. I . . ." Audie's eyes went back to the kitchen door and she felt her chest bunch up in knots. "Nobody told me. I'm so sorry."

Esther shrugged. "The family doesn't make a major production of it. We don't want her to feel like she's peculiar—just a regular little girl who needs a bit of help with her breathin'."

"My God." Audie simply stared at Esther. "I told her I'd watch, but I'm sure she doesn't—"

"She likes for people to see. She likes you. If you told her you'd go, I recommend that you do."

Audie thanked Esther and found herself climbing the back steps. She opened the door to Jamie's kitchen—a symphony of 1970s golds and browns—and found Sheila and Kiley at the table. Kiley was holding a plastic mask over her mouth, but Audie could see her eyes smiling above the rim.

"Hey, Kiley," she said softly. "I'm here to see the treatment you told me about."

Sheila whipped her head around, at first scowling, then letting the tension drop away. She slowly smiled at Audie. "Have a seat. It's a girls-only party."

Audie would not cry. It would not happen. If this little girl could sit there so matter-of-fact, so could she. For some reason, Audie thought she'd read that cystic fibrosis was a fatal disease. But that couldn't be right—Kiley looked so healthy. She acted healthy. She was so bright and happy. It wasn't possible.

Audie suddenly felt a hand reach out for hers and looked up, shocked, to see Sheila smiling at her. "There are wonderful things going on with research right now—great things. It's an exciting time."

Audie nodded like an idiot, feeling the sting of tears she thought she'd talked herself out of. She turned her eyes away and stared at the little machine that seemed to be pushing steam through a tube and into Kiley's lungs, making hissing and clicking noises as it worked.

"She has two kinds of breathing treatments," Sheila went on. "This one is antibiotics to prevent infection. The others are for breaking down the mucus. We alternate during the day."

The kitchen door opened and Michael and Quinn walked in, and Quinn's eyes slammed into Audie's, full of questions and concern.

"Hey! How's my trooper?" Michael leaned over and kissed his daughter on top of her head and reached for her little hand. "Do I get to be the next one to pound on you, squirt?"

Kiley nodded, her eyes smiling at her father.

"About ten more minutes, Mike," Sheila said softly.

"It's a date," he said, leaning down to his wife. Audie watched as he kissed her gently and whispered, "I love you so much, Sheila," before he walked to the refrigerator.

"Dear God in heaven, what are you eating now, Michael?" Sheila called after him.

"Would you get off my back, woman?" Michael huffed. "I'm getting some limes for the guests. You can't have a party without limes." He winked at Sheila on his way out the door and Audie watched a wistful smile spread across Sheila's face.

Quinn was still staring at her.

"I'm going to run to the rest room, OK, Kiley? I'll be right back." Audie felt herself move as if in a trance, rising from the kitchen chair and walking down the hallway. She passed right by the bathroom. She just needed to go stand in a corner for a few moments and let the trembling stop.

She found herself at the front door. She opened the door, closed it behind her, and sat down on the stoop. Then she cried like a coward.

She heard the front door click shut behind her and felt Quinn sit close, his hip right up against hers. "Did you bring any of your hankies, Homey?"

She shook her head violently, hiding her face in her hands.

"You're going to have to start remembering to bring them along, all right?"

Quinn held out one of his white handkerchiefs and waited for her to take it. "That was my mistake. I probably should have told you about Kiley, but it never came up. She's a great kid. She's going to be fine."

Audie wiped at her eyes and stared at him, at a loss for words, listening to the waves of backyard laughter roll along the side of the house. Then she looked at all the neat brick homes lined up so close to one another in this city neighborhood and thought about all the lives pressed together on just this one street—sickness and happiness and rivalry and regret and love. Families.

Her question came out as a rough whisper. "What did

Michael mean when he said he'd 'pound' on her?"

Quinn brushed Audie's hair away from her face and tucked a handful of waves behind her ear, and she saw his green eyes flicker with tenderness.

"They have to percuss her chest—pound on it—a couple times a day. We all went to classes to learn how to do it—Mike and Sheila, Da, Pat, and me. Percussing breaks up all the gunk in her lungs so she can breathe."

She turned her face away from him.

"It's OK, Audie. It's just part of her life. We do what we have to so Kiley's comfortable and happy. Then we just pray a lot."

She turned to stare at him, suddenly very angry. "Pray for what?"

"Well, a breakthrough. The way things stand right now, people with cystic fibrosis are lucky if they live to the age of thirty or so."

Audie's mouth fell open.

"We just try to have faith."

"I can't deal with this." She stood up and began to walk down the sidewalk.

Quinn was behind her. "A walk sounds good," he offered.

She didn't respond, but she didn't resist when Quinn reached for her hand.

"You've got a tender heart, Audie. That's one of the things I like about you. But please don't be sad. Kiley doesn't like it when people are sad for her—it pisses her off, in fact." Quinn started laughing.

"My God!" Audie pulled away her hand. "Do you have any idea how bizarre this whole thing is for me? That your family laughs so much? That they love each other so much? Like the way Michael was with Sheila in there—do you have any idea how strange this all is to me? How overwhelmed I am? How surprised?"

"No. I didn't know." Quinn inclined his head a bit and studied her, his green eyes intense yet warm. The man was so beautiful, Audie's breath hitched.

She started to walk again.

"Hey. Wait."

"How can everyone pretend they're not sad?" She whirled on him. "Aren't your hearts broken?"

"Hell, yes, they are."

She shook her head. "I don't get it."

"Audie." Quinn laid his palm gently against the side of her face. "We're not pretending anything, but if there's a choice between laughing and crying, the Quinns pick laughing every time. It's better for the soul."

She blinked at him, her mind reeling, her heart twisting in big, mysterious knots of emotion—for this man, his niece, the rest of his family, and her own huge, immeasurable emptiness.

"Why did you give me your mother's handkerchiefs?"

Quinn watched as she propped her fists on her hips and jutted out her chin before she continued.

"Stanny-O told me they were Trish's. Why did you give them to me? You hardly know me. I'm nobody to you."

He dropped his hand from her cheek and looked at her for a long time. It was a good question—a damn good question—and for the life of him, he couldn't come up with a logical answer. He was beginning to realize that logic had little to do with his feelings for Audie.

"It freaked me out, Quinn. Tell me why you gave me your mother's handkerchiefs!"

He nodded slowly and took a breath. Her rich brown eyes were fixed on his and she wasn't letting go. This was a big moment, and he didn't want to blow it. Not too much, he told himself. Not too fast or she'd bolt.

"Because I'm tired of washing your snot out of mine?"

Audie closed her eyes and shook her head, trying not to laugh.

"All right, fine. They're actually my grandmother Stacey's, and I gave them to you because I think you're special and I wanted you to have something that was special to me, personal to me. But you already know that's how I feel about you."

Her eyes flew open and she started marching away from him down the sidewalk. At least she wasn't running or flipping him off, Quinn thought. He stayed at her side.

She suddenly wheeled on him. "Your *grandmother's*? God! That's even worse! When we get back to the North Side, I'm giving them back to you."

"I wish you wouldn't."

"I have no business with them."

"And why is that?" He grabbed her by her upper arms. "Isn't it my choice what I do with them? Lace doesn't go with my shoulder holster, anyway."

She blinked, and Quinn watched as a single tear rolled down her left cheek. "What in the hell is happening here?" she whispered, her eyes scanning his face. "I feel like I'm in the Twilight Zone of love or something, and it's making me panicky, like I've got to get out of here, like you're too much for me, your family is too much for me."

Quinn was tempted to pull her close to him and smother her doubt with kisses—but he knew that would only make things worse. He dropped his hands from her body. "Then count to ten and stop your crying, Audie, because I need you for something important."

She frowned and propped her fists on her hips again. "Need me for what?"

"Do you want to do something nice for Kiley? Would you like to see her laugh?"

She nodded. "Of course I would."

"Then come back to the house with me. Pat said the

boys want to get a game going down at Kennedy Park. Want to go kick some ass with me?"

Audie's eyes got wide. "Soccer?"

"Yep. I figure we tell them you've never played before, but you want to learn. That ought to be good for a few laughs." He took her hand and they were walking with purpose back down the street.

"And we let Kiley in on the joke from the beginning?" Audie was smiling.

"My plan exactly."

Quinn watched Sheila and Audie trade shoes—even Audie couldn't get off a decent kick in a pair of flimsy little sandals, he supposed.

And from the sidelines, he watched Kiley squeal and giggle and yell as Audie pretended to be confused and scared of the ball. It was a fine performance, too.

The little girl's eyes nearly popped from her head when Audie finally let loose and jumped and twirled and ran in her short skirt, the sweat running down her face, blowing everyone out of the water.

When Audie scored the first time, Quinn laughed so damn hard at Michael's stunned expression that he thought he'd busted an artery. It was priceless. The other times she scored he just felt proud and cheered her on.

And when she jumped on his back, and took a victory lap—God, Quinn felt like the luckiest man on earth to be holding her, to have her with him.

"Good Christ," Pat whispered to him at one point, slapping his brother's back. "Did you have a chance to winterize her yet?"

"*Pogue mahone*, Stacey," Michael quipped, trying not to laugh in appreciation. "I'll find a way to get you back for this one, believe me."

It was eight-thirty when Quinn and Audie said they

needed to head back, and after nine by the time they made it to the car—there were a lot of people who wanted to hug Audie good-bye. Sheila had a difficult time removing Kiley's arms from around Audie's neck.

Jamie walked them down the street.

"Keep safe, lad. See you Wednesday at the Academy for rehearsal." Jamie gave Quinn a peck on the cheek as his son got in the car.

"Audie?" He walked over to the passenger side and placed his big hands on her shoulders. "You, my dear, are a complete joy. Please come back soon."

"I'd like that."

Jamie wrapped her up in his arms again and gently patted her back. "Take good care of each other," he whispered. Then he kissed her cheek, too.

All she could do was nod.

CHAPTER 10

Audie sat quietly in the car, tingling from Jamie's kiss and his words. Now she knew where Quinn got his unlikely mixture of gentleness and macho swagger—from his father.

"I'm dying of curiosity, Quinn. What's *pogue mahone* mean?"

Quinn laughed. "That's Gaelic for 'Kiss my ass.' "

"Figured it was something like that," she said.

"So did you have a good time today?"

"Oh, fair, Stacey," she sighed. "How about you?"

His chuckle was so warm and soft that it gave Audie goosebumps.

"My family is the best part of my life—my family and friends. I've already told you that." Quinn reached over and brushed his knuckles against the side of her face. "Having you with me today made it even better."

Audie shot him a circumspect look.

"That's all. I'm done. I won't say another nice thing to you the whole way back. I swear it." He dropped his hand to her shoulder briefly, then pulled away to concentrate on the drive.

She sat in silence, staring out at the busy South Side neighborhoods along 103d Street. The cars looked normal. The streets were straight and flat. The traffic lights were red, yellow, or green. It was all quite ordinary.

Then it must be her, she decided, because suddenly she didn't know where she was.

But oh! She sure knew how she'd gotten there!

It started with the anonymous threats. Then Griffin insisted she call the cops. Then the cop sent to protect her ended up seducing her. Then she'd been seduced by the cop's entire family!

And right at that instant, Audie couldn't decide whether to run like hell or jump into this man's arms and beg him to love her forever. How had she let it get this messed up? How could she have put herself in this position?

But there she was—in Quinn's car, in the dark, under some kind of magic spell. Her brain had been addled by an entire day of affection and belonging, and now her mind was wandering light-years beyond basic common sense, and she was thinking about all the wonderful "what ifs" of Detective Stacey Quinn.

What if Quinn was the right man for her? What if he could love her for who she was? What if they got married someday and she suddenly became one of those Quinn people—the laughing, arguing, singing, drinking, loving South Side Quinns?

What an intriguing thought.

If Helen were alive, she'd have a cow, and wouldn't that just be icing on the wedding cake right there?

Audie giggled silently and cast a sly peek at Quinn, then turned away.

Their wedding would be a big, emotional affair. The reception would be loud and wild. All their kids would have Quinn's eyes. She'd quit the column and go back to coaching and teaching. They'd live in Quinn's house and they could fit one of those wooden swing set contraptions in the backyard.

She stole another glance at the poor unsuspecting groom- and father-to-be, his no-nonsense face lit up by the dashboard, all straight angles and handsome planes.

Oh, hell, she might as well admit it—it wasn't just the magic spell of his family. It was the magic of Stacey Quinn himself. He was wonderful. She was fatally curious about him, fatally tempted, fatally interested.

She winced and looked down at her hands. She'd already used the L-word in her mind, hadn't she? It didn't mean she actually loved him. It just meant it might be possible. Or not.

Audie smoothed her hair and pulled her shoulders back. "OK, Quinn. The answer is I'm not exactly sure what I like the best," she said, seemingly out of nowhere.

"Huh?" Quinn looked her way and cocked his head.

"That day on the boat you asked me what I like in bed and I don't really think I know for sure."

"Jee-ay-sus, Audie. You're supposed to warn me!"

She looked over to see him grinning ear-to-ear.

"I'm sorry. You're absolutely right, Detective." She laughed and took a deep breath. "I'd like to talk about sex now. Would that be all right?"

"I've got a few spare minutes."

Audie folded her hands in her lap and bit her lower lip. "Why don't you ask me questions and I'll try to answer them? Do you think that will work?"

"What kind of questions?"

"Sex questions."

"Like a health class quiz?"

"No! Like a get-to-know-you thing."

Quinn snorted. "Pardon me for bringing this up, but the last time I tried to 'get to know you,' you sent me packing to the guest room."

"I know. But this is different."

"So you're ready for me now, Audie?" His voice sounded strained.

"I think so. I don't know. Just ask me questions before I chicken out."

Quinn took the entrance ramp onto the Dan Ryan Expressway, laughing nervously. "I don't think I'm going to be watching road signs in a minute. Don't let me miss the Lake Shore exit."

"No problem."

He adjusted himself in the driver's seat and pulled the car into the stream of expressway traffic. "OK—let's start with a simple one. Uh, how do you like to be kissed?"

"All the ways you've kissed me so far have been quite nice. I got no complaints there."

"Great. Uh, what gets you . . . well . . ."

"Hey! You told me you weren't sexually repressed!"

"I'm not! I just . . . fine, let me backtrack a bit. How do you like to talk about sex?"

"What do you mean, 'how'?"

"I mean do you like flowery words and vague references to, you know, body parts and things people do with them when they make love? Or do you like to talk about sex directly?"

"I wouldn't know. I've never had this conversation before, exactly."

Audie crossed her arms under her breasts and looked out at the shiny river of cars. "I've talked about sex, of course, but usually afterward, and it was stuff like 'That felt nice,' or, 'I liked this or that,' so I'm not sure how I prefer to talk about it right now, with all my clothes on, riding in an unmarked police car." She turned to face him. "How do you like to talk about it?"

"Directly, I suppose."

"Then let's be direct. Keep asking."

Quinn turned up the air conditioning and shifted in his seat. "Are you sexually attracted to me, Audie?"

"Oooh, yeah." She pursed her lips and nodded.

"So it hasn't been all wishful thinking on my part?"

"Not hardly."

"That's a huge relief."

"I'm glad."

"All right. Let's take care of the paperwork first. I'm healthy. No HIV. No herpes. No nothing. The department tests every six months and the last one was in June and since then I haven't been at risk, if you know what I mean. I'm good to go. How about you?"

Audie laughed nervously. "There's been no one since Russell, and I got tested again just a month ago. I'm completely healthy. And I know you're Catholic and everything, but I'm on the pill."

"Wow. Then we could do some serious sinning."

"We could."

"So tell me what gets you sexually aroused."

She laughed. "We're moving right along, aren't we?"

"No point in dawdling." He grinned at her. "I've sinned before, you know."

"Fine. Being within a hundred miles of you gets me aroused, Quinn. Hearing your gravelly voice. Feeling you touch my hand or my cheek or my feet and legs—well, you already know what happens with that."

He did know. Yes, Lord, he did. And Quinn looked at her over there, glowing, round and soft and refreshingly honest, and realized that if this was going where he thought it was, tonight was going to be one hell of a good night.

At that instant, Connelly's warning came to mind, and he knew that no matter how much he wanted Audie, how crazy she was making him—this probably was not a smart move.

But then she turned toward him, those dark eyes sparkling, those plump lips turning up at the corners, and Quinn didn't give a damn what Connelly said. He couldn't even remember what the man looked like.

"And talking about sex with you, Quinn—now *that* gets me plenty aroused."

"It does?"

"Yes."

"Did you say my voice is gravelly?"

"Yes, I did."

"All right then. And how do you know you're getting hot for me?"

"Hot for you?" Audie laughed and then sighed deeply. "Mmmm. Well, I start to tingle all over and I feel all warm inside. My stomach does a little flip. I want to touch my own breasts." She lowered her voice to a whisper. "Then I feel myself getting wet and slippery and I start thinking about how I'm going to get something big and hard inside me."

She heard Quinn take a loud gulp of air. "Holy God in heaven, that was a fine answer."

"Ask me some more."

"Whoa," Quinn whispered. "So when you're like that— all hot and slippery—goddamn!" He turned up the air conditioning another notch. "What do you imagine happening first? What would you want to start off with?"

"Are we talking about right now, with you? Can I answer it that way?"

"Yes."

"I'd like to start with a long, slow kiss. Then lots more of them, because I really like the feel of your mouth on mine—have you noticed we seem to fit really nice on each other?"

Audie heard Quinn gulp. "That I have. And as I recall, my mouth fits real nice in a few other places you got."

"I know it does," she breathed.

Quinn was quiet for a moment, trying to get his synapses to fire. "OK, so we've kissed. What next?"

"Next I'd want you naked, Detective Quinn. I'd want to

take your clothes off—with no help from you—and watch your expression when I look at all of you for the first time ... when I put my hands on you."

"That could be arranged."

"Because you've seen a lot more of me than I've seen of you."

"True enough."

"And then you'd take off my clothes."

"Yes, I would."

"And you'd put your hands all over me."

Quinn sucked in air.

"Keep asking. I'm liking this."

"I noticed." He sat for a moment just listening to the sound of his own blood pounding in his ears. "What makes you come, Audie?"

"Wow. That's a complicated one." She turned in the seat to get a good look at him. His face was very serious and his jaw was tight and hard above his collar. She wondered what else of his might be hard. "You want the honest answer?"

"Honesty is good."

"Well, honestly, it doesn't happen all that often. It can take some time and a lot of direct attention, you know?"

"I do know."

"I think you were on the right track the other night."

"Without a doubt."

"But every once in a while it just happens all nice and mellow for me."

Quinn turned to her with a smug little smile. "That's all going to change, Homey."

"How do you mean?"

"I mean, what you just described doesn't sound all that tremendous."

"It can be nice."

He chuckled lasciviously. "Nice is nice, but here's what

I want to know: Has it ever been so fucking hot that your screaming made the neighbor lady call the cops?"

Audie's eyes flew wide. "Um, not that I recall."

"I think you'd recall something like that."

"I guess I would."

"Well, that's the part I'm gonna change, Homey."

She laughed.

"Or die trying."

She laughed again.

Quinn checked the road, then turned to face her, waiting until their eyes locked in the faint light. "Tell me how you like it, Audie."

"Like what?"

He stared at her, and his voice came out rough and low. "Tell me how you like your sex."

"Oh, boy." She whipped her head around and looked out her window. She wondered if anyone else driving on the Dan Ryan Expressway at nine-thirty on a Sunday evening was having this discussion, in just this way. Somehow, she doubted it.

"I wasn't expecting that one."

"Too bad. You wanted direct questions—I'm asking them."

She turned toward him slowly, and she could barely get the words out. "I've been thinking about this a lot since that night on my couch."

"Me, too. Nonstop, really."

"And I just want the sex to be with you, Quinn."

"Great. Now exactly—"

"Wait! Here's Lake Shore, but you're in the wrong—"

He squealed across three lanes of traffic to make the curved exit ramp, little electric sparks flashing as the front left bumper scraped along a retaining wall.

"Sorry."

Audie hooted. "Man! This is great! OK, next question?"

Quinn shook his head, his heart slamming against the inside of his ribs. "No way. No more questions—I just want the actual sex now."

"But—"

"I need to get inside you—*right now*."

She couldn't stop laughing. "That doesn't sound safe."

"You'd better not be yanking my chain, woman, because I've got no more gentleman left in me."

She was quiet for a moment, then said, "Oh, Quinn. It's ten minutes to my place. Do you think you're gentleman enough to wait that long?"

"That I can handle." He looked over to see her smiling quite brightly. "Have pity on your man, Audie. There's not enough blood in my brain to carry on this conversation."

"That's OK." Audie reached out and touched Quinn gently on the side of his face, trying not to panic at the way his words had just slammed into her heart—*your man, your man*—trying not to panic at how much she wanted him, all of him, everything he had to give her, everything he'd show her.

She let her fingers trail along his jaw to his throat, and she hooked her fingers inside his shirt, circling in the soft down below his collarbone.

"How about I ask the questions now?" she whispered. "I think we've got time for a few, all right?"

The silky touch of her finger caused tiny flashbulbs to pop in front of Quinn's eyes, making driving an even greater challenge. "Just make 'em easy—like ones I can answer with a grunt."

She giggled. "Okay. Here's one I think you can manage." She leaned over and put her lips against his ear. "Are you hard right now, Quinn?"

He swallowed. Her hot breath made him shudder. "God, yes, I'm hard."

"How hard?" She brought her lips to the tender spot under his jaw and kissed.

"Extremely hard."

She scraped her teeth along his neck. "As hard as that night on the sidewalk?"

"Harder."

She bit his earlobe. "As hard as that night on your deck?"

"Harder."

She flicked her tongue under his jaw. "As hard as the other night on my couch?"

"Harder. Longer. Thicker. I've been saving up."

"Excellent," Audie breathed, flopping back against the passenger seat. "That does it for *my* questions."

They barely looked at each other and they didn't speak and they didn't touch—not while they parked the car or rode the elevator to the twenty-eighth floor or walked down the hallway and opened the door to Audie's place.

They didn't talk as they entered the apartment or when Quinn put his hand over Audie's to stop her from flipping on the light switch.

They said nothing to each other as Quinn took her by the hand and led her to the huge black windows overlooking the lake and the northern edge of city lights—the John Hancock Tower, Water Tower Place, Michigan Avenue, all spread out before them like diamonds tossed on black velvet.

Finally, Quinn smiled down at her and broke the silence. "We're going to finish what we started."

She stared into his eyes, bright with reflected light and intense desire.

"I'm going to take down your hair. Then I'm going to kiss you."

Audie nodded helplessly. He wasn't asking her if he

could do any of these things—he was *telling her*.

That worked for her.

Quinn released the clasp she'd used to pull back her hair for the soccer game. The heavy waves now tumbled onto his wrists like warm satin, and he breathed her in. She smelled like spice and flowers and musk. She smelled just like she tasted, if he recalled correctly.

Audie stood very still, breathing fast, watching the re- strained and slow way he moved around her, the ravenous gleam in his eyes. The lion at breakfast was back, but this time she was showing him to the all-you-can-eat buffet.

She closed her eyes and felt the tingle as his fingers moved up into her hair and his palms cradled her head. Then his lips came down on hers, all hot, all wet, all Quinn—and all was lost.

Where did she go right then? She couldn't say, because her world suddenly turned to nothing but sensation, no thought, no care for where her feet were planted. The only thing she knew was that this man's mouth was on hers and his hands were on her and she wanted it bad. She loved it.

She felt Quinn rock her in his arms, back and forth with the press of his loins, his tongue tasting her, taking her. She loved that, too.

Then he stopped kissing her and held her in front of him. He took her hands and pressed them against his shirt, and her fingers began working down the column of buttons.

She stopped and frowned.

"Your gun. I don't know what to—"

"That's the only thing I'm going to help you with, Homey." He reached behind him and removed the nine- millimeter automatic pistol from his waistband, walked away, and placed it on a side table. He came back. "You're on your own now."

She pulled the shirt from his belt and spread it apart across his body, then settled her palms flat on his ribs. She slid her hands up and over his hard chest and flat, silky nipples, across his wide shoulders, and down his arms, feeling each warm, solid inch of him as she went. The shirt fell to the floor.

Audie leaned in and put her lips on his breastbone. She nuzzled close and kissed him, feeling the tickle of his chest hair against her cheek, breathing in the scent of him, sighing with relief to finally be this close to him.

But it wasn't nearly close enough.

She brought her hands to his waist and down across the solid ridges of his stomach, leaving a trail of southward-bound kisses as she moved. She dropped to her knees and looked up at him.

"I love your body, Quinn."

He seemed surprised by that. "This'll work out pretty good then."

She put her hands at his belt and tugged, then felt the zipper slide open under her fingers. She kept watching his face so far above her, seeing the storm clouds gather in his eyes as her fingers pushed away his shorts, as she welcomed him in her hands.

"Oh, God, Quinn." She took a deep breath and let her eyes embrace what she already cradled in her hands—all thick, silky head and stiff flesh. "You're very big."

"Told you I was saving up."

She looked up to his face again, his eyes glittering with the city lights. "Hurry. I want my turn," he said.

She slinked her hands down his narrow hips and along the hard line of his legs, yanked off his sandals, and stood, seeing him there in front of her, all lean and solid and wearing nothing but a lopsided grin and a raging hard-on.

"Turn around, Audie."

A shiver went through her. "Turn around?"

"That's what I said."

She felt him put his hands on her hips and turn her to

face the windows. It was an amazing sight—they were reflected back, floating in all the lights, somewhere in the darkness. She watched Quinn lean down to whisper in her ear.

"Spread 'em, Audie."

She gasped.

With a gentle nudge of his bare foot, he pushed her legs wide apart, then reached around and raised up her arms, placing her hands flat against the glass.

Quinn saw her expression in the window—half shock and half amusement. Perfect.

He leaned down into her ear. "I think I'd better frisk you before I fuck you."

Audie whimpered.

He started by pulling her T-shirt from the waistband of her skirt and pushing his hands up her back and around her ribs, feeling with pleasure how she rippled under his touch. He unhooked the tiny snap at the front of her bra, and the satiny fabric fell loose inside her shirt just as his hands swooped up to cup the freed weight of her breasts. Her nipples immediately rose to hot points in his palms.

"Good Lord," she mumbled, feeling his big penis jab into the small of her back. She dropped her head forward and shuddered.

Quinn's hands were all over her now—moving on the bare skin of her stomach, her ribs, her sides, running little circles around her rigid nipples. She couldn't help it—the feeling was so intense that she arched into him, pushed her breasts into his hands, and pressed her hips back against his cock.

"Looks like we're not messing with any of that 'resisting an officer' shit, are we, Audie?"

She started to laugh but stopped abruptly, because his hands were at the zipper of her skirt, and he was shoving down hard on the skirt and underwear until they caught on her spread upper thighs—too tight to move any farther.

His hands were on her bare bottom now, and she heard herself moan a little, and the oddest sensation ran through her—it was almost as if she'd just had a small, friendly orgasm simply because he was touching her.

But that was impossible.

His hand went to her belly and he pulled her back against him, causing her hands to fall from the glass. Quinn pulled the shirt and bra over her head and dropped them to the floor.

Audie saw herself then, naked breasts and wild hair, her skirt shoved down low on her hips, and Quinn's hands moving on her.

It happened again—the little pleasant flash of heat in her blood. "Wow," she whispered.

"Lean against me, Audie. I won't let you fall."

He pushed aside her hair with one hand and bent his lips to the back of her neck. Audie felt him kiss her there, bite her, his lips hot and wet and his breath so close in her ear. He began rocking her again with the press of his hips, and she thought for sure her knees would give.

He suddenly lifted her off the floor and yanked off the skirt and underwear. While she was up in the air, she flipped off her sandals. Then he set her back down in front of him, nudging her feet apart again.

His hands went everywhere now, all over her, cradling and pinching her breasts, encircling her throat, moving down her sides and over her hips and sliding up and around her ass. She saw everything in the windows, and she felt like hot lava in his hands—no bones left in her anywhere, just heat and slick need.

Quinn slipped his hand down her belly and toward the open split of her sex. His fingertips made the slightest contact with her wet flesh and she jumped and cried out.

"Oh, Audie," Quinn whispered in her ear. "I've been

waiting for this. I've been waiting to come to you, make you mine. I can't wait anymore. I want you so much."

She let her head fall back against him and shivered. She liked the way his words had just spilled out thick and musical from the back of his throat and hot into her ear. She liked the sound of his voice so close, so intimate. She liked that every inch of her skin pressed back against him and that his cock was smashed up against her and his fingers were moving slow and sure along the entrance to her.

With the lightest touch, he coaxed her stiff little bud from its hiding place, pinched her, and rubbed his erection hard against her from behind.

"Do you feel me, Audie?" He kept moving against her.

"I feel you, Quinn," she moaned.

"What do you feel? Tell me."

"I feel how good you are to me," she breathed. "Oh, God, I feel how much you want me—how much I want you."

Quinn slid his fingers from her and pulled her up to her full height, encircling her gently in his arms.

"You're going to get me. Right now."

Yet again, a flash of heat spread through her, and this one was an attention-getter. She saw her eyes fly open in the dark window. There was no mistaking it—Stacey Quinn had just made her come with the barest touch of his finger, the press of his skin on hers, and with his words.

What the hell would happen when he was inside her?

"Come here to me," he said, turning her, taking her hands, and sinking slowly with her onto the Oriental rug. "It's time for sweaty sex on the floor, Homey."

They knelt in front of each other and she stared at him, so close, so gorgeous and intense. She felt his hard desire tap against her belly now. She felt his arms reach around her back and pull her against him. He felt like fire. There was fire in the tongue that licked into her mouth, fire where his fingertips pushed up into her hair. She felt herself become only what his hands wanted from her—nothing but slippery heat and stiff nipples and arching flesh, all for Quinn. Only for him.

"You are so soft. So beautiful," he managed between kisses. "I want you to take whatever you want from me. Take it."

Audie pushed hard into him with her mouth, then pulled back, breathless. She came back to him, running her tongue across his lips, resting her hands on his thighs, then pulled back again.

Quinn smiled at her. She did it again—came to him and kissed him with a sharp rush of need and then pulled away. There was something happening here, he realized, as if she was right on the edge of letting go, on the edge of asking for something, but she didn't know how to go about it.

Just as he suspected.

"Let it go with me, Audie." His voice was warm and his hands cradled her face and she felt herself trembling—from desire or fear she couldn't say.

"I'm not sure I can," she said.

Quinn looked down at her beautiful flushed face, her lips swollen from his kisses, her eyes dark and doubtful.

"Please don't be afraid of me."

She shook her head. "I'm not afraid of you, Quinn. I'm afraid of me—of what I want right now, with you . . . what I want to say to you."

He smiled at her and gently traced his thumb across her full bottom lip. When her wet little tongue came out to greet him, his penis jumped.

"Say it."

She was about to shake her head again when he pulled her roughly to him, smashing her breasts against his bare chest. "I want to hear you ask for it," he said roughly.

With a little sob, she leaned back and looked into his

eyes. "I want it hard, Quinn," she whispered. "I want you to pin me down, and take me until there's nothing left of me. I want you to make me scream."

He let out a surprised laugh, deep and throaty, but said nothing at first. Then his grip on her softened. "Tell me if I hurt you. I don't want to hurt you, sweet lassie."

It was her turn to laugh. "You can't. I think I was made for this—for you, for right now. I think I've been waiting all my life for this." Her eyes pleaded with him. "Do it, Quinn."

"Jaysus."

He laid her gently on her back, and his face was drawn with such raw sexual hunger that she trembled. He hovered over her a silent moment as if to give her one last chance to change her mind.

Like that would happen.

"I want to scream, Quinn," she whispered, and his hands were pressing down on the insides of her thighs, spreading her wide, and she felt him slowly run a finger along the dripping seam of her.

"Holy Christ, Audie," he groaned.

He cupped himself in his hand and rubbed the fat head of his penis up and down the entrance to her. With his eyes hot on hers, he pushed inside her in one long, slow slide and listened to her moan the whole way in.

At first, Audie thought he'd ripped her apart. He felt so huge and hard, and she'd been empty for so long that it was a shock to her. But when he began to move, so slow and deep, all she felt was the pleasure, the swaying pleasure in the putting in and pulling out, the press of his hard weight into her, becoming part of her.

His hands went to her wrists, moving them up over her head and pinning them to the carpet as he began to move a bit harder and a bit faster. Audie looked up into his eyes, so forceful and serious, and she felt conquered like never before, treasured like never before, and the waves started to break in her mind.

She was his. He was inside her. She was getting exactly what she wanted—what she'd always wanted.

Thank God.

Then the words began.

"I'm taking you, Audie. I'm right here. I'm giving you what you want, big and deep and hard. I'd do anything for you. Do you know that I'd do anything for you?"

His words struck like velvet lightning in her blood. She felt herself clenching and pulling as he continued to rain words down upon her in that musical voice—so many words.

"You're mine, woman," he growled, dipping his head to suck and lick at her hard nipples. "I'm never letting you go. I'm taking you hard. Taking your sweet little body."

The man who said so little in everyday conversation was making love to her with words, she realized, bringing her to orgasm with words, words like kisses, words as real and as hard as the cock now fully inside her, reaching her core.

"I feel you coming, Audie. I feel you so hot and sweet— God, you are the sweetest damn thing I've ever seen in my life!"

Where was this place? Wherever it was, she was going fast and rough and it was a rushing, dark place and his words were dragging her there.

"I'm coming!" she whimpered.

That made him smile. "I know you are, baby," he said, kissing her softly. "And I'm going to keep you there, then push you higher." He adjusted himself over her, changing the angle and speed of his thrusts, and the friction was too hot, too good, and she cried out.

Quinn looked down to see her body shimmering with sweat, all softness and sex writhing beneath him, her breasts exposed, her lips parted. She was very close to letting go completely, he knew. And it was going to be good.

"Come here to me." He released her wrists and pulled her up, balancing her head in one arm while supporting himself with the other. He started a slow and sultry rhythm with his hips.

"Don't close your eyes. I want you to look right at me while I split you open. Look at me while I love you. You want me deep inside you, don't you, Audie?"

"Oh, God, yes!" She didn't recognize her own voice.

Quinn pushed into her without mercy then, rough and serious and just a bit faster. "I'm taking you, Audie. I'm taking you with everything I've got, everything I am. Do you want more?"

"Yes! More!" And the words faded into a wail, not a cry, not a moan, but a desperate sound that told Quinn what he needed to know—that this was something new for her and it was surprising and strong. Her eyes began to close.

"Open your eyes and look at me." She did. His gaze locked on hers and she gasped. He was seeing too much. He was asking for too much!

"It's too much. . . . I don't know—"

"Just feel, sweetheart," he murmured. "Just feel us together; feel how good this is between you and me. It's unbelievable. It's *so . . . damn . . . good.*"

He held her head so that she couldn't escape the truth of what she'd asked for and what he was giving her. And Audie didn't know where the force originated—whether it was in her heart or her flesh—but she was drowning in it, dying in it, staring into the penetrating green fire of Quinn's eyes as he showed her what it felt like to feel possessed, taken . . .

Loved.

He watched her face widen in shock and her eyes flash. Then she screamed—and it was wild and reckless and he covered her mouth with his own to swallow it. She arched against him and shook and went rigid, screaming louder, and her hands were tearing at his back, and Quinn absorbed the violence of her surrender.

He grabbed her tight in both his arms, knowing this was too much for him, too intense. "I'm lost," he told her. "I'm yours. . . ."

Quinn came inside her with a roar and the heat blinded him and the world shattered into pieces around them.

They clutched at each other for many long, quiet minutes, their breathing ragged, their bodies slick with sweat and throwing off heat.

Quinn knew he should probably say something to her, but nothing seemed right. Nothing seemed good enough. Important enough. So all he did was whisper her name— *"Audie."*

And right then, he put away the fantasy forever. He didn't need it anymore. He didn't want Carmen Electra. He sure as hell didn't want Martha Stewart. He wanted this woman—he wanted Audie.

He pulled her up as he rose to his knees, then turned so that she sat on his lap. She stayed curled around him, quiet, hiding her face in the crook of his neck. Eventually, she stirred. "Quinn?"

"Mmm?"

"Are you always like that?" She rubbed her cheek against his shoulder.

"Like *what*?" he wondered aloud. Did he usually let his heart crack in two? Did he usually see his soul reflected in a woman's eyes?

"Do you always talk that much?"

He chuckled, slightly embarrassed, gently stroking her back and hip with one hand. "Did I talk a lot?"

She pulled away enough to see his face, so sweet and confused. She ran a finger along his sweaty hairline and smiled at him. "Yes. You talked an awful lot."

He frowned. "That may have been a first. I hope I didn't say anything stupid."

Audie stared at him in silence, then kissed his cheek and tucked her body close to his again, gripping his waist tight with her legs.

So many extraordinary things had just happened to her, but the most amazing was that Quinn had just taken her to a place of blind, raging lust and now he cradled her in his lap, so warm and sweet, worried that he'd said something stupid. She'd never known a man like him.

Suddenly there were tears in her eyes, and she was glad he couldn't see them.

"Nothing stupid, Quinn," she assured him, kissing his neck and hugging him tight. "Just wonderful."

After a long while, he lifted her away from his chest and kissed her tenderly. "I won't be sleeping in the guest room tonight, will I, Homey?"

"No. And not in the hallway, either. I don't think I'm done with you."

"Are you threatening me?" His mouth twitched with the beginnings of a wicked smile.

"Yes, and you love it." She ran a finger across those beautiful lips. "Shall we?"

With a groan she pulled away from him, tucked her legs beneath her, and stood. She offered him her hand, but he just looked up at her, astonished.

"Aren't you coming?"

"I kind of like the view from here," he said, and she looked down to see her thighs glistening with sweat and semen.

"Oh, God."

He jumped to his feet and put his arms around her, rubbing her back. "You look like a woman who's been thoroughly ravaged, and as I recall, that's what you ordered. Wanna take a shower with me?"

When she stopped laughing, she leaned her head back and looked into his eyes, so bright and contented. "I have to tell you something first, Quinn."

"I'm all ears."

"I explained how it is with me, and—"

"I changed all that?"

As ridiculous as it seemed, Audie suddenly felt a little self-conscious. "It seems that way," she whispered.

Quinn grabbed a handful of her thick, wavy hair, grinning. "You did look fairly shocked by the whole thing."

"That's because I was."

He kissed the adorable tip of her nose, then rubbed his cheek against hers as he whispered into her ear, "Tell me how it was different."

She closed her eyes and sighed, wondering how she could possibly explain this to him. She wasn't an expert on the male orgasm, but she didn't think they had the kind of drastic range of responses that women did. After a long moment, she pulled back to look at him.

"OK, Quinn. Have you ever taken a sip of Bud Light and found yourself staring at the can, trying to convince yourself that you'd just swallowed beer?"

His grin spread.

"My usual orgasm is a Bud Light."

He was already shaking with silent laughter. "And just now . . . ?"

"Like sticking my mouth under the Guinness tap and slurping every rich, delicious drop until I blow up, knowing it's a very good way to die."

Quinn laughed hard and clasped her to him so tight that she momentarily couldn't breathe.

"You're supposed to warn me when you're going to talk about beer, woman."

"I forgot again."

"Audie, you make me so happy . . ."

The words came out sure and clear, and though Quinn's arms relaxed around her, she still couldn't breathe. She felt him stroke her hair and caress her back. She nestled closer, listening to his heartbeat, his breath, remembering how he had held her like this on the dock that night, when he first offered her a place in the world where she fit just right.

When she warned him she was a failure at love.

Quinn must have heard her thoughts again, because he whispered to her in his gravelly voice, ". . . until we both dry up and blow away."

CHAPTER 11

September 14
Dear Homey Helen:

I've known people who've used compulsive neatness as a substitute for human connection, for human feelings. My theory is these people keep the mind and hands occupied so the heart doesn't break.

I think you've seen this behavior: Clean, clean, clean. Control, control, control. Do, do, do—all to stay so busy that you don't have time to look around and realize you've wasted your entire life.

And really, what is the point of a spotless house or an orderly desk if your life is in shambles?

—Your most loyal fan

PS: I really enjoy the new "Pet Corner" on your Web site. It's helpful *and* entertaining!

Quinn thought it possible that he was hallucinating. After all, he'd been thinking of nothing but Audie all morning—as he raced home at seven to shower and change his clothes, then while in the shower, then on the drive into the station, and each second he'd been sitting here trying to pretend he was the same Stacey Quinn who sat at this desk on Friday.

But he wasn't. Because this morning he was Autumn

Adams's lover, and the desk sergeant had just escorted her into the detectives' room, and he felt like he did every time he'd ever had the privilege to watch Frank Thomas hit one over the 400-foot center field wall at Comiskey Park—he was awestruck. Just damn glad to be alive.

Stanny-O was up on his feet. "Audie!" He pulled up a chair for her. "Did you recover from yesterday?"

Her eyes flew wide and she stared desperately at Quinn.

"Good morning, Audie," he said evenly. "I think Stan was asking if you liked the party."

"Oh, crap. Hell." She collapsed in the chair and produced a weak smile for Stanny-O. "Yes. I had a great time. You?"

"Always do. Want some coffee, Audie?" Detective Oleskiewicz winked at Quinn as he started toward the coffee island. "You sure look like you could use a cup or two . . . *or five*." He winked at Quinn again.

"I'd love some!" she called after him.

Quinn tried not to smile too much. He tried not to stare at the short tan linen skirt and matching blouse she was wearing. He tried not to reach out and touch her hair or the smooth skin of her thigh just above her kneecap. He tried not to carry her bodily to the supply closet and take her up against the wall next to the copier toner.

"Good morning, Homey," he said softly. He leaned back in his chair and clasped his fingers behind his head. "So you missed me, huh? It's been"—he quickly checked his watch—"three hours and forty-six minutes since I left your place."

It seemed Audie was trying her best not to smile at him, too, and Quinn watched her bite down on her bottom lip and slowly flutter those thick black lashes of hers. He nearly fell over backward in his chair.

Damn, she was something else. Quinn had not exactly led a monastic lifestyle, but sex with Audie had been a mind-blowing experience. And there she sat this morning, trying not to smile or look him in the eye, and his heart was so full it was sore.

What had happened between them last night—all last night—had been intense. Fun. Wild. And extremely important.

So of course he wasn't the same man who'd sat at this desk on Friday, because today he was the luckiest son of a bitch on the planet.

Unfortunately, he also was risking the wrath of his commander and needed to find a way he could stay on Audie's case and still come clean with Connelly. Exactly how he'd manage that remained to be seen. He'd worry about it later. Because just then, Audie decided she'd smile at him.

"Here you are, Audie." Stanny-O placed her coffee on the edge of Quinn's desk and reached into his top right-hand drawer. "To what do we owe this lovely visit? Care for a mint?"

"Oh. Sure. Just a sec." Audie shook her head as if she were shaking loose her thoughts and started rooting around in her shoulder bag. She took out handfuls of hair clips, receipts, trash, crumpled cigarettes, and a balled-up pair of panty hose before she found what she was looking for.

"Here it is. Another one. It was in this morning's mail." She tossed the envelope on Quinn's desk and shoveled all the junk back in her bag. Then she reached for a Frango Mint and popped it in her mouth.

Quinn picked off a few flecks of tobacco from the letter before he unfolded it and read it without comment. Then he handed it to Stanny-O.

"Jeesh," Stanny-O said. "I've gotta tell you, these letters are really starting to piss me off. I mean, what is this?" He held up the note. "Who's he talking about?"

"Well, I'm pretty sure it's not me," Audie said, shrugging and letting her eyes catch Quinn's. "But it might be my mother."

"Tell me why you say that," Quinn immediately asked.

"Well, because that's how my mother was. My dad used to call her a human doing, not a human being. She got very pissed off at that."

Quinn nodded and leaned toward her. "Audie. Stanny-O and I need to talk with you about your case, and I need you to keep an open mind, all right?"

She ran a nervous hand through her hair and shrugged. "Sure. What?"

Quinn watched Stanny-O place the latest letter in a manila envelope and fill out an Illinois State Police crime lab form. Then he turned back to Audie and saw her smile turn to a frown.

"We need your help," he said softly. "We need to know what's in your gut about these letters, Audie."

She blinked at him and squirmed uncomfortably in her chair.

"Whose voice is that right there?" Quinn pointed to the big envelope Stanny-O now held in his hands. "When you close your eyes and hear those words . . . who do you picture saying them? Who talks like that, Audie?"

She sat perfectly still, but her eyes were wild and going back and forth from Stanny-O to Quinn. She shook her head.

"You can tell me, lassie."

She slammed her eyes shut and let her shoulders sag. After last night, she would tell this man anything.

"I go back and forth with this every day and I still can't figure it out," she whispered, returning her gaze to Quinn. "Sometimes I think I hear Drew. I wish to God I didn't. But some letters—like this one—sound just like him when he gets started on something. But then I tell myself Tim

Burke is probably doing this, not Drew, but the letters just don't sound like Tim! None of them do!"

Audie frowned and shook her head. "I honestly don't know what to tell you."

Quinn reached for both of her hands and she grabbed on. The simple touch made his pulse race. "Unfortunately, we don't always know people as well as we think we do. Stanny and I see it all the time in this job." He stroked his fingers over the smooth top of her hand.

"Fine," she said. "Then let's just say it *is* Tim Burke, because I hate myself for even thinking it might be Drew, you know?" She shook her head, miserable. "Drew is my brother."

"And you told me yourself that you're strangers to each other," Quinn said, holding her gaze. "We're going to have to talk with him again. And I need to ask you about something else."

"OK."

"Can you think of any reason why Drew would want to hurt your mother?"

"What?!" Audie ripped her hands from Quinn's and stood up. "Are you trying to tell me—" She lowered her voice to a whisper and caught Stanny-O's eye. "Are you guys telling me you think Drew killed our *mother*?"

"Look. Sit down a minute, all right?" Quinn pulled her chair closer to him and she sat, her bare knees touching his chinos. "There are basically two ways we can look at this, OK? One way is that these letters and your mother's death are somehow connected. Thinking of it that way, it could be either Drew or Timmy."

"But—"

"The other way is to see these incidents separately. Your mother was just a random mugging victim. Your letters are just the sick game of someone who's angry with you. In that scenario, it's more likely Timmy."

"All right."

"But either way, it seems we're right back with the same two suspects, so Stan and I were just talking about getting surveillance on both of them, just to be sure. We'll have eyeballs on them and eyeballs on you—and we'll catch 'em."

Audie looked confused and tired.

"I didn't mean to dump all this on you right now." Quinn's voice was so soft it was almost a whisper. "But what you said about this latest letter may help us. Thanks for bringing it in. Are you all right, sweet Audie?"

She nodded gently.

"Let me walk you to your car." Quinn helped her up, placed his palm flat against the small of her back, and led her out the front door as Stanny-O stared in silence, fascinated.

When they reached the Porsche, Quinn opened the door for her, but she didn't get inside. Instead, she turned toward him, so close that the tips of her breasts brushed against the front of his shirt.

"Hi, Detective." One corner of her plump mouth crooked up in a smile, causing Quinn's heart to shudder, because he now knew exactly what she felt like naked beneath him.

"Hi, Miss Adams." He took a quick look around the parking lot, then leaned into her for a kiss. With his lips against hers, he asked, "Have you recovered from yesterday?"

She chuckled and pulled back from him. "I'll never recover. Besides, some of it was today anyway. This morning, if you'll recall."

"Mmmm. I do recall." His mouth was back on hers and she felt his arms go around her waist.

"Quinn?"

"Yes?" His warm, soft lips had moved to the side of her

neck, the base of her throat, and his fingers were at the top button of her blouse.

"Not here. Are you busy right now? Can you get away?"

His head jerked back and she watched him blink. "Are you asking me what I think you are?"

"Yes. I'm completely depraved."

"Jaysus, that's good to hear." Quinn shot her a crooked grin and let his eyes scan down below her face. "Look what I've done to you, Audie." He buttoned her blouse and ran his hands nervously through his hair. "Don't get me wrong—I'm glad you're depraved. But yes, I am busy right now. I'm also nearly brain-dead with lust for you, but I've got to get back to work."

She nodded.

"Wait. Where the hell is Rick Tinley and why isn't he with you?"

"He *is* here," Audie said, moving her eyes over her right shoulder. "He's in the police car right over there, waiting for me."

"Oh, great."

She watched Quinn acknowledge Tinley with a brusque wave before he sighed deeply. "Well, woman, we've just gone from rumor and innuendo right into the testimony of a credible eyewitness." He gave her a sheepish grin. "You going to be OK with people knowing you're hanging around with a South Side Irish cop?"

She fought back the urge to throw her arms around his neck and scream like a ninny. "I'll survive the shame somehow," she said with a wry smile. "But what about you? Is it all right if people know you're chasing some North Shore Protestant Cubs fan?"

He chuckled deep and low and ran his finger down the side of her face. "You're right. Let's deny everything."

Quinn's green eyes glowed in the morning light, and Audie heard herself sigh with contentment. Talk of murder, stalking, and betrayal notwithstanding, she didn't think she'd ever been as happy as she was right at that instant, with her heart in chaos and her vision filled with nothing but Stacey Quinn.

"What's your schedule today?"

Audie shrugged. "The usual. I've got a National Public Radio spot at noon. I'm going running with Tinley at two. Then I've got the TV segment at five."

"I'll change over with Tinley at the TV studio and we'll get some dinner."

She grinned at him. "Sounds good, Quinn."

"At my house."

"Sounds real good."

He leaned closer to her, and she had to close her eyes because he had so much power over her. He whispered roughly in her ear, "Do you think you'll have time in your schedule to be thoroughly ravaged this evening?"

She produced a tiny squeaking sound and turned her face away.

"I'll take that as a yes."

With Audie safely on her way, Quinn returned to the squad room, where Stanny-O sat, waiting.

" 'Lassie'?" he inquired, slowly stroking his goatee and grinning. " 'Sweet Audie'?" Stanny-O strolled over to the edge of his partner's desk and held up Audie's untouched coffee cup. "You know, she really should have had some of this, Stacey. The woman looked exhausted."

He stood in the shadows of the WBBS studio and watched her. Her head was tilted demurely and she glowed in the perfect pink jacket, discussing the secret to keeping a kitchen garbage disposal smelling clean and fresh.

It was something Quinn knew she didn't give a rat's ass about and never would, and it cracked him up.

He chuckled quietly, shoved his hands in his pants pockets, and wondered if he was already totally, irrevocably, in love with Autumn Adams.

There she was under the studio lights—everything he needed and nothing he'd ever imagined, all rolled up into one gorgeous package.

He could see the peek of her sweat socks and running shoes behind the long anchor desk and watched as she nervously tapped one foot against the floor. Quinn's gut twisted. She was his. This disorganized, accident-prone lapsed Presbyterian was all his, and he could hardly believe his good fortune.

"And as always, thank you, viewers, for another wonderful week of handy comments and suggestions," she said.

Kyle Singer shot a dazzling smile into the camera. "And thank you, Homey Helen—we'll see you again next Monday. In the meantime, don't go away, Chicago—we'll be back with more news right after these messages."

Quinn watched onetime suspect Kyle Singer kiss Audie on the cheek as she unclipped her microphone. An hour with Kyle was all it had taken to convince Quinn and Stanny-O that he was harmless—and as gay as you could get. He had no interest in Audie beyond friendship.

Quinn watched her carefully step off the platform and chat with a producer, all Homey Helen from the waist up and all Autumn Adams from the waist down. Her legs looked long and strong and she stood casually with one hand on her hip—like a jock, Quinn thought.

In his reverie, he was nearly lulled into thinking Audie would make it across the studio without tripping. Then she turned abruptly, smashed into a production assistant, and grunted in surprise as they both went sprawling.

Quinn helped the women to their feet and walked Audie out through the lobby.

"If you keep this up, you're going to end up in a body cast."

"That ought to make things challenging for you."

"That's one challenge I don't think I want," he said.

"I warned you I was a spaz." She turned toward him as he opened the front door and smiled down at her. He was one fine-looking man, this Stacey Quinn, all neatly pressed and self-assured and grinning—and he was *her* man. He'd said so.

She'd felt it.

"Whaddya say we go home and freshen up my garbage disposal, sweet thing?"

Audie laughed hard and swung her arm lazily around his waist, feeling her stride match his down the sidewalk. He squeezed her shoulders.

"Wanna drive my Porsche?" She tossed him the keys and sidled over to the passenger door.

"You planning on taking your clothes off in the car again?"

"Nope. I can wait until we get to your place."

When they got to his place, Quinn handed her a cold beer and told her to relax out on the deck while he cooked. She did as she was told, realizing with a sigh that she could get used to this. She took down her hair, removed her jacket, kicked off her shoes and socks, and let her head sink back against the chair cushion.

The next thing she knew, Quinn was crouched in front of her, patting her knee.

"What?" She bolted to attention.

"Dinner's ready. You fell asleep. I think maybe I wore you out last night."

"Oh." She blinked, trying to focus on Quinn, her eyes opening wide at the sight of the table. "What's this?"

"Dinner." When Quinn stood up, she saw he'd donned a bright green barbecue apron that read: "When Irish Eyes Are Smiling, You Know Something's Cookin'."

"Nice apron."

"Thanks."

He went around to the back of her chair and pushed her closer to the table, then pointed to the serving dishes.

"Grilled salmon with a warm dill sauce. Saffron basmati rice. Mixed green salad with blue cheese, pears, and caramelized almond vinaigrette. I hope you like it."

Audie was quiet for a long moment, trying to keep her mouth from hanging open. Then she looked at him casually spread out in his chair right next to her, in his apron, a satisfied grin on his face.

"You're incredible, Quinn. Thank you for this. You're the only man who's ever cooked for me."

He chuckled and began to help himself to large amounts of food. "I seem to be a lot of firsts for you, Audie." He didn't look at her. "I hope you're OK with that."

She just stared at him, still trying to wake up, still trying to put all this in perspective. He had no idea how true that statement was.

She leaned over and kissed him on the cheek. "Thanks, Stacey."

One corner of his mouth curled up in delight. "It's my pleasure."

Audie served herself some of everything and thought about that statement. "It really is, isn't it? You get pleasure out of cooking and doing things around the house, don't you?"

"Yes." Quinn was chewing and obviously enjoying the fruits of his labors. "My mother taught me to cook. She taught me to take pride in making things organized and clean so that people could be at ease and happy in our home—you know, hospitality. I think that's why I need to have things in order before I feel free to enjoy myself."

Audie closed her eyes in pure bliss. "My God, Quinn. This is delicious."

"Thank you."

"So." She took a sip of white wine. "Hypothetical situation here. Let's say we're done having this delicious meal and we go into your messy kitchen, but I start taking off my clothes right in front of the dishwasher."

Quinn raised his eyebrows. "This is purely hypothetical, of course."

"Of course. So, would you just walk around me to load the dirty dishes or could you let everything sit while you make wild passionate love to me?"

Quinn chewed and narrowed his eyes at her. "How much time would that take, exactly?"

"So it would bug you."

"Yes, it would bug me." He took another mouthful. "I take it that kind of thing wouldn't bother you much."

Audie giggled. "Well, first off, I don't cook. You realize I don't cook, don't you?"

Quinn raised one eyebrow. "I saw the penicillin ranch in your refrigerator, woman."

She snickered. "Oh, yeah, there's that. But even if I did cook, I could easily leave the kitchen till the morning if *you* were standing naked in front of *my* dishwasher."

"This is good to know," he said, taking another bite of salad. "It may ease your mind to know we'll never face that dilemma, because I always clean as I cook."

Audie's head popped up. "Huh?"

"Clean as I go along. I wash what I can while the food cooks and soak the rest after I serve. I put the utensils and measuring cups in the dishwasher. I clean off the counter. That way, when the meal's over, it only takes a few minutes and I can go enjoy myself with a clear conscience."

Audie stared at him. "Wow—I think I read about that in a Homey Helen column once."

Quinn laughed and enjoyed watching her eat for a moment. "I'm just curious, Audie, and I don't want to piss you off, but didn't any of this stuff ever rub off on you? I mean, didn't you ever see your mother do any of this around the house?"

Audie went very still, and Quinn wanted to kick himself for asking that. He didn't want her to be sad tonight. He wanted her to relax and have a good time.

She put her fork down and turned to him. "The truth is Helen didn't have much time for me, even before she and Marjorie started the column. Everything had to be just so—the meals, decorating, cleaning, entertaining my dad's business partners—I always felt like I was in the way.

"Then when she started the column, she hired Mrs. Splawiniski to cook and a whole parade of cleaning ladies to do everything else, and I don't think my mother ever set foot in our kitchen again unless it was to oversee the latest remodeling project or give instructions to the caterers."

Quinn stopped chewing and stared at her.

"So the answer is no. My mother never taught me to cook and never showed me how to make people feel welcome because she didn't have the time—she was too busy telling the rest of the world how it was supposed to be done."

She picked up her fork again and took another bite of fish. "This has got to be the most delicious thing I've ever tasted in my life."

"Was there anything at all you liked about your mother?"

Audie stilled again, then shrugged. "I admired her for being a successful businesswoman. I admired her going for what she wanted in life."

Quinn leaned back in his chair and studied her. Though he thought he knew her fairly well by now, the initial question he had about Autumn Adams was still the one he couldn't answer—why didn't she just bag the Homey Helen routine and do what made her happy? Why didn't *she* go for what she wanted in *her* life?

"I've decided I'm not going to sign the syndication renewal, Quinn." She looked up at him, her toffee-brown eyes wide and hopeful. "I've decided to quit the column and try to go back to the Uptown Alternative School. What do you think?"

Quinn reached over for her hands and held them between his. "I think that's great."

"Really?"

"Really. I've been sitting here trying to figure out why the hell you haven't done it sooner."

Audie laughed softly. "Because I've been a wimp and a fool, Stacey."

"That's not—"

"It's true. I think I've been spending the last year trying to earn the love of a dead woman. Pretty pathetic, huh?"

"I'm sorry."

"Yeah, it is pretty sorry."

"I meant I'm sorry you had to go through that." Quinn stroked her hands gently. "So why now? Is it the letters that made you finally decide?"

"No." She looked right at him. "It was you."

Quinn blinked his eyes as if he'd heard wrong, and his hands quieted. "Me? How do you figure?"

She wasn't sure if this was the time to say this. She wasn't sure if there would ever be a right time, because this was going to be another one of those firsts Quinn had mentioned.

"Because being with you these last few weeks has reminded me what it feels like to be happy. Now I want more, and I can tell you that being Homey Helen isn't the way to get it."

Quinn was watching her carefully, his eyes focused on her face, and Audie knew he was waiting for her to continue.

"And I realize that nothing I do is ever going to make

her love me, because she's gone. If I want to be loved, I think I should stick with living people. The odds are better."

He pulled on her wrists. "Come here to me."

"The kitchen's not clean."

She landed with a thud against his chest, and his deep laughter rumbled through her. He leaned her back into the crook of his arm and kissed her, pressed her close, and he tasted like caramelized vinaigrette and sweet lust, and Audie was powerless against the slam of desire she felt for him.

"How much happiness and love do you think you can stand, woman?" His lips were on her throat and his hands were pulling her silk shell from the waistband of her running shorts.

"I couldn't begin to tell you, Quinn," she said through the giggles. "We'll just have to experiment." She began unbuttoning his shirt.

"I thought you said I was the most aggravating man you ever met in your life. So how can I make you happy?" His hands were sliding up and down the front of her blouse, and her nipples stiffened with each pass of his palms. He leaned forward and began to nibble at her through the slippery fabric, his mouth leaving little wet marks all over the front of her.

"Oh, God, that was weeks ago—now you just make me completely insane." She gasped. "Especially when you do that."

"We're going inside, Homey." Quinn stood up from the chair with Audie still attached to his lap and hurled open the kitchen door. She assumed they were headed for the bedroom, but she was wrong. Quinn set her down on the kitchen counter, right over the built-in dishwasher, right next to the sink full of soaking pots and pans.

"Here's another good reason to clean off the counter as you go," he said.

Audie started laughing, but Quinn's mouth was on hers and, as it often was with him, the line between laughter and bone-melting pleasure blurred. With him, they almost seemed to be the same thing.

"God, what are you doing, Quinn?" His hands were at her hips and he was pulling her running shorts and underwear out from under her.

"I want you naked in front of my dishwasher."

"I'm on *top* of the dishwasher."

"Same diff." He yanked the blouse over her head, then the bra.

By the time he grabbed her legs and hooked them over his shoulders, his eyes were drilling into hers and his smile had grown completely wicked. Audie was nearly hyperventilating.

"How about whipped cream? Damn, I don't have any. Hold on."

"What *do* you have?" It occurred to Audie how bizarre it was to be chatting in this position, naked, sitting on top of a dishwasher, her legs flung over the shoulders of a man in an apron.

"How about some honey, honey?"

"Honey?" Audie let her head fall back because what she was imagining made her brain too heavy to hold upright. Then she felt him shift in front of her, heard him groan. She looked up, and he was opening the cabinet directly overhead. "Perfect."

Next, it occurred to her that despite the fact that she was thirty years old, she was about to have another first.

He crooked his arms beneath her legs and unscrewed the lid to the honey jar. She closed her eyes. Then she heard the utensil drawer slide out to her left and heard him grumbling as he searched for something. A melon baller? A garlic press? She tried not to think about it.

"Now we're cookin' with gas," Quinn muttered in his gravelly voice. Audie opened her eyes to see him dip a little wooden drizzler into the jar until it was heavy with slow-dripping honey.

He was enjoying this—she could tell by the glint in his eye—and he leaned closer to her and whispered, "Say 'Ahhhh.' "

Audie was trembling, but she opened her mouth and stuck out her tongue and the honey was cool and sweet and sticky inside her mouth. Then Quinn was there—hot and slippery and sharing it with her—and she released herself to the heat and the taste and the licking and sucking and swallowing and she realized she'd never see a jar of honey quite the same way ever again.

"You taste like sex and candy," Quinn said, pulling back. "And I'm going to take bites out of you everywhere if that's all right with you."

Audie nodded, running her tongue over the sticky outside of her lips, trying not to shake too much.

"Are you cold?" Quinn put down the honey and Audie realized he was about to lower her legs—which was something she definitely did *not* want him to do—so she locked her ankles behind his neck and pulled him closer.

"I'm not cold, Quinn. I'm very, very hot, and I want to be your dessert."

Quinn's eyes fastened on hers and his shoulders started to shake. "You really are depraved."

"So arrest me." She loosened her grip on him and leaned back on her elbows.

Quinn picked up the honey again, still laughing, and began drizzling little golden puddles on her deep rose nipples. "Where have you been all my life, woman?" He lowered his head and brought his lips to her sticky, puckered flesh.

"I think I've been waiting for you to find me, Quinn," she breathed. "To find me and pour honey on me until I come all over your countertop."

The vibration of his deep chuckle sent little buzzing streaks of heat through her breasts right down to the hot spot between her legs. She watched Quinn's mouth on her, his honeyed tongue gliding out from his smile to lick at her, and she trembled again.

"You're yummy," he murmured, pulling one nipple into his mouth and biting her softly. When she moaned, he did the same to the other nipple, then drew wide circles around her breasts with his tongue, eventually coming back to her mouth, hot and wet and sweet.

His hands suddenly reached under her bottom to pull her closer to the edge of the counter. He put his lips to her ear.

"Audie, baby, come here to me," he whispered, and it was his voice again, his voice and the simple things he said, that was pure sex to her, that made her take the leap from sensible woman to anything Quinn wanted her to be.

As the honey dribbled down into the curls between her legs and trickled deep into the lips of her vulva, she wondered if she'd ever feel safe enough to tell Quinn how much power he had over her. How much she wanted him.

Then she stopped wondering anything at all, because what he was doing was so good, so good, and his tongue was hot and firm, then barely a whisper, then long and slow and all over her.

"Oh, God, this is nice," Quinn thought he heard her say, but the blood thundered in his head so loud that he was nearly deaf. That was fine, because he didn't need his ears for what he was doing right now—all he needed was his tongue and his lips and his teeth and the searing hot place at the center of Audie, pressed up to him.

He pulled her up higher and angled her to his mouth, gripping her around the waist. She was sweet, so sweet, and he used his fingers to spread her wide and put one finger deep inside her, then two, and felt how slick and swollen this woman was and knew he would do anything for her, anything she wanted.

She suddenly clutched and hardened around his fingers and against his mouth. She let out a piercing cry that gave him goosebumps and she was calling his name and he licked into her, pushed his fingers into her deeper, faster, and her arms flailed out to her sides and the spice rack crashed to the stove in an explosion of broken glass and a pungent blast of rosemary, curry powder, and cream of tartar all spewed out in an unalphabetized mess.

"I'm so sorry!" Audie tried to sit up, tried to breathe, but Quinn lifted her off the counter and spun around.

"Is there glass on you?"

Audie could barely focus on his words. Her body was still spinning and clutching, and for a second she couldn't remember why she was naked.

Then she was being carried to the living room against Quinn's bright green apron and she wanted his clothes off, wanted to touch his skin, wanted to feel him against her all hot and smooth and strong.

He put her down in front of one of the big overstuffed chairs and brushed his hands over her skin, and Audie finally came out of her fog.

"Quinn." She grabbed him by the shoulders. "I'm fine and there isn't any glass on me. I'm so sorry I did that."

He stopped and stared at her, tasting her in his mouth and realizing he was hard as steel and wanted her to sit on him—and he didn't give a shit about his spice rack *or* the dirty dishes.

He ripped off his clothes and made himself comfortable

in the chair, his feet on the floor and his erection pointed toward the ceiling.

"I just had a great idea," he said, grinning.

Audie walked toward him slowly, scanning all of his long, lean muscle, his blatant arousal, and the startlingly beautiful face.

"I bet it's the same idea I have," she whispered.

She climbed up on his lap, straddled his thighs, and positioned herself right above him. She leaned down to kiss him softly, then nibbled on his jawline and bit the side of his neck.

"Will you tell me your idea first, Quinn?" she breathed into his ear.

She got what she wanted—the low rumble of his laugh moved through her blood and bone, and she knew she was right where she was supposed to be.

"My idea was I fuck you blind," he said.

She pulled back in mock disappointment. "But I wanted to do that to you," she pouted.

"I'm flexible."

Audie watched the change in his expression as she slid onto him just enough to capture the big head of his penis. She waited, feeling him throb inside her, feeling her body kiss and squeeze him, seeing how he fought the urge to thrust all the way into her.

He was gorgeous. He was sweet to her. And it was magic to watch the surprise and joy on his face when she eased down very slow and took him in very deep.

"I'm so happy when I'm with you, Quinn," she sighed, seeing his grin spread.

Then she wiped the grin right off his face.

CHAPTER 12

Finding out which soundstage would host the Chicago Garda Pipe and Drum Band was the easy part. Getting there on time was proving to be a real challenge.

Human beings of every description were packed into Grant Park in a loud, hot, and airless press of bodies, slithering under a cloud of cooking smoke. Griffin held tight to Audie's hand as they made their way down what was supposed to be the center thoroughfare at CityFest.

"It's a good thing I'm not claustrophobic," Griffin said to her. "Because I'd be flipping out right about now."

"This is nuts!" Audie yelled, pushing her way eastward. "I don't want to be late! Let's try to go faster."

Audie got slammed into Griffin again. "*Ack!* Hurry! Come on!"

Somewhere past the Vietnamese food tent and the chili booth, Audie spied the bandstand where a few men in kilts milled around while recorded Irish music blasted.

She didn't see Quinn anywhere, but as they pressed closer, all the musicians began to file onstage and she heard the unmistakable voice of Jamie Quinn booming over the sound system.

"Welcome to the sixth annual CityFest performance of the Chicago Police Department's own Garda Pipe and Drum Band!"

A cheer went up from the mob and Audie pulled Griffin into the thick of it, worming her way to the front.

"I'm supposed to meet Quinn's family here, but I'm never going to find them in this mess!" she cried.

"We'll be playing a variety of tunes for you today— everything from hymns to reels and jigs and an occasional tear jerker," Jamie said just as they made it to the edge of the stage.

Audie was breathless as she scanned the rows of men and women above her. Her eyes finally landed on Quinn, directly before her, front and center.

"We'll be doing three sets, so hang around, eat a lot, and don't forget to drink. Because you know our motto—"

Every cop onstage and half of the crowd called out in unison: "The more you drink the better we sound!"

"Oh, shit, mon!" Griffin yelled into Audie's ear. "I've died and gone to Irish cop hell!"

Audie couldn't laugh—she was too busy staring up at Quinn in shock. Then her head nearly caved in from the gut-rumbling drone that split the air—the sound of forty-five bagpipes warming up.

"Is this your way of punishing me for all those Saturday nights at the Wild Hare reggae club?" Griffin screamed.

She just smacked his arm and kept staring.

Well now. This was not exactly what she expected to feel, was it? She gawked at the sight before her, realizing that if she considered each element independently, the sight of Stacey Quinn in a skirt, kneesocks, and a dorky little hat should send her into fits of laughter.

But she wasn't laughing. Instead she took in the complete picture of him and her heart jumped into her mouth. He was magnificent. He looked strong and proud and so sexy it should be illegal. And as they began to play, his face pulled in concentration as he blew into the mouthpiece and his fingers flew over a single row of airholes.

The sound was deep and crushing, and Audie looked around to see an audience full of people just like her, looking up with awe. Some were smiling with joy and others were frowning with absorption, but nobody could be bored by this musical assault.

Audie observed how Quinn's mouth and hands caressed the gangly, primitive-looking pipes, and she couldn't help but think of the way he used his mouth and hands on her. She saw the ripple in the muscles of his neck, forearms, and wrists as he coaxed out the notes—much like the way he coaxed out the pleasure in her.

Her body trembled despite the heat.

"You all right?"

Audie turned to Griffin and nodded. "Just a little overwhelmed!" she shouted.

Jamie stood right next to his son, looking like a big gray bear in plaid, his legs as thick as tree trunks. Jamie's face was rigid with concentration and radiated the same delight she saw in Quinn.

They obviously loved doing this, and their joy was contagious. Audie broke out in a wide, happy grin.

Just then Quinn looked down at her and winked, his hands still flying. She winked back.

"You know what these Celtic types wear under their kilts, don't you?" Griffin shouted into her ear.

"Not a thing?"

"That's what I hear."

Audie crossed her arms under her breasts and closed her eyes, letting the music sweep over her, carry her to another place. And before she knew it, the Garda Pipe and Drum Band was done with its first set.

Somewhere in the middle of a song Jamie had introduced as "Roddy McCorley," Audie felt a tug on the hem of her sundress and looked down to the smiling face of

Kiley Quinn, then around to see Sheila, Little Pat, Michael, and Pat crowding around. She introduced Griffin to everyone, caught Kiley when she jumped into her arms, and spent much of the next hour hopping up and down in the hot afternoon sun, Kiley's laughter ringing in her ear.

Sheila took her daughter for most of the third set, and Audie enjoyed the slower melodies Pat said were called airs, and he apparently knew all the words.

"I take it you've been to this show before?" Audie asked him.

Pat's eyes creased in amusement as he smiled at Audie. "Just a time or two," he said, wrinkling his nose.

Just then, Audie felt a set of smooth hands run over her bare arms, and she turned around to see Tim Burke smiling down at her, looking cool, blond, and debonair in his khaki summer suit.

He offered Griffin a firm, friendly handshake that Griffin ended abruptly, then turned to Pat for a much less hearty greeting.

"Pat."

"Timmy."

Audie's entire body began humming with the awareness that something very, very bad was about to happen. Based on just the few details she'd been given, the prospect of mixing Tim Burke with beer and the entire Quinn family sounded downright unsafe.

She had the mental picture of one of her home ec projects gone awry.

Before she realized it, Tim had leaned in and kissed her on her cheek. He let his lips stray to her ear and he whispered hoarsely, "You look good enough to eat today, sweetheart."

Audie jerked away. "What? Get lost. I'm listening to the band." She was also feeling the eyes of every Quinn on her, from Kiley all the way up to Jamie.

Audie risked looking up at Quinn, and his deep green eyes met hers with a flash of something between rage and sadness, and Audie felt sick to her stomach. Then Quinn suddenly lost pressure in the bag and the melody line dissolved in an off-key groan.

Jamie threw his son a look of daggers, and Quinn got back on track.

Audie heard Tim sniggering in her ear. "Oh, yes. They're quite a talented bunch of drunks."

She stiffened, not only at his words but also at the sight of Michael pushing closer, his face red and his body puffed up and ready for a fight.

"I don't understand you, Audie," Tim continued, still close to her ear. "You're sending me mixed messages."

She turned around and scowled. "What mixed messages?"

"Well, you've not returned any of my calls, but then I get one of your nice—"

"Get the hell out of my face! How about that for being clear?" she shouted.

Audie realized that Griffin was slowly backing away and pulling on her arm, his eyes bouncing from Tim to Quinn to Michael to Jamie to Pat and back to her.

Tim leaned into her and touched her hair. "Don't be fooled, Audie. The Quinns are scum. If you want the real thing, come back to me."

Michael was upon them now, his face crimson, and she felt Griffin grab her shoulders and pull her away just as the roar of bagpipes deflated into a sour wail and something— or someone—sailed over her head.

Quinn landed with a thump right on top of Tim Burke, pinning him to the asphalt.

"No fucking way, mon," was Griffin's commentary as Audie stood with her mouth hanging open, shaking her head, watching Quinn flip Tim onto his stomach and slip a pair of handcuffs over his wrists.

The shocked crowd eased back as most of the band members jumped from the stage and pulled their weapons on the vice mayor, now facedown on the sticky ice-cream-and-pizza-smeared blacktop.

"For the love of Christ, put your weapons away!" shouted the man Audie recognized as Commander Connelly. "Get back up on the stage!"

Jamie pulled his son off Tim Burke and glared at him with annoyance. Then he clamped one thick fist around Tim's shirt collar and pulled him up from the ground, releasing the handcuffs.

Tim began to curse and spit with rage and embarrassment.

Jamie gave him a friendly push forward. "Go away, Timmy," he said softly.

Tim staggered toward Quinn, wiping part of a crushed hot dog bun off his cheek, but Quinn stood calmly. He put a shaking finger in Quinn's face. "You're going to pay."

Quinn didn't flinch. "If you come anywhere near her again, I'll kill you with my bare hands."

Tim Burke took one second to stare at Quinn with hate, turned his glare on Audie, then stalked off through the crowd.

Only then did Quinn turn to see Audie. She stood silent, her eyes huge, her mouth open, clutching Griffin's arm.

"Are you all right?"

She gaped at him.

"Audie! Are you all right?"

"Am *I* all right?" Her body was shaking from the sudden drop in adrenaline as she screamed at the top of her lungs, "I'm fine! But you people are completely insane!"

Jamie chuckled at that and moved everyone back up onstage, leaving Quinn to stare at her and catch his breath. "Did he hurt you?"

"Hurt me?" Audie moved from Griffin's side to stand in front of Quinn. The pipes started up again, without their star player, and Quinn had to shout at her so she could hear him.

"Did he touch you?"

"What are you talking about, Quinn? Do you mean to tell me you did all that just because he *touched* me?"

"We'll talk about this after the set."

She shook her head and gestured toward the city skyline. "I don't think so. I'm leaving." She started through the crowd, quickly saying good-bye to his family, Griffin jogging behind her. Quinn yelled after her and turned on his heels, weaving through the press of bodies until he caught up with her.

"Audie." He touched her shoulder and she spun to face him.

"I'll get you an Italian ice!" Griffin shouted in her ear, nodding toward Quinn as he turned away.

"What the hell were you doing?" She knocked her fists against his chest, hitting him in his brass nameplate. "Somebody could have been hurt! The kids saw everything!"

Quinn looked stricken and rubbed a hand across his chin and down the perspiration on his throat. "All I could think was he was going to hurt you."

She started to laugh but abruptly stopped as she understood his words. She stared at him in disbelief. "The letters? You thought Tim Burke was going to murder me right here in front of thousands of people?"

"I'm not sure what I thought, Audie. All I know is I saw his hands on you and I wanted to kill the man."

"God! I can't believe this!" She turned to go, but he reached for her wrist and gripped her tight.

"Please hear me out."

She jerked back from his touch. "No! You're an unstable, gun-toting neat freak! Your little show just now scared me much more than any letters ever have!" Before she knew it, the tears started to well in her eyes. She turned to run.

The pipes were reaching a crescendo and Quinn took a huge breath to shout as loud as he was able, "I love you, Audie!"—and the words exploded from his lungs just as the song ended and before the applause began, perfectly timed for the full appreciation of the CityFest crowd.

"Go for it!" Michael's booming voice rang out behind Quinn, and he cringed. Quinn hung his head as the band cheered him on from the stage.

Audie's arms fell uselessly to her sides and she turned slowly, her head spinning, feeling the eyes of hundreds of beer-swilling, egg-roll-eating Chicagoans now fixed on her and the guy in the kilt.

Quinn looked up from his cower, his eyes pleading. "I couldn't let him hurt you."

"Oh, this is just great, Quinn." Audie shook her head, aware that her knees were feeling weak and she was a hair's breadth away from sobbing. "You *love* me? This is getting completely out of control."

"That happened a few days ago, really," Quinn offered.

She stared, nodded, and felt relief that at least the band had started playing again. It was some kind of happy jig that had people clapping and dancing instead of staring at her and Quinn.

She looked at him for a long moment but couldn't bear what she saw—too much honesty and too much love. She stared down at her sandals until Quinn's spats appeared in her line of vision.

"Look at me, Audie," he said.

She would only hurt him. She knew she would only hurt him.

She raised her eyes. His gaze locked with hers. And though she knew this was the biggest mistake she'd ever make in her life, she reached out and touched his chest, right where she'd so recently pummeled him. His skin felt hot beneath the white uniform shirt. His heart was beating fast.

"Quinn, I—"

A voice boomed down from the heavens. "Hey, Fabio— get your arse up here so we can finish our set!" Jamie's words echoed through the speakers, and the laughter rolled and rocked through the Grant Park crowd.

"Meet me by the stage?"

Quinn's little-boy uncertainty was showing again, and all Audie could do was smile and nod. He started to go, but she grabbed his shirt and popped up on her toes to whisper in his ear.

"What's under your get-up, Detective?" In case he missed the point, she bit his earlobe.

He pulled back, grinning wickedly. "Boxers, Homey. For now, anyway."

He winked at her and she watched him swagger through the crowd, the plaid kilt swaying against his firm butt and muscular thighs with every step.

"He loves me," she muttered to herself, staring after him. Then she smacked herself in the forehead. "Oh, crap! Hell! What a disaster!"

Griffin suddenly reappeared with a half-melted lemon ice.

"I've got a big favor to ask you, Audie." He handed over the leaking waxed paper funnel. "Do you think you'd be all right hanging with the Quinns for the duration?"

He wagged his eyebrows to the left and gave his dreadlocks a little shake, and Audie followed. Griffin's big favor was standing a few feet away, looking beautiful and shy in a white gauze sundress and gleaming dark skin. Audie turned to find Pat, Michael, Sheila, and the kids all smiling at her.

"I think I'll be fine," she said.

When she pushed through the crowd to reach the Quinns, Sheila put her arm around Audie's shoulders and squeezed.

"You OK?" she shouted.

"Fine. Are you and the kids OK?"

"Fine." Sheila looked at Audie and sighed. "Testosterone poisoning," she said. "At least it keeps things interesting."

Quinn opened the back door and Audie pushed past him into the kitchen. She disappeared down the hallway, kicking off her shoes as she ran. He heard her feet move fast on the stairs.

"Where are you going?"

"To the bedroom!"

"I thought you wanted me to tell you about my pipes and kilt!"

"I do! Bring 'em up!"

A few moments later, Quinn found Audie lying on her stomach on his bed, her chin resting on her fists and her bare ankles crossed above her in the air. The little blue sundress was pulled tight across her round bottom, and she was smiling at him, apparently ready to be enlightened.

"Let's get to my lesson, Quinn." She cocked her head and he watched the dark waves of her hair brush against her bare shoulder.

"It will be a pleasure to properly introduce you to the second most beautiful lady in the world."

"Lady?"

"Her name is Philomena." Quinn clicked open the carrying case and pulled out the gangly apparatus. "Here she is.

A Great Highland bagpipe made in Scotland in 1897. She was my grandfather Quinn's."

"Wait. It has a name?"

"Yes. My grandfather named her. In Greek, it's supposed to mean 'one who loves songs.' "

"Philomena." Audie mused over that while she watched him cradle the pipes in his arms like a child.

"You obviously take very good care of it, them—her."

"Sure I do." Quinn grinned at Audie, then bent down and kissed her softly. "I figure if I'm lucky enough to be in the company of someone this beautiful, it's my duty to take real good care of her."

Audie hummed in agreement, not missing the compliment. "So. What's an Irishman doing playing Scottish pipes?"

Quinn laughed. "That's a good question, Homey." He settled the pipes into the crook of his arm and began to give his lesson. "The Irish version are called Uilleann pipes, and they have a softer, more melodic tone. These babies produce the great big roar a man needs for things like parading down State Street and going to war against the English. Some people call them Irish war pipes, but that's not really accurate."

Audie stared, realizing there was apparently a third subject that could turn Quiet Quinn into Chatty Cathy—bagpipes. So it was family, sex, and bagpipes.

"So tell me all about Philomena. I promise I'll try not to get jealous."

Quinn grinned at her again, and Audie felt her stomach flip.

"Well, let's start with her anatomy, shall we?"

She nodded.

"I hold her close to my left side with pressure from my forearm—there's no strap tying her to me. She's got three drones that come out of the top." Quinn pointed to three thin, tall pipes rising above his left shoulder, one much longer than the others.

"Now, one of the things that makes Philomena so special is all the silver-and-ivory inlay on the drones, see?" He brushed his finger along the bands of ornate detail work and smiled. "They don't make pipes like this anymore."

"How much is that worth?" Audie asked, her eyes wide.

"About three thousand, not that I'd ever sell her. She'll stay in the Quinn family."

"That's good." Audie couldn't help but smile at him, and she pictured in her mind how Quinn would teach their kids to play Philomena one day. Their kids—the ones who'd be playing on that swing set right out in the backyard.

She suddenly gasped. She had to stop thinking like this.

"You all right there, Homey?"

"Go on. I'm learning a lot," she managed.

"OK." His eyes sparkled down at her. "This is called the chanter." His fingers rippled along the pipe at the bottom of the instrument. "I cover or uncover the holes to play notes. All the while, the drones up here continue to produce the background hum you always hear in pipe music."

"You do both at the same time?"

"Yes. I use what's called circular breathing—I breathe in through my nose and out through my mouth in a continuous cycle. That way, the pressure stays constant to support the drones and the melody line from the chanter."

"That sounds hard."

Quinn laughed. "It is. You usually have to study for years before you're allowed to play the chanter in a band. Da started teaching me when I was about twelve, so when I joined the force I stepped right into the Garda Band, full of myself and ready to go."

Audie lifted an eyebrow. "You? Full of yourself?"

"Yeah, well, I can't help it that I'm so damn good."

Audie laughed. "OK. So what's the bag made of? I thought it looked kind of different from the other bagpipes."

"Ah. The detective in you again, Homey," he said appreciatively. "It *is* different—most of the newer pipes have Kevlar bags, a plastic material. But I wanted to keep Philomena as historically accurate as possible, so I'm one of a handful of players that use an elk hide bag."

Quinn rubbed his fingers along the rough skin. "See how it's all bumpy here? It's inside out—the inside of the bag is the outer hide, elk hair and all."

"Eeewww, gross."

"Yeah, well, it helps make the sound rich and mellow, not buzzy like the new pipes. Want me to play a little something for you?"

"Please."

"How about 'Itchy Fingers'?"

Audie laughed. "Sounds good."

"I won't be able to talk, all right? I'm going to fill the bag with air and then give her a little slap to get the juices flowing."

Audie cocked her head and blinked. "What did you just say?"

"A slap gets the air moving through the drones. Now you can't be making me crazy while I play, or it won't sound right."

"I wouldn't think of it, Quinn."

The song was light and quick and Quinn was right— Philomena's sound was quite rich—and sitting this close, Audie could appreciate the amount of skill it took to produce the glorious tone.

She sat up on her haunches and clapped enthusiastically when the song ended, then gave Quinn one of her ballpark whistles.

"God, woman, you're going to make me deaf," he mumbled behind his smile, putting the pipes away and closing the case. Quinn stood in front of her, his hands on his hips.

"What next, Homey?"

"Ahhh." Audie flopped down on her side, propping her head with an elbow as she appraised him.

Quinn watched the sundress pull across the curves of her breasts, the slight swell of her stomach, and her round hips. He hoped whatever she wanted to know wouldn't take long to explain.

"The get-up, Stacey. All the doodads you're wearing."

He narrowed his eyes at her. "I'll have you know that everything about the get-up, as you call it, is significant. So treat it with respect."

"Oh, I'm very respectful of it, believe me."

A little flash of heat moved through Quinn at the serious look in her eye. She *did* like the get-up, and it surprised him how happy that made him.

"Where should I start?"

She looked him over carefully and hummed, thinking. "Tell me about the little milkman hat and the story with the shoes."

Quinn laughed big and reached for the black two-edged cap sitting at a jaunty angle on his head. He held it out to her and ran his fingers along the black-and-white checkerboard pattern on the brim. "It's called a Glengarry and this is the black and white of the old Chicago Police Department."

He set the hat on Audie's head, giving her shiny hair a fluff and letting his fingers linger on her cheek a moment.

"You enjoying this, Homey?"

"Very much," she sighed, smiling up at him.

She watched him rake his fingers quickly through his sun-streaked short mane, the entirety of his hairstyling regimen, as she'd already learned.

"And these are spats worn over your standard-issue police shoes." He took off the spats and shoes and placed them under a straight-backed chair near the bureau.

"You look real good in those kneesocks, Quinn."

"They're not kneesocks—they're called hose. And these bright green garter things are called flashes—you fold the tops of the hose over the flashes just below your knee."

"So take them off."

He shot her a challenging look. "I feel like you're going to start sticking dollar bills in my shorts."

She laughed. "If you earn it, I will."

He took off the hose and flashes and folded them neatly on the chair. While he did that, Audie got to look at the defined muscles of his calves and his tapered ankles. He had excellent legs, this man in a skirt.

"Where to next, Homey?"

"The shirt," she said, grinning and rolling back to her stomach, propping her chin in her hands. Quinn watched the Glengarry slide off her hair and land on the disheveled comforter. The sight of Audie rolling around on his bed brought on that tightening in his chest again and in his groin.

His fingers went to the shirt buttons, taking detours to point out important features. "This is, of course, the standard-issue Chicago Police Department summer dress shirt, with the city flag on the right arm here"—he pointed—"and the Garda Pipe and Drum Band insignia on the left. And this little brass plate on the pocket is my name in Gaelic—Cuinn." His fingers pulled out the shirttails from the front and back of the kilt.

"So unbutton the rest of it."

He cocked his head to the side and saw how she watched his fingers pop open the last few buttons. He pulled off the shirt and gave it a series of little burlesque flips through the air before he laid it neatly over the back of the chair.

When Audie was done laughing, she continued her questions. "Does the undershirt have any significance, Quinn?"

"Yes it does, since you ask. Fruit Of The Loom, JCPenney, six for fifteen dollars."

Audie watched him do the one-handed macho T-shirt removal thing and toss it to the chair. And there he stood in front of her, wearing nothing but the kilt and a muscular chest, trim abdomen, and strong arms.

Audie knew she might very well be drooling, but she didn't care. His body was exquisite—powerful, sprung tight, ready for whatever might be required.

She liked that about him.

Quinn crossed his arms over his chest and glared down at her, trying his best to temper his sparkling eyes with a frown. "What now, Miss Adams?"

All she could do was look. She folded her legs beneath her and sat up again, hands on knees, just appreciating him. "Can you let your arms down to your sides?" she asked very softly.

The request surprised him. He couldn't imagine what she found so interesting but did as she asked, watching her watch him.

Audie was fascinated by the single thick vein that ran the length of the inside of each arm, branching off into smaller veins that wrapped around the forearm and wrist. His arms were a soft pink-peach, sprinkled with light freckles and covered with a dusting of hair. The same hair covered his chest and narrowed to a V shape between the ridges of his stomach muscles.

It came as a shock to realize she knew exactly what he felt like in all those places, how warm his skin was, how hard his muscle felt beneath her fingertips. She also knew how bracing he smelled and how smooth he tasted.

She sighed. So what if Quinn was full of himself? He was the most exquisite male specimen she'd ever seen, and beneath the hard-ass cop routine, he was the kindest man she'd ever known.

And he said he loved her, so he must be a very brave man as well.

Audie stared, breathing quietly, feeling the room grow thick with tension and desire. She'd tried to be honest with him. But was she honest with herself?

She told herself she didn't know how to love him—but she desperately wanted him, right now. Was it wrong to want his body? Was there anything wrong with taking what she wanted and giving him what he obviously wanted, too?

"The belt, Quinn," she said, her voice unexpectedly husky and low. She laughed at herself, embarrassed. "I mean, what's in your little pouch, good-lookin'?"

Quinn enjoyed the way her cheeks and chest flushed. "This is called a sporran, Homey, and its made of horsehair, and I keep real important stuff in here, so don't be smart."

His hands went down to the snap and opened it for her, revealing a wilted twenty-dollar bill. "Beer money."

"How about in the back?" Her eyes were expectant and bright.

Quinn twisted the black leather belt around to reveal a second, larger pouch and opened it. He took things out one at a time, held them up for her inspection, and placed them on the chair. "Car keys. Badge. Service weapon. Handcuffs." He unbuckled the belt and laid that on the chair as well.

She harrumphed a little and her brows drew up tight. "Do you always have to carry your gun, Quinn? All the time?"

"Except when I'm in the shower or asleep or naked with you, yes."

She inclined her head thoughtfully and saw him bring his hands to the button at the waist of his kilt.

"Stop right there, buster," Audie said sharply. "Don't move."

She scooted down and let her legs flop over the edge of the bed. Her nose was level with the button in question.

She leaned back on her hands and looked up into his eyes. "Tell me all about the kilt, Stacey." The corners of her mouth rose ever so slightly.

"What do you want to know about it?"

"Absolutely everything," she said, shaking her hair around her shoulders.

The sight of this woman beneath him, her hair spilling out behind her, her breasts just screaming to be touched— that was all bad enough. But then he felt her left toe start to tickle the hair on his right shin, moving higher along the inside of his calf, then around to the back of his knee.

He noticed that to inflict this agony, she had to crook her knee out to the side, and the flared skirt of her dress fell away, revealing lots and lots of bare inner thigh.

"Jaysus, Audie."

"The kilt."

"Yeah. Uh, the colors of the plaid are, uh, Douglas blue for the Chicago Police Department, green for Ireland, and white for the City of Chicago. Do you like it?"

"Lovely," she whispered, removing her toe from his skin. "Could you come a little closer, Quinn?"

He put his hands on his hips, and it was then that Audie noticed a definite change in the neat, straight pleat at the front of Quinn's kilt, as if it was hitched on something, something that was becoming more of a disturbance with each passing second.

She let her eyes travel up to his face and saw how his green eyes burned down at her.

"I'm not going to bite you," she said demurely. "At least not too hard. And I've had all my shots, like Michael."

He took a step closer, and Audie let her fingertips graze

along the backs of his knees. She was surprised when
Quinn shuddered and started snickering.

"Don't tell me you're ticklish, Detective!" Her hands
pushed higher beneath the light wool tartan, her palms resting flat against the long, solid muscles at the back of his
thighs, the warm skin, and the fine covering of hair.

Quinn tried to breathe easy, but he was looking at her
face, and that was not the place to be looking if he planned
on relaxation. She was holding his gaze and bit down on
her bottom lip with a question. Then the little pink tip of
her tongue licked at the very same spot, and Quinn let out
a soft groan.

Suddenly her hands swept higher and cupped nothing
but bare muscle, and Quinn felt his skin burn beneath her
touch.

"So it *is* true," she whispered, smiling up at him with
delight.

"Only on special occasions."

"Such as . . . ?"

"Such as whenever you plan on putting your hands on
my ass—that's special enough."

She tilted her head back and roared, which he watched
appreciatively. "So you knew I was going to do this, did
you?"

"God, I was hoping. I ditched my drawers in the
kitchen."

She laughed some more and then squeezed his hard butt
with her hands. "And how about this, Detective? Did you
hope I'd do this?"

She leaned forward and brought him closer, her hands
clamped on his ass, and began nibbling at him through the
plaid. First she scraped her teeth into the root of him, then
helped herself to a hard mouthful.

"Jaysus," Quinn whispered, his head thrown back and

his eyes closed. He spread his feet a little wider for balance and let his hands drop to his sides.

Audie moved her knees apart and snuggled him in tight, resting her bare legs against the outside of his calves. Her hands still gripped him, held him secure, while her mouth searched and kissed and bit at the big erection threatening to push through the flap of the kilt.

Audie grabbed the edge of the scratchy fabric with her teeth and moved it to the side, and the thick, satiny head of his penis burst through the curtain.

She was there to catch it, and he was inside her mouth, polished-smooth, hard and hot, and she felt his fingers brush through her hair and grab on. His body moved instinctively to take advantage of what she offered.

Audie trailed her fingertips in lazy circles around his bottom and then reached up under his legs to cup his testicles. She felt his entire body shiver under the light touch. She pulled away.

"Wait, Quinn. I'm such a slow learner. I'm supposed to give it a little slap first, right? To get the juices going?"

"Whaaa . . . ?"

She did.

"Holy God, woman. You're going to kill me."

"And then I put my mouth on the reed and blow, right? Then play the chanter with my fingers?" She ran her tongue along the underside of his cock. "It might take some practice before I get the hang of circular breathing. I hope you don't mind."

Her wet lips parted and she welcomed him back inside.

Quinn didn't know whether to laugh or cry and his head was pounding and the room was spinning and all he felt was Audie and it was as if all the power in the universe was concentrated right there in her hot little mouth.

"Audie?" he croaked out, his hands now reaching down to gently touch her face.

She raised her eyes but continued to give him a wealth of slippery, sucking kisses. She stopped when she saw a shadow of unhappiness in his face.

"What is it?" She sat up straight, thinking to herself that she'd done something wrong or she'd hurt him—but she didn't slap him *that* hard—or maybe he didn't like what was happening, though it certainly didn't appear that was the problem. "What's wrong?"

"Nothing's wrong." He knelt down in front of her and placed his big hands around her hips. He leaned in to kiss her with decisiveness, letting his lips and the tip of his tongue trail along her lush mouth, so hot from the recent friction.

He whispered into her ear, "I'm not going to last if you keep doing that. It's too wonderful. I promise I'll make it up to you, though."

She sighed with immense pleasure and held his face in front of her, touching him softly around his eyes and at his temples. "Oh, Quinn," she breathed. "Did you enjoy playing for me today?"

"What?"

"Did you enjoy playing the pipes for me today?"

"Of course I did," he said, smiling sweetly. "I loved playing for you, seeing you enjoy yourself."

"Exactly." Audie kissed him tenderly, overwhelmed by a hot rush of feeling for him that she couldn't stop and didn't want to identify. "So just let me do the entertaining for a while, all right? Now stand up."

"I meant what I said. I love you, Audie."

Love! The word burned in her throat, behind her eyes, in her brain!

Quinn stayed on his knees and gazed at her long and deep. "I love being with you. You make me laugh—more than any woman I've ever known. You're good for my soul."

She shook her head almost imperceptibly and tried to smile, though her heart was splitting apart with fear and dread and panic.

"Quinn, I—"

"Don't." He stopped her abruptly, then softened his voice. "Maybe someday you'll tell me what I want to hear. But until then, don't say anything."

Audie blinked at him, not quite sure what she'd ever done in her whole entire life to deserve a man like Stacey Quinn, if only for a while.

"I told you I suck at love."

A very depraved smile spread across Quinn's face, and he ran a fingertip over her wet lips. "Then, lassie, for the time being let's just stick to the things you do extremely well."

He stood up and stepped away from the bed, smiling as he popped open the waistband of the kilt. It fell to the floor in a heap around his ankles.

"Aren't you going to fold it and put it on the chair?" Audie asked.

"I'll get it in the morning."

It surprised her that she could laugh at a time like this, but she did. Only Quinn could make her laugh while her blood boiled and her heart broke apart.

She gazed at him—his body hard with desire, his eyes so intense they burned through her. She'd always remember him like this.

"Then get your naked butt back over here, Detective. I'm not done entertaining you."

CHAPTER 13

The news wasn't entirely unexpected, but Marjorie was still stunned. The words themselves felt heavy. They settled on her with a loud thud.

"The aneurysm is thirty percent larger than two months ago," the doctor had said. "The medication hasn't worked as we hoped and now surgery isn't even an option. I'm very sorry."

She'd sat motionless.

"It could be any time—days, weeks. But very soon. You'll need to get your affairs in order."

He had no idea.

Marjorie looked around her now and sighed. She briefly acknowledged the brown and wilted plants at the windows, the disorder, disarray, and dust of these once elegant rooms. She could resist the idea of tidying up tonight, as she'd resisted it for over a year now, though the sight of all this disrespect made her sick, sick, sick!

Audie had ruined this apartment—Helen's place, her place—the symbol of everything they'd worked for. And the anger rose in her so hard and so fast that it made her blind the way it sometimes did, like the night she became the person she now was.

Marjorie felt a headache coming.

There was no time to waste. Everything she did from

this moment on must be streamlined, purposeful—and perfect.

She took one last look over her calm black lake and her sparkling city, then walked slowly to the guest room. She lay down upon the bed to wait out the pain now throbbing through her skull.

The bedclothes were neat, but she could smell that detective on the pillowcases. He had defiled her room, her bed, and such awful visions of him and Autumn came to her that she felt ill again! Absolutely sickened! That girl had no right to be happy—no right!

Oh, Helen! How had it come to this?

Marjorie turned her cheek into the soft cotton of the pillow and allowed herself to cry. It was impossible to forget the image—the eyes that burned with a smoky dark fire, the way her hair fell in rich dark waves around her face, that lovely face! And those lips . . . those lips that were at once the essence of joy and the vehicle for betrayal.

For forty-four years, those lips made the world disappear. Then they said things that made it all look so sordid, so wrong, such a mistake.

Of course Helen deserved to die. Just as Autumn did. In fact, sometimes she had difficulty reminding herself that they weren't one and the same—Autumn looked so much like her mother did so long ago.

Marjorie's head was spinning.

They'd been as one since freshman year. All they'd survived! The delicate juggling act that allowed them to explore their passion for each other while keeping Helen academically sound and socially desirable. Then the sham of a marriage to Robert Adams! It was necessary, of course—Robert's presence gave their arrangement legitimacy.

And all they'd accomplished—the combination of Helen's charm and her own brilliance and determination made them unstoppable! How dare Helen decide—after a lifetime together—that she wanted to be with someone else! And a man, no less! *Banner* CEO Malcolm Milton!

Marjorie stared up at the ceiling in the guest room and laughed out loud at her own stupidity. Being Helen's business partner had made her wealthier than she'd ever imagined. And from the beginning, Helen had assured her the column would be hers if anything happened to her. It was only fair, Helen always said.

So when the will specified leaving the column to Autumn first, then Drew, Marjorie was devastated. There she was, dying, finally demanding the recognition she'd always deserved—but all she got was more money. But she didn't want more money. She wanted glory! She wanted to be Homey Helen!

Marjorie heard the sound of her own desperate laughter echo through the guest room. How many times had she gone over this in her mind since then? The absurdity of leaving something so precious to those two idiots!

Autumn? For God's sake. Her life calling seemed to be teaching delinquents to kick a little ball into a big net. And Andrew? Dear God! He was a gutless, indolent twit who was slowly killing himself with alcohol.

Helen's progeny. The offspring of a cold-hearted, selfish bitch and a cuckold.

You'll need to get your affairs in order.

She brought a hand to her head. She wrenched her eyes against the throbbing.

Marjorie didn't like to think about what had happened fifteen months ago, but sometimes the images were so raw that they crashed through her brain like a freight train— unstoppable, loud, and painful. Like now.

She'd suggested they meet after work for a drink. No, things had not been good between them for a while, but Marjorie now had an explanation for the mood swings and her raging headaches and her screaming fits. Helen would understand. Helen would take her home to the Lakeside Pointe condo and hold her, comfort her, remind her of all they'd shared.

She knew that as long as Helen told her she loved her, she could face whatever came next.

An enlarged artery was pushing against her brain stem, she told Helen, and surgery might kill her.

Didn't Helen see how much she needed her right then? Didn't Helen know that she held her heart in her hands?

Helen had looked her in the eye, patted her hand, and said how sorry she was. Then she proceeded to tell her that their relationship was over because she was in love with Malcolm Milton.

Marjorie's professional contribution was vital to the success of the column, Helen went on, so if Marjorie felt well enough, they could continue their working relationship.

"And I am sorry about the timing of all this," Helen added.

Marjorie's hands had turned to blocks of lead beneath Helen's touch, and for the very first time, she saw the ugliness in Helen's lovely face. That's when it started—the shift inside her. She felt her love break away, pull from the foundation like walls in an earthquake, only to be replaced by hate. Looking back, it was almost embarrassing how fast the transition occurred. And how complete it was.

The next night, Helen was dead.

You'll need to get your affairs in order.

Marjorie's head pounded. She groaned.

It had been shamefully easy to accomplish. She signed in at her obedience class, then slipped out the side door, as everyone did from time to time. When the dog has to go, he has to go, right? No one noticed that she didn't return.

She took Mark home and hailed a cab. She used a pay phone to call Helen's cell phone and relayed the news that

Drew was in trouble and needed her—poor Helen was always blind when it came to him.

Helen picked her up on a North Side corner. As Marjorie explained how Drew had gotten himself in a jam in a bad neighborhood—drugs again, maybe?—Helen became so hysterical that Marjorie offered to drive. How perfect could it be?

Helen didn't suspect a thing until it was too late. The vagrant she'd hired to meet them took the first swing and Helen fell unconscious. Marjorie's turn came next. It felt satisfying. It felt final.

Early the next morning, Marjorie found the homeless man, thanked him for his efforts, and shot him. She took what remained of the money she'd paid him the night before, then threw the gun in a Dumpster across town.

Police never connected the deaths—and why would they? Helen Adams was rich and famous and her death was a front-page tragedy. The man disappeared as anonymously as he had lived.

Marjorie rose from the bed and walked to the guest bathroom. She washed her hands and tidied her hair in the mirror—and stared.

Well, she might as well have one last bit of fun. It wasn't as if she'd end up locked in a women's prison for thirty years! She knew how this sordid tale had to end—she had to put an end to the Adamses. Just like they'd done to her.

Drew was already taken care of—she'd seen to that long ago. And in just two days, she'd kill Autumn and put a bullet in her own brain in the ballroom of the Drake Hotel, in front of Malcolm Milton and everyone. Front-page news, most certainly. She'd get her glory after all.

The challenge would be in the details, she knew, in seeing how much damage she could inflict between now and then.

Marjorie chuckled at the reflection in the mirror, watch-

ing the crows'-feet deepen around her eyes. She really was
an attractive woman for her age. It was a shame she'd been
betrayed by her lover and by her own body at the same
time. But the circumstances gave her a freedom she would
not otherwise have, she supposed.

She sighed. Every once in a while she'd feel a flash of
guilt for how she'd tormented Autumn since Helen died.
Slashing her tires. Sending her black and shriveled roses.
The letters. But then she'd notice the liquid brown depth
of Autumn's eyes and the way her hair fell in messy waves
against her shoulders and the guilt would disappear.

With every passing day, that clumsy, ungrateful girl
came closer to ruining it all. With every day, Marjorie hated
her more.

It was ironic that Autumn was in love for the first time
in her life, just as her life was over. Her love for the detective was pitifully obvious, though Marjorie knew Autumn was unaware of the simple truth. All the Adamses
were such emotional invalids.

She'd have her fun with Autumn through Stacey Quinn.
She'd considered simply killing him outright, but there was
always the chance she'd be caught and prevented from
making her grand exit. No, instead she'd throw the detective a juicy bone and make things unpleasant for the happy
couple.

And did she ever know just the bonehead for the job—
Timothy Burke! Oh, she had to laugh. When Autumn told
her about the lifelong animosity between Quinn and Burke,
she could barely restrain herself. This was going to be *so*
entertaining!

She'd never liked Burke, anyway. She'd truly enjoyed
torturing him this past year, egging him on to keep trying
with Audie, sending him little thank-you notes with her
signature and personal invitations to her book signings.

Marjorie giggled. It was shameful how in America these

days a slimy good-looking man always made it further than
an average-looking man with morals, character, and brains.
She preferred to see what she'd done to Tim Burke as an
act of community service.

You'll need to get your affairs in order.

Tomorrow she'd pay the vice mayor a visit and set
things in motion. She'd also need a gun, though she already
knew how easy it was to acquire one in this town. Next
she'd need to make arrangements at the kennel for darling
Mark—the one thing she hated to leave behind.

Marjorie looked one last time in the mirror. It seemed
strange that she appeared so calm on the surface when under the layers of skin and hair and muscle and bone there
was a bomb waiting to go off, a rushing ball of pressure
and chaos straining to be released.

Her life was over. At least with a bullet, she'd have
control of when it happened. And control had always been
important to her.

She needed to get out of the apartment before Autumn
came home. The girl had gone to a baseball game with the
detective and his family today and Marjorie had no idea if
the happy couple planned to shack up here or at his place.
Oh, young love!

Marjorie moistened several squares of toilet tissue with
the rubbing alcohol she kept under the sink and wiped off
the surfaces and stainless-steel fixtures until they gleamed.
She flushed the tissue down the commode. As always, Autumn would never know she'd been here.

Marjorie left, relieved that her headache had lessened,
comforted by the knowledge that at least one room in her
apartment was exactly as it should be.

She'd die knowing at least one thing was perfect.

"You've been quiet since we left Comiskey. Was it the
shock of seeing a baseball team actually win a game?"

"Shut up, Quinn."

As he chuckled, Audie snuggled closer. He'd taken her to her first White Sox game that day, and she'd spent many hours in the company of Jamie and Pat, Michael, and Sheila. She'd felt relaxed and happy and she'd laughed so hard that at times her stomach muscles complained.

They were back at Quinn's now, in his bed, and her heart was full and her body heavy with pleasure. They'd just made love—slow and tender and heartbreakingly intense. And Quinn was right. She'd been very quiet.

Because she was really starting to panic.

At the ballpark, she and Sheila had arranged a Christmas shopping excursion on Michigan Avenue. Audie had invited everyone for a sail before it got too cold. Jamie had asked Audie to consider helping at the Police Athletic League's indoor soccer clinic—in January. And she'd agreed.

Audie reminded herself many times during the day that she was in command of her heart, in command of her life.

But as they were leaving the park, Jamie hugged her tight and told her, "I'm glad my son found you. My only regret is that Trish didn't have a chance to welcome you."

Welcome you?

Oh, crap. Hell. She was in control of nothing, she realized. She had let the situation get completely out of hand.

Why was she making plans with these people? Why was she pretending that she'd still be around in the coming months when in her heart she knew it could never be? Why was she letting it drag on with Quinn when she knew the longer she waited the more it would hurt them both—hurt *everyone*?

She felt like such a fake. She felt like a liar.

She brushed her cheek against Quinn's bare chest, the stiff hairs there tickling her neck. She breathed him in—an elixir of summer sweat, soap, and a warm skin that seemed to dull her common sense as it heightened all her other senses, making her press even closer. At that moment, she couldn't seem to get him close enough.

Maybe just once more.

Audie felt Quinn's lips graze the top of her head and his big hands stroke her shoulders and arms. It astonished her that she'd come this far this fast with Quinn and that she was in his bed, wrapped up in his arms, and in his life.

How did she get so wrapped up in this man's life?

Audie tried to stay calm, but despite the deep thump of his heart beneath her cheek, despite the warm, sensual tingle that still spread through her body, she was far from calm.

She slammed her eyes shut and heard a desperate little groan escape from her lungs. She pulled him tighter.

The problem was, she'd allowed herself to need him. And the force of that need brought her the brightest joy and the darkest fear she'd ever known. Because she knew that when she failed with Quinn—like she'd done with every other person in her life—she'd be failing all of them. In her mind's eye, she saw Kiley's bright little face, and she knew she could never risk hurting her.

Let's face it—she didn't know how to love one man, let alone the man's entire family! She'd have to be insane to risk disappointing all those people! She didn't want the responsibility. She didn't want the grief or the guilt.

She didn't want any of it.

"I'll be right back. I need to go to the bathr—"

Quinn's arms closed around her, and she could feel the steel-hard muscles tighten around her back and waist. "Oh, no, you don't," he said.

She knew Quinn had probably spent the last few minutes listening to the wheels turn in her brain, feeling the tension in her body. He didn't miss much.

She tried to shake off the seriousness. "I'll be gone three

seconds, Quinn. I think even you can wait that long to—"

"Talk to me, Audie."

Her whole body went still.

When he began to soften his embrace, Audie realized he'd been holding her together. As his arms relaxed, the knot of emotions broke apart inside her, her limbs felt weak, and her throat opened to a horrible sound she didn't recognize. Within seconds, she had her face buried in his chest and she was weeping.

"I've got you, lassie. Go ahead and cry." Quinn's whisper was rough but filled with gentleness, and Audie felt his fingers slide through her hair and brush her cheek. He felt solid and warm beneath her and she allowed herself to let it go, only vaguely aware of the loud honking noises she was making.

"I love you," he whispered in between her sobs. "I love you, sweet Audie."

"No! No! Don't love me! I—"

He pressed her head to his chest and began to sing. Audie's eyes flew wide with surprise and she gulped back her cry so she could hear him.

"When a man's in love he feels no cold
As I not long ago
As a hero bold to see my girl
I plowed through frost and snow

"And the moon she gently shed her light
Along my dreary way
Until at length I came to the spot
Where all my treasure lay."

His singing was simple, true, and sweet, filled with the same beautiful cadence as his speaking voice. She lay perfectly still as he continued.

"I knocked on my love's window, saying
'My dear, are you within?'
And softly she undid the lock
So slyly I stepped in.

"Her hand was soft and her breath was sweet
And her tongue it did gently glide.
I stole a kiss—it was no miss
And I asked her to be my bride."

He paused then, and Audie waited, breathless, for the next line. It didn't come.

"Why did you stop?" she whispered.

He laughed softly. "It doesn't have a happy ending."

Audie raised up on her elbow and frowned down on him. Did he understand? Was he telling her that he understood she could never give him what he deserved?

"So what happens?" she asked.

"She punches him."

Audie studied him in the soft light from the hallway and he looked back at her warily. "I'm sorry there isn't a happy ending, Quinn."

When he tried to smile, his face revealed a combination of such masculine power and fine beauty that it made her ache. In such a short time she'd gone from seeing this man as a sexy but aggravating cop to what he was now—probably the closest she'd ever get to love.

"Why were you crying, Audie? Was it the damn photographs again?" Quinn's wan smile slowly faded. "I can cover the wall with a couple of bedsheets whenever you're over."

She shook her head.

"I know being with my family reminds you of what you didn't have. My heart breaks to think you were ever lonely."

His words stunned her. No one had ever spoken to her so plainly, with such intimacy and knowledge. She stared at him.

"It's not fair that your family didn't stand by you and love you. It's not right that you didn't have a bunch of people telling you you were great when you sucked, or telling you that you sucked when you were great . . . like families are supposed to."

She didn't move.

"Audie, you can have my family, they can be your family, too, if you want."

Her throat nearly locked up on her, but she knew she needed to regain control of this conversation. "Like a rental?" she managed.

"I'm serious."

She raised up a little more and scowled at him. Her pulse was racing. "So am I, Quinn. Please don't offer me that."

She started to move away, but he grabbed her by the shoulders and studied her—the plump cheeks and ripe lips, the clean line of her jaw, the delicate hollow at the base of her slim throat. He reached up to brush a few stray locks from her damp forehead and cupped his palm around her frightened, tear-stained face.

Quinn was aware that this would be the mother of all uncomfortable moments for Audie—but she'd live.

"What I'm saying is that you can borrow my family while you decide if you want one of your own—you know, a husband-and-kids sort of arrangement—someday. And if you ever decide you do, be sure to let me know. I'll help you look for them."

Her heart lodged in her mouth. Was all this some kind of backhanded proposal of marriage? These questions? The song? Oh, God, no. Either she was reading far too much into this or she'd waited too long. But it hadn't even been seven weeks!

She forced a casual smile and kissed his cheek, trying her best to hide the terror she felt. "I'll be sure to tell you, Quinn. In the meantime, I really do have to go to the bathroom."

She slipped out of his grasp and escaped the bed.

"Audie. Just one more thing."

She spun around.

"You said something to me on the boat about your parents that I can't get out of my head."

Audie let out an exasperated groan. "You're not going to interrogate me tonight, are you? I'm really not in the mood for—"

"You said your parents tolerated each other." As Quinn straightened and propped himself against the headboard, the sheet fell low on his abdomen. Audie's eyes flew from that tantalizing sight to his face, where she saw a flicker of pain. "Then you said, 'like any marriage.' But that's not true, Audie. That's not like every marriage is. It doesn't have to be."

Audie's breath was coming fast and shallow and her fingers gripped the doorframe. She felt her feet edging backward into the hallway.

"Da and my mother had much more than that, so I know what's possible. I saw it. I saw laughter. I saw—"

Quinn's face contorted in the shadows and the moisture sparkled in his eyelashes. Audie was frozen, reeling with the effort it took not to go to him. Why did she want to go to him? She should be getting out!

"I saw them touch each other a lot, even though that's not exactly normal with Irish couples—but it was a small house. All us boys knew what was going on. He loved her so much, right up to—" Quinn wiped at his eyes with the back of his hand, then looked up at her, his expression determined.

"They had pride in what they'd created together—children, home, friends, memories, a place in the world where they'd come together to make a life. That's more than tolerating, Audie. That's love. I saw it every day as a kid, and I know it's not a load of shit or a fantasy. It's real. *It can be real.*"

"I wouldn't know." Her heart felt as if it would burst in her chest. Her mouth was dry. Her hands were shaking.

"You've just got to have faith."

"I wouldn't know about that, either."

Quinn watched her standing there like a trapped animal, breathing fast. If she took off now, she wouldn't get far—she was wearing only a Garda Pipe and Drum Band T-shirt worn thin by a thousand washings. Her car keys were on the nightstand by his head. Realizing that now was as good a time as any, Quinn made his voice as soft and soothing as he could.

"Faith is believing in something when there's no possible way to guarantee it. Like believing that Kiley will get to live a full life. Like believing you and I are together for a reason. Faith is taking a chance, Audie."

"No, Quinn." She didn't recognize the sound of her own voice—it was gritty and strained with emotion. She stared at him all stretched out on his bed, gorgeous and honest and in love with her, and knew that time had run out. In that strange voice she said, "I'm so sorry. I wish things were different. I wish *I* were different."

Audie was trembling. She brought her arms tight around herself to stay steady. "I'm sorry," she said again.

It was painfully quiet for a moment. Then Quinn let his head fall back and he looked down his nose at her, his eyes half-shuttered and grim. "So, this is how you do it?" he asked. "You just say 'sorry' and walk out and either let the poor bastard chase after you awhile or watch him crawl into a hole and lick his wounds?" He rocked his head against the headboard. "Damn. I never thought I'd say this, but I think I actually feel sorry for Timmy Burke."

Her jaw fell. Her arms collapsed to her sides. "Excuse me?"

It was then that Quinn saw how her body was framed in the doorway, lit from behind by the hallway light, every delicious curve and swell of her nakedness in relief under the thin fabric, her breasts rising and falling with her agitated breathing.

Quinn realized he was getting hard as a railroad spike just looking at her, making this the only time he could recall getting a hard-on while getting the heave-ho.

"Did any of the others ask you to marry them?" he whispered. "Or was I the only one? Is it more difficult because I love you? Does that make things harder at all for you, Audie? I'm curious about that."

"What in hell are you talking about?" Even as she said it, she knew what was coming next. She'd walked right into it!

"The green and slimy problem, sweet thing." He leaned forward and Audie watched him dangle his beautiful arms over bent knees. "Nobody ever ran from you—did you think I wouldn't figure that out? I'm a cop, for God's sake!" He let go with a harsh laugh. "*You* were the one who ran, Homey. *You* ran from the green and slimy and hairy thing with eleven eyeballs that lives in your heart and makes you afraid of love—afraid of life. And your mother put it there."

Her feet were shuffling backward into the hallway. She was blind with the need to get out of Quinn's house.

But he sprang out of the bed, and Audie watched in horror as Quinn advanced on her, naked and mightily aroused, his green eyes locking on hers with a combination of fury and yearning. Her hand reached out behind her to make sure the escape route was clear.

"Do you think I'm letting you off the hook?" He flashed

a brief, but lascivious, grin before he frowned at her. "Do you think I'm the kind of man who falls in love just for the hell of it? Do you think I'd tell a woman I love her because I've got nothing better to do that day? Would it surprise you to know that I've never said that to another woman in my life? Not Laura? Not anybody?"

He stepped closer.

"How about if I told you that I'm convinced you're the right woman for me? That you're my shot at getting what my parents had?"

She took several additional steps backward, but he followed her.

"I'm talking to you, Miss Adams." He was so close, she could feel the heat pulsing off his naked body. "And I deserve an answer."

"I warned you, Quinn." She felt a single hot tear fall down her cheek and lodge at the corner of her mouth. This was so awful—worse than it had ever been! Worse than she could have imagined!

Audie closed her eyes and willed herself to go numb inside. All she needed was the presence of mind to get through the next few moments and she could put this behind her. She told herself it was just like soccer—you see the shot in your mind's eye; you kick; you score; you're done.

"I can't love you, Quinn. It's over."

He nodded. "So it was just for sex?"

She gasped. She gawked at him. How dare he say that? How dare he stand there all smug with his lips curled up like that? She abruptly closed her mouth and squared her shoulders. If that's the way he wanted to do this, fine.

"Yes. It was just for sex. I'll be leaving now."

Quinn leaned his head back and roared, and that was the last straw for Audie. She spun away from him and managed one step toward the stairs before she was knocked off her feet.

"What the hell are you—"

He picked her up, twisted her around in his arms, and brought his mouth down on hers, hard and hungry and hot. He held her against him with one big arm locked around her waist while the other hand cradled the back of her head. He walked forward until her back thudded against the wall.

She struggled to turn her face away, but he had her pinned. She was kicking violently—a futile effort now that he'd immobilized her with the press of his entire body.

The first picture that fell off the wall was the one of John in his Cub Scout uniform. Quinn watched with detached curiosity as it hit the floor near his right foot. The next picture down was of Michael and Sheila's wedding day, followed by a baby picture of Kiley and then Pat's ordination portrait.

The walls were shaking as Quinn shoved the T-shirt up around Audie's neck and she enthusiastically wrapped her legs around his hips so that he could push into her over and over, deeper and deeper.

"Was it just for sex?" he rasped between thrusts.

"No . . . no!" She could barely form the words. "I like you! I really do . . . but . . . I don't love you. . . . I don't know how."

Quinn thought that was funny. And when he stopped laughing, he put his lips to her ear and spoke in time with each slide into her flesh. "All right, then. Leave me. Add me to your list of lover boys." He shoved into her harder. "Because I don't just want in your pants, Homey. I want in your heart. I want it all. I want *everything*."

He cupped her bottom with one of his big hands and let the other roam down to where their bodies joined. She was pulled so tight around him, stretched so thin.

He felt her shake and heard her whimper as he ran his

finger along the hot velvet rim of her, then moved up to the top of her sex to let his finger spin loops around her clitoris. He knew exactly where she was desperate for his touch, but he merely circled, letting his fingertips slide everywhere but where she needed it most.

Her hips began to buck under him, and this time the big wedding portrait of the Quinn great-grandparents bit the dust, the old glass cracking on impact with the wood floor. He shuffled a bit to avoid the splinters.

"Oh! My! God!" Audie cried. Her mouth searched for him. He welcomed her tongue as it slid over his, tangled with his, begged for more. Then he forced her mouth wider and invaded her.

Everywhere.

His thumb flicked at her stiff little nub, then rubbed it without mercy. His penis hammered into her, big and rough. His mouth devoured her.

It gave him a great deal of satisfaction to feel her jerk so harshly, scream from deep in her chest the way she was, going on and on like she'd never stop. And when he grabbed on with both hands and exploded into her harder than he'd ever come in his entire goddamn life, the big Chicago cityscape fell off the wall and crashed to the floor in a shattering blast of glass.

A moment later, Quinn could barely remain upright, his knees were shaking so badly and his heart was so full. He didn't risk moving yet, because he'd have to be surefooted in all this glass. Quinn sighed—like most things pertaining to Autumn Adams, this last bit was going to take some very careful maneuvering.

Audie's head lolled on his shoulder and she was breathing fast, mumbling as if in a trance. He loved her so much. And he knew this was going to hurt him more than it would hurt her. But it had to be done.

He cautiously stepped back, separated their bodies with

agonizing abruptness, and found a spot to set her feet on the floor. He yanked the T-shirt down over her trembling body, providing a bit of dignity. She was going to need it.

"Don't move," he said, turning back toward the bedroom.

He appeared an instant later, her clothes, purse, and car keys piled in his hands. "Here you go, Homey," he said, guiding her by the elbow to the stairs, watching to make sure she made it down safely.

"Lock the kitchen door on your way out, would you?"

Drew was on a roll. It was late, but he was almost done with the final chapter, and he couldn't remember the last time he had felt so electrified, so alive!

This had certainly been liberating—so much better than therapy ever was. Soon he would deliver the manuscript to his agent and she would send it to the publisher and his advance would be in the mail.

Thank God. Audie had been right—he had some serious cash-flow problems.

But the real joy would be walking into the Chestnut Street office tomorrow and hand-delivering a copy to that miserable little fiend. Then afterward maybe he and Audie could go out and get a cup of coffee. They needed to talk. He needed to prepare her for the fallout.

It probably wouldn't hurt to apologize for being the world's worst brother, either. Better late than never.

It was long past time he told Audie the truth—at least the part he knew of it. He was fourteen years old the day he had walked in on his mother and Marjorie and his life was ruined.

Marjorie had looked up from what she was doing—and what she was doing scared the *living hell* out of him—and glared until he silently closed the home office door. And from the age of fourteen on, that woman owned him. She set him up for a marijuana arrest that she hid from Helen in exchange for his silence. Then she seduced him—a fifteen-year-old kid who had no idea what was going on with his body or his brain—and told him he was sick and twisted. She screwed him up *but good*.

Well, fuck you, Marjorie Stoddard, you lying, manipulating, poodle-loving lesbian control freak! Andrew Adams has finally grown a spine, and it's going up the middle of four hundred pages of shocking, lewd, in-your-face truth about Homey Helen!

Hope you like it.

Man, did this ever suck.

Griffin was out on a date. Marjorie wasn't answering her phone. Stanny-O hadn't returned his page. Some uniformed cop Audie had never seen before was asleep on a straight-backed chair outside her door, the poor man.

Audie was so desperate for someone to talk to that she'd even briefly considered calling her brother—then she remembered there was a chance he was a psychopath.

It hardly mattered. Because contrary to all common sense, the one person she needed the most right then was the very same person who'd made her miserable in the first place! Stacey Quinn just threw her out of his house! Out of his life!

Audie paced up and down the hallway, absently batting the soccer ball between her feet.

What a jerk.

How could he have been so wildly, unbelievably, fabulously carnal with her and then just send her packing like that—like she didn't mean anything to him? Like he didn't love her? Like he'd never given her his grandmother's handkerchiefs?

How could he *do* that to her?

Audie stopped. She felt her heart plummet to the soles of her feet.

Well, duh! That's exactly what she'd wanted all along. Wasn't it?

No promises she couldn't possibly keep. No pain. No words she didn't mean. No chance of failing.

She gulped down a mouthful of air, and despite the fact that she was nearly dehydrated from two hours of crying, she feared she could start up again at any moment.

This was ridiculous. He was testing her, of course, the cocky bastard. He wanted her to come running after him, like she had on the lakefront that day. He wanted her to beg for it, like she had the first night they'd made love.

He was giving her a taste of her own medicine. He wanted her to break down and say she loved him. *Loved* him!

He wanted it all!

Who did he think he was?

Audie smacked herself in the forehead.

Oh, God! Stacey Quinn was *her man*, that's who he was!

He *knew* her! He knew how her mind worked and what made her laugh. He knew exactly what scared her the most. He knew how to make her feel so damn good she screamed!

He *loved* her! He was patient with her. He told her his most painful secrets. He cooked for her and rubbed her feet and sang to her. He held her when she cried.

And the most amazing thing of all was that he'd asked her to *marry* him! He'd offered his family to her! Sure he asked for everything, but that's exactly what he offered her in return, wasn't it? A family, belonging—love?

Love.

Oh, crap.

Audie kicked the hell out of the soccer ball and it went whizzing across the apartment until it hit the built-in refrigerator and pinged around the kitchen, finally rolling to a stop in the middle of the Italian marble floor.

She stood in the hallway, blinking back the latest rush of tears, and wrestled with the monster-sized ball of stubbornness and terror that stuck in her throat. She wondered how she'd get through the rest of the night without hearing Quinn's laugh, seeing his smile, and feeling his caress.

Let alone the rest of her life.

CHAPTER 14

Like most Chicagoans, Marjorie had seen the photo of Tim Burke's furious, wiener-bun-encrusted face on the *Banner*'s front page. So it was perfectly understandable that now, sitting with the vice mayor in his grandiose office, she had to struggle to keep from laughing.

In addition, she was nearly giddy with how well her plan was progressing, and it made her wonder if the boy was as blindly in love with Audie as he claimed or merely rendered stupid by his own vanity. Perhaps it was both. It hardly mattered, just so long as he followed her lead. And so far, Tim Burke was blithely traipsing down the path Marjorie had prepared for him.

Tim gazed at her now, his long fingers steepled as if in prayer, tapping against a haughty smile. With an abrupt nod, he uncrossed his legs, got up from the leather club chair, and began pacing the room.

"I just don't want her to be hurt in this."

"And that's exactly what will happen if we don't step in, Tim. My God, I just can't bear to watch. . . . Oh, I'm sorry. . . . I've really gotten myself worked up over this, haven't I?"

Marjorie dabbed at her eyes with a tissue and waited for Tim to return to her side. He did and patted her knee.

"Tim, I don't mean to be all doom and gloom, but with-

out her mother there is no one in the world to look out for
Audie except me. God knows Helen would agree with me
on this—that detective is not what Autumn needs!" Marjorie blew her nose daintily and then laughed. "I mean,
really! Can you picture Stacey Quinn as her escort to something like the *Banner* Ball tomorrow? It's laughable!"

Tim shook his head in disgust.

"She needs a man who's her equal in the public realm,
who understands fame. She needs you, Tim. You are perfect for each other! Those times when I saw the two of you
together my heart would just leap! And I'm sure if we can
only get rid of that pit bull, she'll open her eyes—and
you'll be the first thing she sees."

Tim leaned back into the chair and he appeared to be
thinking. Not too much, Marjorie hoped.

"You know, I've really appreciated how you've kept in
touch with me. If it weren't for your encouragement and
the note here and there from Audie, I think I would have
given up, I really do. She's been so unpredictable—a sweet
card one week or an invitation to one of her book signings,
and then she slams the door in my face! But you really
think . . . ?"

"Absolutely, Tim. I hate to say this, but I think Stacey
Quinn may even be violent. You hear all the time about
policemen being mentally unstable—you know, abuse of
power." She stopped suddenly. "But I suppose this is not
news to you."

Tim snorted, looking around the room, and for a moment
it seemed he was wrestling with a critical concern. Then he
broke into a dazzling smile. "Let's do it." Then Tim's smile
abruptly lost its warmth. "I'd love to put him in his place,
Marjorie. There's bad blood between us."

"I know. Audie told me all about the two of you."

Tim's brow arched. "Really? She must tell you everything."

Marjorie tilted her head and smiled at him. "And that's why I'm so sure this will work, Tim—she's told me how she feels about you."

His eyes widened hungrily. "What exactly did she say?"

"That she struggles every day with whether she's ready to love you. It's a huge step for her."

"I know," he said with reverence. "So we won't be forcing anything, then?"

"Just speeding up the inevitable," she said, smiling sweetly.

"But what happens when she denies it?" Tim looked worried.

"Then we have to make the evidence so inflammatory that Stacey Quinn won't even give her the time of day, won't listen to her denials."

"He has to be blind with hurt."

"Exactly."

Tim nodded, but Marjorie still saw a remnant of doubt in his eyes. "There's one thing," he said.

"Yes?"

"The letters. That's the part that bothers me. Quinn thinks I've been sending them, as ridiculous as that is, but I'm worried about Audie. Have there been any more lately?"

Marjorie sighed. "A couple. But I think they're close to making an arrest."

His head snapped to attention. "Really? Any idea who?"

Marjorie hesitated, scanning Tim's face with what she hoped looked like deep concern. "If I tell you, can you keep it in confidence? Nothing can interfere with him being taken into custody—Autumn isn't safe until he's behind bars."

Tim exhaled with seriousness. "Of course, Marjorie. You have my word."

"Well, I'm afraid it's her brother, Andrew."

"Holy shit. Well, I can't say I'm surprised."

The tissues came out again, and Marjorie let her head fall into her hands. Tim stroked her shoulder as she continued.

"I think Helen's death, then this latest divorce just sent him over the edge. It's heartbreaking. I've known him since the day he was born."

"I'm sorry." Tim encouraged her to raise her head and looked at her with compassion. "I thank you for putting me in your confidence, Marjorie. Your loyalty to Audie is refreshing—I wish there were more people like you in the world. Hey!" He grinned at her playfully. "If you ever decide to leave the column, I could find you a place here in City Hall—you'd be perfect in the public relations office."

She laughed him off. "I'll think about it."

They agreed it wouldn't take much to send Quinn into orbit but debated how to go about it. Marjorie didn't dare come right out and suggest that she forge Autumn's handwriting—lest Tim make the connection with the mysterious thank-you notes—but God bless him, the boy was putty in her hands.

"Do you have access to her personal stationery?" Tim's question came out as a guilty whisper. Marjorie could tell she was expanding the vice mayor's horizons.

"Oh, well, yes. When I'm in the office the next time I'll . . . wait! Oh, Tim, you won't believe this!" She sprang open the clasp to her black leather attaché and began a feigned search for . . . "Yes! I have some right here!"

Tim grinned at her. "I know exactly what will do it for poor Stacey, but I don't want to embarrass you, Marjorie. This might be pretty tasteless."

She frowned at him and reached for another tissue. "The whole situation is tasteless. I'm just so glad we're not too late to do something about it."

They put their heads together and came up with a note

that satisfied them both. Marjorie signed Audie's name with a practiced flourish and folded the note in thirds just as Tim's secretary knocked on his door and peered in.

"I said I wasn't to be disturbed!"

"It's the mayor," she whispered. "He said 'now.' "

"Oh, shit." Tim rose instantly, straightening his tie and running a nervous hand through his hair. "I'm so sorry about this, Marjorie. Do you think . . . ?"

"Oh, heavens! You go right ahead! I'll just look over this again and leave it on your desk and we'll talk Monday. No rush."

"Fabulous!" Tim stooped to kiss her cheek. "You're a wonder, Marjorie. Take your time. I'll talk to you Monday."

No, you won't, you buffoon.

Marjorie smiled at the secretary as she closed the door, then laughed at her own good fortune. She spent the next five minutes downloading all nineteen threats from a floppy disk onto the hard drive of the vice mayor's computer, then unfolded the love letter and left it on top of his desk.

One anonymous call to 911 from a pay phone downstairs, and the fun would begin.

Getting her affairs in order *indeed*.

Two hours later, the evidence technicians were removing Tim Burke's computer equipment from his office. The vice mayor had retreated to the sofa, where he glared silently at Quinn and Stanny-O.

Quinn didn't know which was more entertaining—Timmy's brief spurt of out-of-control ranting or this prolonged silence. Obviously, his attorneys told him on the phone to shut his mouth until they got there. Which would be any second.

Outside the vice mayor's door, Quinn could hear a crowd gathering, and he wondered how many minutes he had until the City Hall press corps got wind of the search warrant and descended on them like sharks in a feeding frenzy. How many minutes did they have before the mayor himself was rousted from his committee meeting?

When the evidence techs got the last of the equipment, Quinn closed the office door behind them, leaving just himself and Stanny-O alone with Tim. Stan was looking through the desk drawers. Quinn took a seat across from Tim.

"Can I tell you something off the record?" Tim asked, smiling. "Just a little something between old friends?"

Quinn shrugged. "Have at it, Timmy."

Tim leaned forward and whispered, "You're a bigger idiot than I thought."

Quinn grinned at him. "I'm crushed to learn you feel that way about me."

Tim's shoulders began bobbing with laughter and he shook his head. "I just hope you've got other job skills to fall back on—bricklaying or driving the big rigs or something—because you're going to be unemployed real soon, boy-o."

Quinn's eyebrows shot up with amusement. "You don't say?"

"Oh, boy."

Quinn turned around to see Stanny-O leaning on both palms, staring at the surface of Tim's cluttered desk. Stan raised his head and glanced toward Tim, then locked a pair of startled eyes with Quinn's.

"I think you'd better have a look at this, buddy."

The instant Quinn saw the single sheet of elegant off-white stationery, individual words popped from the page like they were in 3-D, and his hand began to shake. His gaze flew to the familiar messy display of a signature at the bottom of the page, and for a moment he couldn't remember how to breathe. He couldn't think. He couldn't feel.

Quinn looked to Stanny-O, but his partner only frowned and shook his head, stunned. Then ever so slowly, Quinn turned his gaze toward Timmy.

The vice mayor sat comfortably against the leather cushions, legs crossed casually, a shit-eating grin spreading over his face. "Life's a bitch, ain't it, Stace?"

Then the mayor burst through the door, which was the only reason Tim lived long enough to be taken into custody.

Marjorie's gray head popped cheerfully through the office door. "There's a Sheila Quinn here to see you, Autumn," she whispered. "Do you want me to tell her you've got a lunch date and don't have time for visitors?"

Audie looked up in disbelief. "Sheila?"

"Yes. That's what she said. Isn't she the detective's sister-in-law you told me about?"

"She is." Audie stood up from behind her desk, so dizzy she thought she would faint.

It had been fourteen hours and a thousand years since Quinn had thrown her out. He hadn't returned her calls. He wouldn't answer his door or see her at the station house. And it was downright pathetic how often she'd checked to make certain her new answering machine was working.

But why was Sheila here?

Audie wondered how much Quinn had told his family about what had happened between them. Maybe Sheila drew the short straw and was sent out as the Quinn family emissary, here to put Audie under an ancient Irish curse or something.

This could be bad.

"Autumn?" Marjorie stood poised at the door. "Mrs. Quinn is waiting."

"Tell her I'll be right out."

Marjorie nodded and was about to leave when she turned around, tapping the door shut. "Are you feeling any better, honey? I worry about you."

"I'm fine," Audie said with a sigh. Marjorie had been so supportive this morning, assuring her it was all for the best, telling her things always happen for a reason.

Audie was suddenly seized by an enormous rush of guilt. She'd been so distracted that she hadn't even told Marjorie about her decision on the column. She owed this woman everything. She owed her the straight story. Homey Helen had been Marjorie Stoddard's life.

"Marjie? Do you think *you* could be my lunch date today? I think we need to spend some time together."

The older woman tapped her temple with an index finger and grinned. "My hunch is you're going to tell me you're through with the column and that you're not re-signing with the *Banner*."

Audie's mouth fell open.

"Honey, it doesn't take a mind reader to see how miserable you've been. I'm sixty-three years old. I'm ready to slow down. I was expecting this, really, and I only want you to have all the happiness you deserve."

Audie still couldn't say anything.

"We'll have plenty of time to talk. What is most important to me right now is you don't get yourself all riled up about that detective. I'm sure you'll forget about him soon, like all the others." Marjorie had her hand on the door.

Audie tried to smile. "You think so?"

"I know so."

Audie's eyes glazed over. Could she ever forget Quinn? Why would she even want to?

She couldn't sleep last night. In the dark, she could see his intense green gaze. She could hear his gravelly voice

saying, "Come here to me." She could still feel his hands
move on her skin and his . . . his . . . Oh, crap! Hell! She
could still feel him hot and hard inside her!

This was no way to live!

"Autumn?" Marjorie grabbed on to her wrist. "What
about Sheila?"

"Right."

At that moment, Audie did something quite out of character for her. She pulled Marjorie close and hugged her,
feeling with a shock how thin she seemed, how delicate.
Maybe she really did want to slow down.

"Thank you," she whispered, stepping back.

Marjorie seemed too overcome to look Audie in the eye
and walked into the front office.

After taking a few moments to steel herself, Audie
peered out to see Sheila sitting quietly on the sofa, nearly
dwarfed by the coffee-table floral arrangement. Sheila
looked up with those expressive blue eyes and Audie
watched as she smiled, obviously in spite of herself.

Audie had never had many girlfriends—usually just her
soccer teammates in high school, college, and the adult
leagues. The reason was simple: From what she'd seen, it
looked like hard work. The process of finding and keeping
women friends seemed fraught with twists and turns and
chances for bad mistakes that she'd just prefer to avoid
from the start. In fact, it seemed almost as difficult as dating.

But Sheila's friendship had been so easy, so relaxed. It
had been one of the many perks of being with Quinn. And
now what?

As she watched Sheila stand up and walk toward her,
Audie went down the list of possible reasons for this visit—
she was here to yell at her or to cry or to ask a lot of
questions that were none of her business. Or maybe she
had a message from Quinn!

"Hi, Sheila. Come on in." Audie nodded toward her office and offered her a seat in one of the chairs by her desk. She took the other one.

"Did the maid take the day off?" Sheila asked, one dark eyebrow arched high as she surveyed the room.

Audie laughed. Maybe this wouldn't be so excruciating after all. "She took the year off. The decade."

They sat quietly for a long moment, just examining each other as if unsure where they stood. Audie watched Sheila's pleasant face slowly go hard with anger, and she braced herself.

She knew Sheila was tough, direct, and stubborn as hell. She had to be. She was married to Michael Quinn. She took care of a sick child all day, every day.

"Where's Kiley?" Audie managed, her voice distinctly strained.

"With Da." Sheila's mouth was turned down and trembling. "We need to talk."

With a groan, Audie let her shoulders slump and her head fall forward into her hands. She'd been sitting like this a lot in the last fourteen hours.

"What the hell happened with you two?"

Audie raised up. "That's between me and Quinn."

A deep frown furrowed Sheila's brow. "You've destroyed him."

Audie laughed. That was a bit much. "I didn't mean to hurt him."

"Bullshit!" Sheila's berry-blue eyes bored holes into Audie. "I thought you two really loved each other—no, I was *sure* of it. We all were."

Audie watched Sheila shake her head in disbelief, her knuckles going white around the strap of her big straw purse. "What kind of person are you, Audie? How could you do that to him?"

"Do *what* to him? Try to be *honest* with him?" Audie

was angry now, too. Sheila was overreacting and it was really none of her business anyway. "Listen, Sheila. I never wanted to hurt him—that's the whole point to this. I let him go because I thought it was the kindest thing I could do for him. I'm just not sure I'm the right woman for him."

Sheila let go with an ugly laugh. "I don't believe how smooth you are. You lead the guy on. You make him fall in love with you. You make all these nice plans with all of us. And all the while you're screwing Timmy Burke behind his back? Do you do this kind of thing all the time? Is this how you get your jollies?"

Audie stared blankly, blinked once, and forced her tongue to function. "What the *hell* are you talking about?" The question came out in a harsh whisper. "What did you just say to me?"

Sheila stood up and glared down at her. "I said Stacey found out you were sleeping with Tim! They found your letter this morning when they arrested him! God! How could you do that? How do you live with yourself?"

Audie jumped to her feet and glared at Sheila's hard little face. "I have absolutely no idea what you're talking about."

"Yeah, right." She turned to leave, but Audie grabbed her arm.

"You're not going anywhere, Sheila. You sit your little butt down in that chair and tell me what's going on! Tim was arrested? For what? What letter? What the hell is going on?"

Sheila's mouth formed a small round shape and she exhaled the word, "Oh."

Audie waited, her blood pounding.

"They haven't called you yet?"

"Called me? Who?"

"Oh, Lord. Sit down."

"I'm not sitting anywhere! Tell me!"

"Fine." Sheila squinted up at Audie and pulled her mouth tight. "They arrested Timmy Burke this morning for sending you the letters. They found them stored in his computer at City Hall. He's being held at the station right now and apparently it's a huge political mess. Stacey called Da to ask for his advice and told him about what you'd done and Da told me. I got so goddamn mad that I came right up here—even though Da said you weren't worth the trouble."

The room was spinning and Audie held on to Sheila's shoulders, not just out of frustration now, but out of necessity. She thought she might fall over. *Not worth the trouble?* Jamie Quinn said that about her?

The words hit her chest with enough force to knock the wind out of her. The tears were immediate, and they flowed hard. The sense of loss took Audie by storm.

Sheila continued. "There wasn't anything you could have done that would have hurt Stacey more, but you knew that, didn't you?" Sheila reached out with her purse and whacked Audie on the shoulder. "Let go of me."

Audie dropped her arms.

"Stacey is one of the finest men I've ever known, and you . . . you are the most cold-hearted bitch I've ever met in my life and I can't *believe* I fell for your act! I'm usually not wrong about people, but . . . ." Tears were falling down Sheila's cheeks. "Boy, did I screw up this time!"

Audie's shoulder stung and her face was wet and she wasn't thinking clearly, but still, she knew there was one part of this conversation that baffled her more than the rest—the letter. What letter?

"What letter, Sheila?"

Sheila just glared at her.

"Listen to me, Sheila. I didn't betray Quinn with that scumbag Tim Burke and I have no idea what you're talking about. What letter?"

Sheila remained silent.

"I would never do that to Quinn. I—" Audie screeched to a halt, nearly gagging on the words. "I care about him. *Oh, my God, I love him!*"

"Bullshit. Again."

"Please, believe me!" Audie's heart was hammering. Did she just say what she thought she'd just said? She tried to concentrate on Sheila's mean little face. "I'm going over to the station right now and sort this out."

Sheila shook her head. "Don't bother. Da said Stacey never wants to see you again."

Audie began to tremble. In a matter of minutes, her world had imploded. It was no longer a matter of pride or hang-ups or mind games between them. Quinn never wanted to see her again because he thought she'd been with Tim Burke! Good God! Quinn had said he loved her and wanted to marry her and now he thought she'd betrayed him with his lifelong enemy!

Just like Laura did.

She wanted to scream! She wanted to rip something into shreds!

"Good-bye, Audie."

"No!" Audie blocked Sheila's progress toward the door. "You're going to tell me what you know. They arrested Tim? He sent me those letters? But it doesn't make sense! What lies did that bastard tell Quinn and why did he believe him?"

Sheila sighed and closed her eyes. "The game's over, Audie. They found your letter saying how you couldn't get enough of Timmy—in the car, at your place, on the boat— absolutely gross. It was all right there in your handwriting."

"My handwriting?" Audie whispered.

"I'm out of here."

Audie grabbed Sheila's upper arm and shook her.

"You're the only real girlfriend I've had in years. Did you know that?"

Sheila's mouth opened in surprise. "What?"

"Quinn is the most incredible man I've ever met. I was fantasizing about marrying him someday and having kids with him and putting up a wooden swing set in his backyard."

Sheila said nothing.

"When I was a little girl, my dad used to pull me out of school and take me to Wrigley Field for an afternoon Cubs game. He'd buy me a hot dog and a Coke and . . ." Audie was blubbering and shaking and couldn't stop talking. ". . . and I'd sit there thinking that I could live with all the emptiness in my life, because I knew there would be a few days like that—perfect days where I felt like I belonged somewhere, belonged to someone."

Sheila was dumbstruck.

"The days I had with Quinn and you and your family felt just like that to me! Maybe even better! And Quinn told me I could borrow all of you, and I was seriously thinking about it."

"Then why—?"

"Because I don't know anything about the right way to love people and he scared me, Sheila—you all scared me! And I said some things I shouldn't have and backed away. But I didn't do anything with Tim Burke. I can't stand the sight of him. Somebody set me up."

Sheila shook her head. "I don't want to hear any more."

"Please don't go—"

Audie and Sheila both jumped at the sound of a man shouting in the front office.

"You deserve everything you're about to get!" the voice said, and Audie was at the door, flinging it open on its hinges in time to see Drew rushing into the hallway.

"Drew?" Audie ran into the reception area just as Marjorie shoved something in her desk drawer. "What's going on, Marjorie?" she shouted. "Are you all right?"

Marjorie looked up, wide-eyed and pale, then put her face in her hands and cried.

"I'll be right back." Audie swiveled around to see Sheila standing in the doorway to her office, her face stricken with sadness. "Stay with Marjorie for a minute."

Audie raced out the office door, down the steps, and out into the bright sunshine of the sidewalk, looking to her right and left for any sign of her brother in the crowds of shoppers and businesspeople. He was nowhere to be seen. He must have run, which would be a first for Drew.

Suddenly Sheila was behind her, coming out the brownstone's front door.

"Sheila, wait!"

She didn't. She pushed her way past Audie and ran across the street. Marjorie flew by an instant later, heading down the sidewalk with her briefcase, not responding as Audie called after her.

Audie groaned in exasperation and collapsed onto the building's front steps, dropping her face into her hands.

Was this what it felt like to lose your mind? It wouldn't surprise her if a spaceship suddenly materialized overhead and a little gray man beckoned for her to walk up the ramp.

With every last bit of strength she had, Audie rose to her feet—and came face-to-face with the alien! No, wait. It was Russell. She'd forgotten their appointment.

"You look awful, Audie." Russell peered into her face. "Have you been crying or something?"

She snorted and turned to go up the steps. "Something," she said. "Let's hurry up and get this over with."

"Mind if I smoke?" Audie asked as Russell got settled in his chair.

"Not in the least. Mind if I have a complete mental breakdown?"

His sternly handsome face looked haunted today, but she was going to help the guy out. With this one conversation, she'd put him out of his misery once and for all.

"Did you sign the contract?"

"No, Russell, I did not." Audie stared quizzically at the stray cigarette she found in her desk drawer and threw it in the trash—it didn't even tempt her. She clasped her hands on the desktop. "Look. My life is falling apart right now and I really need to be on my way, so I'm just going to get right to the point. I asked you to come over today because I've decided not to sign it. I don't want to be Homey Helen anymore."

Russell went perfectly still, except for a slight tremor at the left corner of his down-turned mouth. "You're fucking kidding me, right?"

"I've never been more serious about anything in my life. I want out. It's over. I'm not sure exactly what comes next, but please do whatever it is you have to do to sell it. Drew won't be taking over. That I can tell you. Just take care of it, please."

His words came out dreamily. "But we just sent out your new publicity shots. You looked so good with your hair down."

She sighed. "Keep it together, Russell. I've made my decision. I'm going back to my old job."

"You're going to do *what*?"

"Coach. Teach. I'm going to do what I enjoy—what makes me happy. Uptown has agreed to take me back starting in the winter semester, and I'm putting the Lakeside Pointe condo on the market. I've already started house-hunting in Wrigleyville."

He began nodding absently and let his eyes scan her office. "You're insane."

"Not anymore, I'm not."

Russell whipped his head around and gave her his best look of disapproval. "So you're going back on your word to your mother?"

This wasn't an unexpected tactic, but Audie couldn't hide the weariness she felt. She was barely holding on to rational thought—all she wanted was to find Quinn. Talk to him. Make him listen.

"My mother is dead, Russ. She's been that way for over a year and I think it's safe to say she doesn't give a crap what I do. The only person I need to answer to is myself."

"But the *Banner* reception is tomorrow night! The column—"

"I'll go to the party and I'll do the column until the last day I'm obligated, which is October first from what I can tell. Your firm will be compensated for everything related to tying up the loose ends."

"But, Audie—"

She reached for the file folder on top of a teetering stack of newspapers. "Here's the contract, with my letter of resignation attached. Just think, Russ—you won't have to deal with me anymore. Maybe your ulcer will go away."

Russell took the folder from her, staring blankly, then placed it back on her desk. "I'm not doing your dirty work. You can give your resignation to Malcolm yourself." He turned to leave but glanced over his shoulder. "You know, I just can't believe you're throwing all this away—the fame, the TV spots, the money. I don't understand you at all, Audie."

She smiled sadly. "I know you don't, Russ. That's OK."

Russell's eyes suddenly narrowed. "I won't let you do this. I'll find a way to make you stay."

"God, don't go there, all right? Think this through a minute—my mother made you an obscenely rich man, but the party's over. Besides, I was a public relations disaster waiting to happen, and you know it, Russ."

Audie stood up behind her desk to make her point. "How long before somebody found out I don't own a vacuum? That the one year I tried to roast a Thanksgiving turkey I left the plastic bag of giblets inside and the whole thing tasted like a trash can liner? That I wouldn't know silver polish from Polish sausage? So think of this as me doing you a huge favor, and just let it go. Let *me* go."

Audie saw his face brighten, as if he'd had an epiphany.

"This is your way of getting back at me because I slept with Megan Peterson, isn't it? I apologized for that, Audie. I really did want it to work out between us—I still wish it had."

She was stunned, and it took her a moment to realize she was hearing the sound of her own laughter. Since she really could use a rip-snorter right about then, Audie threw her head back and roared.

Unfortunately, Russell stalked out before she could say good-bye. When she'd stopped laughing, she poked her head out of her office, suddenly remembering that Marjorie was gone. That was bad—because she had no idea why Marjorie had been crying.

Besides, she needed Marjorie's help cleaning up the enormous mess her life had suddenly become.

Who wrote that letter on Tim's desk? Why? How could she convince Quinn to talk to her? Had Tim really been threatening her? What did Drew say or do that upset Marjorie so? And why did he run off like a crazy man?

What the hell was going on?

Well, he'd made a debacle of that, hadn't he? It was the shock of seeing her, he supposed. He hadn't laid eyes on the crone for over a year, since she'd stood stiff as a two-by-four at Helen's funeral, the tears running down her face.

He shouldn't have run off like that. His calves were still cramping from the three-block race from Chestnut Street to the parking garage. He should have stayed there and talked to Audie.

But he had freaked. Confrontation was not his forte. And now he had the creepiest feeling—a premonition almost—a sickening kind of dread that made his mouth dry. Between that and his leg cramps, he was a wreck.

Drew limped over to the bar, made himself a drink, then sat down in his favorite chair and closed his eyes.

When his gaze had locked with Marjorie's, an electric shock sliced through him and the hairs stood up on the back of his neck. She sat behind the big, polished desk like she was a Supreme Court Justice, and the look in her eyes was creepier than he'd ever seen.

She accepted the manuscript calmly. She didn't even seem surprised. The only thing she said was, "Good title."

As he looked down at her cold expression, he had a brief wild thought that Marjorie was the one sending those threats to Audie. It was in her eyes.

But then he'd shaken off the idea. *He* was the one Marjorie hated, not his sister. The disgust in Marjorie's eyes was for him, not Audie. Audie had never done anything to Marjorie. Marjorie protected Audie. Marjorie loved Audie.

Didn't she?

Drew propped his drink on the armrest and blinked into the growing darkness.

What did he know about his sister's relationship with Marjorie? What did he know about his sister, period? When was the last time he'd really talked with her, really listened to her?

He couldn't remember.

Drew sighed and pinched the bridge of his nose with his fingers. He'd been a real ass the day she'd come to ask about the boat. He remembered how she stood there in the library, looking scared and confused, asking him if he wrote the threats to get at the Homey Helen assets.

He let loose with a nervous laugh, feeling the dark room begin to close in around him. Jesus Christ, even his sister didn't like or trust him! Right then, Drew realized that he'd never felt more wretchedly alone in his whole life.

And that was saying something.

Drew drained his drink and picked up the phone. When Audie greeted him with surprise and a touch of fear, it broke what little remained of his heart.

"Audie, we need to talk."

CHAPTER 15

On the evening of September 22, Audie found herself in the grand ballroom of the Drake Hotel, surrounded by gold filigreed columns, lemon-yellow walls, tuxedos, and sparkling crystal chandeliers.

So much for being chopped into itty-bitty pieces and shoved inside freezer bags, she thought. Her body was one big miserable chunk of living flesh tonight, on display in a strapless port wine gown Marjorie had selected for the occasion.

At least it wasn't pink.

But so what if her body was in one piece? Her heart was bashed to smithereens. She was so sad that her skin felt sore to the touch. Her head ached. Her feet hurt inside a pair of beaded red evening shoes. She felt like she was going to cry again.

Audie wandered toward the open bar across the room, glad that she'd let Drew escort her tonight and wishing he'd hurry back. That morning, she'd gone for a sail—alone with her brother, out on the water, for hour after hour.

She couldn't remember the last time they'd talked like that. Probably because they never had. It was like going on a blind date—they had to start from scratch. There were so many surprises, yet she sensed that Drew was slowly working himself up to something big—something that was horribly painful for him. She promised him that when he was ready, she'd listen.

The biggest shock of all came when he told her he'd always wanted to do the Homey Helen column. She thought she'd heard wrong, and then when he repeated it, the two of them nearly died from the laughter. At some point it disintegrated into plain old crying—crying for their mother, their father, for everything they could never get back.

At one point Drew made this observation: "We probably should have talked a long time ago."

"Yeah," Audie said. "That might have been good."

Now what was taking him so long? She'd asked him to run to the office to get her letter of resignation, which she'd forgotten to bring along. Their plan was to talk with Malcolm together, but if Drew didn't hurry, she might have to face Malcolm without him.

Besides, the truth was that without Drew at her side, she felt quite alone and out of place in this sea of people. All she wanted was to tie up loose ends and escape without too much drama. Then she could go home and get out of this dress and get on with her life.

A life without Homey Helen.

A life without Quinn.

"What kind of beer you got?"

"Beer?" The young bartender looked shocked.

"Yes. *B-e-e-r.*" Audie rolled her eyes and nearly said out loud, "What? Can't a woman in a strapless red gown have a beer?"

"On tap, we've got Killian's, Beck's, and Old Style. In bottles we've got Heineken and Sam Adams."

"Killian's, please."

She took her beer and wandered out into the press of beautiful people. The *Banner*'s annual fall fling was always a predictably elegant and stuffy affair, and Malcolm spared no expense in entertaining his staff writers and syndicated

columnists. With a small smile, she realized it was an ex-
clusive club she was honored to un-join.

She looked around at the opulence and only half-listened
to the din of laughter and chatter. After tonight, there'd be
no more of this, she knew—Homey Helen was going to be
history, and Autumn Adams was just going to be herself.

She lifted her glass and whispered a private toast.
"Here's to the first day of Autumn."

How else could she celebrate her freedom? Drew already
had said she was welcome to sail every day she wanted
until the end of the season. She'd join her winter indoor
women's soccer league, as usual. Maybe she'd look into
taking a few continuing ed classes at the Learning Annex—
cooking, gardening . . . bagpipes?

She shook her head so hard that her French twist came
de-Frenched, and she tried to fix it with one hand. Then
she groaned out loud. How many hours had it been since
Quinn had made her laugh? Since she'd seen his eyes?
Since she'd been thoroughly ravaged? She groaned again.

The strangest part of this whole miserable mess was that
every time she thought of Quinn, she smiled. She felt it
happening again—the tiniest smile was turning up her lips.
Maybe it was just the residue of bliss—his gift to her. She
headed back to the bar.

"Another Killian's, please."

"Did you drop it?" The bartender looked young enough
to be a college kid, but he was quite cute in his tuxedo,
and his smile was big and devilish.

"I chugged it, babe." She took the glass, tilted back her
head, drained it, and set it down on the bar with a thud.
Then she belched demurely.

"Excuse me."

The young man's face went slack. "Dude! Aren't you
Homey Helen?"

"Actually, that was my mother." Audie grabbed a cocktail napkin and dabbed at her mouth. "I'm just a soccer coach with a broken heart."

The young man frowned. "Who in the world broke your heart?"

She belched again. "Broke it all by myself."

"How did that happen?"

"Oh, you know." Audie waved her hand in the air. "I couldn't say the L-word to the most wonderful man I've ever known and now he's convinced I did something really awful that I didn't do and he won't talk to me. Won't answer my calls. Won't answer his door. Your basic nuclear winter."

"Ouch." He leaned across the bar. "I bet I could heat things up for you."

Audie laughed. "Just get me another beer, dude."

When she turned back to face the room, she saw her loose ends walking right toward her. It was show time, with or without Drew.

"Hello, gentlemen."

Malcolm Milton took her hand warmly and patted her shoulder. "You look lovely as usual, Autumn. Now tell me why in the world you haven't taken care of our little house-keeping matter. I refuse to believe the rubbish Russell has just been telling me."

Audie winced. "I should probably confess that I've never been very interested in housekeeping, Malcolm. I think we need to have a chat. Do you have the time now?"

His face fell, and the CEO turned to Russell, and Audie watched Malcolm's mouth became smaller, paler, and tighter. With each passing second, Russell looked closer to tossing his cookies.

It might have been the Killian's. It could've been the rush of being herself after so long. But on her way to the white-linen–covered table with the huge fall centerpiece, Audie felt like jumping up and down and hooting.

The second they all were seated, she made her position clear. There would be no reconsidering. She was finished.

"Thank you for your generosity and support, Malcolm, and for helping my mother with her career from the very beginning. She liked and trusted you very much." Audie took a deep breath and continued. "But here's the good part—Drew wants to do it."

Russell made a sound in between a laugh and a scream of horror. Malcolm sat quietly, his face completely blank; then he got up and walked away.

"I take it he's not thrilled with the idea?" Audie said half to herself and half to Russell.

"Oh . . . my . . . God." Russell was obviously in shock, and Audie watched his pulse beat bang at the tight white collar of his tuxedo shirt. "When did you find out about this?" He turned fierce gray eyes in her direction.

"Today. He's going to give you a call Monday. He's very excited—wants to make a bunch of changes. Good luck, Russ."

Audie reached out her hand and waited until Russell, in shocked silence, offered his. She pumped it hard and smiled at him. "Later."

She turned toward the curved carpeted stairs that led from the ballroom floor to the sitting rooms and lounges. Just a few more steps and she'd be free of this room. Of this life. She'd wait for Drew out front. She'd mail her resignation to Malcolm on Monday.

Audie felt someone reach for her wrist, and she pivoted quickly to see the bartender.

He flashed her a toothy grin. "Just wanted to let you know I'm going on break. Would you like to come with me?" He opened his tuxedo jacket to reveal two Heinekens stuffed in an inside pocket.

Audie laughed, surprised and flattered by his determination. She studied him a moment, admiring just how cute he really was—greenish eyes, sandy straight hair, a wide, sensual mouth . . . "Oh, hell!" she groaned.

"Hey, I'm twenty-one, if that's what you're thinking. Whaddya say, soccer coach?"

Audie sighed. "Look, thanks for the beers and the offer, but no. I need to go home."

"With or without company?"

Jeez, the guy was stubborn, and for a second she was tempted. But it would only be a pale imitation of what she really wanted, and no amount of wishful thinking would turn this kid into Quinn.

She popped up on her toes and kissed his cheek. 'Go find a girl to love. She's out there. Have faith."

She went running up the stairs, holding up her long skirts as she went. Maybe Drew was on his way in the front door. That would mean three minutes and they'd be at her car. Fifteen minutes and she could get out of this stupid dress and stupid shoes that made her look like Dorothy in the Land of Oz. She couldn't wait to get the hell out of Oz.

"Audie?"

What now? She spun around only to find herself staring at . . . Tim Burke?

Somebody just shoot me.

The run did nothing for him. Nearly ten hard and fast miles along the sticky, dark lakefront, and he didn't even feel tired. There was no sense of peace in him. Just fury, loneliness, and a stomach-churning dose of doubt.

Quinn peeled off his sweat-soaked clothing and stepped into the shower. He never thought he'd say this, but he missed Rocky Datillio. He'd been a roommate in name only, but now that he was married and gone for real, the house felt empty.

Maybe it was just that somewhere in the back of Quinn's

mind he'd pictured Rocky moving out and Audie moving in.

He'd pictured a lot of things.

Quinn let the water rush over him and he shuddered. The last two days had been wild. The last two days had nearly done him in.

Timmy Burke was looking at nineteen counts of felony assault and two counts of stalking. The mayor went apoplectic. The reporters were salivating all over themselves. Commander Connelly told him that he and Stanny-O had done fine work, but they'd taken ten years off his life expectancy.

Then Quinn came clean to Connelly about his relationship with Audie, and the commander got so red in the face that Quinn was afraid he'd have a stroke on the spot. He had no idea what Connelly was going to do to him on Monday, but it wouldn't be pretty.

At the initial hearing that morning, Tim had been released on a $100,000 bond and told to stay away from Audie. It was what they expected.

After the hearing, Quinn went back to work—it may have been Saturday, but he didn't know what else to do with himself. The congratulations he kept hearing only annoyed him. He and Stanny-O had done their jobs—they'd made an arrest in an important celebrity harassment case. The added bonus was that Timmy Burke had finally gotten what he deserved.

Yet none of it mattered to Quinn.

Because all he thought about was Audie. And all he felt was awful.

Quinn let the cool stream hit his face straight on, hard enough to smack some sense into him, he hoped. Da and Michael and Pat came to see him at the station house today, and Michael had been downright *nice* to him—a sure sign that he'd become an object of pity.

What a god-awful scene that had been, admitting to them that he hurt like hell.

"We're right here with you, boy-o," his father had said.

Quinn felt like punching something.

He raked his fingers mercilessly through his hair, scruffing up the shampoo, groaning as the water cascaded down the top of his head and along his shoulders.

He couldn't stop picturing the words he'd seen above Audie's signature, and the more he tried not to think about the words, the clearer the mental images became. He knew no amount of running would ever shake the pictures loose from his brain.

Audie had called several times yesterday and today, crying to Stanny-O and begging to talk to Quinn. Rick Tinley drove her out to his house early that morning. But he couldn't face her yet—not until he knew exactly what he wanted to say.

Because the truth was that just two days ago he'd asked Autumn Adams to marry him. But today he almost wished he'd never met her.

Quinn turned and let the water beat down on his back. The nightmares last night had been wicked.

The first was Audie in danger, running from something just beyond his vision, screaming out his name. And though he could see her and hear her, he couldn't reach her, and all he could do was watch helplessly as she cried out.

He woke up nauseous, drenched in cold sweat. And he was angry—so damn angry at himself for failing her.

When he went back to sleep, the torture only intensified. His hands were filled with her warmth and her curves and his fingers were trailing along the hollow of her throat, running down the silken slope beneath her ribs, dipping into the slippery center of her, so ready for him. He was lost in her scent and her heat and was disappearing into everything she was when he woke up—his body in agony.

Despite everything, Quinn ached for her touch and her laugh. He wanted to hear the way she said his name—"*Stacey*"—half a private joke and half an endearment.

Goddamn it, he missed her. Despite everything, he loved her. And she loved him—he couldn't be wrong about this. He could not be wrong about Audie.

Then what *was* he wrong about? Because he was sure as hell wrong about *something*.

Quinn turned and closed his eyes under the stream of water, feeling the dread grip his heart and squeeze it dry. Something didn't fit and he damn well knew it—he'd known it the instant he and Stan set foot in Timmy's office with the search warrant. But he'd ignored his gut because of the hard, cold evidence that stared him in the face. Besides, Connelly told him his gut couldn't be trusted when it came to Timmy Burke, right? He also had to admit that the prospect of sending Timmy Burke to jail was damn near intoxicating.

So what had he missed? Where was the piece he'd not seen?

Quinn walked through the series of events in his mind for the hundredth time.

Fact: An anonymous call from a City Hall pay phone claimed that the vice mayor's computer contained threats to Homey Helen. The voice was muffled but was possibly that of a female. The message got relayed to Quinn and Stan.

Question: How did the caller get access to Tim's personal files? What motivated the caller to read through them and decide to contact the police?

Fact: The threats were right where the caller said.

Question: Was Timmy so stupid that he'd compose those notes on his office computer? Was he so arrogant he thought he'd never get caught?

Fact: Tim Burke was stalking Audie. Quinn saw him at the library book-signing with his own eyes, and Tinley saw him at the coffee shop. Plus, there was the other hard evidence—the flower delivery receipts, the security video of Audie's apartment building, the phone records.

Question: If Timmy was sleeping with Audie, what motive would he have for stalking her? It ran contrary to everything he knew about the psychology of stalkers—people obsessed with "proving their love" to someone who had rejected their advances. That love letter described a lot of activities, but rejection wasn't one of them.

Fact: Timmy hated Quinn. Audie's letter had been lying right on top of the desk for the world to see, and Timmy surely wanted Quinn to read it and go insane with jealousy—which was exactly what had happened.

Quinn rubbed his eyes and his groan of frustration echoed off the bathroom walls.

Why the hell had Timmy taken everything so calmly? Why didn't his lawyers raise a stink about anything? It was almost as if Tim *wanted* to be arrested, *wanted* to go to jail.

Quinn raked his hands through his wet hair. Maybe he needed to look at this another way, keep the two pieces of evidence separate. First the love letter. Was it possible— just *possible*—that the love letter was a fake put there for his benefit? Was it meant to distract him? Keep him away from Audie?

Quinn's heart was hammering in his chest. Was it possible that Timmy was willingly taking the fall for someone else? But who? Andrew Adams? And why? It made no goddamn sense!

Quinn hung his head and let the water fall like a curtain over his eyes. The uneasy feeling he'd been carrying around for two days was now a screeching, piercing alarm going off in his brain. And it was telling him to look at whoever had picked up the phone and called 911.

The caller may have been a female—was she the perpetrator? This female would have to have known everyone involved and know exactly how to make all the pieces fit together. She had to know Tim Burke. She had to know enough about Audie's life to use it against her. She had to have access to Audie's stationery.

Quinn slammed off the shower, bashed his fist against the tile wall, and hung his dripping head. Jaysus God.

Marjorie Stoddard?

He didn't know why or how, but he knew he was right.

The next few moments were a blur. Quinn raced around the house naked and wet, making one call after the next. First Audie's home—he got her answering machine. Where was she? Next he paged Stan, Connelly, and the state's attorney's office. He threw on his clothes, ran out through his backyard, and got into his car.

"Goddamn it!" he hissed, spinning out of the alley. Didn't Audie say she was going to some ball tonight? Where? The Drake? He called for backup at the Drake and requested officers be sent to Marjorie's home address.

As he blew through red lights and snaked through weekend traffic, Quinn realized with rising fear exactly what Marjorie Stoddard was capable of. He thought of her competence. Her thoroughness and attention to detail. He remembered how she'd looked him in the eye and asked whether Audie had constant police protection.

Not tonight she didn't, thanks to Quinn. He'd pulled the uniforms off duty once Tim was charged—just in time for September 22.

He suddenly saw it so clearly—Marjorie had killed Helen Adams. Why and how, he couldn't say yet, but she'd done it. Marjorie was a killer. A killer with big plans for Audie.

Quinn slammed the gas pedal to the floor and felt the fury build inside him.

What had he done? Had he been too busy fighting with

Timmy Burke to protect someone he loved? Was history about to repeat itself?

Had he just let Audie die?

Drew flicked on the lights.

He could count on one hand the number of times he'd been in this place and he'd hated every moment of every visit—because *she'd* always been there. Tonight it was the silence that made it eerie. He shivered.

Drew headed straight into Audie's office. He hadn't seen it since Helen died, and he didn't know whether to laugh or cry. My God, it was amazing that Audie had held up as long as she had! Drew had to give her credit. He was proud of his sister for trying so hard.

He spied the legal-sized folder on top of a precariously balanced pile of . . . debris, really, and smiled to himself. Things were certainly going to be different around here from now on, now that he was going to be running the show.

The first mistake to be corrected would be Marjorie. The next thing to go would be the god-awful name Homey Helen. He'd give Griffin a trial run, see how things went. He seemed like a decent enough guy.

Drew strolled back into the front office and headed for the door, but something caught his eye. A plain white envelope sat propped up against the back of Marjorie's desk chair. In flowing cursive writing he saw the words "*Getting My Affairs in Order.*"

A tingle spread through Drew's body, and he found himself standing over the chair, staring, reaching toward the envelope in slow motion with a shaking hand.

The sickening sense of dread was back and his mouth went dry as he opened the envelope and a pair of earrings fell out into his palm—small, elegant gold twists he'd given to his mother for her birthday several years ago. But these were the ones the police said were never recovered . . .

As Drew's eyes raced across the first sentence, he knew he didn't have a second to waste. He called the police, ran out of the building, and prayed that Audie wasn't already dead.

Tim Burke's hair and smile were perfect and he was wearing an outrageously expensive tuxedo accessorized with a surgically enhanced blonde, and Audie smiled—it was like looking at Satanic Ken on a date with Hose-Bag Barbie!

"Tim Burke," she chirped. "Is prison food as bland as they say?"

"Audie, please." His voice was soft and tortured and it was the last thing she expected. She turned slowly to see that he was absolutely stricken. "Please. One minute."

Tim whispered to his date and she went down the stairs without him.

Audie's heart was thumping and she could barely breathe. "The clock's ticking."

"I didn't threaten you with those letters, Audie. Please believe me."

"Good-bye."

"Audie!" He gripped her arm—hard. "I love you! I've loved you since the first minute I saw you!" He lowered his voice to a whisper, aware that people were starting to stare. "I would never hurt you, sweetheart, but I think you really are in danger—it's Marjorie."

Audie's jaw dropped and she shook her arm away from his. "You're sick. And your girlfriend's waiting."

He shook his head sadly. "She means nothing to me, and I'm not the one who's sick. Marjorie is. I hate to say this, but I'd stick close to the police for a while if I were you. She put those letters in my computer yesterday, Audie. She forged that love letter to me. She wants to hurt you."

Audie began to tremble.

"I'm real worried about you."

Tim was absolutely sincere, Audie realized. He was tell-ing the truth—at least what he thought was the truth—and the questions whirled around in her mind and her heart until she could hardly breathe. Then Tim said, "I'll never stop trying with you, Audie," and he reached for her hand.

That did it. Her brain snapped to attention. She almost fell for it! "Are you threatening me?" she whispered.

"I'm telling you that you deserve so much better than Quinn. I'll wait as long as I have to."

Suddenly the fear disappeared and she started laughing, somewhat hysterically.

"Let me see if I've got this straight," she said, still laugh-ing. "You're innocent. Marjorie is a head case. And you're going to wait around until you're a better man than Stacey Quinn? Is that it? 'Cause that means you'll be waiting for all eternity, Timmy—like until the Cubs win the World Series!"

"Wha—"

She realized she was yelling at the top of her lungs now, but she couldn't stop.

"You will *never* be as fine a person as Stacey Quinn, or anyone in that family. Give it up!"

Tim stared at her in quiet shock for a moment, then sneered. "I see you fell for Quinn's 'retarded little brother' sob story. Works like a charm. I wish I had a dollar for every blow job he's gotten out of—"

Audie shifted her weight, cocked back her right arm, and made solid contact with the left side of Tim Burke's face. He went sprawling to the floor in a puddle of tuxedo—in front of the full contingent of Chicago's media elite.

She heard the whir and saw the flash of cameras all around her.

"That was from the Quinns, you total sleaze!" She headed for the ballroom exit and shouted over her shoulder,

"And if you ever bother me again, you'll regret it!"

Her hands reached out to push open the doors but encountered a solid male chest instead. She whipped her head around to find Quinn blocking her way, frozen, his mouth open, his eyes wide, and his gun drawn, Drew panting at his side. Right behind them were four uniformed Chicago police officers.

So much passed through her in that instant of contact—heat and love and so many desperate questions and so much regret—that all she could do was let out an incoherent sob. Her hands fell away from his chest.

"Nice cut," he said.

She found her voice. "How long—?"

His eyes were intense. Determined. "Long enough, Homey."

Audie began to shake her head, trying to remember where she was, who she was, and whether she was asleep or awake. Then she became aware of the deafening silence of the ballroom, saw the cops run to help Tim Burke off the floor, and saw Quinn staring at her with his lion-at-breakfast look—and the world dissolved into a blur around them.

Audie watched as Quinn, without a word, grabbed her hand and slid his mother's *claddagh* ring off his pinkie and onto her left ring finger. Then his warm hand grasped hers. He smiled at her. And out of the corner of her eye, Audie saw Marjorie coming toward them.

It all happened so fast that later, when she'd try to sort through all the events of that night, it would seem like a single flash of time to her—an instant that contained a lifetime of joy and fear and horror.

Marjorie had a gun.

Audie got the briefest glimpse of Marjorie's empty, cold face before Quinn threw his body against her and she heard the *pop!* and her overwhelmed mind explained it away as a tire blowout or fireworks, but then the screams began and a dozen *pop-pop-pop*s exploded from behind her. Audie couldn't breathe ... couldn't breathe ... because Quinn had fallen on her, dead weight on top of her, and it was then that she felt the heat seeping through the fabric of her dress.

He was bleeding all over her.

Audie held his hand in hers and squeezed.

Drew's face was ashen. He looked broken and ill, but he'd stopped crying. And Audie was suddenly filled with a rush of love for her brother she had never thought possible.

The last few hours had provided answers to questions Audie didn't even know she had. Drew had told her everything that he'd been through. The police had made a copy of Marjorie's suicide note for them, and they'd read and re-read the horrible truth about their family and their mother's death until it finally seemed real.

For the first time, Audie could look back on the arc of her life and *understand*. She didn't like most of what she saw, but at least it made some sense. No wonder her parents' marriage seemed strained! No wonder Drew had been so bitter and unpleasant. No wonder Helen didn't have time for her daughter—she was too busy living the world's most elaborate lie!

Drew and Audie sat for several moments in stunned silence, only vaguely aware of the busy humming and clanking of the hospital just outside the door. The police had found a quiet office for them, and except for Audie's frequent trips to the nurses' station for news on Quinn, that's where they'd stayed.

Audie looked down at herself again and groaned with sadness. Her gown was saturated with Quinn's blood, though it was hardly visible. Not for the first time, she wondered if Marjorie had intentionally selected a dress that wouldn't show bloodstains. Marjorie's own preference for the evening had been white. And she'd been shot so many times . . .

"I'll go up there with you if you want, Audie."

She blinked away the gruesome image. "What?"

"I'll go with you to see the Quinns."

She smiled at him and shook her head. Drew was right. It was time for her to face the Quinns and whatever huge crowd had formed in the surgery waiting room. The problem was, she had no idea what awaited her up there.

Did the family think she'd slept with Tim Burke? Did they know Quinn had taken that bullet to save her life?

She closed her eyes and wiped a tear from her cheek.

"Audie. He's going to make it."

She nodded silently.

"You're perfect for each other."

Her eyes went wide. "Huh?"

Drew chuckled a little at the shock on her face. "The guy's funny and smart and he loves you. I knew it the first time I talked with him. Go for it."

She stared at him.

"Go on up there. You're wearing his ring, and if you're going to marry him, you'll have to deal with the Hibernians from hell sooner or later. So go."

"You'll be OK?"

"Fine. Please call me at the house when there's news."

She kissed Drew on the forehead and left. On the way to the bank of elevators, she saw a wooden door with a stained-glass window and a brass plaque that read simply: "Chapel." She sucked in her breath and slipped inside.

Audie slid into a pew toward the back and listened to the steady mechanical breath of the air-conditioning vents as her eyes adjusted to the darkness. She saw a few solitary forms toward the front.

OK. She was going to try to have faith now. So she folded her hands and tried to say a prayer.

Not that she'd ever prayed for anything in her life. She didn't know who or what to send her prayer to or what words to use or feelings to feel. Maybe God would understand that she sucked at prayer.

She bowed her head and gripped her hands tight in her lap, and the tears plopped from her eyes onto the dark silk of her dress.

Quinn would live. She had faith. He had to live.

It was ridiculous, she knew, but when she thought of Quinn she saw just two things—the green fire in his eyes when he pulled her close and said, "Come here to me," and the wooden swing set in his backyard.

Stupid. Quinn's face in passion and a swing set—but that's all she saw, all she felt, all she was, and she focused on those images as if they would save her, save him.

"God, please let him live," she whispered out loud, not caring if anyone heard. "Please give me a chance to love him."

Next, she asked for courage—a lot of it. Then she took the elevator to the waiting room to face the Quinns.

The place was packed. She saw Jamie, Michael, Sheila, Kiley, and Little Pat, Aunt Esther, plus Stanny-O and Commander Connelly and an assortment of faces she recognized and many she didn't, and she realized she was just standing there, her chest heaving, her heart breaking, a ridiculous woman in a ball gown the color of blood, standing where she suspected she wasn't welcome.

Suddenly little Kiley stepped out from the row of chairs against the wall and ran to Audie, gripping her skirt.

She took in a sob of breath to ask the only question that mattered. "Is there any news?"

Michael narrowed his eyes at her and answered in a wooden voice, "Nothing more."

She nodded. Staring at her were at least two dozen members of the Garda Band, many of the Beverly neighbors she had met at the party, several Area 3 detectives, and a half-dozen uniformed officers.

Audie began to absently stroke Kiley's dark curls, hoping the rhythm would remind her to breathe, then lowered her head. "Oh, God. Quinn," she whispered to no one.

Pat then entered the room and stood off to her side. She looked up at all of them, stopping on Pat's face. He seemed the most receptive.

"It's my fault."

The tears poured down her cheeks and trickled down into the bodice of her gown, but she didn't have the energy to brush them away. "If it weren't for me—my stupid case, my stupid life—he wouldn't have been shot. I'm so sorry."

Nobody moved. Nobody breathed.

Audie looked to Sheila's pale and trembling face and then to Michael, who'd been transformed into a stranger by the pain. She couldn't even think of looking at Jamie.

She sought out Patrick again and said, "I screwed up. I'm not very good at this—at love—and I made a huge mistake. I was scared. I was scared that there was something wrong with me and that I'd only hurt him one day—hurt *all* of you—so I ran away from him." She choked back a sob. "And I ended up hurting everyone anyway."

The room was utterly silent. Everyone stared at her blankly, waiting. Audie was certain they could hear her heart pounding and her blood roaring.

"But at no time did I betray Quinn with Tim Burke." Audie raised her trembling chin. "That I did not do."

How ironic was this? She didn't have the courage to admit that she loved a man as they lay in bed, alone, in the dark. So this is what it got her—she had to spill her guts to a hostile crowd that included children and strangers, in a public place, under fluorescent lights!

"I love Stacey Quinn," she announced in a steady voice, looking from face to face. "He's the first man I've ever loved, and it's the most frightening thing in the world for me to admit, but also the most magical experience of my life. I love him more than anything in the world, and I'd do anything—" the tears kept coming "—*anything* to get one more chance to earn his love and forgiveness. And yours."

Her shoulders were shaking. She barely heard her own plea. "Just one more chance to love him."

They remained silent.

Then Kiley looked up at her, her eyes brimming with tears, and she said, "I've missed you, Audie. Can you stay this time?"

Pat was moving toward her with one hand extended, but Jamie threw out an arm to block him, and his voice filled the room. "I'll do it, Patrick."

Kiley let loose and ran back to Sheila.

This was it.

Jamie was a huge man, a man in agony—a man who had said Audie wasn't worth the trouble. What had Sheila once said about him? "If you're stupid enough to go back on your word or hurt one of his boys, God help you."

Audie stood tall, ready for whatever was about to happen, when Jamie grabbed her hand and pulled her fingers up to his chest. He stared for a moment at the ring on her finger—the one he'd given his wife so long ago—and with an unreadable expression, gently released her. His palm was coming toward her face, and she braced herself.

"Put your head here, lassie," he said.

Jamie pressed Audie against his chest as a big, cool palm stroked her cheek and her hair. Then he brought both arms around her and squeezed. Kiley returned to her place on Audie's legs, and Little Pat was holding one of her hands and Sheila and Mike and Pat and Aunt Esther and Stanny-O had gathered around them in a circle, all clutching to one another.

Audie breathed in Jamie, heard him whisper, "Please forgive me, dear girl," and allowed the dam to break inside her heart, once and for all.

Audie's body shook with sobs of sorrow and joy and she clung to him, clung to everyone, as the realization washed over her.

She wasn't alone anymore. She was one of the Quinns.

"Excuse me."

The voice cut through the safe cocoon of Audie's brand-new world and she stiffened. Everyone pulled apart to stare at the waiting room doorway, where Tim Burke stood alone, visibly trembling.

Michael was already stumbling toward him in a rage. "Of all the unholy—"

Jamie's big paw reached out and grabbed his son.

"I came to inquire about Stacey." Tim's voice was soft and shaky, and he sent a grateful nod toward Jamie.

Tim looked wilted and pale. His tuxedo shirt was missing several studs. His bow tie was lopsided. He appeared deflated—like somebody had stuck a sharp pin in his ever-ballooning opinion of himself.

It was then that Audie noticed the angry red swelling around his left eye and cheekbone. Quinn had been right—it *had* been a nice cut.

"I came to apologize, set things right for Audie's sake, but it looks like she's done OK on her own." Tim straightened his shoulders, and for the first time in more than a year, Audie saw a trace of something redeemable in Tim Burke. Something that approached decency.

He met her direct gaze. "Marjorie has been forging little notes from you all year—saying you missed me, thanking me for the flowers, inviting me to your appearances. Honestly, Audie, I never would have harassed you. I just thought you were taking a while to make up your mind about me."

Audie took a step toward him, Kiley still hanging on her dress. She knew he was telling the truth—just like he had on the ballroom steps.

"I sincerely apologize for my behavior. I never intended to hurt you." Tim dropped his gaze to the mauve indoor-outdoor carpeting under his feet and tugged at his shirt collar. After a moment he raised his head, his expression bleak, and directed the next remarks to Jamie.

"I did mean to hurt Stacey, however. Marjorie and I made up that letter from Audie, Mr. Quinn. I wanted him to be jealous. I wanted him to turn away from Audie and never look back. I wanted—"

Michael was breaking free from his father and Commander Connelly had to add his muscle to Jamie's.

"But Marjorie . . ." Tim shook his head in wonder and moved his eyes to Stanny-O. "I turned my back for five minutes and that crazy old bitch copied all those notes in my computer. Then when you and Stacey showed up with the search warrant, I realized she'd handed me the opportunity I'd been looking for! I mean, all I had to do was keep my mouth shut for as long as it took for you two to drag my ass to jail, charge me, and sacrifice me on the altar of modern journalism, right? Then I could turn Marjorie in, sue the pants off everyone for slander and false arrest, and ruin Stacey's career, all while earning the sympathy of every goddamned registered voter in the city of Chicago! I couldn't have planned it better myself!"

Tim shrugged. Then his voice softened. "Jesus—I had no idea what Marjorie had up her sleeve, but Stacey figured it out on his own and ended up getting shot. Believe me, I didn't mean for that to happen. Anyway, I thought I owed you the whole story."

The room was deathly silent except for the sound of

Michael's labored breathing. Audie suddenly felt the little hands on her skirt relax and watched in amazement as Kiley marched right up to Tim Burke.

Kiley's fists were balled at her sides and she raised her chin to look into his eyes.

"You're nothing but a double butt face," she said with conviction. "Nobody here respicks you very much. You better go home."

Tim nodded and left the room.

"The doctor's coming out."

All heads whipped around at Stanny-O's announcement, and for a second Audie wondered if she was strong enough to stay standing. But Sheila's arm came around her waist and Jamie's hand covered hers in a vice grip.

"He's stable," were the only words the surgeon could get out before the room erupted in cheers. It took a full minute before it quieted enough for her to continue.

"Detective Quinn is a very lucky man," the surgeon said, untying a mask from behind her head. "The bullet went into his flank and caused a great deal of damage. He's going to be one kidney short of a matched set, but he'll make it."

With those words, the room exploded in cheers again and Jamie Quinn fell to the floor on his knees, taking Audie with him, where he proceeded to cry like a baby in her arms.

In the morning, Quinn asked to see his family. They went in together and there was a lot of messy tears and swearing and laughing—entirely too much noise for a hospital room, Audie thought.

She remained near the door to give everyone a chance to see him, but Quinn began asking for her and they stepped aside so she could get closer.

She touched his hand and stood by his side, not moving

or breathing, just drowning in relief at the feel of his warm fingers on hers.

"Thank you for not dying," she said, which greatly amused everyone. Quinn gave her fingers a squeeze and tried to smile.

"Let's give them a few minutes, all right?" Jamie bent down and kissed his son on the cheek. "We'll be outside, boy-o."

As Pat brushed by Audie, he whispered in her ear, "I see that your prayer worked." She watched in amazement as he winked at her, then softly shut the door behind him.

She turned her eyes to Quinn. He was pale and still and hooked to tubes and wires. His lips were dry and cracked. But his eyes were alive—he was alive—and she stroked his brow to let him know it was all right to rest.

"I'm glad to be here, Audie," he said, barely a whisper.

"Oh, God, you have so many people who love you!" she blurted out, embarrassed at the desperation in her voice. "I mean . . . I just . . . I don't think they could have . . . if you didn't make it, they . . . Oh, God!"

Audie's lips were shaking and her chin was trembling and she grabbed his hand in both of hers. When he opened his eyes, she saw how tired he was, but there was laughter there, too, and it reassured her. If he was laughing, he was going to be fine.

"Tell me who loves me," he croaked, clamping down on her fingers with surprising strength.

She inclined her head a little and smiled at him. "You want me to give you a list of everyone who loves you?"

He nodded, eyes half-closed.

"Do they have to be in alphabetical order?"

He smiled weakly. "I need to hear the names," he whispered.

"All right. There's Kiley and Little Pat, of course. Father Pat. Mike and Sheila. Jamie. Aunt Esther. Commander

Connelly. And Stanny-O, who said the only reason you survived was the amount of Guinness in your blood."

He smiled bigger and grimaced.

"Then there's everybody at District Eighteen and at Area Three. Everybody at Keenan's Pub. Everyone in the Garda Band. And all the people from the neighborhood—I can't remember anyone's name except for Belinda Egan, the lady with the worm in her brain—and those are just the people out there in the waiting room."

He nodded, so tired now. "Is there one more?"

Audie leaned close to his ear, kissed him softly, and whispered, "Have faith, Stacey Quinn. I'll love you until we both dry up and blow away."

Audie watched him lose the fight against exhaustion, a lopsided grin spreading over his face even as his eyelids closed. She felt his fingers search hers until he found it— the *claddagh* ring—just where he'd put it the night before.

Quinn sighed deeply. He was nodding off. "One question?"

"Anything," she said.

It came out gravelly and weak, but she heard it just the same.

"Marry me."

Then he fell asleep, the smile frozen on his face, apparently confident that she'd say yes.

Audie smiled down on him and smoothed his hair. "Dream on, you cocky bastard," she whispered.

EPILOGUE

Audie stopped to stare at all the pictures on the wall—so many faces! She reached up to touch the photograph that seemed to hang right in the center of everything.

The brilliant color image was of a man and a woman on their wedding day, caught unaware by the camera, their faces alive with laughter and joy. They were surrounded by a mob of people—so many people who loved them.

She could still feel the pipes rumbling through the church eaves as Drew walked her down the aisle. She could still feel the fragile antique ivory lace against her skin, its cool whisper a gift from Trish and her mother before her.

She could still picture the scene at the altar: Pat struggling to remain priestly and official behind his huge smile; Michael and Stanny-O's giggling; Sheila fidgeting and weeping in her place as matron of honor; and, unfortunately, the sight of Griffin in his vintage powder-blue bell-bottomed tuxedo.

She remembered her first glimpse of Quinn. He waited for her at the center of the altar in his dress kilt, the delight and seriousness at war in his expression. He offered her a warm and steady hand as she took her place beside him.

More than a year had passed since their wedding day, but for Audie, the memory was still so sharp and so beautiful that it could make her cry.

And oh, dear God! The reception! The police would've been called if they weren't already there.

Now she was laughing and crying at the same time, which was not a good sign, and she took a deep breath. She needed to pull herself together. Drew and his new girl-friend were due for Sunday dinner, and Quinn had been cooking most of the day.

She wondered if Drew was bringing Mark and groaned. The last time Drew brought the damn poodle, it ate three issues of *Bon Appetit* off the coffee table and then pro-ceeded to vomit them up in the middle of the kitchen floor. Quinn was not happy and spent the next half hour mopping.

Well, this was Drew's special day and he could bring his dog if he wanted, she supposed. After all, how many times does a person win the Pulitzer Prize for commentary and have a book on the *New York Times* best-seller list at the same time?

It had been such fun watching Drew's fame grow this last year. One critic described the "Don't Ask Andrew" syndicated column as "jarring, ill-mannered and horribly funny," and *60 Minutes* dubbed him "the voice of a pissed-off generation." And *Clean Laundry, Dirty Secrets: The True Story of Homey Helen* had made him a literary star.

Drew had long ago become a star in Audie's eyes: he gave her the *Take a Hint* as a wedding present and told her he loved her.

With a great sigh, Audie let her hands settle on her big, round tummy. Each day she wondered who this person in-side her would be—his or her own person, of course, but she couldn't help hoping the child would get the best from the Adamses and the Quinns.

With any luck, the kid would grow up to be a pipe-playing sailor with a quick wit, a love of baseball, and a wicked corner kick. For its own sake, Audie prayed the child would grow up to be only reasonably neat and tidy.

She closed her eyes and made the baby this silent promise: *You'll know what it's like to be loved. You'll know what it feels like to have people throw their arms around you just because they can.*

Audie headed toward the stairs and smiled to herself. Her students had given her a maternity leave send-off Friday afternoon, and she'd been overwhelmed with the realization that her life was filled with kids and soccer and happiness.

And any day now, this child.

The tears were coming again, and as she wiped her eyes she caught a glimpse of Quinn downstairs, his face pulled tight with concern and love. Suddenly he was taking the steps two at a time to get to her.

"I'm fine. I'm fine." Audie patted his arm. "You know what a hormonal spaz I've been lately."

"Would you like me to rub your feet?" He led her down slowly, one hand at her back and another cupping her elbow.

"No way," she laughed. "That's how we got into this mess in the first place."

When they reached the bottom of the stairs, Quinn put an arm around her, pulled her snugly, and kissed her hair. "I love you, sweet Audie."

"And I love you." She leaned back to look at him and knew that one lifetime would not be enough to tell this man just how much she loved him.

He reached in his pants pockets and pulled out a handkerchief, dabbing her eyes with gentleness. Audie frowned, ripping the soft linen from his hands, and the tears gushed.

"Oh, crap! Hell! I did it again! I mixed the whites and the darks! All these were white before you married me! I've ruined all your beautiful, perfect handkerchiefs!"

Quinn rubbed her back. "I didn't marry you for your laundry skills, Homey. Come here to me."

She fell against him, immediately comforted by his heat on this cold and snowy March day, immediately finding her place in his arms. She breathed in the scent of whatever he was cooking, and it smelled heavenly. So did he. She sighed and snuggled closer.

"Can I ask you a question?"

He rubbed his cheek against her satin-soft hair and chuckled. "Anything."

Audie tried not to ask too often, but she needed to hear it today—the hormones, no doubt. Her voice was very faint.

"Why, Stacey? Why are we here like this, you and me?"

Quinn stroked both sides of her huge belly and smiled.

"Because you're good for my soul and I'm good for yours. And our love is good for the world."

She stared into his handsome, kind face and smiled through her tears. "We're really going to be a family, aren't we, Quinn?"

"I've got a little hint for you, Homey." He kissed her softly and breathed his words into her ear.

"We already are."

Read on for an excerpt from

TAKE A CHANCE ON ME

Another wonderful novel by Susan Donovan—
available from St. Martin's Paperbacks!

CHAPTER ONE

It Only Takes A Minute

Emma gasped when she entered the exam room, though she couldn't say which of the two creatures there alarmed her more.

Was it the tiny, shivering collection of skin and bone, skittering around the linoleum on long toenails, eyeballs bulging and urine squirting?

Or was it the six-foot-forever package of man in a power suit, pivoting his blond head, one steel-gray eye narrowed as if to take aim directly at her hormone-secreting glands?

"Good morning, gentlemen. I'm Dr. Emma Jenkins." She pulled a portable exam table from the wall and took a steadying breath before she faced them again. "I understand we're having a few problems?"

"That's correct." The man's voice was as stiff as his posture. "Potentially serious problems, I'm afraid."

Nodding, Emma looked from Mr. Dudley Do-Right to the dog—yes, she'd graduated first in her class and was almost certain the animal on the floor *was* a dog—and back again.

Hoo, boy! This had to be the most mismatched human–canine pair she'd ever seen—and she'd seen some doozies.

These two were Butch Cassidy and the Saint Vitus' Dance Kid. Hairless and Mod. Batman and Rodent.

"I'm glad you came to see me." Emma turned to wash her hands, and felt Studly Dudley's eyes boring holes into the back of her neck. He continued to stare as she bent down for the dog, placed him on the stainless steel table, and peered into the little, frightened face.

"So what's happening, Hairy?"

She already had a fairly good idea. The new patient questionnaire said "Hairy" was an adult male Chinese Crested of unknown age, six pounds, six ounces of quivering anxiety and incontinence. His owner—a business consultant named Thomas Tobin according to the form—was referred by a Baltimore colleague to her Wit's End Animal Behavior Clinic.

"Let's have a look, okay, little man?" She bent closer and scratched the dog behind one fuzzy, Yoda-like ear. With a sigh, Emma removed the collar of sharp metal prongs from around the dog's neck, and watched relief flood Hairy's dark eyes.

And she wondered what kind of *complete moron* would put a pinch collar on a puny, terrified creature like this?

She straightened to her full height, bringing her eye-level with the moron's red power tie.

"Mr. Moro—Tobin." She let her gaze travel over the clean-shaven chin and the pale, stern mouth. She studied the slight bend in his nose that hinted of familiarity with flying fists and blood, then met his piercing silver eyes.

There was a tiny scar above his right eyebrow shaped just like a semi-colon.

It certainly gave her pause.

Lordy! Why had this seriously big, seriously bad boy stuffed himself into a suit? With another quick survey, Emma decided he'd be more at home in a black leather jacket and threadbare jeans. The image gave her heart palpitations.

She needed to hold her ground. So she held up the offending piece of metal.

"This pinch collar might be a bit severe for a toy breed, Mr. Tobin." She flung it into the waste can with a resounding *ka-ching!* "And inflicting pain really isn't the way to get a dog to walk alongside you—even the biggest, most aggressive animals. Besides—" She scanned Semi-Colon Man from his wingtips to the tips of his golden eyelashes and grinned. "You look like you might be able to handle a bruiser like Hairy without the aid of metal spikes."

Thomas Tobin stood ramrod-straight near the examination table, aware that he himself was being examined. Clearly, this pet psychiatrist chick had been giving him hell since the second she walked in here, and he didn't much like it.

How in God's name was he supposed to know what kind of dog collar to buy? He spent his life plotting bloody murder with adulterers and psychopaths—he didn't exactly have time to serve as equipment manager for the Butt-Ugly Dog Club!

"Thank you for that update," he said flatly.

Then for some odd reason, Thomas found himself seized with the need to prove to this woman that he wasn't entirely insensitive. So he reached over to pat Hairy's head the way he figured any pet owner would.

The dog cringed with each pummeling.

"Mr. Tobin!" Emma grabbed his wrist, suddenly clutching a rock-solid twist of heat, bone, and muscle. "Could you be a little gentler, do you think?"

He stared at her.

She stared at him.

The drum of his pulse hammered against the pad of her thumb and vibrated all the way down into the pit of her belly. And as they remained linked and the seconds ticked by, everything inside her—every cell, every chromosome, every piece of mitochondria—went on alert.

Sexual Alert.

"How—?" She blinked. The man's skin was on fire. She swallowed and tried again. "How long have you had this dog? Is this the first dog you've ever owned?"

"Ten days," he said. "And yes. This is definitely a first for me."

Emma decided his eyes weren't cruel, but they were solemn and powerful and seemed to pin her down and dissect her without her permission. They didn't frighten her, exactly, but they certainly made her feel a bit off-balance.

He pulled his wrist from her grasp. "Hairy is mine by chance, Dr. Jenkins."

"That's a difficult way to begin a relationship, Mr. Tobin."

"You don't say?" He tilted his head and locked his gaze on hers. "The question is what are we going to do about it?"

For an instant, Emma was not entirely sure what they were discussing. *The dog*, she reminded herself. *We were discussing the dog.*

With a sigh of relief, she moved her attention from the two-legged enigma to the four-legged one, and bundled Hairy in her arms. She brushed her fingers behind his ears and along his spindly neck.

These itty-bitty, exotic, hairless breeds had never been her favorite—too prone to rashes, respiratory problems, dental malformations, and any number of behavioral disorders the blame for which she'd like to place squarely in the lap of greedy breeders. And Chinese Cresteds were an acquired taste, most definitely.

But as she looked into Hairy's big, sad bug eyes, she felt a rush of warmth for the tiny dog. He was a living creature. He was scared and anxious and cold and so boldly, unabashedly homely that he was very nearly cute.

She ran her fingers down his back, studying the baby-smooth hide of pink blobs and black spots that looked like bloated raisins floating in puddles of watered-down Pepto-Bismol.

This motif was accented with a scraggly poof of black hair at the tip of his bony tail and a troll-like shock of white fur at the peak of his skull and around his ears. His snout was pointy, like a ferret's.

"Well, now. Have you got it goin' on or what, you little devil?" she murmured into the side of his neck.

Emma felt the heat of Mr. Sexy's gaze, looked up to find him studying her in bewilderment, and wondered again how the hottest man to ever set foot in her clinic had ended up with the world's most unattractive dog.

Then she felt a hot trickle spread down her shirt.

"Piss happens." She smiled and shrugged, reaching for the paper towel dispenser above the sink. Studly beat her to it, and suddenly, one of his big hands was roaming over her damp shirt, rubbing and squishing her breasts with a clump of brown paper towel.

Hell-o! Emma felt her nipples zap to life under his clumsy assault. She was so aroused that she feared flames could be shooting out of her underpants. She'd never been so mortified in her life.

She grabbed his hand. "I've got it."

"Yes, you certainly do," he muttered, stepping back, looking at the floor. "Sorry."

The sound of paper towel brushing over cotton roared like an oncoming freight train in Thomas's ears. He stared at his shoes.

Okay—he'd just felt up the veterinarian. Maybe Rollo was right—he'd gone way too long without a woman, no matter how legitimate his reasons.

Thomas watched, embarrassed, as the molestee tossed the paper towel in the trash and regained her professional composure. Then she began a physical examination of his . . . his . . . dog. After ten days of cohabiting with Hairy while trying—and failing—to find a real home for him, maybe he should just see the picture for what it was.

It was the picture of a chump and his dog.

Thomas shifted his weight, rubbed a hand over his face, and groaned internally, the only place he allowed himself to groan or shout or laugh these days, it seemed.

He watched the way the vet stroked the dog with the gentlest touch, and noticed that Hairy's trembling eased with each moment he spent in her hands.

He could see how that might happen.

The vet was extremely pretty, in a farm-girl kind of way. The creamy skin of her face, neck, and hands looked warm and silky. Those guileless eyes were the exact shade of her blue jeans. Her smile was genuine and sweet and pushed her whole lovely face into an expression of welcome.

It was pointless, of course, but Thomas couldn't help but wonder what it would feel like to grab hold of that thick braid and yank her up against him. He couldn't help but wonder what all that gorgeous hair would feel like once he'd unraveled it—would it be straight and glossy like polished wood? Would it be wavy and fall in heavy sections in his hand?

As the woman bent over his dog, he let his eyes peruse the rest of her—subtly, of course. He was highly trained in the art of covert observation, after all.

She filled out those battered jeans quite thoroughly, from where the denim stretched over her round hips and curvy thighs all the way down to where the straight legs ended in a pair of scuffed-up leather clogs. A nice, full, and hospitable package of feminine flesh she was, not all bony and pointy like some women. And under that long-sleeved T-shirt, he could make out the soft but sturdy shoulders, the ripe swell of her breasts, the inward curve of her waist.

It was painfully obvious that those weren't buttons he'd felt poking up beneath the paper towels. This Emma Jenkins, DVM, was easy on the eyes—and the hands. Maybe the DVM stood for "Damn Voluptuous Mama."

Then he stopped himself, as he always did, and wondered what the doctor's dark side looked like. Sure, the woman was pretty, but he knew all too well that even pretty people had ugly sides, and they could be mighty ugly indeed.

Which one of the four great appetites had ensnared the lovely Emma Jenkins? he wondered. Guns, drugs, money, or sex?

She didn't look like a gang-banger, but after running the Murder For Hire Task Force for seven years, he wasn't surprised by anything anymore.

She didn't look like an addict or an alcoholic, but he'd known plenty who managed their masquerades just fine—scout leaders, teachers, ministers—you name it.

No, in his experience it was usually money that motivated women to make stupid choices. Less often it was sex. So the question was which of those two evils did Emma Jenkins serve, and how low did she go?

If it was money, maybe she had a habit of bouncing checks. Maybe she shoplifted steaks from the Super Fresh butcher case. Or maybe, desperate for prestige and a comfortable lifestyle, she'd cheated on her vet school admission tests.

Or it might be more complicated for her, Thomas thought, like a combination of material greed and the desire for sexual control. Maybe the lovely Dr. Jenkins had lied to some rich loser about being pregnant, then trapped him into a marriage he didn't want!

He nodded silently, watching the vet bend toward Hairy's shivering body and listen with the stethoscope. That had to be it—the poor bastard! But she didn't wear a ring, so maybe he'd discovered her deception in time to make a clean break. Good for him.

Thomas sighed, bemused by the truth of it: A man couldn't afford to turn his back for one damn minute.

Which brought him right back to sex—perhaps the greatest weakness of all. How many men had he seen sit across a table from him babbling, crying, driven to acts of sheer idiocy simply because of a *woman*? Too many to count.

He'd seen sex turn brilliant businessmen into cretins. Powerful men into milquetoasts. Moral men into felons.

He'd seen it turn decent lives to shit.

Thomas checked his watch, then crossed his arms over his chest. How much longer could this possibly take? Wasn't this where she handed him some puppy uppers, collected her outrageous fee, and sent them out the door?

But the vet was now peering into Hairy's eyes, nose, ears, and throat. Then she closed her own eyes in concentration and felt along the dog's ribs and into its soft belly.

Resigned to waiting a bit longer, Thomas leaned back against the cabinets and allowed himself to watch her work, watch how her slim, sure fingers moved, how she breathed quietly, how the little frown line puckered between her pretty eyebrows. Thomas felt himself go still inside.

Strangely quiet.

And he wondered how good it would feel to have her stroke *his* belly, maybe while he rubbed his cheek against hers, breathing in the faint flowery scent that seemed to pulse from her skin and hair.

He wondered how glorious it would be to settle in for a nap with his face buried in those stupendous breasts, so comforting, so welcoming, so female—so damn erotic . . .

"So is he eating well?"

"What?" Thomas yelped.

"Eating. Food. Does Hairy do it?"

He straightened. He shoved his hands in his trouser pockets. Why the hell was he fantasizing about the breasts of a lying, cheating, sirloin-stealing man-hater?

"Uh, not much eating, actually. He doesn't seem hungry."

"And what are you feeding him?" Emma noticed that Thomas Tobin had taken a step toward her, and that he was frowning.

Thomas could barely remember her question. "Uh, dog food?"

She winced, then continued the examination. "Could you be a little more specific, please?"

"Sure. Those hard crunchy things. The forty-pound bag."

Emma straightened up and put her hands on her hips. "Thrifty is fine, Mr. Tobin—and forty pounds ought to take care of Hairy for a good portion of his natural life—but how big are the individual pieces of food? Did you purchase kibble designed for the smallest breeds? What brand? And do you soak the food in warm water before serving it?"

He tried not to gape at how the stethoscope hung straight down from her neck, separating the two luscious, all-natural spheres straining under wet fabric. They looked like two fresh baked cupcakes, topped with cherries, covered in a tight film of cellophane.

His blank stare was all the answer Emma needed, and she sighed. Who in God's name would hire this guy as a consultant? He might be eye candy, but he was about as sharp as a bucket of mud.

"Have you ever tried to chew a baseball, Mr. Tobin? Have you ever, say, while drunk at a fraternity party, tried to shove a baseball in your mouth and chew on it?"

He blinked. "Not that I recall."

"Well." Emma pursed her lips. "Hairy needs teeny-weeny pieces of food for his teeny-weeny mouth. A lot of Cresteds aren't even blessed with a full set of choppers. Here. Have a look-see."

She pulled back a pink speckled lip to expose a random display of teeny-weeny teeth.

"Got it," he said.

She sincerely doubted that.

"I could use a hand here. Please hold him—gently—while I clip his nails. How long has it been since you trimmed his nails?"

"I never have," he said.

She reached behind her for a small set of clippers, then bent her head to the task, coming so close to Mr. Buy-in-Bulk that she caught the whiff of smooth, woodsy aftershave mellowed on warm male skin.

"I really didn't know I had to trim them." His voice was almost apologetic and nearly a whisper, and she felt it brush hot over the tiny hairs at the nape of her neck. She continued to clip, trying to keep her hands steady.

One paw down. Three to go.

"Some Cresteds need to have their nails trimmed each week, Mr. Tobin. The nails are fragile and can break off too close to the artery and cause bleeding. See how this—" She turned her head and found him waiting for her, his face so close, his lips slightly parted, his right eye closing lazily as if he was ready to pull the trigger.

Then he moved in even closer and he dropped his gaze to her mouth. And for the briefest, wildest, most implausible second of her life, Emma thought for sure this very strange, very sexy man was going to kiss her.

Oh, *daddy!*

She turned back to the clippers. "Uh . . . and you really need to bathe Hairy once a week in a medicated soap to keep his skin free of pustules. I'll write down the name of the brand I prefer, if you like."

Her pulse was thumping like the tail of a Labrador retriever. Was it her imagination, or were there really great arcs of heat lightning shooting from this guy right into her ovaries? Did she really just say the word *pustule?*

This was bizarre. *He* was bizarre. And *she* was a wreck!

"I would like that very much," he said, his voice thick and raspy and still so close. "I think I would appreciate your recommendations on just about anything, really."

Three paws down. Heart still pounding.

"And Cresteds are always cold, Mr. Tobin. Did you notice the shaking?"

"Of course."

"When you, uh, acquired the dog, was he wearing any kind of sweater or coat?" She finished the last paw and stood, sighing in relief.

"A sailor suit, actually." He gazed up at her, one eyebrow arched in what Emma thought might be the beginnings of actual playfulness. "Navy blue with white trim. And a matching cap."

Emma stared. He was on the verge of a real smile, and in that instant, Emma realized that this somewhat slow guy was not only gorgeous, he was downright adorable! Did she see the beginnings of dimples? She felt light-headed!

"A sailor suit?"

"Yes."

But then he stood up, and any humor or warmth drained from his face, which made her inexplicably sad.

"Seems the previous owner was a complete flame . . . er . . . a flamboyant type of person. He had lots of different clothes for Hairy. Jogging suits. A leprechaun outfit. Evening wear."

Emma stared at the man in amazement. The things he said were hilarious, but he wasn't even smiling. How could a normal person not be laughing? And why did she have the strangest feeling that he was pulling her close while pushing her away at the same time? What was going on here?

As a rule, she tried her best not to alienate the owners of her patients, because she had yet to meet a dog that could sign a check. But she couldn't hold it in anymore with Thomas Tobin. She let her mouth fall open, and she laughed. Loudly. It was one of her snorting laughs, too, the kind that made people look sideways at her in restaurants.

Mr. Tobin gazed at her blankly.

Emma wiped her eyes. "Okay, the thing is, Hairy needs to wear *something* because he's got no hair, right?"

"Oh." Thomas rubbed a hand along his jaw. "I didn't know the outfits were for heat retention. I thought they were, well, you know, fashion statements." He didn't bother mentioning that Hairy's owner was wearing an identical sailor suit at the time of his death.

Emma picked up the chart and began scribbling notes to herself, still chuckling. "Let's see what we can do to make Tom and Hairy get along a little better, shall we?"

"Thomas."

She raised her eyes to him.

"My name is Thomas. Not Tom."

"I see. And I'm Emma." She held the pen in mid-air as they stared at each other awkwardly. It soon became apparent that Mr. Personality had nothing to add.

"All righty then, Thomas. Let's go over the specific behavior problems you've encountered. On your form you say that Hairy isn't quite cutting it in the house-training department, is that correct?"

Thomas nodded.

"Unfortunately, that's rather common with male Cresteds. I'll order a urine analysis and an ultrasound to rule out any medical conditions, such as bladder stones. And when was the dog neutered, Mr. Tobin?"

"Neutered?"

"Yes. The dog has been neutered—his testes were surgically removed. Do you know how old he was at the time?"

Thomas stared at the dog in horror. "I have no fu—uh— idea," he mumbled.

She suppressed a smile while glancing at the form. "I've heard some Crested owners find it helpful to secure a maxi pad over the dog's penis while working on house-training. I'm told it cuts down on cleaning projects."

When Mr. Tobin made no comment, she raised her eyes to him. His face had gone white. His eyes were huge.

"Do *what*?" he whispered.

Emma tried not to laugh. "Tying a sweat sock around the hips with a pad placed sideways seems to do the trick. Be sure to get a brand with adhesive backing so it stays in place."

He continued to stare blankly.

Emma reviewed the rest of the list. "He shakes and howls whenever you run the hair dryer, the vacuum, or the coffee grinder?"

Thomas nodded, his gaze moving absently out the window to the parking lot.

"And he keeps you awake at night with pacing and whining. He chewed the molding around your front door, clawed holes in a wall and a carpet. Your neighbors left you notes that he cries and barks all day when you're gone. Anything else?"

Thomas shoved his hands deep in his trouser pockets. "Isn't that enough?"

Emma hugged the chart to her chest and smiled at him, then glanced down at the frightened dog. Clearly, the first order of business was to convince Hairy that he was safe with Thomas—and that was going to be a tough sell.

She'd already observed that the man hadn't managed to form any kind of bond with the animal in ten days. He hardly looked at the dog. The dog shied away from the man. And every time Thomas's voice contained the least bit of agitation or disapproval, Hairy's trembling escalated.

On the bright side, Thomas seemed to have an open mind about all this, which was more than she could say about some of the owners she encountered. Many people waltzed in here with their minds already made up about how to keep their pets in line, already well on their way to a tragedy.

At least Thomas Tobin was listening.

His eyes remained locked on hers, and she thought she noticed the briefest flash of something deeply human in his expression. Then he looked away.

Had it been loneliness? Longing? Whatever it was, it looked so out of place on that he-man face that she'd probably just imagined it.

"Has Hairy exhibited these behaviors in the past, Mr. Tobin?"

"I have no earthly idea."

She nodded. "Okay. First and foremost, the dog is having trouble adjusting to his new home. I believe Hairy is experiencing severe separation anxiety and panic attacks."

Thomas stared out the window, picturing the scene again. He'd found Scott Slick on his kitchen floor, dead for days, the ugly dog keeping guard at his owner's side, shaking like a leaf, hungry and scared. It was the most pitiful thing he'd ever seen.

Yeah, separation anxiety and panic attacks sounded right on the mark.

"Dogs always do things for a reason," Emma continued. "In Hairy's mind, these behaviors make perfect sense—they accomplish something for him. Will his former owner be taking him back any time soon?"

"I sure doubt it," Thomas said, turning back to her.

Emma offered him a reassuring smile. "I realize Hairy is a challenge right now, but with relaxation exercises, a consistent house-training regimen, medicine, and a little time, I think everything's going to be fine."

Thomas looked down on the shivering dog and winced. What had he done? Why had he taken this damn dog home with him? How long would he be stuck with him? Would the dog really have to wear a Kotex?

He started to feel queasy.

"Do you have any questions at this point?"

"No."

"Are you all right?"

"Perfect, thanks."

Emma spent the next forty minutes demonstrating the relaxation exercises and working with Thomas and Hairy until they got it right. She was pleasantly surprised to see that Thomas caught on rather quickly.

After making sure the urine test results were normal, she

walked Thomas and Hairy to checkout, where she gave
them their discharge instructions, shopping list, follow-up
schedule, and prescriptions.

Then she slipped into the back hallway, leaned against
the wall, and closed her eyes tight.